Dark Currents

Dark Currents

AGENT OF HEL

JACQUELINE CAREY

A ROC BOOK

ROC
Published by New American Library, a division of
Penguin Group (USA) Inc., 375 Hudson Street,
New York, New York 10014, USA
Penguin Group (Canada), 90 Eglinton Avenue East, Suite 700, Toronto,
Ontario M4P 2Y3, Canada (a division of Pearson Penguin Canada Inc.)
Penguin Books Ltd., 80 Strand, London WC2R 0RL, England
Penguin Ireland, 25 St. Stephen's Green, Dublin 2,
Ireland (a division of Penguin Books Ltd.)
Penguin Group (Australia), 250 Camberwell Road, Camberwell, Victoria 3124,
Australia (a division of Pearson Australia Group Pty. Ltd.)
Penguin Books India Pvt. Ltd., 11 Community Centre, Panchsheel Park,
New Delhi - 110 017, India
Penguin Group (NZ), 67 Apollo Drive, Rosedale, Auckland 0632,
New Zealand (a division of Pearson New Zealand Ltd.)
Penguin Books (South Africa) (Pty.) Ltd., 24 Sturdee Avenue,
Rosebank, Johannesburg 2196, South Africa

Penguin Books Ltd., Registered Offices:
80 Strand, London WC2R 0RL, England

First published by Roc, an imprint of New American Library,
a division of Penguin Group (USA) Inc.

First Printing, October 2012
10 9 8 7 6 5 4 3 2 1

LIBRARY OF CONGRESS CATALOGING-IN-PUBLICATION DATA:

Carey, Jacqueline.
    Dark currents: agents of Hel/Jacqueline Carey.
        p. cm.
    ISBN 978-0-451-46478-1
    1. Police—Fiction. 2. Murder—Investigation—Fiction. I. Title.
    PS3553.A66855D37 2012
    813'.54—dc23   2012007049

Set in Stempel Garamond
Designed by Alissa Amell

Printed in the United States of America

PUBLISHER'S NOTE
This is a work of fiction. Names, characters, places, and incidents either are the product of the author's imagination or are used fictitiously, and any resemblance to actual persons, living or dead, business establishments, events, or locales is entirely coincidental.
    The publisher does not have any control over and does not assume any responsibility for author or third-party Web sites or their content.

Acknowledgments

Thanks to my editor, Anne Sowards, for embarking on this new journey with me, and to my agent, Jane Dystel, for her continued excellent guidance. Thanks to my family and friends, and to all the denizens of the real-life Pemkowet. You know who you are. And no, you're not in the book.

Dark Currents

One

It was an idyllic summer evening in Pemkowet the night the Vanderhei kid died. No one could have guessed that the town was hovering on the brink of tragedy. Well, I suppose that's not technically true. The Sphinx might have known, and the Norns, too, come to think of it. But if they did, they kept it to themselves.

There's some sort of Soothsayers' Code that prevents soothsayers from soothsaying on a day-to-day basis, when it might, you know, avert this kind of ordinary, everyday tragedy. Something about the laws of causality being broken and the order of creation overturned, resulting in a world run amok, rivers running backward, the sun rising in the west, cats and dogs getting married. . . .

I don't know; don't ask me.

I don't pretend to understand, especially since it *wasn't* an ordinary, everyday tragedy after all. But I guess it didn't rise to the standard required to break the Soothsayers' Code, since no sooth was said.

Anyway, I'm getting ahead of myself.

So, it was an idyllic evening in Pemkowet, the little resort town I call home. A mid-July Michigan evening, soft and warm, not too muggy, one of those evenings when the sunlight promises to linger forever.

It was a Sunday, and I had plans to meet my best friend, Jen Cassopolis, for Music in the Gazebo. Los Gatos del Sol, a Tex-Mex band, was playing. They say music hath charms to soothe the savage breast, and in my experience, it's true. Also, I'd seen the promo poster, and the guys in the band were pretty cute.

Hey, it doesn't hurt.

Mogwai didn't come when I called him, but he was a cat of independent means and he'd been pissed at me since I'd given in to pleas from my friends in animal rescue and had him neutered. I'd hated to do it, since he wasn't really *my* cat so much as a streetwise buddy who dropped by on a regular basis, but there were an awful lot of feral Moglets running around town. I filled his bowl on the back porch and made sure the torn screen that served as a cat door was ajar.

It wasn't the most secure arrangement, but I didn't worry too much. For one thing, my apartment was on the second story above Mrs. Browne's Olde World Bakery. Mogwai's route to the screened porch involved a series of feline acrobatics, Dumpster to fence to porch, that I doubted many humans could duplicate.

As for nonhumans . . . well. Those who were my friends, I trusted. As far as I knew, those who weren't didn't want much of anything to do with me.

I slung my folding chair in the carrying case over my shoulder, locked the apartment behind me, and headed down the stairs into the alley alongside the park. In front of the bakery, there was a line of tourists spilling out the door and down the sidewalk. There always was at this time of year. Most locals would avoid the place until after Labor Day.

It was quiet in the rear of the bakery. That was where the magic happened, but it happened in the wee hours of the night, after the bars had closed and the last tourist had staggered home, before the sun rose.

Cutting through the park, I headed for the river, dodging meandering families pushing strollers, small children clutching ice-cream cones that melted and dripped down their chubby hands.

It could be a pain if you were in a hurry, but I wasn't, so it made me smile. I still remembered my first ice-cream cone. It was Blue Moon, a single scoop in a kiddie cone. If you've never had it, I can't even begin to describe it.

Truth is, for all its quirks and flaws, I love this town. I wasn't born here, but I was conceived here. And when my mom returned here four years later, a desperate young single mother with a half-human child who couldn't manage to fit into the mundane world outside, Pemkowet took us in.

Twenty years later, I'm still glad to be here.

My feeling of benevolent well-being persisted the entire two blocks it took to reach the gazebo. The gazebo was perched in a smaller park alongside the river. It was a fanciful structure of white gingerbread wicker strung with white Christmas lights, dim in the still-bright daylight. The band was setting up, and a good-size crowd had already gathered, locals and tourists alike. The river sparkled in the sunlight. It had its own unique smell, dank and green and a little fishy, yet somehow appealing.

The hand-cranked chain ferry, its curlicued canopy also painted white, was making its way across the river, the big chain rattling as a pair of small boys hauled furiously at the crank, their efforts encouraged by the amused operator in the best Tom Sawyer tradition. I'd begged for a chance to turn the crank when I was a kid, too. Beside the ferry landing, a massive weeping willow trailed an abundance of graceful branches into the water. Beneath its green shadow, tourists fed popcorn to the ducks, the adults hoping for a glimpse of something more eldritch and exotic, the children delighted to settle for greedy mallards.

Life was good.

A vast affection filled me, making me feel warm and buoyant. I held on to the feeling, willing it to last.

It didn't.

The moment I caught sight of Jen, it fled, leaving me feeling as shriveled as a pricked balloon. Envy rushed in to fill the empty space it left behind.

I'm okay with being cute, honest. I shouldn't complain. I recognize the fact that there's a certain irony in it. On a good day, I can aspire to pretty.

Jen's pretty on an ordinary day, and on a good day, she can aspire to gorgeous. She's got that perfect Mediterranean coloring, with dark hair and olive skin, and she's one of those girls who always look sort of glossy. When we were both teenagers, my mom said she looked like Phoebe Cates in *Fast Times at Ridgemont High*. I'd never heard of the movie, which shocked Mom, so she rented it from the library and we watched it together. We watched a lot of TV and videos together, Mom and I. Turns out it was a pretty good movie, and she was right.

Anyway.

Jen was having a good day, in part because the light was hitting her just so, and in part because she was flirting with a guy who obviously found her attractive, mirroring it right back at him. A guy I knew.

Oh, crap.

In a small town, practically everyone knows one another. When you combine the entire population of Pemkowet, East Pemkowet, and the outlying township, it's only about three thousand people. Between the tourists, the cottagers, and the boat owners, that triples during the summer, but they don't count in the same way people you went to high school with do.

I not only went to high school with Cody Fairfax, I worked with him at the Pemkowet Police Department, where he was the youngest patrol officer on the force and I was a part-time file clerk. Or at least that was what I'd started out as. I did a lot more behind the scenes, but that was mostly between me and the chief.

Unfortunately for me, I had a whopper of an unrequited crush on Cody Fairfax, who was currently lounging on a blanket at my best friend's feet, propped on his elbows, legs crossed at the ankles. Unfortunately for him, I also knew exactly what kind of closet case he was. When it came to women, he had a reputation for being a player that he'd earned fair and square, but there was a reason behind it, and it wasn't fear of commitment.

Cody was afraid of being found out.

Envy and anger, two of the Seven Deadlies. I could feel them coiling deliciously in my gut, wanting to rise and consume me. I had to be careful with that sort of thing, especially anger. When I lost control of my temper, things . . . happened. With an effort, I made myself envision the emotions as a glass filled with roiling liquid, and imagined myself emptying it slowly on the ground.

Bit by bit, my mood eased.

While the band tuned their instruments, I picked my way through the throng, unpacked my folding chair, and plunked it beside Jen's.

She glanced over at me. "Hey, Daise! It's about time."

I made myself smile in response. "Yeah, sorry. I was hoping Mogwai had forgiven me."

Jen laughed. "After you had him snipped? Not likely."

Cody acknowledged me with a studied casualness. "Good evening, Miss Daisy Jo."

"Officer Fairfax." I shot him a covert glare. He raised one eyebrow in response.

Members of the eldritch always recognize one another, and we can usually identify one another by nature or species in time. Cody knew perfectly well that I knew what he was. After all, in some circles in Pemkowet, it was common knowledge. But the soothsayers aren't the only ones with a code. There's a code of honor in the eldritch community, too. You don't out one another. Everyone in town knew about me because the story had gotten around when I was conceived, even before Mom and I moved back here. It was different with the

Fairfaxes. And I wouldn't out Cody for spite or any other petty reason. I'd catch some serious flak if I did, and his reclusive clan was rumored to be pretty dangerous, too. But that didn't mean I was about to let him work his wiles on Jen. She'd had a hard enough life.

I just wished he weren't so damn good-looking and that I didn't have a crush on him.

I couldn't help it. For me, it went back to the fourth grade. Cody was in the seventh grade, and we rode the school bus together: me to the mobile home community alongside the river out in the marshy sticks where Mom rented the double-wide she owns now, him to his clan's place out in the county woods.

There were bullies on the bus, and if I wasn't exactly afraid of them, I was afraid of the reaction they might elicit from me. They had heard the rumors. They made it a point to pick on me.

Cody made them quit.

It was as simple as that, and I'd been infatuated with him ever since. Even through his transformation from a promising young JV basketball star to a semidropout loser and alleged stoner, through his myriad high-school-and-after conquests, none of which ever lasted longer than a month or two, and through his surprising rebirth as an officer of the law.

Once, he had protected me.

It was enough.

"Ladies, I should be going." Uncrossing his legs and hoisting himself from propped elbows, Cody rose to his feet. He did it in one effortless movement, the kind you might expect of someone who had been a JV basketball star. Or, say, a feral someone who occasionally howled at the moon and turned into something wild, untamed, and bloodthirsty, possibly quite furry. "I'm on duty tonight."

I glanced surreptitiously at the sky, where a crescent moon hung pale in the fading cerulean. The chief and I had never discussed it, but I was pretty sure he scheduled Cody for patrol duty very, very carefully.

"Call me?" Jen asked hopefully.

Cody's gaze slid sideways toward me. He had light brown eyes speckled with gold, a distinctive topaz color. There was a hint of phosphorescent green behind them that only I could see. "We'll see."

He left, and the locals in attendance retrieved various prohibited adult beverages they'd hidden from his view.

"Jeez!" Jen muttered under her breath. "Call or don't call, but you don't have to be a jerk about it." She paused. "Do you think he'll call?"

I shrugged. "I guess we'll see."

Two

The band was good.

And that was a good thing, since it helped distract me while Jen went on and on and back and forth about Cody Fairfax, and whether or not he really was a jerk, whether or not he might call, whether I thought she should go out with him if he did. . . .

Well, that was an easy one.

"No," I said. "I don't."

She eyed me suspiciously. "So he *is* a jerk?"

I sighed. Lying isn't one of the Seven Deadlies, but I tried to avoid it. When you're condemned to go through life worrying about being the spawn of Satan, you learn to avoid anything that leads you down a dark path. "Not exactly. It's just . . . you know his track record."

"Yeah, but people change." Jen scanned the crowd, looking for her eleven-year-old brother. "Brandon! Stay where I can see you, okay?" Lowering her voice, she turned back to me. "Is it true that Cody only became a cop so he could make sure his family doesn't get busted for growing pot in the county woods?"

"No," I said honestly. "I'm pretty sure that's not true."

"They're a little like the Joads or something, aren't they? Like one of those inbred redneck families Mr. Leary made us read about." Jen nibbled on a manicured thumbnail, caught herself doing it, and stopped. "But Cody's different." She shrugged. "Anyway, who are you or I to talk about family, right?"

I didn't say anything. Jen's family was no prize. Her father worked as a caretaker and handyman for a bunch of wealthy families with summer homes. He could fix almost anything, and when he was sober, he had a reputation for being a reasonably decent guy. But he wasn't sober often, especially at home. He had a chip on his shoulder that grew ten times bigger when he drank, and he took his temper out on Jen's mother.

Still, compared to my father, that was nothing.

"Sorry." Jen made a self-deprecating face. "You know what I mean. Your mom's great. You know I love her."

"Yeah." I smiled at her. "I know."

It was true. Ever since Jen and I had become friends in high school, when I helped her track down her older sister, Bethany, at the House of Shadows and make sure she was okay, or as okay as she could be under the circumstances, Mom had taken Jen under her wing, doing her best to make sure Jen didn't get into the same kind of trouble. Which is sort of ironic if you think about it, since dating a werewolf might fall under that category. On the other hand, I knew plenty of girls who'd dated Cody Fairfax without suffering any side effects worse than common heartbreak, so I guess it's no-where near as dangerous as becoming a blood-slut out at Twilight Manor.

By the way, if you're ever conversing with an actual vampire, do *not* refer to the House of Shadows as Twilight Manor. There's a rea-son vampires aren't known for their senses of humor. If you acciden-tally do so, I'd say run, but it's probably already too late.

Los Gatos del Sol ended one song and went straight into another rollicking number. It's hard to stay moody when you're listening to a good Tex-Mex band, and they were cute, especially the accordion player. Funny how accordion players are dorky in a polka band, but kind of sexy playing Tex-Mex or zydeco. This one was working the whole smoldering-Latino thing, tossing his head to keep an errant lock of black hair out of his eyes. Catching my gaze, he winked at me. There was a faint sheen of sweat on the brown skin of his bare throat, and I imagined myself licking it.

A jolt of lust shivered the length of my spine, making my tail twitch.

Yeah, I said tail.

No horns, no bat wings, no cloven hooves, and Mom swears I don't have a birthmark that reads 666 on my scalp. Since I trust her, I haven't shaved my head to check. Mostly, I take after her. I have her pert nose, her cheekbones, her chin. I inherited her fair skin and that white-blond Scandinavian hair everyone thinks comes from a bottle.

But I have my father's eyes, which are as black as the pits of . . . well, you know. And a cute little tail, which I've learned to tuck as carefully as a drag queen tucks his package, only back to front.

For the record, I'm not actually the spawn of Satan. My father's name is Belphegor, lesser demon and occasional incubus. Here's another piece of advice: If you're vacationing in Pemkowet, or anywhere on the planet with a functioning underworld, do *not* mess around with a Ouija board. The spirit you summon might just pay a visit. Mom learned that the hard way, and I'm living proof of it.

Daisy Johanssen, reluctant hell-spawn. That's me.

At any rate, there's a fine line between desire and lust, and unfortunately, lust *is* one of the Seven Deadlies. With my emotions roiling under the surface, it wasn't safe to skirt around the edges of it; not to mention the fact that casual hookups for me tended to go south at some point. There are circumstances under which it becomes very difficult to conceal a tail, even a small one. Believe me, that's an awkward conversation to have.

"Check it out." Jen nudged my arm, jerking her chin at the accordion player. "He's checking *you* out."

"Yeah." Ruefully, I folded up the image of my licking his throat and packed it away in a mental suitcase, zipping it closed. "But it's complicated."

"Yeah, I know." Jen was quiet a moment. "I'm sorry."

"Thanks." I was grateful for her understanding.

In the west, the sun sank slowly behind the tree line. Los Gatos del Sol took a break. The *Pride of Pemkowet*, a replica of an old-fashioned paddle-wheel steamboat, churned down the river to catch the sunset, laden with sightseers. There was a splash, and then oohs and ahhs from the tourists aboard the boat. They'd caught a glimpse of something this time: a flash of a naiad's pearl-white arm, maybe, or an undine's hair trailing like translucent seaweed. The locals stayed seated while the tourists in the park rushed to the dock to see, returning in muttering disappointment. Whatever it was, they'd missed it.

By the time the band began its last set, the dusk was luminous. I watched the children at play.

It was a lovely sight, and only a little bittersweet. I missed the careless unselfconsciousness of childhood, when a boy on the bus could be a hero and nothing more complicated. The youngest kids flitted around the park like dragonflies. There were little girls forming friendships on the spot, one in a flounced polka-dotted skirt, one decked out in tie-dye by latter-day-hippie parents. There was a young gymnast showing off, turning cartwheel after perfect cartwheel. Jen's brother, Brandon, was hanging out with a couple of buddies, trying to look like they were too cool to play with the little kids. He was a surprise baby, what they call a change-of-life baby.

There was a dad letting his three daughters spin around him like a maypole, making themselves dizzy until they fell tumbling onto the soft grass. A few yards away, a boy who couldn't have been older than five or six was swiveling his hips like a miniature Elvis. There was a giggling blond girl with a doll in the crook of one arm leading another little girl in gingham by the hand toward the bushes—

Oh, crap.

My skin prickled. One of those kids wasn't a kid. Reaching into my purse, I eased out my police ID and stood slowly.

"What's up?" Jen asked.

My tail twitched again, this time in a predatory reflex. "Hang on. I'll be right back."

I followed the little girls behind the curve of the ornamental hedge, catching them just as the one was handing her doll to the other.

"Don't take that, sweetheart," I said to the girl in gingham. "That's not a nice doll."

She gave me a confused look.

"We were only playing!" the blonde said in a sweet, piping voice. She had pink, rosy cheeks and blue eyes set in a heart-shaped face.

It takes an effort of will to see through a glamour, and not everyone can do it, but I can. The angelic-looking child before me turned into a milkweed fairy, all sharp-angled features and tip-tilted eyes, a halo of silvery fluff floating around its head, tattered, translucent wings springing from its shoulder blades. The baby doll it clutched had become a ripe milkweed pod oozing sticky white sap. I held up my ID. "Play somewhere else."

The fairy hissed at me, baring a mouthful of needle-sharp teeth. "Thou hast no authority over me! I do not yield to a piece of plastic!"

"No?" I held up my other hand, my left hand, palm outward, displaying the rune written there, invisible to mundane eyes but plain as day to a fairy's. "How about this?"

The fairy recoiled, but held its ground. "Hel should never have granted an ill-gotten half-breed such license!"

For the record, that's Hel the Norse goddess of the dead, unrelated to the hell from whence my father came. Ironic, I know. An eldritch community needs a functioning underworld to exist, which makes Hel the number one supernatural authority in town. And I just happen to be her agent.

"But she did." Anger stirred in me, and this time I let it rise, molten hot and delicious. I could feel the pressure building against my eardrums. On the other side of the hedge, someone let out a startled yelp as a bottle of soda popped its lid. The scent of ozone hung in the air, and electricity lifted my hair. I bared my own teeth in a smile, my tail twitching violently beneath the skirt of my sundress. And since you're probably wondering, no, I don't wear panties. "Do you yield?"

With another hiss, the milkweed fairy vanished.

The little mortal girl in the gingham dress burst into tears.

"It's okay, sweetheart." Reaching down, I took her hand and let my anger drain away. "What's your name?"

She sniffled. "Shawna."

"That's very pretty." I smiled at her. "Okay, Shawna. Let's go find your mom and dad, shall we?"

Within a minute, I had her restored to her parents. Mom and Dad were a nice young couple visiting from Ohio. Caught up in the idyllic mood, listening to the band and watching the antics of the many children, they hadn't even noticed their daughter's fleeting absence. It had been so brief, I couldn't blame them. It was easy to let your guard down on a beautiful evening in Pemkowet.

"Listen." Lowering my voice, I nodded toward the public restroom, a squat cinder-block building rendered charming by virtue of a colorful Seurat painting replicated on its walls. While tourists emptied their bladders inside, nineteenth-century Parisians strolled and lounged on the island of La Grande Jatte. "This may sound strange, but I strongly recommend you take Shawna to the bathroom and turn her dress inside out."

Ohio Mom blinked at me. "I beg your pardon?"

I laid one hand on Shawna's head, stroking the wispy brown hair escaping from her ponytail. "It's just a precaution. But your daughter caught a fairy's attention. Better to be safe than sorry."

Ohio Mom turned pale. Ohio Dad laughed. "Relax, hon. It's just a publicity stunt." He winked at me. "Fairies, huh?"

Tourists, gah!

"It's not a publicity stunt." I couldn't keep a hint of irritation from my voice. "Trust me, you don't want to wake up in the morning and find nothing but a milkweed pod lying on Shawna's pillow."

Which could very well have happened if little Shawna had taken the doll. That was all the fairy would have needed to make a changeling. Oh, we would have tracked her down eventually—I would have known what had happened as soon as I saw the missing persons report, which was how I came by my special role in the department in the first place—but it would have resulted in some seriously bad publicity.

Plus, there's no telling how it might have affected the kid. People who get abducted by fairies come back . . . changed.

It took a bit of convincing, but Ohio Mom decided to humor me. I went back to rejoin Jen.

"Errant fairy," I explained briefly.

She nodded. "Did you get them to turn the kid's dress inside out?"

"Eventually."

Jen made a face. "Tourists."

"Yep."

It wasn't entirely their fault. The Pemkowet Visitors Bureau actively cultivates paranormal tourism. They don't offer any guarantees—most visitors never catch more than a fleeting glimpse of a member of the eldritch community, or they fail to recognize those of us who pass for human—but the PVB isn't exactly candid about the potential dangers, either.

What with being a goddess and all, albeit a much diminished one, Hel keeps most of the eldritch folk in line. The rune inscribed on my left palm is a symbol that I'm licensed to enforce her rules and act as her liaison between the underworld and the mundane authorities. It works pretty well most of the time, at least with the eldritch who respect order. Unfortunately, there are plenty who prefer chaos.

Especially fairies, of which we have many.

Los Gatos del Sol wrapped their last set. The crowd began to disperse into the warm night. Jen retrieved her brother, Brandon, and we discussed plans to schedule a good old-fashioned movie night with my mom, or maybe a *Gilmore Girls* marathon.

I was relieved that she didn't mention Cody again. Generally speaking, Jen and I didn't keep secrets from each other. My crush on Cody was a glaring exception. It was tied up with keeping *his* secret, which I was honor-bound to do.

By the time I made my way back to my place, the young couple in the front apartment were making loud and vigorous love, which I could hear on the landing; but on the plus side, Mogwai had decided to make an appearance. I turned on the stereo and poured myself a couple inches of good scotch, my one grown-up indulgence, then lit a few candles and curled up in the love seat on my screened porch to mull over the evening.

Mogwai settled his considerable tricolored bulk in my lap, kneading and purring his deep, raspy purr.

"Not too bad, Mog." I stroked him absentmindedly. "One changeling scenario averted. Hel would be pleased."

He twitched one notched ear in a cat-quick flick.

I sighed. "And yeah, one hopeless crush flirting with my BFF. But it's not really any of my business, is it?"

He purred louder in agreement.

On the stereo, Billie Holiday sang good morning to heartache, her voice fragile and almost tremulous, and yet there was a fine steel thread of strength running through it, a strength born of suffering and resolve. Of all the music in the world, nothing soothes my own savage beast like women singing the blues. The year I discovered it, I was twelve, and my mom was dating a bassist in a local jazz band, the only serious boyfriend I'd ever known her to have. He introduced us to a lot of music. His name was Trey Summers, and he was killed in a car accident that winter. I still missed him, and I know Mom did, too.

I petted.

Mogwai purred.

Outside, the night was filled with the sounds of a resort town in full revelry: partying tourists frequenting the bars, bass beats thumping. Inside, with profoundly poignant resignation, Billie Holiday invited heartache to sit down.

I blew out the candles and went to bed.

Three

It was almost four in the morning when my phone rang. Living downtown, I'd grown accustomed to tuning out a lot of noise, including the sirens.

But the phone woke me.

I reached for the nightstand across the warm, furry mass of cat pressed against me, grabbing my cell phone. " 'Lo?"

"Daisy." It was the chief's voice, low and gravelly. "We have a situation. I need you here."

I sat bolt upright. "Where?"

"Downtown. By the gazebo." With that, he disconnected.

Displacing a disgruntled Mogwai, I turned on a light and scrambled into street clothes: jeans and a black T-shirt, plain and unobtrusive. Skirts were more comfortable for me, but I'd long since learned I was taken more seriously in pants, and the chief sounded deadly serious. Whipping my hair into a ponytail, I headed out the door and clattered down the stairs.

Below my apartment, the ovens were cranking in the bakery's kitchen, and Mrs. Browne was working her magic, tantalizing aromas of yeasty bread and sweet confections spilling out into the night.

Hearing the side door bang, she came over to tap on the window, an inquiring look on her wizened face. I gave her a quick shake of my head, setting out through the darkened park at a fast jog.

There were two squad cars parked on the street alongside the gazebo, lights flashing, and an EMS vehicle sitting motionless. Not a good sign. On the river beyond, I could see the outline of the fire department's rescue boat. The searchlight wasn't sweeping the water, so whatever they were looking for, they'd already found it.

There weren't any onlookers at this late hour, but Bart Mallick, one of the older officers, was posted on the perimeter.

"Daisy." He tagged me with the beam of his flashlight, his shadowed face impassive. "You shouldn't be here."

My well-tucked tail twitched. "Chief says otherwise," I said in an even tone. "He called for me."

With a heavy shrug, he let me pass.

On some level, everyone in the department knew I had an arrangement with the chief. But the kinds of cases I helped out on were usually small: pickpocketing bogles, will-o'-the-wisps leading tourists astray, that sort of thing. This was bigger, and I had a sinking feeling in the pit of my belly.

Over by the EMS vehicle, a couple of first responders were tending to a pair of soaking-wet figures, wrapping them in blankets and speaking in hushed, soothing tones. Behind the gazebo, there was a body on the ground, and Chief Bryant and Cody Fairfax were standing beside it. Cody was drenched, too, his dark blue officer's uniform plastered to his body and his hair slicked back. His boots and his utility belt lay on the grass at his feet.

The chief beckoned me over. He was a big man, thick and solid, with sleepy, hooded eyes that reminded me of Robert Mitchum on the Turner Classic Movies channel. Right now, they held a look of grave sorrow and regret.

I made myself look at the body.

The drowning victim was a few years younger than me, a college kid, judging from his T-shirt. In the light of the chief's flashlight, his skin looked grayish and mottled. His mouth was agape, whether due to the slackness of death or the futile attempts to revive him, I couldn't say. There was white foam crusting his lips and nostrils. His eyes were open, which creeped me out. You might think that being a hell-spawn would make me less squeamish about death, but you would be wrong.

"What—" The word emerged as a squeak. Clearing my throat, I tried again. "What happened?"

"According to his friends, they got drunk, and young Mr. Vanderhei here bet them he could swim across the river and back. They called nine-one-one when they realized he was in distress. It's happened before, I'm sorry to say." The chief knelt heavily on one knee. "But the timeline doesn't make sense. There's something off about their story. And look at this."

Reaching into his pocket, he pulled out the watch I'd given him and dangled it above the kid's chest. It rotated in a quivering circle, the hands on its face spinning backward with manic violence.

Magic.

The watch was genuine dwarf workmanship, and it responded to the residue of eldritch presence. Whatever else was true, this was more than an accidental drowning.

The chief glanced up at me. "I don't know who or what was responsible for this, but I mean to get to the bottom of it." His voice was grim. "If someone assisted this boy to an early grave, I *will* find out. No one and no*thing* gets away with murder in my town. Are you willing to help?"

I took a deep breath. "Yes. Of course."

Cody spoke for the first time. "Are you sure that's a good idea, sir?"

Oh, crap.

Rising to his feet, the chief fixed Cody with an implacable stare. "It's pretty damn clear that I need someone with ties to the eldritch community on this one, son. Someone else in the department you'd care to nominate?"

After a brief hesitation, Cody shook his head. "No."

"Good." The chief tucked the watch back in his pocket. "Since you caught the call, you can take the lead on the inquiry. But I want you to work with Daisy. The medical examiner's on his way and I've asked him to make this a priority." He jerked his chin toward the EMS vehicle and the victim's friends. "You can start by taking those two down to the station and taking their statements. Maybe you can get the truth out of them."

"Do you want me to notify the victim's parents?" Cody asked. He hoisted an evidence bag containing a wallet. "They're just over in Appeldoorn."

"No." Chief Bryant squared his shoulders. "I'll handle it myself."

It was a tense ride to the station. The victim's friends were in shock, white faced and shivering, still wrapped in the blankets the EMTs had given them. Although he'd donned his belt and boots, Cody was still soaked. All of them smelled like river water, and in a closed squad car, there was nothing at all pleasant about the odor.

"Who got to him first?" I asked softly. "You or the fire department?"

He shot me a look. "I did."

"I'm sorry."

A muscle in his chiseled jaw twitched. "I'm sorry I didn't get there sooner."

Pemkowet's police station is small. We parked the victim's friends in the front office under the supervision of the night clerk, while Cody ducked into the rear office to change into a spare uniform, summoning me to join him.

"Listen." Unbuttoning his shirt, he stripped it off to reveal a lean, muscular torso. A flicker of inappropriate lust stirred in me at the sight of those washboard abs. Apparently even death couldn't deter the Seven Deadlies in a hell-spawn. And Cody Fairfax had a treasure trail leading from his belly button to parts south. Great, now I'd have that image stuck in my brain. He shook himself all over like a dog, water spraying. "This is serious business, okay? So for now, just keep your mouth shut and take notes."

"Okay," I said mildly. "I'm not an idiot."

Cody ran his hands over his damp hair, smoothing it. There was a hot, feral gleam in his topaz eyes. "This could be really, really bad for the community, you understand?" he said in a low voice. "All it takes is one incident to set off a lynch-mob mentality. It's happened before in other places."

"Is that why you're so . . . private?" I asked.

He grimaced. "I come from a long line of people who like their privacy."

Right, along with hunting illegally in the county woods and game preserves during the full moon. "I'll make you a deal. I'll do whatever you say. Just don't mess around with Jen Cassopolis." I paused. "Unless you really do like her, enough to be honest with her. I mean *totally* honest. Then it's none of my business."

He shrugged into a dry uniform shirt. "Deal. Now get out of here while I change my pants."

We interviewed the victim's friends separately, hoping to catch them up in any discrepancies; which is to say that Cody interviewed them while I recorded their statements on the department's only working laptop.

Mike Huizenga was the first interviewee, a hulking defensive tackle at nearby Van Buren College. He had a broad, doughy face and a shell-shocked look.

"Just walk me through your evening," Cody said gently to him. "You said you were barhopping. Where did you start?"

He rubbed his nose with one fisted hand. "Um . . . well, we did some front-loading, you know? Pounded a couple of six-packs."

"Was that at the victim's parents' house?" Cody checked himself. "I'm sorry. At Thad Vanderhei's house?"

"No." He shook his head. "The frat house."

"Triton House?"

"Yeah."

I knew it by reputation as the base of a hard-partying local frater-nity with notoriously dangerous hazing rituals. Even in the summer, Triton House was party central. All three were members, and the kind of guys who were one of the reasons I never went to college.

According to Mike Huizenga, the three amigos got loaded on cheap beer, then drove down to Pemkowet to pick up drunken tour-ist chicks. They hit happy hour at the Shoals, where they downed a few more beers, then worked their way around town in a circuit, do-ing tequila shots at every establishment. No fights among them, no quarrels, just a night that ended in a bad idea and a tragic outcome.

The second interviewee, Kyle Middleton, told the same story, only the bars were in a different order. He was a skinny, jumpy little guy, someone used to being comic relief, now in over his head. I felt a bit sorry for him, but only a bit. Something was definitely wrong with their stories.

Cody borrowed the laptop and consulted my notes. "So you ended up at Bazooka Joe's?"

"Yeah, I think. That's what it's called, right?"

"And you struck out."

"Yeah." Kyle shrugged. "We struck out."

"Too bad."

"*Not*," I muttered.

Cody shot me another look, and I shut my mouth. "See, here's the thing that confuses me, Kyle. Last call's at two a.m. It was three twenty-four a.m. when you called nine-one-one. What were you guys doing for over an hour?"

"Oh . . ." Kyle squirmed. "Just screwing around, you know? Thad had a bottle of scotch he took from his parents' bar. Like a ten-year-old single-malt. Really good stuff. It was his idea to go drink in the gazebo until sunrise. He heard sometimes you can see those, whaddya call 'em, river nymphos at dawn. We got bored waiting. That stupid bet was his idea!" His voice rose and tightened. "It was *his* idea, okay? I never wanted anyone to get hurt!"

My tail twitched.

"Who got hurt, Kyle?" I asked.

He shut down.

"Kyle?" Cody asked in a soft voice. "Were you talking about Thad? Or someone else?"

He looked away. "Can I go home?"

Cody and I exchanged a glance. "One last question," he said. "Did you and Mike and Thad go to the Wheelhouse tonight?"

"No."

"You're sure?" He held up a plastic evidence bag with a sodden matchbook with the Wheelhouse's logo on it. "Thad had this in his pocket."

Kyle's eyelids flickered rapidly. "I don't know anything about it."

"Huh." Cody contemplated the evidence bag. "There's a phone number written on it. Was there someone in particular Thad was trying to hook up with tonight?"

"No. I don't know." He shrugged. "He must have gotten some girl's digits in one of the bars."

"Why wasn't he carrying his phone?"

"I don't know." His voice was taut again. "It must have fallen out of his pocket in the river."

"He jumped into the river with his phone?" Cody sounded skeptical.

"I guess. I don't *know*! We were drunk, okay?"

"Can I see your phone?"

Kyle handed it over. I watched his expression while Cody examined the phone, just as I'd watched Mike Huizenga's when Cody had gone over the same line of questioning with him. Whatever they were hiding, it wasn't on their phones.

"Okay." Cody returned the phone. "Look, I'm sorry to put you through this, but we have to treat any death very seriously, you understand?"

There were tears in the kid's eyes. "It was an *accident*!"

"It certainly seems that way." Cody tapped the evidence bag. "But things aren't always what they seem in Pemkowet. Isn't that right, Daisy?"

A twenty-one-year-old kid had died tonight, and his friends were covering up the truth. It wasn't hard to access a well of simmering anger. I held Kyle's gaze, feeling the air pressure in the room change. "It certainly is."

"Don't worry." Cody rose. "Whatever happened, we'll get to the bottom of it."

Four

Since Kyle's parents lived out of state, Mike Huizenga's parents drove down from Appeldoorn to retrieve both witnesses. They were stalwart descendants of Dutch settlers, rightfully horrified at the death of their son's friend, wrongfully furious that Mike and Kyle had been detained for questioning.

"It's standard procedure, Mr. Huizenga," Cody said patiently. "We're very sorry for the Vanderheis' loss. I'm sure they'd want us to do everything by the book."

"Do you think Jim and Sue Vanderhei will take comfort in knowing their son *died* in this ungodly den of iniquity?" Mrs. Huizenga shouted at him, her chin quivering. "And your response was to harass his grieving friends? I want to file a complaint!"

"They ought to raze this place to the ground," her husband muttered.

Did I mention that Appeldoorn is a highly conservative community that enjoys an extremely uneasy relationship with Pemkowet? Well, it is.

Unseen by the good Dutch folk, a hint of phosphorescent green flashed in Cody's eyes. It gave me a private thrill to see him struggle with his temper, and, strangely, I found it calming. Perverse, but true.

"I'm so very sorry, Mrs. Huizenga," I said in my most soothing voice. "If you'd like to file a complaint, I'd be happy to help you. I'm sure Chief Bryant would be glad to call you and discuss your concerns in person. But it's late, and your son and his friend have had a terrible night. I can't imagine how they're feeling right now." I gave them a sympathetic smile. "Maybe it would be best for everyone if you just went home and prayed on it."

She hesitated.

"She has a point." The husband put his arm around his wife's shoulders. "Let's get the boys home."

The boys nodded with guilt-and-grief-stricken agreement.

It was a relief to see them go, although I had a bad feeling that we hadn't heard the last from the parents.

Cody slumped back into his chair, heaving an exhausted sigh. "Go home and pray on it. That's rich, coming from you."

I perched on a corner of his desk. "You think I can't talk the talk? You think the words are going to turn into poison in my mouth?"

There were tired shadows smudged under his eyes, and his bronze-colored hair had dried rumpled, reminding me of the boy on the bus he had once been. "Apparently not."

I swung one leg. "I didn't choose to be what I am any more than you did. It's what we do with it that matters, right? That's what my mom always said. Isn't that why you stood up for me all those years ago?"

He shook his head. "I hate bullies."

Oh.

"Is that why you became a cop?" I was still curious.

"In part." Cody yawned. "Listen, I need you to pull some photos of those kids so I can ask around, see if their story checks out."

"Do you think it will?"

"No. Do you?"

"No." I shook my head. "I think they're lying, but I don't have the slightest idea why. Do you think they got in a fight or something?"

"No." He rubbed his chin, which glinted with stubble. I thought about his treasure trail, and put that thought out of my mind. "We'll have to wait for the autopsy report to be sure, but I didn't see any obvious signs of a fight on the body or on the witnesses. No bruised knuckles, no black eyes, no knots or lumps." He fought to suppress another yawn. "Thing is, I think they *were* telling the truth about it being an accident. It's what kind of accident it was that they're lying about."

"You think it could have been a water sprite that drowned him?" I asked slowly.

"I don't know." Cody met my eyes. "It's the most obvious possibility. Sirens used to lure sailors to their deaths, didn't they?"

"At sea, yeah, but we don't have sirens here. Not in freshwater." A memory from Mr. Leary's myth and literature class struck me. "There is one drowning-by-naiad incident on record."

"Check it out," he said decisively. "Have you got an in with them?"

I made a face. "Not exactly. But I know how to summon them." Rising and parting the blinds, I peered out the window. "It's too late today already. Sun's already rising. Those kids were on the right track; it has to be done at dawn."

"What about sunset?"

"Not here," I said. "Too many tourists on the river that time of evening. Cody, if it was a drowning-by-naiad, why lie about it?"

"Not a clue."

"What about the number on the matchbook?" I asked.

His mouth quirked ruefully. "Illegible, all but the first five digits. Water damage. I was hoping to find a partial match in the call log on one of their phones."

"No luck?"

"Nope." He paused. "Do you have to report this to, ah, the powers that be?"

"Good question." I shivered a little. I might be Hel's liaison, but let's face it, she's scary. "I'd rather wait until we know more."

Cody nodded. "Your call. Any chance that the chief's magical watch made a mistake?"

"It never has before. But for all we know, it's picking up on the fact that some bogle or puck stole the kid's phone, and his friends are lying for totally unrelated reasons."

An odd look crossed his face. "What would a bogle or puck want with a cell phone?"

"I don't know," I said. For a werewolf cop, he really was surprisingly naive. "They just like messing with mortals. Hell, for all I know, maybe they wanted to hack his Facebook profile."

"Huh. Okay." He pointed at the laptop. "Go ahead and file their statements, and get me those photos from the DMV. I'll finish up the report. We'll get a few hours of sleep and start canvassing as soon as the bars open."

"We?" It surprised me.

Cody shrugged. "Chief wants us to work together, and it doesn't hurt to have a pretty girl on hand when you're questioning bartenders. They're going to be paranoid, afraid we're after them for overserving those kids."

"Maybe we should be."

"Maybe." He rasped one hand over his stubbled chin. "But we did find an empty bottle of Macallan at the scene, so that part of their story checks out. They kept drinking after last call."

"Yeah, but did the bottle come from the Vanderheis' bar?" I asked.

"Good question." Cody gave me an approving look, which faded quickly. "Not one I look forward to asking the bereaved parents."

"No," I murmured. "I wouldn't think so."

After that exchange, we worked together in silence. I took the opportunity to write up a quick report on the milkweed fairy encounter for the Pemkowet X-Files, which is where I keep records of incidents that are eldritch in nature and don't exactly fit into the mundane criminal-justice code. That one already seemed as if it had taken place ages ago. By the time we had finished, it was nearly seven in the morning. The rumor mill was in motion and the phone had begun to ring. I felt sorry for the night clerk, and even sorrier for Patty Rogan, the day clerk coming in to replace him in an hour. It was going to be a long, unpleasant day.

At seven o'clock sharp, the chief lumbered in to conference with us and draft an official statement for the press. He looked haggard and drawn, and I felt sorry for him, too. I wished we had something concrete to tell him, but we didn't.

Not yet, anyway.

It was broad daylight when I left the station. I was tired and my eyes felt gritty. I walked the four blocks to my apartment. Most of the retail shops were still closed, but the bakery was already open, a buzz of speculation spilling through the screen door.

Speaking of buzzing, my phone was doing just that. As soon as I closed my apartment door behind me, I fished it out of my purse. "Hi, Mom."

"Daisy, baby!" Her voice was strained. "Are you okay?"

"I'm fine."

"Mrs. Browne said you ran out of the apartment at four in the morning."

I managed a tired smile. "Do you have her keeping tabs on me?"

"She cares about you." A gently chiding note. "A lot of people in the community do. Is this about what happened?"

"What's that?"

Mom lowered her voice. "Sandra Sweddon told me a boy drowned in the river last night."

Thad Vanderhei's lifeless face flashed behind my eyes, his skin blue-gray and mottled. "I can't talk about it. But I'm fine; I promise. I just need a little sleep."

That made her solicitous. "Be careful, sweetheart. Take care of yourself."

Have I mentioned that my mom is a totally awesome person, despite having made one really bad life choice? One of the awesome parts is that she never, ever makes me feel that she regrets it.

"I will."

"Come see me when you can. I'll read the cards for you."

I nodded, too tired to remember she couldn't see me. "I will. That's a good idea, thanks."

"Anytime," she said before hanging up, blowing kisses into the phone. "Love you always, Daisy, baby."

"Me, too."

I set my alarm and slept.

Five

Two hours later, my clock radio blared to life, shouting out tunes from a classic rock station. Not my usual choice of music, but it does the trick. I jolted into wakefulness and slapped it off, then dragged myself into the shower. The hot water invigorated me. I stood naked beneath the spray, twitching my tail back and forth in a luxuriant manner, letting the water wash me clean.

Okay.

Fresh jeans and a scoop-necked T-shirt, check. Cereal for breakfast, check. Call in vain for Mogwai and fill his bowl, check.

I was meeting Cody at the station at eleven o'clock a.m. That gave me twenty minutes to run an errand.

Plenty of time. Or, at least, it would have been if Casimir had what I needed.

The Fabulous Casimir—I think he'd trademarked the name—was our resident head witch and the proprietor of Sisters of Selene, Pemkowet's local occult store. He was as shrewd as he was flamboyant, and his affinity for cross-dressing had roots in a number of shamanic traditions; although, truth be told, I think he probably would have done it anyway. I'd done business with him a number of times. In fact, the watch I'd bought the chief came from his shop. He greeted me effusively when I entered, the chimes on the door ringing. "Daisy, *dahling*! It's too horrible for words! Tell me, is it true?"

I blinked, still a bit sleep-deprived. "Is what?"

Blinking back at me with long artificial lashes, he lowered his voice. "The Vanderheis' oldest son?" He drew one manicured fore-finger across his throat. "Last night? He went glug-glug?"

Anger rose in me, setting the door chimes to shivering faintly. "For God's sake, Cas! It's not a joke!"

He looked contrite. "I'm sorry. I didn't mean it was. So it is true?"

I sighed. "Yes. And I need a strand of freshwater pearls."

Casimir shook his turbaned head. "Don't keep them in stock, *dahling*. Sorry. Try the bead shop down the street. They're damn near putting me out of business. Stupid mundanes, don't know qual-ity from crapola."

"Will they work?" I asked him. "For a summoning?"

He struck a pose, tilting his chin and weighing invisible scales on his hands. "*Comme ci, comme ça*. Maybe. It depends on their mood, Miss Daisy. *You* know."

I glanced at my watch and decided I could hit the bead shop later. "So what do you know about the Vanderhei kid, Cas?"

He shrugged. "Nothing, really. I know more about the family in general. Very conservative and *very* wealthy. The rumor I heard is that Jim Vanderhei was one of the major backers behind the Prop Thirteen resolution two years ago. Remember?"

"Um . . ." I didn't follow politics closely. "A little help?"

"Oh, girl!" Casimir sighed dramatically. "You can't afford not to pay attention to these things. Prop Thirteen? The one that would have required registered voters to get DNA testing to prove they are a hundred percent human?"

"Oh, right. But it didn't pass."

"Not that time, no. It doesn't mean they won't try again." He nar-rowed his eyes at me. "What do you want with freshwater pearls,

Miss Daisy? I heard the boy drowned by accident." He paled beneath his artfully applied foundation. "Oh, sweet goddess, tell me a member of the community wasn't involved! Because that is *all* the Vanderheis need to turn personal tragedy into a political crusade."

Oh, crap.

Glancing around, I made sure no one else had entered the store. "I don't know, Cas. On the record, we're just covering all the bases. But between you and me, the chief's watch was spinning like a top."

Casimir's Adam's apple bobbed up and down as he swallowed hard. "Best you try to keep that under wraps, girl."

"I know." I pointed at him. "You, too. But if you hear anything, let me know."

He nodded. Casimir might put up a frivolous front, but you don't get to be the head of Pemkowet Coven without being able to keep a secret. Matter of fact, even I don't know who all the members of the coven are. "You be careful out there, Miss Daisy. You know there are folks in the community who are none too fond of you and what you do."

"Yeah, I know. I got hissed at by a milkweed fairy yesterday." It seemed like ages ago. "But if I hadn't intervened, we'd be scouring the dunes for a missing child on top of everything else. What can I say, Cas? I believe in the rule of order. A society as mixed as ours can't function without it."

He raised his hands. "You're preaching to the choir, girl. Just remember there are plenty who believe otherwise." He lowered his voice again. "And *they're* not going to worry that messing with you could breach the Inviolate Wall, Miss Daisy."

I shrugged. "This might turn out to be nothing. I hope it does."

"I hope so, too." Casimir looked worried. "Just watch your back."

"I will," I promised. "And don't worry; I'm not working alone. Cody Fairfax is the lead officer on this case."

"Officer Down-low?" He fanned himself. "Girl, he's all kinds of fine, but you watch him, too. Those furry clans protect their own. If

it gets hot, and he has to choose between having your back and outing himself, I wouldn't trust him to do the right thing."

"I'll keep it in mind," I said. "Thanks, Cas."

The Fabulous Casimir recovered enough of his aplomb to blow
me a kiss. "Anytime, Miss Daisy!"

I mulled over his warning on the walk to the station.

Casimir was right about the rumors about the Inviolate Wall not
protecting me. In eldritch terminology, the Inviolate Wall is what
divides the mortal plane from the divine forces of the apex faiths, the
major living faiths: Christianity, Islam, Judaism, Hinduism, Bud-
dhism, etc. In theory, it means that the divine forces of the major
living faiths can't act directly on the mortal plane, only indirectly
through their millions of adherents. But in places like Pemkowet, the
wall is thinner, not so inviolate. There are cracks, and things slip
through them. Kind of like my father slipped into my mother.

And . . . technically, my existence represents one of those chinks.
And if I were to supplicate my father, Belphegor, for my demonic
birthright, it could cause a full-blown breach and unleash . . . well,
hell on earth.

Which in turn could free up the forces of heaven to combat them,
unleashing . . . well, Armageddon, basically.

Knowing that, one might wonder why the eldritch community
suffers my existence. That's where it gets tricky. According to Hel—
again, that's the Norse goddess, not the infernal plane—if an immortal
deliberately caused my death, it could *also* bring on Armageddon,
because in accordance with ancient laws, my father would have the
right to seek vengeance on earth, thus creating a significant breach in
the Inviolate Wall.

Like I said, tricky.

In a sensible and orderly world, that would mean no one would
ever think it was a good idea to kill me, and it would be in everyone's
interest to keep me happy and complacent, so that I was never
tempted to give in to the dark side and invoke my birthright. Alas,

we do not live in a sensible and orderly world. Ordinary humans have their sociopaths, terrorists, and anarchists capable of destroying everything around them, and laughing while their worlds fall to pieces.

So do we, and the stakes are considerably higher.

It was good to be reminded of it.

I realized my tail was untucked and lashing in my jeans—I buy them a little loose out of necessity—and wrestled my emotions under control before the tourists on the sidewalk behind me began to wonder why the blond girl's butt was trying to escape its denim confines.

Officer Down-low was waiting for me at the station. He did indeed look all kinds of fine after a few hours of sleep, a shower, and a shave.

Even though we worked in the same department, I didn't often see him, since Cody usually worked night shifts. Affinity for the nocturnal and all. It was the first time since grade school that we'd be spending any length of time together. I wondered how long it took his stubble to grow, and whether men of the howl-at-the-moon persuasion had to shave more often than most people.

Or whether, indeed, most bothered. The older members of the Fairfax clan did keep to themselves, but I seemed to remember a couple of them being sort of hairy—not in a Joaquin Phoenix–losing-his-marbles-and-growing-a-long-scraggly-beard way, but more in a sexy Hugh Jackman–as-Wolverine-unexpectedly-rocking-the-muttonchops way.

"Daisy Jo?" Cody waved a file folder at me. "Ready?"

"Huh?"

He thrust the folder into my hands. "Let's canvass."

We hit the town on foot. Downtown Pemkowet is small enough that it's easier to walk than drive. Unfortunately, we struck out left and right. None of the bartenders on duty this early in the day had been working last night. Whether out of genuine disinterest or an instinctive desire to protect their own, everyone we spoke to claimed not to know who had been working.

I staged a detour at the Fabulous Casimir's retail nemesis, Baubles & Beads, where I bought a long strand of freshwater pearls. Mission pearl, check. The salesclerk eyed Cody and me with mild curiosity as I looped them around my neck. I guess women didn't usually shop for cheap pearls with uniformed cops in tow.

"I can get reimbursed for this, right?" I asked him.

"Hell if I know," Cody admitted. "Keep your receipts."

"I will."

His stomach rumbled, and he grimaced. "Daise? We're not getting anywhere at this hour. What do you say we get a bite to eat?"

I smiled. "I say yes."

Every town has its local cop shop, and Pemkowet was no exception. Callahan's Café was only a block and a half away from the station. It was one of those places that for inexplicable reasons, or maybe proximity to the police station, proved tourist-averse and attracted a local clientele instead. Their coffee sucked, but they offered a bottomless cup of it in the age of Starbucks, and they did good things with red meat. Plus, I had a soft spot in my heart for the place. My mom waitressed there for years, and I have fond memories of spending long hours sitting quietly at a corner table with a coloring book. That was when the chief first took a semipaternal interest in me.

I ordered the meat loaf special, because who doesn't love meat loaf? Cody got ribs. And yes, I enjoyed watching him gnaw on them with his strong, white teeth. Most people leave shreds of meat clinging to the bone. Not Officer Down-low.

It gave me a shivery feeling deep in my belly, and made my tail twitch. Those teeth . . . *gah!*

Focus, Daisy.

I cleared my throat. "So . . ."

"Hmm?" Cody looked up from his plate of ribs.

I willed the most titillating of the Seven Deadlies to subside, casting around for a topic that didn't involve discussing the case in public. "You never did say whether you like Jen enough to . . . you know."

"I don't know her well enough to say." He gave me a level gaze. "And since I keep my word, I suppose that means I never will."

I flushed. "I didn't mean—"

Cody interrupted me. "Look, I respect your wanting to protect a friend. But why are you so sure I'd be bad for her?"

Anger flickered. "Oh, you mean other than the obvious? Because you've never dated the same woman for longer than a month or two! I know Jen; she's got a self-destructive streak. She needs someone stable in her life, someone she can depend on."

He looked away. "That's not true."

"I think I know her better—"

"Not that." He looked back at me. "I dated the same woman for over a year."

"Who?" The milk in my coffee curdled as I began ticking his girlfriends off on my fingers. "Sarah Holcombe, Beth Wilcox, Julia Morales—"

"It's no one you know. She lived in Canada." Cody nodded at my coffee mug. "Better simmer down there."

I took a deep breath, imagined myself pouring out a glass of curdled anger. "I don't like being bullshitted, okay? She lives in Canada? Please. That's the oldest gimmick in the book."

Something hard surfaced behind his eyes. "I said *lived*."

Oh.

Suddenly I felt about six inches tall. I opened my mouth, then closed it. I cleared my throat a few times, scrambling to find a shred of grace. "I'm sorry. I didn't know. Was she . . . What happened? I mean, if you want to talk about it."

Cody shook his head. "Not here." Polishing off his ribs, he wiped his fingers on his napkin. "Sam at the Shoals said Brent Timmons was on duty last night. If that's the first place they hit, there's a good chance he'd remember them. It doesn't get that busy until later."

I reached for my phone, glad to have something constructive to do. "I'll look up his address."

"Don't bother." Cody took out his wallet. "I know where he lives."

Six

We drove a way out of town into the countryside, a few miles southeast, but still well within the circle of Hel's influence. It's strongest in Pemkowet, where it's centered, but it actually extends in a ten-mile radius.

Halfway there, Cody spoke without preamble. "She was killed. Shot by a hunter." The muscle in his jaw jumped. "He claimed it was self-defense. The game warden didn't find him at fault."

"Game warden . . ." I inhaled sharply. *Wow.* Okay, I guess it was out in the open now. "She was a werewolf?"

"Why does that surprise you?" His voice was dry. "Ultimately, we have a duty to our clan to mate with our own kind. It's the only way our species can survive."

"What was her name?" I asked.

"Caroline. Caroline Lambert." Although Cody's voice remained calm, his knuckles whitened on the steering wheel when he said her name. "We met at a gathering of the clans in Montreal the summer I was twenty-one."

"Montreal?"

"It has an underground city and a functioning underworld." That muscle in his jaw twitched again. "And a narrow but deep streak of conservative Catholicism that would like to see, like Mr. Huizenga, that very underworld razed and destroyed. The hunter happened to be of that persuasion."

"You think he did it on purpose."

"I'm sure of it," he said grimly. "The Montreal clan weren't discreet, and they had human enemies."

"Did the police investigate?" I asked.

He shook his head. "Caroline was killed during the full moon. Nothing to investigate about a wolf carcass."

"Yeah, but . . ." A sense of indignation swamped me. "Cody, she was a *person*, too! Couldn't her clan have done something?"

"They tried," he said briefly. "The police weren't interested."

I put two and two together. "That's why you became a cop." Mistress of the obvious, me.

Cody gave a curt nod. "We've always existed on the fringes, Daisy, walking the line between human and animal, between civilization and wilderness. It makes us vulnerable in ways that don't affect others in the community. Hunters have always killed wolves. And contrary to popular belief, it doesn't take a silver bullet, just a bullet. As a police officer, I'm in a position to help protect my clan."

I had a feeling there were some serious flaws in his logic, and it occurred to me that if he was serious about the whole mating-within-his-species thing, there was no way he was interested in a real relationship with Jen, but I also had a feeling this would be a good time to keep my mouth shut, so I went ahead and did that.

We drove along the bluff above the river, passing the road down to the mobile home community where my mom still lived. I saw Cody glance briefly in that direction before making a left turn, and I was glad he remembered.

Brent Timmons lived in a ramshackle old farmhouse in the country. He came shambling up to the door when we rang the doorbell, scratching his bulging belly beneath an impressive overhang of bushy black beard.

"Cody, man!" His eyes lit up, and he stuck out one big, hairy mitt of a hand. "Whassup? How's life on the straight and narrow?"

Belatedly, I recognized his name and remembered that Cody and Brent had been in the same graduating class at Pemkowet High.

"Could be better, could be worse." Cody clasped the proffered hand. "Hey, Big B. You mind looking at a few photos for us?"

"Sure, man." Brent nodded amiably. "C'mon in. You want to smoke a bowl?" He glanced at Cody's uniform. "Um . . . just kidding. Maybe crack open a cold one?" He noticed me. "Oh, hey! Hi, there, Pixy Stix." He gave his belly another scratch, peering down at me. "You want to party?"

Oh, blech. My tail lashed.

For the first time since I'd inadvertently evoked the memory of his murdered girlfriend, Cody's lips curved with amusement. "Sorry, Big B. Maybe another time. Pixy Stix and I are on duty. You were working happy hour at the Shoals last night?"

"Yeah." Big B looked bewildered. "So?"

Cody slid the three photos out of the folder. "These guys come in?"

He studied them. "Nah."

"Are you sure?"

"This is about the drowned kid, isn't it?" Brent's gaze sharpened. "No, man. I heard about it this morning." He stabbed the uppermost photo with one thick forefinger. "I always keep an eye on those frat-boy types. More often than not, they're mouthy shits who end up starting trouble they can't even begin to finish. None of them in the bar last night, not at happy hour."

"You're *sure*?" Cody pressed him.

The beard wagged up and down. "Uh-huh. Abso-fucking-lutely, bro."

Another handclasp ensued. "Sorry. Didn't mean to doubt you."

Brent Timmons enfolded Cody in a major bear hug. "No worries, amigo. Don't be a stranger."

"I won't."

We got back into the patrol car. Cody reported in to the dispatcher on duty, then checked his watch. "We've got time to kill before hitting the bars on the list again."

"You don't believe Brent?" I asked.

"I do, but I'd like to get as much confirmation as possible." He rubbed his chin. "And I'd like to show those photos around at the Wheelhouse. There's got to be a reason the kid had that matchbook in his pocket."

I shivered a little. "You know it's a major ghoul hangout?"

Cody shot me an amused look. "Some big, bad hell-spawn you are. Got anything else on your agenda?"

"Maybe," I said. "My mom offered to read the cards for me. We're going right past her place."

His fingers drummed on the steering wheel. "Tarot cards?"

"Ah . . . not exactly," I admitted. "But she's got this knack. Mrs. Browne says it's not uncommon for humans with an affinity for the arcane to come from a long line of psychics and seers."

In most places, this would not be a logical course of investigation, but this was Pemkowet. Cody shrugged. "It can't hurt."

Retracing our path, we drove down to Sedgewick Estate. Yeah, it's kind of a fancy name for a mobile home community, but the truth is, the place has its own charm. The tidy row of units faces a marshy expanse of river dense with tall, waving grass and dotted with willow trees. Most have decks or screened porches added onto them where one can sit and watch the gleaming currents wind their way through the grass.

Mom greeted me at the door with an effusive hug. "Daisy, baby! I'm so glad to see you." Catching sight of Cody, she widened her eyes. "Officer Fairfax! Is everything all right . . . ? No, of course it's not. I mean . . ."

I smiled. "It's okay. We're working together."

"Hmm." Mom's face took on a crafty look, or at least as crafty as it ever got, which wasn't very. Unlike Jen, she knew all about my long-standing crush. As far as I was concerned, moms were exempted from the eldritch code of honor, especially when they were pretty much honorary members of the community. "I see."

"We were passing by, Ms. Johanssen," Cody said politely. "Your daughter said you offered to read the cards for her."

She waved one hand. "Marja, please. Call me Marja. Come in, come in."

As always, Mom's place was something of an organized mess. Jars of canned fruit were stacked on the tiny kitchen counter. Novelty Christmas lights in the shape of starfish were wrapped around the top of the walls. She was in the middle of a project, and there was a half-draped dress form in one corner, lengths and swatches of fabric strewn over every available surface.

"I'm doing the dresses for Terri Sweddon's wedding," she said in response to my inquiring glance. "That's what her mother was originally calling about this morning. You know she's marrying the youngest Dalton boy?"

"I heard."

Mom busied herself clearing a mass of tulle and pins from the old Formica dinette. "I began teaching myself to sew when Daisy was born," she said brightly to Cody. "I had such a hard time finding onesies with enough room for her tail. Over the years, I've managed to turn it into a full-time job. Would you like a cup of coffee?"

He choked out a cough. "Ah, no. No, thank you."

She dusted off a chair and went to fetch her cards from a drawer in the hutch. "Have a seat."

I winced a little at Cody's expression when he saw the well-worn deck of cards, brightly colored and smaller than regulation size. "Aren't those—"

"*Lotería* cards," I confirmed. "She's had them since taking Spanish class in high school."

Cody blinked.

Mom gave him a stern look, although her stern looks weren't very stern, either. We look a lot alike, fair-skinned Scandinavian blondes, but unlike mine, Mom's eyes are as blue as a cloudless sky, and they reflect her innately sunny disposition. "Symbolism is symbolism, and these cards have a rich historic tradition."

"Also, she couldn't afford a tarot deck back in the day," I added. "So she made up her own system with these."

"Which works very well," Mom said.

"Okay," Cody said in a mild tone. "No offense intended."

All of us sat at the dinette, Mom and I facing each other. I picked up the familiar deck and fanned it to find my significator, *El Diablito*, the little devil, placing it faceup on the table. Then I shuffled the deck carefully, holding the image of Thad Vanderhei's drowned face in my mind. When it felt right, I cut the deck three times and passed it back to my mom.

She turned over the first card, laying it in what would be the center of the spread: *La Calavera*, the skull.

"This is your victim." Her gaze met mine. "I have a feeling this reading's going to be pretty literal, sweetheart."

I nodded. "Anything you can tell us might help."

"The underlying influence." Mom turned over the second card: *La Botella*, the bottle.

In his chair, Cody stirred. "Did you talk to her about the case?" he asked me.

"No!"

"Is there a bottle involved?" Mom asked.

Cody sighed. "I can't comment on it."

"*La Botella* could refer to any kind of substance abuse," she said pragmatically. "Under the circumstances, I'd interpret it as referring to the victim, not the questioner. But if there's an actual bottle, it means this reading *is* uncommonly literal, and you should pay close attention to the symbols themselves."

He nodded. "Duly noted."

She turned over a third card: *La Araña*, the spider. "The deeper cause. Your victim was drawn into someone's web."

I tried to recall whether there were any literal web spinners in the eldritch community. The myth of Ariadne came to mind, but wherever she lived, if she yet lived, it wasn't anywhere near Pemkowet. I thought there might be some Native American myths about spiders, and made a mental note to visit the library or ask Mr. Leary about it. My old myth and lit teacher had retired a couple of years ago to dedicate himself to serious drinking, but he was still one of the best sources of arcane information I knew.

"The destination." Mom turned over the fourth card: *Las Jaras*, the arrows. She frowned at it for a moment, then shook her head. "The arrows generally represent a goal, a target or ambition. It doesn't tell us much in this context."

"Unless the perp was a vampire," Cody suggested, leaning over the table to study the cards, caught up despite himself. "You said to think literally, and an arrow's pretty close to a wooden stake." He flushed. "Ah . . . assuming, of course, that there *is* a perp. We're a long way from making that conclusion."

Mom smiled at him. "Don't worry. All readings are strictly confidential." She turned over the final card. "The culmination."

It was *La Sirena*, the mermaid, but the card was upside down, or reversed, as actual tarot readers say.

"An alluring woman," Mom murmured. "But she's in distress."

I touched the strand of freshwater pearls looped around my neck. "Could it be a naiad or an undine?"

"It's possible." She looked worried. "There's something bad going on; that's for sure, Daisy, baby." She gathered up the cards, shuffled, and squared them, setting them back on the table. "I'm willing to try, if you'd like me to do a reading for you, Officer Fairfax, but the cards usually only get vaguer when they're questioned twice on the same issue."

He shook his head. "I'll defer to the expert, but call me Cody."

"Cody." A hint of a smile returned to her blue eyes. "I'd be happy to do a reading on a more personal matter."

He cut the deck and glanced at the uppermost card: *La Luna*, the moon. Of course, that would so totally be his significator. "Another time, maybe."

Her smile deepened. "Anytime."

Seven

"Your mom's not what I expected," Cody commented on the drive back toward the town.

"How so?"

He gave me a sidelong glance, topaz eyes glinting. "Oh, I don't know. She's really . . . nice."

I yawned, slumping a little in my seat. "Meaning I'm not?"

"Let me put it this way," he said, not unkindly. "You've got a short fuse."

I gazed at his hands on the steering wheel. Cody had good hands, nicely shaped, with long fingers, strong and sinewy. Rather like the rest of him, from what I'd seen. "Tell me something I don't know."

He concentrated on the road. "What we talked about earlier . . . You're right about Jen Cassopolis. Her sister's still out at Twilight Manor, right? I'd forgotten about some of the crap she went through. She deserves better."

I sat up straighter. "Hey, now! I didn't say *better*."

Cody shrugged. "It's what you meant, and you were right. It's okay. I'll call her. I'll do the old 'it's not you; it's me' routine. After all, it's true."

"Is it because of the whole mating-within-your-species thing?" I asked.

He didn't answer.

I let the silence ride a while, but I couldn't help being bedeviled with curiosity. "Did you love her?"

"Caroline?" His mouth twisted. "Honestly, I can't say. Long-distance relationships are tough, and there's a lot we never got a chance to find out. But I liked her a lot, Daisy. An awful lot."

"I'm sorry," I said honestly.

He gave me another glance, his expression softening. "I know. Thanks, Pixy Stix."

My tail twitched with indignation. "What's that all about, anyway?" I grumbled. "Why the hell did Brent call me that?"

Cody chuckled. "Hell if I know, but it's funny."

We passed the turnoff to downtown Pemkowet and headed for the rural highway. I grimaced. "You're taking us to the Wheelhouse?"

"Yep. I told you." Cody turned onto the highway. "It's okay. You can stay in the patrol car if you're scared."

"I'm not *scared*," I protested. "I just don't like ghouls."

"Who does?"

"Skanks," I said morosely.

"One man's skank is another man's alluring woman in distress," Cody said philosophically, pulling into the parking lot. "Since you value it so highly, I'm trying to pay attention to your mother's advice. Are you coming or staying?"

I unbuckled my seat belt. "Coming."

Okay, a word about ghouls. Yes, fine, I'll admit it: They do actually scare me quite a bit. The thing is, with vampires, it's a straightforward transaction. Vamps provide you with hypnotic pleasure in exchange for sucking your blood. If they deem you worthy, in time, they might deign to change you and make you one of them. If they don't, like

Jen's sister, Bethany, you're a blood-slut until they get tired of you and either kill you, which fortunately hadn't happened to anyone since I'd been working for the department, or cut you loose, at which point in time you're like any hopeless addict.

Ghouls are different.

By and large, ghouls are as deathless as vampires, but they feed on their victims' *emotions*, which is why they're drawn to the most vulnerable, abused members of society. And that scared me, because in a deep, dark part of me, I could see the appeal of it. I struggled to control my emotions on a minute-to-minute basis. The thought of relinquishing that control . . . Well, there was something sinfully, mindlessly, blissfully appealing in it.

Also terrifying. Because, for better or worse, my emotions defined me.

I took a deep breath before I got out of the car. A handful of gleaming motorcycles were parked outside the bar, mostly Harleys. Because yes, as if ghouls weren't intimidating enough in the first place, most of them belong to biker gangs.

Although truth be told, the bikes themselves were works of art, gleaming and gorgeous. Fighting a perverse urge to try on the nearest for size, I sidled past them, shoving my hands in my pockets.

Cody gave me an odd look. "What are you doing?"

"Didn't you ever see *Pee-Wee's Big Adventure*?" I asked him, envisioning the row of bikes toppling like dominoes.

"No."

I shrugged. "Never mind."

Inside the Wheelhouse, it was dark and seedy. There were a half dozen patrons: four rough-looking guys wearing black leather vests with Outcast motorcycle club patches, and a couple of . . . well, skanks. The sound of clanking pool balls and gruff banter gave way to dead silence as Cody and I entered the bar.

The bartender exchanged a glance with the patrons, then ambled over toward us. He was a wiry guy with ornate tattoos peeking out beneath his rolled-up sleeves, and full muttonchops, a look he was definitely *not* rocking. "What can I do you for, Ossifer?"

Cody opened the file. "I'd like you to look at a few photos, let me know if you recognize any of them."

Muttonchop gave him a tight smile. "Nope, not a one."

Cody's brows rose. "You haven't even looked at them."

Muttonchop glanced toward the back of the bar again. A fifth guy I hadn't noticed before, seated in the shadows, nodded at him. He thumbed through the photos. "Nope, sorry. Can't help you."

"No problem," Cody said pleasantly, moving past the bartender. "I'll just ask these ladies and gentlemen to have a look."

I stuck tight behind him. One of the pool players, a big guy with a walrus mustache, moved to intercept us.

The bartender wasn't a ghoul, but this guy was. Ghouls don't have that underlying deathly white pallor that vampires do, maybe because they're not prone to ignite in sunlight, but you can always tell that their skin tone is a few shades paler than it was when they were alive. And their pupils are always too dilated, their stares too intense. There's something inhumanly *avid* about their eyes.

Walrus Mustache blocked Cody's path with a pool cue. "Mind telling us what this is about, Officer?"

"Just need you to look at a few photos, tell me if you recognize anyone."

He gave the photos a dismissive glance. "Nah, these look like college boys. What are some college pussies doing in a place like this?"

"You tell me," Cody said in an even voice.

"Lemme see." One of the skanks pushed her way forward. She was twenty-something going on forty, haggard before her time. "I seen some college boys in here a couple of weeks ago."

Walrus Mustache rounded on her. "You do what you're told, Loretta!"

Fear flared in her eyes, then faded, replaced by a vacant contentment. "I'm sorry, Al. I didn't mean nothing by it."

A rich, molten tide of anger rose in me, driving out fear. The atmosphere tightened as I stepped out from behind Cody. Behind the bar, the bartender swore as the seal on one of his kegs burst.

I raised my voice. "Let her look at the photos, you big fucking bully!"

Al the Walrus turned that avid gaze on me, his pupils glittering as he licked his lips with a thick tongue. "Says who?" I felt my anger draining against my will, and a sheen of pleasure glazed his eyes. "Oh, you're a tasty morsel!"

A spike of terror jolted me. I willed it to feed my anger, loosing a barrage of fury I hadn't indulged in since adolescence, and held up my rune-marked left hand. "Hel's liaison, asshole!"

Fear flickered in his eyes, and his pupils shrank.

Cody plucked the pool cue deftly from the Walrus's hand, a glint of phosphorescence in his own eyes. "Would *that* be an authority you'd respect?"

From the back of the bar came a deep chuckle. The man sitting in the shadows rose and came toward us, moving with a practiced fighter's loose-limbed ease. "Stand down, man." He clapped one hand on the Walrus's shoulder. "No feeding on the unwilling, remember? They're just doing their jobs."

The man from the shadows had a hint of an accent I couldn't place, something Eastern European, maybe, worn smooth by the patina of time. Definitely not a local. He was tall and broad shouldered, well built without being muscle-bound. Like the others, he wore a leather vest with an Outcast patch over a T-shirt and jeans, but somehow he made it look more of a fashion statement, less of a lifestyle choice. He had high, rugged cheekbones, black hair he wore a little too long, and pale ice-blue eyes, the kind you see on husky dogs sometimes.

Okay, that's a terrible comparison, but the point is, he was gorgeous.

He was also a motherfucking ghoul.

I swallowed against a surge of attraction and fear, altogether losing my grip on fury. Beside me, Cody bristled. I stood, braced in numb horror, expecting the man from the shadows to drink my emotions, but he only waited with an expression of patient amusement while I wrestled myself under control.

That avid spark in his ice-blue eyes was there, no mistaking it, but this ghoul was no slave to his appetites. I had a feeling he was very, very old.

"Better?" he asked.

I nodded.

He turned to Cody, looking him up and down. "Interesting. Very interesting. May I have a look at those photos, Officer?"

Cody handed over the file. "Don't think I've seen you before. You got a name, son?"

"Son." The ghoul laughed deep in his chest. "Yes, Officer. My name is Stefan. Stefan Ludovic. I haven't been in Pemkowet long, but I hope to stay here." He scrutinized the photos. "I'm sorry. I haven't seen these boys." He beckoned. "Loretta?"

Loretta came forward with alacrity, peering at the photos. "Yeah, them's the ones. Them two, anyway." She pointed at Thad Vanderhei and Mike Huizenga. "They was asking for Ray D. I don't remember the skinny little guy."

I whipped out my notepad, jotting notes.

"Ray D." Cody rubbed his chin. "Is he dealing meth again?"

"Not in my territory." Stefan the ghoul's voice went flat, his pupils shrinking. "The nectar of chemically induced emotions is poisonous."

Cody gave him a speculative look. "So you're new in town, but this is already *your* turf?"

Stefan waved one negligent hand. "Does anyone dispute it?"

No one did, although a couple of them, like Al the Walrus, didn't look too happy about it.

By the time Cody was through questioning Loretta, it was established that Thad and Mike had been in the bar looking for Ray D two weeks ago Saturday, but had failed to find him, because no one had seen Ray D for several months. No one knew where he was living or how to contact him, and no one knew why a couple of college kids were looking for him, or at least no one would admit to it. As far as they were concerned, no one even knew whether Ray D had a last name.

New-ghoul-in-town Stefan was adamant that Ray D wasn't dealing on his turf, and the weird thing was, I thought he meant it. There's a long-established connection among ghouls, biker gangs, and drug dealing, what with a lucrative illegal activity that sows misery being the perfect confluence of ghoulish interests, but Stefan appeared dead earnest about the whole poisonous-nectar business.

Also weirdly, I found that sort of hot in a creepy way. I know. So wrong, but true.

"Thanks for the cooperation," Cody said to Stefan. "It's appreciated."

The ghoul inclined his head. "Anytime, Officer." His ice-blue gaze settled on me, his pupils dilating. "And it was a pleasure to meet you, Miss . . . ?"

"Johanssen," I said. "Daisy."

He gave his deep chuckle. "Daisy?"

"Uh-huh." The way he was looking at me made my insides squirm, not entirely unpleasantly.

"Daisy," Stefan repeated. "I hope our paths cross again." He smiled. "For less unfortunate reasons, of course."

"I think we're done here." Cody's tone was brusque. "We'll be in touch if there's anything further."

"Of course."

On the way out of the bar, I spied a fishbowl filled with matchbooks and grabbed one, figuring it couldn't hurt to compare it to the matchbook found in Thad Vanderhei's pocket. The muttonchopped bartender, busy mopping up a prodigious amount of spilled beer, startled and then glared at me. I guess my little temper tantrum caused more than one keg to blow its seal. I gave him a half-assed apologetic shrug and followed Cody out the door.

No, I did not successfully fight the urge to look back and see if Stefan the hunky ghoul was watching me, and yes, he was.

Eight

"Okay, you were right; that was productive," I said as we pulled out of the parking lot. "We've got an actual lead."

"Mm-hmm." Cody didn't sound as pleased as I'd expected. "What?"

"If Loretta's telling the truth, Thad and Mike came into the bar looking for Ray D. They claim no one's seen him for months; no one knew how to get in touch with him." Cody reached over and tapped the matchbook I was holding. "But Thad and Mike appear to have left with a phone number."

"So someone's lying," I said.

"Maybe." He shrugged. "Or maybe they got the number from someone who wasn't there today, and Loretta didn't see it."

I flipped open my notepad and glanced at the list I'd made of all the patrons Loretta remembered being in the bar that afternoon. "Are we going to question all of these people?"

"If we have to."

It had already been a long day of questioning witnesses, and we had all the other bars to revisit. It made my head ache. "I didn't realize regular police work would be quite so tedious," I admitted.

Cody smiled. "You watch too many movies."

"You don't watch enough," I retorted. "I can't believe you haven't seen *Pee-Wee's Big Adventure*! It's a classic."

"If you say so."

"Yes, Mr. Laconic. I do." I studied his profile. "So what did you think of Stefan Ludovic?"

He stopped smiling. "Didn't like him; don't trust him." He glanced at me. "For someone who claims not to like ghouls, you gave a pretty convincing performance to the contrary."

Ooh, alpha-male jealousy! A tingle ran down my spine, culminating in a burst of pleasure at the base of my tail. "What are you talking about?" I scoffed disingenuously. "I barely spoke to him."

"Uh-huh." Cody's expression turned wry. "Thing is, I can't figure out if he was being helpful to pull rank in the Outcasts or just to impress you." He drove across the bridge and crossed into the left lane, signaling for the turn to downtown Pemkowet. "Or maybe it's something else altogether. Maybe he's trying to throw us off the scent."

I shook my head. "I get the impression he's clever enough for it. Loretta, not so much."

"Good point."

It felt good to earn Cody's nod of approval—not in a needy, daddy-issues kind of way, just in a general-validation way. "So far, we don't make too bad a team, do we?"

His lips twitched. "I have to admit, I liked the way you stood up to Al."

That had felt good, too, but I couldn't help wondering what would have happened if Stefan hadn't intervened.

We parked at the station and made another round of the bars on foot. By now, word had spread, and the bartenders and waitstaff were expecting us. Tim Bradley at the Merryman was fairly sure he hadn't served any of the three, but a waitress named Lucy Briggs working the outside deck thought she might remember them. No one at Bob's Bar and Grill could make a positive ID. Rosalind Meeks, the first bartender we asked at Bazooka Joe's, where the threesome had allegedly been for last call, just laughed at us.

"End of the night? Are you kidding me?" She gestured around. It was a vast, cavernous space smelling of stale beer and mildewed carpets. "If they came in *now*, sure, I might remember them. But last call?" She shook her head. "This place is wall-to-wall with college kids, and let me tell you, they all look alike after a while."

Cody leaned forward. "You know we're not looking to get anyone in trouble, right? We're just trying to verify these kids' story."

Rosalind gave him a world-weary smile. "Honey, you don't need to whisper sweet nothings to me. I understand there's a boy dead." She took another look at Thad Vanderhei's photo. "Twenty-one years old, probably still excited he could get into a bar legally. But I'm sorry; I honestly can't say."

"Thanks for trying." Cody gathered the photos.

"Anytime." This time, her smile had more wattage. "You're Caleb Fairfax's younger brother, right? I went to school with him. How's he doing?"

"Good."

"Married?"

Cody nodded. "Married, two kids."

"Ah, well." Her wattage dimmed. "You tell him Rosalind says hi. We dated for a month or two, you know."

"I'll be sure to tell him."

We got the same story when we questioned the rest of the bartenders, waitstaff, and bouncers on duty, and I didn't have the sense any of them were lying. Truth was, there was nothing especially distinctive about the trio. Three average-looking white boys in college T-shirts, board shorts, and flip-flops. You couldn't throw a rock without hitting one of those in Pemkowet in the summer.

The lack of resolution was frustrating, and by the time we finished, I *felt* like throwing a rock at someone.

"Why couldn't one of them have flaming red hair?" I muttered. "Or a birthmark, or a distinctive tattoo, or . . . or six fingers on one hand or something."

"Is that from a movie?" Cody sounded tired.

"Don't *tell* me you never saw *The Princess Bride*." I stifled a yawn. "I swear, when this is over, I'm going to make you come over to watch a movie marathon with Mom and me."

"I can think of worse fates." He glanced at his watch. "Look, it's been a long day, and we're both operating on a few hours' sleep. You've got your . . ." He gestured at the strand of freshwater pearls still looped around my neck for the sake of convenience. "Your naiad summoning at dawn?"

"Yeah," I said. "You want to meet me in the parking lot of the nature preserve? We can hike from there."

Cody hesitated. "No, I trust you to handle it on your own. That's the kind of thing the chief brought you on board for. Go home. You can type up your notes later in the morning. I'll meet with the chief and give him a verbal rundown."

"Okay."

I had a feeling Cody was reluctant to venture any deeper into the eldritch community than he already had; although he'd been quick enough to suggest going to the Wheelhouse, a known ghoul hangout. But then, that was only following the evidence.

Oh, hell, who knew? I didn't pretend to understand men.

Maybe I should ask my father, I thought, and the thought almost made me giggle. The ironic thing was, I *did* have the means. Belphegor, lesser demon and occasional incubus, had made a pact with my mother. If I summoned him, he would answer.

I knew; I'd done it once, when I turned eighteen. I won't do it again, not ever. I just had to know whether or not it was true. And it doesn't summon him to the mortal plane, in case you were wondering. I'm not that stupid. It's more like . . . Skyping with the infernal realm.

The problem was that Belphegor's idea of fatherly advice consisted of attempting to convince me to invoke my demonic birthright, at which time great powers of temptation, seduction, and destruction would become mine to wield, and men would fall at my feet in supplication and adoration.

He kind of glossed over the whole part about it causing a full-blown breach in the Inviolate Wall, leading to Armageddon.

I still hear his voice sometimes. When the wall that divides us is especially thin, my not-so-dear old dad likes to show me what I call temptation scenarios.

"Daisy?" Cody snapped his fingers in front of my face. "Lost you there for a minute. See you at the station?"

"Huh?" I shook myself out of my reverie. "Yeah, right. Sorry. I'll be there as soon as I can tomorrow."

I walked the few blocks to my apartment, where I was surprised and pleased to find Mogwai waiting for me. I spent a few minutes scratching under his chin while he purred and regarded me with a cryptic look; then I filled his bowl. Too tired to bother with cooking, I microwaved a bowl of ramen noodles for myself—hey, when you're in your twenties, that's a perfectly acceptable dinner—then sat down with Mogwai on my futon to watch some mindless TV.

At a little after nine, my phone buzzed. I glanced at it and picked up. "Hey, Jen."

"Hey, Daise." My best friend's voice was listless. "I just wanted to call and see if you were okay."

"I'm fine. Just tired." Tucking the phone under my chin, I picked up the remote and muted the TV. "What's up? You don't sound good."

There was a silence on the other end. "I don't want to bother you. You've got a lot going on."

"You heard?"

She gave a faint snort. "Are you kidding? Who didn't?"

"Well, then you know I can't talk about it, so you might as well tell me. What gives, girl?"

"Nothing."

I stroked Mogwai. "Jen."

She sighed. "Cody Fairfax called to apologize for leading me on last night. He actually gave me the whole 'it's not you; it's me' shtick. Can you believe it?"

"Maybe it's true," I said.

Another silence, longer than the first one. When she spoke, there was an edge of suspicion in her voice. "Did you say something to him?"

"Jen—"

"Don't fucking 'Jen' me! I know you're working with him now."

"It's just . . ." I made a face. This would have been a lot easier if I could have told her the whole truth. "Yeah, okay, I told him you needed someone stable, someone you could depend on. And that if he wasn't going to be that guy, if he wasn't interested in a real relationship, he shouldn't mislead you."

"You don't *know* what might have happened! You had no right!" Her voice dropped. "But you're not exactly a neutral third party, are you? You've got your own reasons for warning him off me."

"Don't—"

"Oh, fuck you!" She hung up the phone.

I tried calling back, but she wouldn't pick up. Guilt pricked my conscience. I cared a lot about Jen. She'd been my best friend for a long time, my only real friend in the ordinary mundane community. Ever since I'd helped her out with her sister, Jen had had my back, defending me through thick and thin. She'd put herself on the line for me more than once. In the cutthroat world of teenagers, that was a big deal. There were times in high school when I might have gone full-blown Carrie-at-the-prom if it hadn't been for Jennifer Cassopolis; and yes, that's another movie Mom and I watched together. Call it a cautionary tale if you will.

Crap.

Jen was right: I wasn't neutral. She knew me too well, and I hadn't kept my secret as well as I'd kept Cody's. And it was stupid, because based on what he'd said today, even if he were interested in me, it could never go anywhere. I thought he was a serial dater because if he got too close to anyone, they'd start to realize he vanished once a month during the full moon.

Hell, if I was honest with myself, I didn't know how much of my attraction to him was because he wasn't a full-blooded human. I'd dated a few guys over the years . . . Well, no. Even that wasn't really true. I'd never had an actual boyfriend. I'd hooked up with a few guys over the years, but there had usually been a fair amount of drinking involved, at least on their end. Ultimately there was always a spark missing, a level of passion I hungered for that went beyond the mere mortal. And yes, there was usually a point where they freaked out on me, and yes, it had a lot to do with the tail. Well, that and what it represented, I guess.

At least a guy who turned into a wolf once a month wasn't likely to freak out over one small posterior appendage. But that was no reason to throw my BFF under the bus. For all I knew, Cody and Jen might have dated for a month and parted amicably. Or maybe they would have fallen in love, and he would have bucked clan tradition.

I doubted it.

More likely Jen would have ended up like the bartender Rosalind who dated Cody's brother, still wistful and pining fifteen years later.

I sighed and turned off the TV.

I could tell myself that all day long, but even if it was true, I hadn't done the right thing. My loyalty should have been to Jen, not to Cody and an unspoken eldritch code. I shouldn't have interfered. I should have told her the truth and let her make her own choices.

Too late now.

I poured myself a couple inches of scotch and put Nina Simone on the stereo. She sang in a lower octave than most women, deep and soulful. Throughout her life, she'd struggled with the mortal demons of mental illness. Tonight, the sound of her voice soothed an ache in me. "It's nobody's fault but mine," Nina sang, commiserating with my guilty conscience.

Wandering onto the porch, I watched the afterglow fade in the west, and listened to the sounds of Pemkowet on a summer evening.

It sounded just like last night.

A young man was dead, and most of the world went on, oblivious. I went back to the living room, flipped open my own case file. Thad Vanderhei stared up at me from his DMV photo, a bland smirk on his face and a faint impression of a circle flattening his hair, suggesting he'd taken off a baseball cap to have the photo taken.

On the stereo, accompanied by a spare, haunting piano arrangement, Nina confirmed in a mournful tone that if she died and her soul was lost, it was nobody's fault but hers.

I brushed Thad's face with one fingertip. "What did you do?" I murmured. "What were you up to, and whose fault was it?"

No one but Nina Simone answered.

Nine

Once again, I was awakened from sleep in the wee hours of the night, this time by Mogwai turning from a warm, dense ball of fur curled against my side into a hissing, spitting, feral creature uttering a low, unearthly wail. Leaping from the bed, Mogwai dashed toward the screened porch.

I sat bolt upright. "What the—"

Outside the screened porch, there was a clatter and a clash, followed by the sound of a door banging open, a rising guttural roar, an alarmed human-sounding shout, and the sound of running feet pounding down the alley.

Yanking on a pair of jeans below the tank top I slept in, I grabbed my phone, unlocked the door to my apartment, and ran downstairs.

Mrs. Browne was in the alley, a broom clutched in her gnarled hands and raised like a club. There was no trace now of the sweet little old lady she usually appeared to be. The lines on her wizened face had hardened into something ancient and fierce and dangerous, filled with all the righteous fury of a brownie protecting its household.

That was another reason I usually felt safe in my apartment at night.

Left to their own devices and provided the appropriate offerings—in Mrs. Browne's case, a fully stocked and prepped bakery kitchen— brownies are benevolent, domestic souls. When threatened, they can and will defend their chosen household with the strength of ten.

"Daisy, lass." She lowered her broom, her expression easing. "Are ye well?"

"I'm fine, Mrs. Browne. Did you see what it was?"

She shook her head. "I heard the ruckus and came a-running." Her broad nostrils flared. "Mortal by the smell o' him, with a skinful o' beer." She pointed toward the west end of the alley, where it curved past the Christian Science church. "He went thataway. Do ye reckon it were just a burglar or a creepin' Tom?"

There was a soft thud from that direction, then a movement in the shadows that made me jump. Mogwai stalked out, his fur bristling.

I relaxed. "I don't know. I'd like to think so, but . . ."

"But there's ill doin's afoot." Mrs. Browne peered at me beneath her furrowed brow, her deep-set eyes as dark as bog water. "Have ye spoken to the nixies yet?"

"Not yet." Nixies fell into the same category as naiads and undines. "I'll go at dawn."

She patted my hand. "I've a nice tray of buns fresh from the oven. Come inside and have one, child. It will help settle your nerves."

It wasn't an offer anyone in their right mind would refuse, no matter what the circumstances. Pocketing my phone, I followed her in through the back door of the kitchen, Mogwai winding around my ankles.

I perched on a stool, nibbling on the warm cinnamon bun Mrs. Browne gave me. Trust me: If you think you know what heaven in the form of a fresh cinnamon bun tastes like, you're mistaken. This was cloud-light and soft as a pillow, laced with subtle layers of butter and cinnamon, just the right amount of icing melting atop it, miles away from the immense, glutinous blobs of dough drenched in cloyingly sweet icing you get at those Cinnabon franchises that permeate malls and airports. Aside from inducing a passing concern that I might be succumbing to gluttony, it did indeed help settle my nerves.

"Do ye reckon this was about the boy who was killed?" Mrs. Browne asked, pouring some cream into a bowl for Mogwai. He lapped it eagerly.

I took a bite, chewed, and swallowed. "Do you know for a fact he was killed?"

"Nay." Her look turned shrewd. "But I know for a fact you'd not be looking into it if there weren't somewhat off about the boy's death. The regular police, aye. Not you, Daisy, lass."

I took another bite. "It may be nothing. But if you hear anything about it in the community, you'll let me know?"

Mrs. Browne huffed. "Don't go offendin' me, now! Of course I will. But no one I've spoken to knows aught." She upended a large bowl of bread dough onto the counter, dusted her strong, nut-brown hands with flour, and began pummeling the yeasty mass. "You do know your dear mother's worried about you?"

"I know." Smiling, I finished my cinnamon bun. "That's why she's got you looking out for me, isn't it?"

She didn't return my smile. "You be careful, child. I do what I can to protect my own here." She waved one floury hand in the direction of the door. "There's naught I can do out there."

Hopping down from the stool, I kissed her wizened cheek. "I know, Mrs. B. Thank you. If you hear something out back in a few minutes, it's just me."

She huffed again, flapping her hand at me. "Go on with ye, then."

With Mogwai trotting at my heels, I went upstairs to fetch my flashlight, then back downstairs to have a look around.

There was a dent in the plastic lid of the bakery's Dumpster. Scanning the ground beneath it with the beam of my flashlight, I made out the faint impression of a footprint in the dusty patch between the alley and the Dumpster. It was facing away from, not toward, the disposal unit.

Someone had climbed onto the Dumpster, then jumped down and run away, scared off by Mogwai's caterwauling and Mrs. Browne's wrath.

My tail twitched with nervous energy.

Fishing my phone out of my pocket, I glanced at the time. A quarter hour short of three o'clock in the morning. That meant it could have been nothing, an energetic drunk meandering home unusually late from the bar, hopped up on vodka and Red Bull and bent on idle mayhem. I squatted lower and studied the footprint, measuring it against my own. It definitely belonged to either a man, or a woman with unfortunately large feet. Given the odds, I'd bet on the former. The imprint had been left by a sturdy industrial tread, maybe a work boot.

Or a motorcycle boot.

Oh, crap.

I knocked on the back door of the bakery kitchen before poking my head inside. "Mrs. Browne?"

"Eh?" She cocked her head at me.

"You said you thought it was a mortal," I said. "Any chance it could have been a ghoul?"

I was hoping she would say no.

Instead, she looked thoughtful. "Well, now, that would depend on its diet, Daisy, lass. Those what exist on pure emotion, more often than not they reek of misery. But there's ghouls that walk among us and pass for ordinary folk. They can eat and drink like mortals; it's only that they take no sustenance from it. One of those . . ." She shrugged. "Aye, one of those might have fooled my nose."

I sighed.

Her expression hardened. "Don't tell me you're mixed up with the likes o' them, Daisy Johanssen!"

"No, no." I willed away a quick vision of Stefan Ludovic and his disturbingly patient ice-blue gaze. "Just checking."

Back outside, I stood uncertainly before the Dumpster, thumbing through the contact list on my phone.

I wanted to call Cody.

But lingering guilt stayed my hand. Also, I didn't have the first piece of evidence that my late-night maybe-would-be intruder had anything to do with this case. Hell, we didn't even know whether it *was* a case yet.

So I settled for splitting the difference. Treating it as a possibility, I used my phone to take photos of the dented Dumpster lid and the dusty boot print.

"Good enough?" I asked Mogwai.

Mogwai answered with a low, distressed howl followed by a gagging sound, his sides heaving as he hunched over in the alley, opened his jaws, and barfed a prodigious mixture of kibble and rich cream all over the boot print. Distancing himself from the mess, he shot me an embarrassed look.

I'd had a feeling that bowl of cream was a bad idea, but so is refusing a brownie's hospitality.

Oh, well.

"Never mind," I said to him. "At least you puked outside, big guy. C'mon; let's go back to bed."

Approximately two hours later, my alarm rousted me from the warm confines of my bed, Creedence Clearwater Revival informing me that there was, in fact, a bad moon on the rise.

"No shit," I mumbled, slapping at the snooze alarm. "Tell me something I don't know, huh?"

Seven minutes later, Mick Jagger told me that while he was so hot for me, I was so cold, like an ice-cream cone.

"As if." This time I turned the alarm off and hauled myself upright. "You're an old man, Mick Jagger. When's the last time you had an ice-cream cone?"

The clock radio remained silent. Nestled into a tangle of sheets and blanket, Mogwai purred obliviously.

It was a bit after five o'clock in the morning and still dark outside. Yawning, I dragged myself into presentable clothing. Naiads are particular about appearances. A short skirt of summer-weight gray wool, check. A sleeveless white cotton shirt, check. Freshwater pearls looped around my neck, check. Given the hike ahead of me, I opted for sensible footwear, shoving my feet into a pair of white Keds and hoping the naiads would overlook them.

My old Honda Civic hadn't been driven for a couple of days, and it whined in protest when I turned the key in the ignition before catching. It wasn't that far to the nature preserve, but after last night, I didn't feel like walking the streets alone.

Even in the car, I found myself glancing nervously in the rearview mirror, but the town was empty.

Five minutes later, I pulled into the parking lot of the Ellsworth Nature Preserve. It, too, was empty. You might think that would be a given at this hour, but the preserve was a favorite haunt of bird-watchers, and those people are crazy.

Flicking on my flashlight, I set out along the marked trail that led to the river. That was the easy part. When I reached the river, I departed from the trail and plunged into the undergrowth.

I'd spent a lot of time playing along the river as a kid, but that had been years ago, and it seemed I'd lost the knack of moving effort-lessly through nature. Twigs caught at my hair, and vines tangled my feet. I blundered underneath low-hanging branches and tripped over fallen logs.

By the time I reached my destination, a broad, secluded bend in the river, there were streaks of orange and pink in the sky, mirrored in the still surface of the water. A shy green heron took issue at my approach, tall-stepping carefully away into deeper cover among the reeds. Dragonflies were beginning to stir, darting about on translu-cent wings.

I took a moment to drink in the beauty and tranquillity of the place, then removed the string of pearls and broke it with a sharp yank, pouring the tiny iridescent beads into the palm of my hand.

"Sisters of the river!" I called. "I come bearing offerings!"

With that, I flung the pearls toward the river. They fell in a shimmering rain, pebbling the smooth surface of the water.

I didn't have to wait long before the river roiled in answer, dozens of lithe figures flitting through the water in response to my summons: naiads with milk-white skin, undines with hair trailing like glassy kelp, quicksilver nixies darting like minnows. They dived deep into the green waters in pursuit of my offering. I'd never seen so many in one place, and the sheer loveliness of it made my heart ache a little. That lasted for as long as it took the head cheerleader of the aquatic mean girls to open her mouth and speak.

A naiad surfaced before me, her alabaster shoulders bobbing above the water, disdain on her beautiful face. "What manner of offering is this?" she demanded, holding up a bead between thumb and forefinger. "These are *cultured* pearls."

Inwardly, I sighed.

"Forgive me, sister," I said aloud in a humble tone. "They were the best I could obtain on short notice." I gestured at an undine behind her who was threading pearl beads through her glimmering hair. "Do they not enhance your beauty?"

The naiad gave a sniff, her gaze skating over me and lingering pointedly on my white Keds. "What do you seek, halfling?"

"A young man drowned in the river the night before last," I said. "I would know how."

The naiad reared up in the water, baring a pair of coral-tipped breasts I had to reluctantly admit were pretty exquisite. Capable of luring a man to a watery doom? That, I couldn't say. *"Do you accuse us?"*

"No." My voice hardened. I held up my left hand, revealing Hel's rune. "Look, I've observed the protocols out of courtesy, but I have the right to ask. What do you know of the events that transpired that night?"

Pursing her lips, the naiad called to the others in a foreign tongue, silvery and lilting. The others responded in kind. In the golden light of dawn, their faces were inhuman, lovely, and utterly unconcerned.

"I know it was naught to do with us," the naiad said dismissively.

"Okay, but what happened?" I persisted. "According to his friends, he entered the river of his own volition, and began having difficulty swimming about halfway across. Can any of you confirm it?"

The naiad assumed a look of outrage. "Now you accuse us of failing to come to his aid?"

"I'm not saying that!" I said with irritation. "I'm just asking you to bear witness. You must have seen—"

She jerked her chin at me. "We have answered your question, Hel's liaison! Nothing more is required. I am sorry a mortal boy is dead, but I swear to you on my oath, it had naught to do with us."

"Yes, but—"

"You have my oath, halfling! You come to us bearing *cultured* pearls, shod like a peasant, and think to earn our goodwill?" The naiad's eyes flashed with annoyance. "Farewell." With a flicker of movement, she turned and dived, and like a shoal of fish, the others followed suit.

Within seconds, there was nothing more than gilded ripples on the surface of the water to mark their departure.

I swore, my tail lashing in frustration. "I'll be back!" I called. "Your oath isn't enough! I need to know what you *saw*, you heartless bitches!"

In answer, a rill of silvery laughter hung in the air.

Naiads, gah!

Ten

Disgruntled, I reported to the police station.

It wasn't a good scene. Patty Rogan, the day clerk, beckoned me aside as soon as I entered the station. Behind the frosted glass on the door to the chief's office, I could make out several figures and hear raised voices.

"What's up?" I whispered to Patty.

"The chief and Cody are in there with a reporter from the *Appeldoorn Guardian*," she whispered back. "The Vanderhei family's making a stink in the papers. They're demanding that the chief either disclose details of the investigation, or rule it an accidental death and order the kid's body released."

Oh, crap.

"Do we have the autopsy results?" I asked.

Patty shook her head. "The ME's office is backed up. It might be a couple of days yet."

With a reporter in the station, I decided this would be a good time to keep my head down and concentrate on paperwork. I grabbed a seat at the corner desk and typed up the notes from yesterday. When the reporter departed fifteen minutes later, I didn't even look up. As soon as the door had closed behind him, the chief called me into his office.

"Daisy." Chief Bryant took a seat at his desk, his chair creaking beneath his weight. His face looked old and careworn. He gestured at Cody, whose expression was tense and guarded. "I've heard about the results of yesterday's investigation. Anything new to report?"

I shook my head. "The naiads and the other water sprites say they had nothing to do with the Vanderhei boy's death, and that I believe. Beyond that, I'm afraid they were uncooperative."

The chief sighed. "So we can neither confirm nor deny any of the circumstances surrounding the boy's death with absolute certainty?"

"At this point, no," Cody said bluntly. "I'm sorry, sir."

"Not your fault, son." Chief Bryant gazed into the distance. "I just wish it wouldn't be so goddamned easy."

"Easy?" I echoed.

His gaze returned, sharpening. "To rule it an accident. Close the book on it and move on. It's what it looks like. It's what the family wants. It's what the county sheriff's office wants. Hell, it's what everyone wants. And if I don't, it could bring a shitstorm down on Pemkowet. Is it worth it?"

I glanced at Cody.

He looked away.

"What we know doesn't add up," I said. "Not yet. As far as the naiads go, there are . . . other avenues I can pursue to get them to talk. Or at least one that I can think of. But it's up to you, sir." I paused. "How big a shitstorm?"

The chief grimaced. "Big."

"With all due respect, sir, fuck 'em," Cody said softly. "This is *our* town."

For that, along with myriad other reasons, I could have kissed him.

"Yes, it is, goddammit!" Chief Bryant slammed his hands down on his desktop. "All right. I'm going to lean on the ME's office. Brody Jenkins is taking heat, too. I have a feeling he's stonewalling us on the results of the preliminary. Fairfax, follow up on yesterday's leads. Track down Ray D and find out what those college boys wanted with him. Johanssen . . ." His gaze slewed my way. "You look nice."

I flushed. "Thanks."

He cleared his throat. "Go ahead and pursue your . . . other avenues. But before you do, I'd like the two of you to restore the victim's personal effects to the bereaved parents." He reached into a drawer and plunked the evidence bag containing Thad Vanderhei's wallet onto his desk. "Reassure them. Let them know we're on the job, working every angle, tracking down every possibility. See what you can find out about their son's activities." He paused. "And while you're at it, ask if they're missing a bottle of Macallan."

Double crap! Not an assignment I looked forward to.

I caught Cody's eye and made myself nod. "Will do."

Since there was no point in putting it off, ten minutes later we were in a squad car heading north toward Appeldoorn. "Chief's right," Cody said to me. "You do look nice."

I'd taken the time to stop by my apartment and exchange my Keds for a cute pair of strappy sandals before I went in to the station. "Thanks."

He didn't mention calling Jen, and I didn't bring it up. Instead, I told him about my late-night visitor.

Cody listened in silence, his expression turning grim.

"Do you think it might be related?" I asked him.

"Hard to say." He glanced at me. "Do you?"

I shrugged. "I don't know."

"There's no telling what kind of hornet's nest we might have stirred up." Cody turned down the old country road toward south Appeldoorn. "Maybe you should think about staying somewhere else for a few days. Maybe stay with your mom or your friend Jen."

I grimaced. "Yeah, I don't think that second one's exactly an option right now. And if I've picked up a stalker, I sure as hell don't want him following me to my mom's place. It's okay; I can take care of myself."

He cocked a dubious brow at me. "If you say so, Pixy Stix."

There was no mistaking the fact that the Vanderhei family was wealthy. Their house, situated on Big Pine Bay, could only be described as a mansion. The grounds were beautifully landscaped and maintained. A three-car garage faced the street, and the driveway was made of some kind of fancy paving stones instead of poured concrete. Although it wasn't in Pemkowet township, it actually lay less than half a mile beyond the outermost limits of Hel's sphere of influence, an invisible boundary nonetheless marked by a tangible sense of loss and listlessness as Cody drove past it.

I wondered how the Vanderheis felt about the proximity.

The doorbell was answered by a teenage boy with dark shadows smudged beneath his eyes and a marked resemblance to Thad Vanderhei, maybe sixteen or seventeen, slender, good-looking in a forgettable way.

"Good morning, son," Cody said in a gentle tone. "I'm Officer Fairfax, and this is my associate, Miss Johanssen. You must be Ben."

"Benjamin." The boy's Adam's apple bobbed as he swallowed. "You're here about my brother?"

"We've come to return his personal effects," Cody said. "And we have a few questions for you and your parents. Are they here?"

Benjamin Vanderhei turned away. "Yeah. Come in."

He led us through a foyer with marble floors and a marble table containing a towering floral arrangement that probably cost more than a month's worth of my wages. A multitude of smaller arrangements were arrayed on the table around the base of the stand, sympathy cards protruding from plastic stake holders. I did my best to walk softly, acutely aware of intruding on a family's grief.

Mr. and Mrs. Vanderhei received us in a sitting room that was bigger than my entire apartment. It had a picture window that looked onto the wind-ruffled waters of Big Pine Bay, a baby grand piano, and a bar with half a dozen crystal decanters on it, silver tags identifying the spirits within them, something I'd only ever seen in movies.

There were more floral arrangements on every surface, a further reminder of the family's loss.

The word that Jim Vanderhei evoked was *patrician*. He was tall and lean, with a thick head of silver hair, his face lined and distinguished. His face was expressionless as he heard out our condolences, and he accepted Thad's water-damaged wallet without a word of thanks, his gaze flinty. "When can we have our *son*?"

"As soon as the medical examiner releases his findings, sir," Cody said. "We're so very sorry for the delay. The chief's on the phone with him as we speak."

His wife, Sue, seated on the couch, choked back a sob. She was some ten years younger than her husband, rail-thin, with birdlike features and blond hair pulled into a chignon so tight it looked painful. "Thad drowned! For God's sake, it was an accident! I don't understand why you're being such ghouls about this!"

"I'm sorry, ma'am," I murmured, ignoring the accusation's sting and her unfortunate choice of insults. "We're just trying to be thorough."

Cody cleared his throat. "Forgive me for asking, but did any of you notice anything unusual about Thad's activities in the past few weeks? Any new friends? Unexplained absences? Uncharacteristic behavior?"

"No!" Her voice rose, and she dabbed at her eyes with a tissue. "Do you think I don't know my own son?"

Jim Vanderhei glowered. "Exactly what in the hell are you trying to cover up down there?"

A flicker of anger stirred in me. I tried to tamp it down and failed, a faint scent of ozone creeping into the air around me. "No one's trying to cover up anything, sir. We're *trying* to get at the truth. And you're not helping."

He stared at me in disbelief.

In the shocked silence, their younger son, Benjamin, took a seat at the piano and began playing a single, halting musical phrase over and over, his head bowed. It helped me regain my focus.

"I'm sorry," I said again. "That was uncalled-for."

"Miss Johanssen is upset by your son's death," Cody said. "As we all are. I apologize for her behavior."

The younger Vanderhei boy kept playing.

"Benjamin!" His mother's voice rose again, cracking and breaking on a shrill note. "Stop it. Stop it this instant!"

He stopped.

"I'd like you to leave now, Officer." In contrast to his wife's voice, Jim Vanderhei's was flat and controlled. "You can tell Chief Bryant that either he can give us our son and let us mourn in peace, or he can give us answers and stop protecting whoever or *what*ever unholy conspiracy he's trying to hide. Until he does, I will continue to bring the full scrutiny of the press down upon him. I'll have his badge and his resignation before this is done. And that's just a beginning."

I opened my mouth.

Cody's hand settled on my shoulder. "Duly noted, sir. I assure you, there's no conspiracy. We're just trying to do our job. One last question. Is there a bottle of scotch missing from your bar?"

"No," he said automatically.

"You're sure?"

Jim Vanderhei strode over to the bar, pulling out the stopper on the crystal decanter marked SCOTCH. He took a sniff. "Present and accounted for, Officer. Would you like to try it for yourself?"

Cody glanced around the room. "Do you keep additional bottles in store?"

"We do not." His voice was stony. "This isn't Pemkowet, Officer. Temperance and moderation are virtues."

I gritted my teeth.

Cody's hand tightened on my shoulder. "Understood," he said. "Once again, I apologize for troubling you."

Jim Vanderhei gave him a brusque nod. "I want my son back. Tell your chief he's on borrowed time. Ben, please show our guests out."

Without a word, the boy rose from the piano bench. We followed him back through the marble foyer. Beneath my lightweight skirt, my tail was lashing uneasily. "What was that you were playing?" I asked. "I liked it."

"Ravel." Benjamin glanced at me with his shadow-smudged eyes. " 'Pavane pour une infante défunte.' "

I blinked.

"Pavane for a dead princess," he clarified. "Not exactly gender-appropriate, but . . ." He shrugged. "It gets the point across." He opened the door. "Thad was part of a secret society. You should look into it."

Cody and I exchanged a glance. "The Tritons?" I asked. "We know about the fraternity."

Benjamin shook his head. "No. Everyone knows about them. But there's a secret society *inside* the Tritons. I don't really know, but I heard Thad mention it on the phone a couple of times when he thought no one was listening. I didn't mean to eavesdrop, but I did. Something about the Masters of the Universe." He hesitated. "There's a guy, a Triton alum—he hangs around the frat house a lot. Matthew Mollenkamp. He's older. Whatever it is, I think maybe he had something to do with it."

"Did you ever hear Thad mention someone named Ray D?" Cody asked.

Benjamin gave his head another shake. "Sorry, no. That's all I know. Whatever Thad was up to this summer, he was pretty secretive about it."

"Thank you," I said softly. "That's a big help."

He looked at me with tears in his eyes. "Do you think maybe Thad did something bad down there?"

"I don't know," I said honestly. "I hope not."

I did, too. But I wasn't sure.

Eleven

Cody and I drove in relative silence back to Pemkowet.

"Sorry about that," I said at length. "I didn't mean to lose my temper."

One corner of his mouth quirked. "Short fuse. I can't say I blame you. It doesn't matter; Jim Vanderhei's not going to back down until he gets his way."

"I don't get it. Why are they so uncooperative? Their son died! You'd think they'd want to do everything possible to find out the truth." I frowned. "Do you think the Vanderheis are hiding something?"

"Could be." Cody shrugged. "But not necessarily. It could be they honestly believe it went down the way the other boys said, and they just want the chance to grieve and move on. Could be they think we're muckraking, trying to drag their son's name through the dirt as payback for their supporting Prop Thirteen."

"You know about Prop Thirteen?" It surprised me a little.

He glanced at me. "I'm not stupid, Daisy. It could have affected my entire clan if it passed."

"True."

"Anyway, it could also be that the Vanderheis don't *want* the truth uncovered. They might not know what it is, but they have a bad feeling about it." Cody turned in the direction of Pemkowet. "I lean toward that theory."

I thought about my mother's reading. *La Botella*, the bottle. "At least we know the boys were lying about the scotch."

"Mm-hmm. But they could have gotten it anywhere. All three of them were old enough to buy."

"So why lie about it?"

He sighed. "Good question, but it's going to have to wait, along with the Masters of the Universe. Once we get some more leverage, we can try questioning the boys again. Right now, I've got to concentrate on tracking down Ray D—and speaking of uncooperative, you're still on naiad duty. What's your plan for getting them to talk?"

"Oh . . ." I temporized. "I have a friend who has some influence with them."

Cody glanced at me again. "What kind of friend?"

"Oh, no." I shook my head. "If you don't know, I'm not telling, Officer Down-low."

"He's in the closet?"

"Not exactly, not in the eldritch community." I pointed at him. "But you are, or at least your clan does its best to stay there. And my, um, friend has a better reason than most to be discreet. You can't expect to receive a trust you don't extend to others."

"Fair enough." He gave a slight nod. "For what it's worth, I trust *you*."

"You do?" That surprised me, too. A lot.

"Yeah." Cody pulled into the alley alongside the bakery. "At least, I'm starting to. Call me later; we'll touch base." His gaze drifted toward the dented Dumpster. "And think about what I said about staying somewhere else for a few nights."

"I'll think about it."

His gaze hardened, green flashing behind the topaz. "If it happens again, if you hear *anything* suspicious, call me immediately, okay?"

Sunlight was glinting on the bronze stubble on his jaw in a distracting manner. I fought the urge to touch it, reminding myself that Jen wasn't speaking to me for this very reason. Okay, fine, I actually sat on my hands. "I will."

Leaning across me, Cody opened the squad car passenger door. "Good."

I dashed upstairs to the apartment to put on fresh lipstick and run a brush through my hair. Lurine Hollister isn't judgmental like the lesser water elementals, but trust me when I say she's *not* someone you want to encounter while looking distinctly subpar. It has to do with preservation of the ego. Even for me, and Lurine had known me since I was barely out of training pants.

After filling Mogwai's bowl, I trotted back downstairs and fired up my mostly trusty Honda Civic again, heading for the lakeshore.

There were a lot of spectacular homes along the tree-lined Lakeshore Drive in Pemkowet, every bit as imposing as the Vanderheis' place, and most of them considerably older. Once upon a time, most had been modest summer cottages, but over the years, far too many quaint cottages sitting on large plots were torn down and replaced with mansions that occupied every inch of space that local zoning laws allowed. The only thing they retained of their original character was their name: names like Sans Souci, Pinehaven, or Gray Gables, proudly displayed on hanging placards at the end of winding driveways, adorned with coats of arms either real or invented. Due to erosion, none of the houses along this section of Lakeshore Drive directly overlooked Lake Michigan. They were set back on the opposite side of the road, but all of them enjoyed lakefront access, usually in the form of a long series of wooden steps and decks leading down to private beaches.

A lot of them were still euphemistically called "summer homes," as they served as seasonal residences for wealthy citizens of Chicago,

Detroit, or St. Louis, but as far as I was concerned, they were mansions.

For sure, Lurine's place qualified.

I couldn't help but feel out of place as I turned into her drive and pulled up to the gated columns. Rolling down my window, I pressed the button on the loudspeaker and announced myself. "Um . . . hello? Hi. Daisy Johanssen to see Ms. Hollister."

It was silly. I'd known her since she was Lurine Clemmons, living in a mobile home in Sedgewick Estate, establishing her current identity. She lived two units down from my mom, babysat me regularly when I was a kid, and served as a willing confidante when I was a teenager, before she moved out to Los Angeles. On the surface of things, Lurine was one of those friends every young person should have: old enough to serve as a role model, young enough to identify when a parent couldn't.

Still, a lot had changed since those days.

My tail twitched restlessly while I waited for a polite voice to reply over the speaker, "Ms. Hollister will see you, Ms. Johanssen."

There was a buzzing sound, and then the gates parted silently, swinging open on well-oiled hinges. I drove through them, and they swung silently closed behind me.

Lurine Hollister, née Clemmons, née God-knows-what in the early days of history, had done very, very well for herself. As far as I could tell, she always did.

"Ms. Johanssen." Lurine's—what? her manservant? housekeeper? butler? I guess he was all of the above—greeted me at the door. He had a closed, lugubrious face and impeccable manners. "Welcome." He inclined his head in a slight bow. "Ms. Hollister is enjoying herself in the pool. She bids you join her there."

"Great, thanks."

I made my way through the house, past the movie stills, the promotional posters, the larger-than-life portrait in oil paint featuring Lurine in an ivory satin gown, her shoulders bare, her décolletage on pulchritudinous display.

Yeah, okay, it was kind of tacky, but in a totally awesome way.

It was painted shortly after Lurine left her career as a B-movie starlet to marry octogenarian real-estate tycoon Sanford Hollister. Naturally, there was some Anna Nicole Smith–esque tabloid scandal when he died within the year and left his fortune to her, but unlike the sad train wreck that was Anna Nicole, Lurine kept a low profile. As soon as the challenge to the will was overturned, Lurine retreated from the media spotlight altogether, returning to Pemkowet to live a fabulous and idyllic life.

For the record, I don't actually know if she was responsible for her husband's death, and I really, really don't want to.

"Daisy, baby!" Lurine's languid voice called to me as I opened the French doors onto the pool terrace. "There's champagne in the fridge. Be a doll and bring a bottle and a couple of glasses, will you?"

"Sure."

It was one of those high-end refrigerators that doesn't even look like a fridge, with silky wood paneling on the doors. One whole section contained a built-in wine rack. I pulled out a bottle of Moët & Chandon, plucked a couple of champagne flutes from the gleaming, glass-fronted cupboard, and carried them out to the terrace.

Lurine's house was situated on two wooded acres. The backyard, with its garden terrace and immense pool, was utterly secluded.

For most former B-movie starlets, that would afford the opportunity for sunbathing in the nude. For Lurine, it meant that she could luxuriate in the pool in her true form.

"Good to see you, cupcake." Lurine lolled in the deep end of the pool, her arms slung carelessly along the edges, wet tendrils of golden hair spilling artfully over her deservedly famous breasts. At some point during the course of history, I'm pretty sure those boobs *did* lure men to their doom, possibly watery. She gave me a slow, lazy smile that hadn't changed a bit since her mobile home days, dispelling any lingering unease I felt. The vast, sinuous length of her lower half filled the rest of the pool, looped and entwined coils gleaming with shifting hues of green and gold and blue, interspersed with iridescent crimson spots. It stirred the water with effortless, muscular grace, and my own little tail gave an involuntary twitch of envy. "To what do I owe the pleasure?"

"I need a favor," I admitted.

She patted the edge of the pool. "Bring that champagne over here, sit down, and tell me all about it. Ooh!" Her cornflower-blue eyes widened. "Is this police business? Is this about the boy who drowned?"

"Yes, and yes." Kicking off my sandals, I sat next to her and dangled my feet in the water. "But you *cannot* repeat anything I tell you."

"Cross my heart." Lurine suited actions to words, then uncorked the champagne with a deft twist and a muted pop, filling both flutes. "Now tell."

I laid out the bare bones of the case, and my dilemma with the naiads and other water elements.

"Dumb bitches," Lurine commented, her voice taking on an unfamiliar edge. "Don't they know if any one of us is involved, it could mean trouble for all of us?"

"Apparently not." I sipped my champagne. Yeah, I know, I shouldn't on duty. But it wasn't like I was an official badge-carrying cop, and there's the hospitality thing. It's very important in the eldritch community. "Will you talk to them for me?"

"Of course," she said promptly, studying me. "You seem kind of down, cupcake. Is it just the case, or is something else bothering you?"

I shrugged. "It's stupid."

And yet within ten minutes, I'd spilled the entire story of my long-standing crush on Cody, and how I'd interfered with him and Jen, and now Jen wasn't speaking to me. Lurine was a good listener; she always had been. Not all of her gifts were obvious ones.

"See," I said when I'd finished. "It's stupid! Seriously, it's like I'm still in high school!" I put my head in my hands. "And I can't believe I'm even thinking about it at a time like this."

"Oh, baby girl!" Lurine said with sympathy. "It's okay. Life goes on even at the worst of times, and there are some ways no one ever grows up, no matter how long they live or how many lifetimes."

It made me feel better. "Really?"

"Absolutely." She pointed at my purse. "Now you get out your phone, call your friend, and apologize to her. If she won't answer, leave a message. Or text her. Isn't that how you kids today communicate? Get it off your chest. If she's a good friend, she'll forgive you sooner or later."

After I'd done it, that made me feel better, too, even though Jen didn't pick up. "Thanks, Lurine. Any advice on the Cody situation?"

Her look of sympathy returned. "What can I tell you? Those clans keep to their own kind, cupcake. If you go chasing after him, you're likely to get your heart broken." Her shoulders rose and fell. "Then again, you're young. There are worse things in the world than heartbreak. Finding that out is a rite of passage."

"Great," I said glumly.

Lurine poured herself away from the edge of the pool in one fluid movement, diving below the surface. The water roiled, slopping over the sides as she undulated from one end and back in serpentine glory. Resurfacing, she gave me her slow, lazy smile, this time with more than a hint of wickedness in it. Her gleaming coils stirred suggestively around her. "You want to come to mama, baby girl? I'll make you feel *all* better."

A shiver ran from the nape of my neck to the base of my tail, making it spasm involuntarily.

Okay, here's the thing. When it comes to ordinary, mortal humans, I'm pretty much straight, but the eldritch have a whole different Kinsey scale.

Yes, it's twisted.

And yes, I find Lurine in her lamia form kind of hot. I can't help it. Something about those deadly coils . . . *gah!* I can't explain it.

I looked away, feeling my face get warm. "Oh, for God's sake! Cut it out! You know, you used to babysit me."

"Age is relative, cupcake." There was a prodigious splash as Lurine heaved herself out of the pool. "Isn't that what I was just saying?"

I sneaked a glance at her and relaxed. Lurine had assumed her human guise and stood two-legged, barefoot and dripping on the sun-warmed concrete, looking amused and pleased with herself as she wrapped a towel around her *Playboy*-centerfold figure.

That, I could handle. "Okay, so, dawn tomorrow?"

"Tomorrow?" She twined a second towel around her wet hair in a turban. "Why wait?"

Twelve

I'd known that Lurine carried a lot of clout among the water elementals. I hadn't known exactly how much.

At her suggestion, we drove over to Sedgewick Estate.

"It's all the same river," Lurine said in a pragmatic tone. "And it's secluded enough out here in the sticks. We'll get Gus to stand guard."

Of course, we had to visit with my mom first. She and Lurine exchanged greetings like long-lost friends, even though I knew they talked on the phone every week. But I guess that's not the same as meeting face-to-face. They had a bit of a falling-out when Lurine tried to give Mom a check big enough to pay off the mortgage on her lot and then some, but that was years ago.

"How's the investigation going? Have you found the spider yet?" Mom asked me, a little furrow between her brows.

"Spider . . . ?" I remembered her reading again. "No, not yet. We're here to question the naiads."

She nodded in understanding. "I'm sure Gus will be happy to make sure everyone keeps their distance."

Sedgewick Estate is a pretty tight-knit community in its own little way. It's always drawn a fair number of eldritch folk, maybe because it's a bit isolated and close to nature. Still, for Lurine's sake, it would be better not to have an audience.

Gus's unit was the farthest one on the estate, a single-wide situated under a big willow tree. The exterior was draped in camouflage netting, giving it a sort of cavernous, moss-covered-hillock appearance, which was appropriate, since Gus was an ogre.

To the best of my knowledge, Gus hasn't eaten anyone in the last century or so, at least if we're talking people.

Cats and dogs, I'm not so sure about.

Gus answered our knock right away, unfolding his mammoth seven-foot-tall frame through the doorway and ducking under the netting. To the mundane eye, he looks a bit like Andre the Giant, and if you don't know who that is, you really need to watch *The Princess Bride*. To the eldritch eye, he looks like Andre the Giant if Andre the Giant were hewn from boulders and stitched together with leather.

"Good evening, ladies," he said in a deep rumble, baring teeth like smaller boulders in a shy smile. "What can I do for you?"

"Lurine's going to summon the naiads," I said. "Can you make sure we don't draw any spectators?"

His smile broadened. "Of course." He glanced at Mom with puppy-dog eyes. "Present company excepted, I hope?"

Um, yeah. Gus the ogre has a crush on my mother.

"Of course Marja's welcome." Lurine patted Mom's arm. "She's an honorary member of the community."

I fidgeted. "This *is* a police investigation."

"It's okay, honey." Mom smiled at me. "I'll stay on the shore with Gus, out of hearing range. I just want to watch. It's been a long time since I've seen a naiad; they don't usually come out this far."

I sighed. "Fine."

We trooped down toward the river. Some yards away from the shore, Gus planted his looming figure on sentry duty. It was late enough in the day that the sun was riding low in the west, beginning its slow descent toward sunset, and a few people were out on their decks, manning barbecue grills.

Gus raised his hands and cupped his mouth. "Better you should go inside for a little while, okay?" he boomed. "Go inside and close your curtains! Important community business here!" There were a few groans and catcalls, but everyone obeyed. For an ogre, Gus is an amiable fellow, but not someone you want to cross.

"Ready, cupcake?" Lurine asked me.

I nodded. "Yep."

At the river's edge, Lurine shucked her sundress and waded into the murky water, her bare feet stirring up eddies of muck. "Let me call them first. I'll come back for you."

"Okay."

In the blink of an eye, she shifted, her shapely human lower half giving way to those vast, glistening, muscular coils. If you crossed a giant anaconda with a rainbow, that's pretty much what the bottom half of a lamia would look like. Propelled by her undulating coils, Lurine glided across the surface of the river through a thicket of sedge grass, her torso disconcertingly upright and towering in the air. When she reached open water, she halted.

Her immensely long, powerful tail thrashed, churning the water. She raised her voice and summoned the naiads in a foreign tongue, every word precise and ringing with bronze-edged irritation.

I don't know what she said, but she sounded pissed.

There was a long moment of silence, echoes dying across the bay. And then the water rippled with myriad arrow-headed wakes as the naiads, undines, and nixies came in swift answer to Lurine's summons, rising to bob in the river, heads lowered in acknowledgment.

Lurine's tail snaked back toward me and proffered a loop, the iridescent tip beckoning. Not exactly what I'd expected when she said she'd come back for me. When I hesitated, she glanced over her shoulder with mild annoyance. "I'm not playing, Daisy. Are you coming or not?"

"Coming." I pried off my sandals and stepped onto the offered loop of her tail. It dipped slightly beneath my weight, and I nearly slipped. "Whoa!"

A coil wrapped around my waist, steadying me. "Gotcha, cupcake."

Okay . . . *gah!*

Lurine retracted her coils, me within them, and in one swift rush I was floating above the river and the aquatic mean-girls club, securely encased in a lamia's grip. Yep, definitely hot—also pretty exhilarating, like the weirdest amusement park ride ever.

The head naiad bobbed and glared at me beneath her lashes. I cleared my throat. "Um . . . hi again." I raised my left hand, the one marked with Hel's rune. "Remember me?"

Her voice was subdued, but icy. "Yes, of course. The sun has not set on our brief acquaintance."

Lurine's tail thrashed in warning. I rode out the convulsions, my bare toes gripping her water-slick coils, one hand clutching her shoulder. "Level with me. A boy *died*, okay? Just tell me what you saw."

They conferred in their silvery voices. The sun sank lower, turning the rippled surface of the water to hammered gold.

At last a pair of timid undines with pearls from my morning's offering twined in their translucent hair came forward. "The boy didn't drown in the river," one of them said in a faint, wispy voice. "They put him there."

My heart skipped a beat. "Who did? His friends?"

They exchanged a glance. "We don't know. It was dark," the other one said. "They were in a boat without lights."

"How many people?" I asked. "Human or eldritch?"

"Four," the first undine said. "Two were human. Two were not. The two who were not put the boy in the river."

"You said the boy didn't drown there." I frowned, thinking. "So he was already dead, then?"

The undines nodded in unison. "Drowned."

"Drowned, but not in the river? You're sure?"

"All of us know what drowned men look like, halfling," the head naiad said with disdain. "We have seen many hundreds of them."

"No doubt." I wouldn't be surprised if she was responsible for a few of them. Ignoring her, I concentrated on the undines. "Okay, the two who weren't human. What were they?"

"Pale," one said.

"Hungry," the other offered.

"Vampires?" I hadn't considered the possibility that the kids were blood-sluts in the making. But by the look of him, Thad Vanderhei hadn't been drained, and I'd never heard of vampires drowning anyone.

The undines shook their heads. "No."

I grimaced. "Ghouls?"

They did their nod-in-unison thing again. I wondered whether undines were a bit simple. It might explain why the naiads were so bitchy, having to share the river with them. "Maybe," one said. "Not for sure."

"Okay, so they put the boy in the river. Then what happened?"

"We don't know," the other said. "We swam away as fast as we could."

Lurine muttered something under her breath, the end of her tail lashing ominously. The undines looked scared.

"It's okay," I assured them. "I don't blame you. I would have run away, too. Can you tell me anything else about the people in the boat? Were the humans the boy's age?"

"Yes," both of them said. "We think so."

"Good, very good." I nodded encouragingly. "What about the other two men? The maybe-ghouls?"

"Not men," one corrected me. "One man and one woman."

Huh, interesting.

I pressed them for as many details as they could remember. All I got was that the man and woman were not young, but not old either. The man had dark hair, but they weren't sure about the woman. The boat was a small motorboat, not a sailboat or a houseboat, but the kind you would take on a short pleasure cruise or fishing trip. Since that described a hundred boats in Pemkowet, it wasn't a lot of help.

Still, it was tons more information than I'd had an hour ago.

When I couldn't think of any further angles to pursue, I thanked the undines for their help. "I appreciate it. This is very, very helpful." I glanced from them to the head naiad. "Why were you so reluctant to share it? Why did you make it so difficult?"

The undines were silent.

"Because it is dangerous to get involved in such affairs, halfling," the head naiad said with exasperation. "We do not know who killed the boy or why. There are those who have hunted our kind for sport over the ages." She waved one alabaster arm, indicating the broad sweep of the river. "In this age, it would be altogether too easy to take vengeance on us. Mortal folk have all but poisoned the waters through carelessness. Imagine what one of the soulless ones could do out of spite."

As much as I disliked her, I had to admit she had a point. "I'll do my best to keep my sources off the record."

The naiad gave me a tight smile. "That may work in the mundane world. In the eldritch community, everyone will know it was a water elemental who gave you this information."

"Yeah, and most of them will be grateful for it," I pointed out to her.

She tossed her hair. "It is the ones who will not that concern us."

Lurine said something foreign and scathing. Her coils stirred, waving me absentmindedly in the air and making my stomach lurch. Remembering my presence, she steadied her coils and switched back to English. "Your concerns are small and selfish, little sister. You do not understand the stakes. If those who did this are not brought to justice, the eyes of the mundane world will turn to Pemkowet." Her eyes flashed. "There will be talk of rooting out evil. There will be talk of destroying the underworld, of razing the city beneath the sands. If that came to pass, Hel would perish, and the rest of us would follow. As below, so above. Do you understand?"

This time the naiad really did look chastened. "Yes, *kyria*. I understand."

"All of you?" Lurine persisted. "And if there is anything else you remember, anything else you learn, you will come forward with it?"

There was a silvery chorus of agreement from the bobbing figures of undines, naiads, and nixies.

"Are you done with them, cupcake?" Lurine lowered me so she could look me in the eye.

"Yeah, thanks."

She dismissed the assembled water elementals with a foreign word that sounded like a thunderclap. Once again, they scattered like minnows—like scared minnows. I had to admit it was infinitely more satisfying this time.

Thirteen

Back at the river's edge, Lurine deposited me gently on solid ground before shifting back to her human guise, the imposing millennia-old monster resuming the form of every heterosexual fourteen-year-old boy's wet dream.

I'd always been fond of Lurine, but I had a whole new respect for her.

"Did you get what you needed, baby girl?" she asked me.

I nodded. "More than I'd hoped. Thanks, Lurine."

"Anytime." Lowering her voice, she gave me a serious look. "Sweetheart, if you need backup, don't you hesitate to call me. You might be getting in over your head here. I'll keep my promise; I won't say a word about this, not even to your mother, but it sounds like we're talking about a murder, doesn't it?"

"Yeah." I swallowed. "It kinda looks that way."

She sighed. "Goddamn ghouls."

It seemed to genuinely disturb her. I wondered fleetingly about Lurine's wealthy octogenarian husband's death, and pushed that thought firmly away. Still really, really didn't want to know. And then I thought about dark-haired ghouls who were neither young nor old, and Stefan Ludovic's patient, piercing, ice-blue gaze.

I shivered a bit. Didn't want to know if he was involved in this, either. Or at least I didn't want it to be true.

"Daisy, baby!" Mom hurried over to the shore, a pair of clean, dry towels over her arm. "Are you cold? I brought towels."

"I'm fine." It was true; I didn't have a drop of water on me.

"*You're* not." Since Mom couldn't fuss over me, she fussed over Lurine, who bore it with amused fondness. "Look at that muck! You don't want to get it all over your pretty sundress." Picking up Lurine's discarded dress, she eyed it critically, examining the seams. "Is this a Marc Jacobs? Because you know I could make it for you at a fraction of the price with twice the workmanship."

"It's from last season. Don't worry about it." Having wiped the river water and clinging bits of rotten plant matter and other unidentified muck from her legs, Lurine held out her hand. Mom hesitated. "Okay, fine. Let's talk about a commission, but *not* at a fraction of the price. I don't want to have this fight again. Can I get dressed now?"

"Yes, please!" Gus's voice boomed in answer. He was still standing sentry duty, now with his massive back pointedly turned and a ham-size hand shielding his eyes. As it happened, the ogre was a gentleman. "Can she get dressed?"

"Hey, Gus! Can we come out now?" someone called from one of the mobile units, peering cautiously through the curtains. "I've got hungry kids and burgers turning to charcoal on the grill."

I laughed.

Nothing was funny, not really. It was just that the absurdity of the exchange in the midst of some very scary and ominous goings-on reminded me that I loved this place and these people.

"It's okay, Gus." I patted his arm, which unsurprisingly was a lot like patting a boulder. "They can come out now."

"Do you have time for a cup of coffee, honey?" Mom asked me in a hopeful tone.

I shook my head. "I need to touch base with Cody."

She did her best to look crafty. "Oh, of course."

Lurine took my mom's arm in hers. "If it's no trouble, I'd love a cup of coffee, Marja. We can talk clothes." She glanced at me, her gaze light, masking her concern. "Don't worry about me, cupcake. I'll call my driver to pick me up."

"Okay."

In my car, I slid my phone from my purse. No reply from Jen—oh, well. The ball was in her court now. Suppressing the tiniest pang of guilt, I called Cody. He answered right away, sounding disgruntled. "What's up, Pixy Stix?"

I cradled the phone against my ear. "No luck?"

"No," he said shortly. "You?"

"Yeah." I nodded. "And it's a pretty major development. Do you want me to tell you, or do you want to meet?"

There was a pause. "You had dinner?"

"I never even had lunch," I said, only just now realizing it.

"Me neither. Meet you at Callahan's in ten." He hung up.

It turned out to be more like twenty. Parking in downtown Pemkowet is a nightmare in the summer, and I had to circle the block several times before, miracle of miracles, a car pulled out of a space right in front of Callahan's Café just as I was about to begin another circuit. I whipped into the space and was fumbling for my purse, which had fallen onto the floor, when someone rapped on the passenger-side window, making me jump.

Cody's face peered at me. I leaned over to unlock the door. He opened it and squeezed his tall figure into the passenger seat.

"Change of plans?" I asked.

"No, I just thought you could give me a quick rundown." He nodded at the café. "Too busy for privacy tonight."

I told Cody the gist of what I'd learned. He heard me out in silence, an increasingly dark scowl on his face.

"Damn!" He pounded the dashboard with one fist when I'd finished. My poor little Honda rocked under the impact. "Sorry. I was really hoping this would turn out to be nothing sinister." His face looked grim. "Now I've *really* got to find Ray D. I don't suppose your mysterious friend has any pull in the ghoul community?"

"No, sorry."

"Too bad." Cody searched my face, his gold-flecked topaz eyes unnervingly intense. "How sure are you about this info, Daisy?"

"Pretty sure," I said reluctantly. "Those undines really didn't want to talk about it. None of the water elementals wanted to get involved. They're scared. They wouldn't have given it up if Lur . . . if my friend hadn't made them. I don't think they'd lie."

"Undines." He ran a hand over his chin. I couldn't help but notice that his stubble was gone. "God help us. That'll stand up in court." He took a deep breath. "Okay, Chief says we ought to have the autopsy report tomorrow. Hopefully, that'll give us something more substantial to go on."

My stomach grumbled. "Can we still get dinner?"

"Yeah." Cody's expression eased into a smile, the corners of his eyes crinkling. "I think we'd better. I'm starving."

"Me, too." Unable to resist, I brushed the line of his jaw with one fingertip. "Plus, you shaved, didn't you?"

"I might have," he admitted.

"And you smell good." I did successfully resist the urge to sniff his neck. Yay for me! "Is that aftershave? What is it?"

"Ralph Lauren's Polo." Cody made a face. "It was a gift, okay? No special occasion—I just didn't want it to go to waste. Don't read anything into it."

"I won't." I paused. "A gift from a lady friend?"

He wagged a finger at me. "None of your business, Pixy Stix. C'mon; let's get a bite to eat."

It was a nice piece of lighthearted banter and a welcome counterbalance to the day's grave revelations. And on that note, both of us exited the Honda and headed for the door of Callahan's . . .

. . . just in time to encounter Jen and her friend Greta Hasselmeyer standing on the sidewalk and staring at us, having just emerged from the café.

Oh, crap.

"Hey!" My voice came out overbright and chipper. "Oh, hey, Jen!" I cleared my throat. "I've been trying to call you. Did you get my message?"

She continued to stare at me for a long moment, then slowly and deliberately shifted her gaze from me to Cody and back. "Yeah." Her tone was flat. "Thanks. I got it. Loud and clear, Daise."

I winced. "It's not—"

Jen held one hand out. "Whatever."

"It's just work!" I protested.

She walked away without a word, her dark, shining hair hanging down her back and swaying like a river. A pissed-off river. Greta Hasselmeyer, who worked alongside Jen in the Cassopolis family industry of caretaking and cleaning for the privileged and wealthy, folded her arms over her chest and shook her head, voicing her disapproval in equal silence.

I probably shouldn't have stroked Cody's jaw.

Crap.

We entered the café and took seats across from each other in a corner booth. "Sorry," I muttered.

"Not your fault." Cody studied the menu, although, like me, he probably had it memorized. "I called her. She wasn't too thrilled by the 'it's not you; it's me' routine."

"I know."

He glanced up at me. "Oh?"

I pretended to study the menu, too. "It is my fault. I shouldn't have intervened."

"You did it for the right reasons."

I coughed. "Not entirely."

"Oh?"

Honestly, this laconic thing could drive a person crazy! "I like you," I admitted. "I can't help it, Cody. I've liked you since I was ten years old and Freddie Cooper tried to pull my pants down on the bus to see if it was true that I had a tail. You told him to stop, and when he wouldn't, you punched him in the head. Remember?"

His eyes crinkled. "Uh-huh."

"So . . ." I gestured helplessly.

"Daisy." Cody reached across the booth, capturing and stilling my hands. "That was a long time ago. You know enough to understand why it wouldn't work now."

"Time is relative," I murmured, trying not to feel hurt. "Rather like age."

"What?"

I shook my head. "Nothing."

He squeezed my hands, and let them go. "Let's talk about something else. Tell me . . ." He hesitated, searching for a safe topic. "Okay, tell me this. *Daisy?* What the, um, hell kind of name is that for a hell-spawn? Where did that come from?" Despite everything, I laughed. "I'm serious!" he insisted. "You can't tell me it isn't a little odd."

The waitress drifted over to our table, bringing glasses of water. Cody ordered ribs again. I ordered the spaghetti-and-meatball special.

"It's from a book," I said. "My name, I mean."

Cody looked perplexed. "If it's *The Great Gatsby*, we read it in Mr. Leary's class, and no offense, but I don't get it."

I sighed. "Not Daisy Buchanan. *Princess Daisy*." Cody looked blank. "It's the title of a romance novel. A big, sprawling one with dethroned royalty and secret twins and incestuous half brothers."

"Still not getting it," he commented. "Possibly more than ever."

"Not a lot to get. It was guilty pleasure reading for my mom and my grandma back in the day, long before I happened. That was one of their favorites." I tugged on a lock of my pale Scandinavian hair. "It has a blond-haired, dark-eyed heroine, okay? And a happy ending. My mom's a big believer in happy endings."

"Ah." Cody's expression changed. "That must take a special kind of strength."

"Yeah." I drew a line through the condensation on my water glass with one fingertip. "She was nineteen when Belphegor knocked her up," I said without looking at Cody. "A freshman in college, the first person in her family to go. One of her roommates' parents rented a cottage in Pemkowet over spring break. The girls thought it would be fun to use a Ouija board. No one knew enough to warn them. At three o'clock in the morning, they found Mom levitating several feet above the bed in the act of, um, congress with a shadowy figure with glowing eyes, bat wings, and a tail."

"Yeah, I heard." His voice was low. "She told you herself?"

"Not that part, no." I fell silent as our food arrived, then busied myself twirling spaghetti around my fork. "Two months later, Mom found herself pregnant. She dropped out of college to have me. Grandma and Grandpa weren't happy about it, but they stood by her. Pretty much everyone else tried to convince her it wasn't a good idea to carry the baby to term." I glanced at him. "Either because they believed her, or because they didn't and they thought she was mentally ill and that the pregnancy would totally unhinge her."

"I'm sorry," Cody said quietly.

"It's okay." I gave him a wry smile. "I'm here, right? Mom refused to listen to any of them. She decided I was her baby, dammit, and she was going to love me no matter what. And that that was all that mattered, no matter who or what my father was. And if part of that was naming her little black-eyed hell-spawn after her favorite character in her favorite book, no matter how silly or inappropriate it sounds . . ." I stuck a forkful of spaghetti into my mouth, chewed, and swallowed. "You know what? I'm okay with it."

Cody picked up his ribs. "Better to light a candle than curse the darkness."

"Yeah." I nodded. "Exactly." I pointed my fork at him. "What about you, Officer? I know what made you turn your life around the second time and become a cop. But in eighth grade, you were a JV all-star. A year later, you were a burnout. What happened?"

He tore a hunk of meat from the bone with his teeth. "Puberty."

I waited for more. "That's it?"

Cody didn't elaborate. "Yep."

Okay, then.

I thought about it while we ate our meals. I didn't know a lot about werewolves. They were too clannish, too secretive. But I knew adolescence was hell on wheels for me, trying to control my temper, trying to cope with unexpected desires. There had been a few . . . incidents. A few things had spontaneously combusted or burst in my presence, most memorably the hot-water pipes in the girls' locker room.

I got suspended for that one. So did Jen, for defending me from the girls who'd been taunting me. Well, actually for threatening to cut off Stacey Brooks's hair in her sleep if she didn't shut up.

The memory drew a reluctant smile from me, accompanied by a pang of guilt.

Anyway . . .

If it was at all the same for werewolves, no wonder Cody had sort of dropped out. Real life isn't like the movies. If he'd gone all *Teen Wolf* on the basketball court, parents on the opposing team's side would have been screaming for an animal control unit, and the entire Fairfax clan could have been outed against their will.

"I get it," I said. Cody looked up at me from his dwindling plate of ribs. "I'm curious. As an adult, do you have full control?"

He glanced around. The café was emptying and no one was seated near us. "Depends on your willpower and self-discipline."

"Do *you*?"

"Yeah." He gave me an unexpected grin that it's only fair to describe as wolfish, sending a shiver down my spine and setting my tail a-twitch. "Twenty-nine days out of a lunar month. The chief would never have hired me if I didn't. Do *you*?"

I sighed with regret. "Me? Not even close."

Fourteen

After dinner, Cody insisted on escorting me home.

"I want to take a look at that Dumpster," he said in a pragmatic tone when I objected. "And I'll sleep better knowing at least you got home safe. You're in the thick of it now, Daisy Jo."

"Oh, fine."

We poked around the Dumpster behind the apartment. No one was lurking back there. Cody shone his flashlight beam on the dented lid to examine it. I had to warn him not to step in the puddle of dried Mogwai puke that obscured the boot print, but I showed him the photo I'd taken of it. Across the street, a handful of guys were playing a late game of pickup basketball beneath the streetlights over the court, the ball thudding rhythmically, a poignant reminder of Cody's younger days.

"Looks like it may have been a peeper," he said. "I still don't like it. You're sure you won't stay at your mom's tonight?"

I nodded. "No way I'm putting her in danger."

"What about the other friend you mentioned?" he asked. "The one who helped out with the naiads?"

"Yeah, um . . ." The memory of Lurine's coils wrapped firmly around my waist was a little too fresh. I felt my face grow warm, and cleared my throat. "For reasons I'd rather not go into, no. Not tonight."

Cody gave me a dubious look. The light above the side door that opened onto the stairway leading to the apartments upstairs did him all kinds of favors, casting shadows on his chiseled features, glinting on a new growth of stubble that I very much wanted to touch again. Plus, he still smelled good. "Okay. You've got my number?"

I clasped my hands behind my back, concentrating on willpower and self-discipline. "Yep, sure do."

He shrugged. "Then I'll see you at the station in the morning."

I waited until Cody was out of sight to open the side door . . .

. . . and froze.

Al the Walrus, the big pool-playing, mustache-sporting ghoul from the Wheelhouse, loomed above me on the bottom stair. His eyes glittered, all pupil. He lumbered toward me, his hungry eyes like twin abysses. "There you are!" His voice was low and grating. "Give us a taste, just a taste!" His nostrils flared, and I felt my terror drain unnaturally, and spike again. "Oh, yes! More!" He licked his lips with his thick tongue. "More and more and more!" He leered at me, coming closer. "You've got all kinds of *more*, don't you?"

I unfroze enough to back away, raising my voice. "Get the fuck out of here!"

"That's right." He kept coming. "Go ahead, get angry." He made a nasty slurping sound. "I *like* angry."

In a panic, I let my anger rise, feeling my hair lift. The lightbulb in the lamp above the door burst with a popping sound.

Al the Walrus moaned, draining my anger. "Oh, so delicious! Keep it coming, little girl!"

Gah, gross! I could *feel* my emotions going into him, and it was disgusting, like a part of me was trickling into a sewer. Also terrifying.

Since I didn't know what else to do, I screamed. High, loud, and piercing, like a victim in a slasher film.

Across the street, the thudding basketball went silent.

Cody came tearing around the block, moving so fast he was a uniformed blur, his eyes flaring phosphorescent green. I caught a glimpse of his face, and it was distorted with fury. Like, really distorted, as in he was beginning to shape-shift. With a growl, he flung Al away from me and up against the wall of the bakery, pressing one forearm hard across his throat.

The big ghoul laughed. "Oh, he's an angry pup!" He licked his lips again, eyes glittering. "I'll take that, too."

Cody backed away uncertainly, shaking his head in confusion. "No feeding on the unwilling." His voice sounded thick and strange, maybe because his mouth suddenly had too many pointed white teeth in it. His ears were awfully pointy, too. And furry. He bared his teeth and laid his ears flat against his head. "You know the rules."

"Yeah." Al's pupils shrank, then dilated. His gaze fixed on me, his leer returning. "But rules were made to be broken."

From across the street came the sound of running feet. "Hey!" one of the basketball players called. "Hang on; we're coming to help!"

I grabbed Cody's arm. "Mundanes coming, Officer Down-low." He glanced at me in the dim light, his ears twitching slightly. I gave his arm a shake. "Better rustle up some of that famous self-discipline and get ahold of yourself."

In the few seconds it took him to reassert control, Al the Walrus took off across the park at a dead run, moving surprisingly fast himself for a bulky guy, and the basketball players arrived. From the far side of the park came the distinctive sound of a Harley-Davidson roaring to life.

"Hey, hey, everything okay?" one of the ballplayers asked anxiously. "You okay, lady? We heard a scream."

"I'm fine." I made myself smile at him, keeping my grip on Cody's arm. "Just some pervert. I was lucky Officer Fairfax was just around the corner."

"Yeah." The ballplayer glanced at Cody with awe. "Dude, that was sick. You've got some mad speed."

"I shouldn't have let him get away." Cody sounded disgruntled, but his voice was normal again. So was his face. Full control, huh?

"It's okay." I squeezed his arm. "We know where to find him. Thanks," I said to the ballplayers. "Everything's okay, really."

"You're sure?"

I nodded. "Positive. But I appreciate it. You were collectively awesome."

"Thanks, guys," Cody added, extricating his arm from my grasp. "Nice work. I'll take it from here."

They drifted amiably back across the street, four college-age kids by the look of them, frat boys maybe, not much different from Thad Vanderhei and his friends. Except these guys had run to the aid of a lady being attacked by a ghoul, even if they hadn't known that was what they were doing, and Thad Vanderhei and his friends had done . . . what? We still didn't know, except that it involved ghouls and ended with dumping Thad's body in the river.

"That settles it," Cody said.

"It does?" Lost in my thoughts, I had no idea what he was talking about.

"Pack a bag." He nodded at the side door. "You don't want to stay at a friend's place, fine. You're not staying here, not until we pick up Al."

"And charge him with what?" I asked.

"Assault."

"He never laid a hand on me," I said. "The police can't enforce Hel's rules, Cody. That's *my* job. If this Stefan Ludovic is really in charge of ghoul territory here, that's who I have to report Al to."

That muscle in his jaw twitched. "You expect *him* to do something about it?"

"Yeah," I said. "I do. If he wants to stay in charge, he has to."

"Unless he's at the bottom of this business," Cody said grimly. "We didn't have this kind of trouble before he showed up."

I stifled a yawn. "Well, if he is, then I'll have to report him to Hel. If he's broken mundane laws, we'll have to negotiate between authorities. But right now, I'm not going anywhere but to bed."

"Right," he said. "So pack a bag. You're staying at my place."

Another time, I would have jumped at the opportunity. But I was tired and cranky. I'd started my day at the crack of dawn being insulted by naiads, and ended it with a totally creepy encounter with a hungry ghoul who'd apparently fixated on my tasty, tasty emotions. In between, I'd learned that it looked like we were dealing with a murder; I'd managed to further alienate my estranged best friend; and Cody's response to my declaration of affection could pretty much be summed up as dismissive.

"No," I said. "Look, I don't think Al's coming back tonight. I'll keep my doors locked. Mrs. Browne will be here in a few hours." I put my hand on the doorknob. "I'm staying."

Cody placed his hand flat on the door, holding it shut. "No, you're not."

"Yeah, I am."

He raised his voice. "No, you're *not!*"

Before I could summon a suitably immature retort, a dune buggy pulled into the alley.

Oh, crap.

Cody lifted one hand to shield his eyes against the glare of headlights. "Hey, there!" he called out. "This isn't a through street."

The headlights blinked out, and a large figure climbed out of the buggy, raising its left hand. The spear-headed rune Teiwaz, indicating one of Hel's guards, shimmered silvery on its palm. "Daisy Johanssen?"

I sighed and lifted my left hand in answer. "Yeah, hi. Nice to see you again."

The figure inclined its head. Now that I wasn't blinded by headlights, I could make out who and what it was. To mundane eyes, it would appear to be an ogreishly tall, long-haired, and bearded man

sweating profusely—and I do mean profusely, actual rivulets running down his skin and dripping from his beard to puddle on the
concrete beneath him. I, on the other hand, saw an ogreishly tall
man with bluish skin rimed with melting frost, his eyes as pale and
colorless as dirty slush, icicles dripping from his head and chin to
puddle on the concrete.

Cody's hand dropped instinctively to his holster. "What in the
hell is that?"

"Frost giant," I said. "His name's Mikill. It means 'big,' right? Or
'large'?"

"True." Mikill lowered his hand. "Daisy Johanssen, I am bid to
summon you to an audience with Hel."

Great.

Fifteen

At least it put an end to my argument with Cody. Even a stubborn werewolf on the down-low knew I couldn't ignore a summons from Hel herself.

"I don't mean to belabor the obvious, but will he"—Cody lowered his voice—"*melt*?"

I shook my head, climbing into the passenger seat of the dune buggy and putting on my seat belt. "Not anytime soon."

"So, you'll—"

"I'll see you at the station!" I had to shout the words as Mikill clambered into the driver's seat and turned the key in the ignition. "Tomorrow, okay?"

"Okay!"

A wash of cool air, accompanied by a pelting of icy droplets, rolled off Mikill and gusted over me as we headed out of town.

"Forgive me." The frost giant shot me an apologetic look. "It cannot be helped."

I shivered. "I know."

Steering with one massive hand, Mikill reached into the tiny storage area in the back and hauled out a thick fur coat. "Here."

I draped it over me, snuggling under it. "Thanks."

The Pemkowet Dune Rides was a mile or so north of downtown, its gaily painted sign promising thrilling family-friendly fun, vistas of the lake, and even a glimpse of Yggdrasil II, the famous world tree. At this hour, it was closed for the night, all the big, tricked-out dune schooners in their stables, the windows of the gift shop dark. Mikill gunned the engine and roared around the establishment on a narrow side track before plunging into the wooded dunes beyond. Bouncing involuntarily in the seat, I clung tight to the roll bar as we hurtled into the darkness, careening around steeply banked curves at death-defying speeds. In daylight it might be exhilarating. At night, lit only by the buggy's headlights, it was pretty much heart-stopping. I admit, I closed my eyes a few times.

The official Dune Rides trails were graded and maintained, both for the sake of safety and the environment. They had to be. Sand dunes are sort of like living things. They don't stay put, moving and shifting, especially if they're not anchored by indigenous flora.

This fact escaped the attention of the settlers of Singapore, who built a logging town here on the shores of Lake Michigan in the 1800s.

Yeah, a *logging* town. Brilliant, right?

And once they'd cut down a sufficient number of white pine trees, the dunes rolled over the town and pretty much swallowed it. Talman "Tall Man" Brannigan, the lumber baron responsible, slaughtered his entire family in a fit of madness and despair. Supposedly, the Tall Man's ghost roams the dunes wailing for forgiveness, and if you see him, it means you're going to die.

According to local legend, Hel moved into town during World War I. It is a fact that the most powerful earthquake ever recorded in Michigan took place in the late summer of 1914, which was when Yggdrasil II was first spotted erupting from the sands. It's pretty tough to hide a pine tree the size of a large missile silo.

And yes, I know, the original Yggdrasil was an ash tree. Like any immigrants, even goddesses have to adapt. Apparently the species of tree wasn't as important as having the Norns water its roots. I don't know; I'm not an expert.

Altogether too soon we crested a rise, and the buggy's headlights tagged the mammoth tree in the distance. This was where the tourists would be let out to gape at Yggdrasil II and enjoy a photo op, and the schooner driver would tell them about Garm, the terrible hellhound who guards the world tree, warning them not to *think* of getting any closer.

I'm not sure about the Tall Man's ghost—that's one of those urban legends where everyone knows someone whose friend's cousin's brother knew a kid who saw the Tall Man and died three days later. Garm, however, is another matter.

"Hold fast," Mikill advised me unnecessarily, gunning the engine again as he departed from the graded trails.

The dune buggy flew and jounced over the sands. Dune grass whipped at the sides of the vehicle. I narrowed my eyes as a hail of icy pellets from the frost giant's dripping beard stung my face. Ahead of us, there was a deep-throated howl.

I poked around at my feet. "Mikill? Where's the offering?"

"There is a loaf of bread in the rear of the vehicle!" Mikill shouted, both hands gripping the steering wheel hard. "You must reach behind you to retrieve it!"

Another howl arose, drowning out the sound of the engine.

Oh, great. Again.

Holding the fur coat in place with one hand, I rummaged awkwardly behind me with the other. Easy enough for a frost giant to do, but I could barely brush the crusty surface of the loaf of bread with my fingertips.

At fifty yards away, Yggdrasil II loomed out of the darkness like a colossus. A piece of the darkness seemed to detach from it, bounding toward the dune buggy, yellow eyes aflame.

"Daisy Johanssen!" Mikill called. "Now!"

"Yeah, yeah! Just don't crash, okay?" Reluctantly, I released the catch on my seat belt, craning my upper body backward. The buggy bounced on its oversize tires, and the top of my head hit the roll bar. "Ouch!"

Garm howled, a long, belling peal, the sound of a hunting dog on the trail, if the hunting dog had an awesome sound system.

"Now!" Mikill repeated impatiently. "I do not wish to do battle with the hound."

Lurching, I managed to get my hand around the loaf. "Got it!"

The frost giant slowed and downshifted as Garm bounded toward us, jaws slavering. The hellhound was approximately twice the size of the buggy. Why it attacked the very denizens of Hel's realm of Niflheim it was meant to protect, and why it was pacified by a loaf of bread, I could not tell you. I asked the first time and was told that was simply the way it was. Happens a lot in the eldritch community.

"Good doggy, good boy," I said encouragingly. "Want a treat?" Garm halted, regarding the loaf of bread with flaming yellow eyes. I hurled it as far as I could. "There you go!"

And like that, Garm the hellhound took off after the bread, bounding into the dune grass, where a contented snuffling and munching sound arose.

"Well done," Mikill said.

I dragged my arm over my forehead, wiping away anxious sweat and frost-giant residue. "What did I say last time, Mikill? Put the bread up front!"

He glanced at me. "Forgive me. I had forgotten the lack of stature that comes of human blood."

I sighed. "Just drive."

Mikill put the buggy in gear. "Keep your limbs well inside the vehicle during the descent."

He wasn't kidding.

I've never been to California, but I've seen pictures of giant redwoods with a hollow so big you could drive a car through it. Yggdrasil II was bigger. You could drive a car *into* it.

Which is exactly what we did.

The path to Niflheim spiraled downward and downward, hewn into the living wood inside the trunk of Yggdrasil II itself. How far down it went, I couldn't say. Local legends say the town of Singapore settled deep beneath the sands during the earthquake of 1914. They don't say *how* deep.

I kept my elbows tucked firmly at my sides, ignoring the curving wall of heartwood rushing past me inches from my face.

An icy mist arose from the distant realm below. The deeper we went, the colder it got. Mikill stopped dripping, his icicled hair and beard hardening with crackling sounds.

Shivering, I huddled under the fur coat.

At last we reached the bottom, emerging beneath a vast canopy of spreading roots tended to by the three Norns, who drew water in wooden buckets from a deep wellspring beneath the very center of the canopy and poured it lovingly over the massive, fibrous roots. One of them glanced at me as we passed, smiling. She looked like a kindly old grandmother, except her nails were long and curved like talons.

"Ma'am—" I began to call out to her, hoping for a little soothsaying as long as I was here.

Shaking her head, she laid a taloned finger against her lips.

The frost giant grunted and gassed the dune buggy. "They have no counsel for you, Daisy Johanssen."

"Why?"

He shrugged. "To undertake a hero's quest, you must first become a hero. That is the way it is."

See what I mean?

There's not a lot to the buried town of Singapore, also known as

Niflheim II or Little Niflheim, or, if you're feeling really flippant safely aboveground in the daylight, Deadwood. Basically, it's one road and a handful of buildings. Thanks to the stabilizing presence of Yggdrasil II's root system, as well as the prodigious efforts of the *duegars*, or Old Norse dwarves, it's . . . well, stable.

It's also dark, cold, and misty.

The dune buggy's headlights cut through the mist. Mikill pulled up beside the abandoned sawmill that served as Hel's headquarters and killed the engine. "We have arrived," he announced.

I climbed out of the buggy and shrugged into the fur coat. Its long sleeves hung well below my hands, and its hem trailed on the ground, making me feel like a little kid playing dress-up. Still, it was better than freezing.

Mikill ushered me into the dark, cavernous interior of the saw-mill, the only light source patches of glowing lichen on the walls. I actually see pretty well in the dark, but it takes my eyes a minute to adjust.

"Daisy Johanssen." A sepulchral voice tolled out of the murky dimness. "Welcome, my young liaison."

I took a knee and bowed my head. "Thank you, my lady."

"Rise."

I obeyed.

The goddess Hel was seated on a throne made from immense saw blades salvaged from the abandoned mill and repurposed through the cunning of dwarfish craftsmanship. It was hard to look at her, or at least half of her. The right side of Hel was fair and beautiful, a white-skinned woman with a clear, smooth brow and a benevolent gaze. The left side of Hel was black and withered, like a charred and burned corpse, only it was a black so dense it seemed to drink in what little light there was. In a sunken eye socket, her other eye glowed like an ember. A handful of shadowy attendants stood beside her throne.

"It has come to my attention that a mortal boy has died," Hel said. "And you are making inquiries among my subjects."

"Yes, my lady."

Her ember eye closed in one long, slow blink. "Is one of them complicit in the boy's death?"

"I don't know yet," I said. "I know there are ghouls involved, but I don't know how or why. One of them attacked me tonight."

"It is very important that you uncover the truth, Daisy Johanssen."

"I'm trying, my lady." I held out my hands, my long sleeves dangling. "Do you have any counsel for me?"

Hel was silent a moment. "Ghouls. What do you know of *ghouls*, young one? It is an unkind name that the age of modernity has accorded them."

"Not much," I admitted. "I know they subsist on human emotion, and they're more or less immortal."

She inclined her head. "In a sense, they are tragic figures. They are beings who were once ordinary mortal humans, slain at the height of great passion and rejected by heaven and hell alike. Because they are immortal creatures born of surpassing passion, they require emotion to sustain their existence. I possess an imperfect knowledge of the particulars, for they did not exist in my own cosmology. But it is true that they can no longer be killed by mortal means. It is well that you know this."

I swallowed. "Am I . . . Are you saying I'm going to have to kill ghouls, my lady?"

The fair side of Hel's mouth curved in a faint smile, while the wizened, charred side didn't move. Creepy, yet at the same time, oddly reassuring. "I am not omniscient, Daisy Johanssen. Such is not my gift. The time has come when you may venture into danger in my service. I would be remiss if I did not offer you a measure of protection." Raising her black, shriveled left hand, Hel beckoned, and a pale blue frost giantess stepped forward, a bright, shiny little dagger lying across both her cupped hands. She offered it reverently to the goddess, and Hel's claw closed around the hilt. "*Dauda-dagr.*"

I blinked. "I beg your pardon, my lady?"

"It means 'death day.'" She surveyed the dagger, the length of it etched with runes, then reversed it, grasping the blade. "When first you swore yourself into my service, I marked you with the hand of life, did I not?"

My left palm itched, and I closed my hand into a fist beneath my sleeve. Almost a year ago, Hel had traced the rune onto it with her forefinger, her right forefinger. Ansuz, the rune of the messenger, the liaison between worlds. "Yes, my lady. You did."

Proffering the dagger's leather-wrapped hilt, Hel extended her left arm. It hung in the murky, misty air like a dead tree branch. "Tonight, I offer you a gift from the hand of death." This time, it was the ruined left side of her mouth that lifted in a grim rictus. Definitely so not reassuring. "*Dauda-dagr* can slay even the immortal undead."

"Oh?" The word came out sort of squeaky.

"Come and take it from me, Daisy Johanssen." There was a hint of impatience in Hel's voice.

"Um . . . okay." I made myself approach the throne, putting one foot in front of the other, trying not to trip over the hem of my fur coat. Hel sat motionless, her right eye closed, long lashes curling gracefully. "You're sure about this, my lady?"

Her ember eye gave me a baleful glare. "Take it!"

Pushing back my overlong sleeves, I grasped the dagger's hilt and felt a frisson of pure cold pass through the weapon as Hel relinquished it.

"Well done." Her other eye, her compassionate eye, opened. "I hope that you do not have need of *dauda-dagr*, young one, but it is best that you have it in your possession. Order must be enforced, lest we all be imperiled."

I took a deep breath.

The dagger was heavy, heavier than I had expected. Also bigger. Hey, everything looks small in a frost giantess's hands.

"Find the truth," Hel said in an implacable tone. "Find it and report it to me, Daisy Johanssen. If you need to dispense justice, you have my leave."

Great.

I dropped to one knee, bowing my head. "Thank you, my lady. I'll do my best."

Sixteen

Mikill the frost giant drove me home, dripping all the way.
I was quiet, holding *dauda-dagr* awkwardly in my lap, thinking about what had transpired. For the first time since I'd become an agent of Hel, I felt the full weight of the responsibility vested in me, coupled with the realization that I had a lot to learn. Also, I was really, really tired. It was kind of overwhelming holding a conversation with a goddess who could casually reference having her own freaking *cosmology*. How did that even work, anyway? Trying to wrap my head around it just made my brain hurt.

By the time Mikill dropped me off in the alley, I was yawning. I thanked him and gave him back his fur coat.

Mrs. Browne was hard at work in the bakery, and her presence and the warm glow of light spilling into the alley from her windows was comforting. She spotted me and gave me a cheery little wave as I skulked past to check behind the Dumpster, where I found nothing. Yay.

That left the stairs to my apartment.

Opening the door gave me a sinking sensation in the pit of my stomach. Feeling only a little silly, I clutched the leather-wrapped hilt of *dauda-dagr* tight in my right hand, and used the left to turn the doorknob, jumping back as the door swung open.

Also nothing.

I heaved a sigh of relief.

Upstairs, I hurried into my apartment and locked the door behind me. A scrabbling sound from the screened porch made me jump again, my tail lashing with nerves, but it was only Mogwai, forcing himself through the torn screen and complaining vociferously about his empty food bowl.

"Hey, big guy," I said fondly, filling his bowl. "You scared me."

Ignoring me, he chomped at his kibble.

"Long day." I sank onto my futon couch and kicked off my sandals, fishing my phone out of my purse and checking it. No messages. No wonder. It was late. Having eaten, Mogwai deigned to come over to settle onto my lap and purr. "Hey, Mog?" I showed him *dauda-dagr*, runes shimmering the length of its blade. "Hel gave me a magic dagger. What do you think of that?"

Unimpressed, he kneaded my thighs with his paws, claws pricking a bit.

I thought about displacing him and going to bed.

Instead, I fell asleep.

I awoke to the sound of my phone chiming insistently and bright sunlight streaming through the windows, a sure indicator that I'd overslept. At least after the past twenty-four hours, I figured I got a pass on worrying about sloth. Glancing at my phone, I saw that the call was coming from the main desk at the station. "Hello?"

"Daisy, where are you?" Patty Rogan sounded harried. "The chief's having conniptions."

"Sorry." I rubbed the sleep from my eyes. "Long day, late night. I forgot to set my alarm. What's up?"

She lowered her voice. "There's a detective here from the sheriff's department. And we got the autopsy report."

That made me sit up straight. "And?"

"Oh, for God's sake, Daisy, *I* don't know." Her voice took on an irritated note. "Just get down here as fast as you can, okay?"

"Will do."

I showered at top speed and yanked on a linen sheath dress so I wouldn't have to take the time to worry about coordinating an outfit, then wolfed down a stale doughnut, eating it over the sink so I wouldn't get powdered sugar on my dress. *Dauda-dagr* was a problem. Having been entrusted with it, I was pretty sure it was incumbent on me to carry it. How, exactly, was I supposed to accessorize a dagger as long as my forearm? I settled for switching out my purse for a woven straw satchel big enough to conceal it.

Phone, check. Keys, check. Magic dagger, check.

By the time I reached the station, Chief Bryant was wrapping up a conference with all the patrol officers, of which there were a grand total of six, and a plainclothes detective from the county sheriff's office whom I vaguely recognized. The chief gave me a dour look as I sidled into the conference room, making me feel unwarrantedly guilty. A late-night summons from the Norse goddess of the dead was a pretty good excuse for being late to work.

Okay, maybe I do have a few daddy issues.

The chief dismissed all the officers but Cody Fairfax and the plainclothes detective. "Daisy, you remember Tim Wilkes from Sheriff Barnard's office. He's here to provide assistance and oversight." His voice was neutral. "Detective Wilkes, Daisy Johanssen."

"A pleasure." The detective shook my hand, looking a bit bewildered. He was one of those average-looking Midwestern guys, mid-forties, with mild brown eyes, sandy hair, and a tidy mustache. "May I ask in what capacity you're involved?"

"You can ask," the chief said. "Not sure I can give you a satisfactory answer. Unofficially, Miss Johanssen is a special consultant on . . . unusual cases."

Detective Wilkes processed that in silence a moment. "Chief Bryant, I do have to request your complete cooperation in this investigation," he said. "And your complete candor."

The chief nodded. "Understood. And I have to request your discretion, and possibly a willing suspension of disbelief. You've been assigned to the region long enough to understand that circumstances in Pemkowet are . . . unusual."

The detective made a noncommittal sound. "You know I can't cut any corners for you, Dave."

"Not asking you to." Chief Bryant held up one broad hand. "Daisy . . . Miss Johanssen . . . has uncovered a significant development I haven't divulged yet."

"Oh?" Detective Wilkes raised his brows.

I fought the urge to squirm in my seat. I was dying to know what was in the autopsy report. Cody, seated at the conference table with an expression of stoic patience, gave me a warning look.

I fought the urge to stick my tongue out at him.

"We have witnesses who report seeing the Vanderhei boy's body dumped in the river," the chief said.

Detective Wilkes's mild brown eyes took on a keen spark of interest. "I'll need to see their statements. Maybe question the witnesses myself."

The chief cleared his throat. "They're undines."

Tim Wilkes looked blank. "What?"

"The witnesses are undines," I said, unable to restrain myself. "I didn't take a formal statement because . . . well, they're undines. There's no point. It wouldn't hold up in court." I shook my head. "You can't even establish an official identity for a water elemental, let alone admit testimony."

"I see." Contrary to his words, Tim Wilkes continued to look blank. "Undines. Yes. Definitely . . . unusual."

Chief Bryant leaned back in his chair, which creaked. "You see why I'm asking for a measure of discretion?"

"Yes." The keen spark returned to the detective's gaze. "I do."

"If you're willing, I'd like you to work in conjunction with my people." The chief gestured at Cody and me. "Officer Fairfax has done a fine job leading the investigation. And I suspect you'll find Miss Johanssen's connections in what we call the eldritch community to be invaluable."

Tim Wilkes scrutinized me. "How is it you come to be so well connected, Miss Johanssen?"

My tail twitched with irritation and impatience. "That's considered an impolite question in the community."

Cody coughed, hiding a chuckle.

"You're one of them." It was a statement, not a question. At least the detective was shrewd.

I sighed. "Yes, I'm one of them. I'm also the goddess Hel's liaison between mortal and underworld authorities, and I assure you, she's very interested in seeing the truth come to light." I rubbed my left palm. "I'd show you my badge, but you wouldn't be able to see it. Since you're here, I assume the medical examiner has ruled Thad Vanderhei's death a probable homicide." I glanced at Chief Bryant. "Chief, I'm sorry I was late, but can I please, please know what was in the autopsy report?"

He gave me a slow nod. "Your undines were right. The Vanderhei boy drowned, but not in the river."

"Where?" I asked.

He shook his head. "Don't know. But he drowned in salt water, not fresh."

My jaw dropped. "Seriously?"

Taking pity on me, Cody slid a copy of the autopsy report across the conference table. "Read it for yourself, Daise."

I glanced briefly at it and saw a lot of scientific jargon. Bottom line, there's actually a physiological difference between the process of drowning in salt water and in freshwater. Also, they tested the fluid in his lungs for saline content. Definitely not river water. Scanning further, I saw other details noted.

"Internal temperature suggests time of death may have been several hours before the discovery of the body," Cody said helpfully. "Which corroborates your undines' testimony."

"He had scratch marks on his back." I looked up. "And they found *scales* under his fingernails?"

He nodded.

For a brief, sickening moment, I thought of Lurine. She wouldn't do that, would she? I was pretty sure she wouldn't. And if she would, why would she have helped me with the investigation?

Reaching across the table, Detective Wilkes turned a page for me. "The ME's office consulted with a biology professor at Western," he said. "He identified them as fish scales, but he couldn't pinpoint the species. On his recommendation, we're sending them to an expert ichthyologist. Hopefully, that will help narrow down our search." He tapped the page. "For now, we're thinking fish tanks."

I let out my breath. "Fish tanks?"

"Any other ideas?"

"No," I said honestly. Snake scales would have been bad; snake scales might have meant a lamia, or *the* lamia. As far as I knew, there was only one. I was just glad it wasn't snake scales. "And I don't see how this connects with the ghouls."

"Ghouls?" Again with the blank look.

This time it was the chief who coughed. "We have a statement from an eyewitness—that is, a *human* eyewitness—confirming that two of the boys were seen at the Wheelhouse two weeks prior looking for a ghoul known as Ray D. The victim was found with a Wheelhouse matchbook in his pocket, and an illegible number on it. And if I understand correctly, Miss Johanssen's undines tentatively identified two of the party in the boat as ghouls."

"Also, one of them attacked me last night," I added. The chief shot me a dumbstruck look. "I'm not sure if it's related."

"Sorry, sir," Cody murmured. "I didn't have time to report it."

Detective Wilkes scribbled in a leather-bound notebook. "Okay,

okay," he muttered to himself. "Got a bit of a learning curve here."
He glanced up at us. "I've never worked a case with a—what do you
call it?—*eldritch* angle before. You're going to have to bring me up to
speed on a few things."

"Where do you want to start?" I asked.

He tossed the question back to me. "Where do *you* want to start?"

I patted my straw satchel, emboldened by the presence of *dauda-
dagr* inside it. "I'd like to have a few words with the new head
ghoul."

"So would I," Cody said in a flat tone.

Detective Wilkes brushed his finger over his neat mustache,
thinking. "All right, I'll tell you what. Give me an hour to study the
case file and make a few calls to my team. I'd like to get them started
running background checks on everyone involved and looking into
local pet stores or aquarium maintenance services." He pointed at
me. "I'd like to see your full report on the, um, undines' testimony.
I understand it isn't written yet?"

"No," I admitted.

"Not to mention this ghoul attack." The chief glowered. "Daisy,
if this is getting dangerous—"

"It's not the kind of attack you can report, sir," I said. "Not to
mundane authorities. It was a violation of Hel's rules. Unless you
can charge a man with attempting to feed on the emotions of the
unwilling?"

He sighed.

Tim Wilkes looked slightly pale. "So that's what ghouls do?"

"That's what ghouls do," Cody confirmed.

"Not usually." I don't know why I felt compelled to defend them,
except maybe for the memory of Stefan Ludovic's ice-blue eyes.
Tragic figures, Hel had called them. In Stefan's case, I could almost
believe it. Or maybe I just wanted to. The others, not so much. "Usually, they feed on the willing."

"Who are willing because they're miserable, and *want* to have their emotions drained," Cody countered. "A vicious cycle most ghouls are only too happy to perpetuate."

"None of which even remotely begins to explain how and why a twenty-one-year-old boy apparently drowned in salt water a thousand miles from the nearest ocean," Chief Bryant interjected in a hard voice. He tossed a copy of today's *Appeldoorn Guardian* on the conference table. The headline screamed,

PEMKOWET CHIEF OF POLICE
CONTINUES TO STONEWALL
Should Legislative Action Be Considered?

"I suggest you get to work before the shitstorm intensifies."

Briefly, I entertained an unwelcome vision of Garm the bread-loving hellhound lying shot and bleeding on the dunes, Yggdrasil II hewn down with a thundering crash by an army of chain saws, and Little Niflheim excavated with backhoes. "Duly noted, sir."

"Good."

Seventeen

A little more than an hour later, Cody, Detective Wilkes, and I set out to pay a visit to Stefan Ludovic at the Wheelhouse, having first confirmed with a phone call that the head ghoul was on the premises and willing to receive us.

There were at least a dozen motorcycles in the parking lot, which seemed a bit excessive for not quite noon on a Wednesday. I wondered whether Stefan had called for backup. He didn't strike me as the nervous type, but he didn't strike me as the type to shy away from a show of force, either.

There was also a shiny black Lincoln Town Car with tinted windows sitting in the lot, its engine idling. I wondered what the hell *that* was all about.

I didn't have to wonder long. As soon as we exited the car, a driver in a suit and tie got out of the Lincoln and opened the door for his passenger. A pair of long, shapely legs in stiletto heels emerged with the elegance of considerable practice, followed by the rest of a familiar figure.

"Hey, baby girl!" Lurine greeted me. She wore oversize sunglasses and a formfitting dress with a bold, graphic print. "Long time no see."

"Is that . . . ?" Cody sounded stunned.

Lurine lowered her sunglasses enough to peer over them, looking him up and down. "Oh, my, you *are* a fine-looking specimen."

Detective Wilkes's voice was faint and incredulous. "Are you, um, Lurine Hollister, ma'am?"

She winked at him. "Guilty as charged."

I sighed. "Lurine, what are you doing here?"

"Let's just say that I had a feeling you'd turn up here today." Lurine slung an affectionate arm over my shoulders. "Your mom's worried about you, cupcake. And I promised to look after you a long time ago."

"You know Lurine Hollister?" Cody turned his stunned expression in my direction.

"Uh-huh."

"Ever since my little cupcake here was hardly more than a baby." Lurine planted a smacking kiss on my temple. "Right, Daise?"

"Yep."

"Is she . . ." The detective lowered his voice. "One of *your kind*?"

Lurine gave him a mild glance. "And what kind do you suppose that might be, cutie-pie?"

He flushed. "I've no idea, ma'am."

She patted his arm with her free hand. "That's probably for the best, don't you think?"

"I've seen all your movies," Cody blurted. "You were great in *Revulsion Asylum*, and *Return to Revulsion Asylum*."

Lurine smiled at him. "You're sweet."

Cody blushed, too. "What can I say? I'm a fan."

Oh, gah!

"I can't believe your taste in movies," I said to Cody. "That's what you watch? Seriously?" Realizing what I'd said, I grimaced and checked myself. "So sorry, Lurine. No offense intended."

She squeezed my shoulders. "None taken, cupcake. Shall we go inside?"

"You don't have to do this," I said to her. "In fact, you really *shouldn't* do this."

Releasing me, Lurine rummaged in her purse and withdrew a neatly folded handkerchief, which she used to blot the crimson lipstick imprint she'd left on my brow. "Oh, don't argue with me." Surveying her handiwork, she gave my temple a final swipe and stowed her handkerchief. "I've been bored lately. This will be fun."

"Ma'am." Detective Wilkes cleared his throat. "Ah . . . Ms. Hollister. This is highly irregular."

She gave him another wink. "That's what makes it fun."

I think the detective would have tried to stop her if he dared, but he didn't. Lurine sauntered toward the door of the Wheelhouse, and the rest of us fell obediently in line behind her.

"I can't believe you know *Lurine Hollister*!" Cody whispered to me. I punched him unobtrusively in the shoulder. "Ow! What was that for?"

"Nothing."

This time, there was no clatter of cue sticks and pool balls to go silent when we entered the bar. It was already silent.

But it got . . . more silent.

I counted seven or eight rough-looking ghouls with pale skin, glittering eyes, and doting women near them. To my relief, Al the Walrus wasn't among them; to my covert disappointment, neither was Stefan Ludovic. There were another four or five mortal men, also members of the Outcasts, wearing their colors with sullen pride. The same skinny human bartender with the muttonchops was on duty, wearing a sleeveless black concert T-shirt that showed off the tattoos on his wiry arms.

Since we'd called ahead, they had been expecting us.

They hadn't expected Lurine.

See, here's the thing. Like I said, members of the eldritch community always recognize one another as kin of a sort. Sometimes it's obvious; sometimes it's not. If there's a glamour, we can see through it. Even if there isn't, as is the case with half-breeds like me or shape-shifters like Cody, there's a palpable sense of *otherness*.

On the other hand, recognizing someone as *other* doesn't neces-sarily translate into knowing exactly what that *other* is. But if it hadn't been evident enough last night, today I realized Lurine was in a category by herself.

Predators recognize one another, too. And the ghouls in the bar that day may not have known exactly what Lurine was, but they sure as hell recognized her as something bigger and badder and older than themselves.

"Hello, boys." She took off her sunglasses. "So nice of you to see us. Is the boss in the house?"

Frozen, no one replied.

I nodded toward the back of the bar. "He's probably lurking in the shadows. He likes to make an entrance."

"He's a show-off," Cody agreed.

Lurine pursed her carmine lips. "So predictable."

From the shadows came a low chuckle.

"I'm really not in control of this investigation, am I?" Detective Wilkes mused to himself. He blinked. "Did I say that out loud?"

Unexpectedly, the muttonchopped bartender banged an empty glass on the service bar. "Hey, Stefan!" he hollered. "Your fucking cops are fucking here again! Are you gonna talk to them or not?"

Raising her eyebrows a fraction, Lurine turned her gaze on the bartender.

He returned it impassively, mopping the bar with a dingy-looking rag. "What are you lookin' at, Goldilocks?"

"I'm not sure." Her tone was thoughtful.

Stefan Ludovic chose that moment to make his entrance, com-ing forward from the shadows with loose-limbed grace. He paused briefly at the sight of Lurine, and then circled her, his head slightly cocked, his longish black hair brushing the collar of his leather vest. His ice-blue eyes were curious, their pupils waxing and waning. She remained where she was, looking sublimely un-concerned.

Definitely some kind of predator face-off. Or a mating ritual. Possibly both.

Detective Wilkes consulted his notes. "Um . . . Mr. Ludovic?"

Stefan ignored him. "Have we met before?" he asked Lurine. "Perhaps in Prague . . . some time ago? Or somewhere else?"

Lurine smiled at him. "Oh, I don't think so, sweetie."

His nostrils flared, and he said something in a foreign language. She replied in kind.

And then he said something in *another* foreign language; or at least that was what it sounded like to me. Lurine answered him in that one, too.

"Oh, for God's sake!" My impatience got the better of me. "We've got a few issues to discuss. Can we talk, please?"

Stefan inclined his head. "Step into my office."

His office was surprisingly luxurious and well-appointed, a back room in the bar with lots of dark wood paneling and leather-upholstered furniture. Nice recessed track lighting, too.

Stefan took a seat behind the desk, indicating a pair of chairs in front of it. "Ladies, gentlemen. What can I do for you?"

Lurine sat, crossing her legs. After an uncertain glance at Cody and the detective, I took the other seat. "First off, one of your ghouls attacked me last night," I said. "I came home to find him waiting in the stairwell of my apartment. He tried to . . . um, feed on me."

His pupils contracted to pinpoints. "I'm very sorry to hear it," he said in a clipped tone. "That is unacceptable. Can you identify him?"

"Yeah," I said. "Al. The big guy with the mustache."

"Ah." A complicated expression crossed Stefan's face. "When you were here before, he tasted you, did he not?"

"Um . . . yeah." *Ick.*

He nodded. "As a result of your, shall we say, mixed heritage, your emotions are unusually powerful, Miss Johanssen. For one of our kind . . ." His pupils expanded in a rush, giving me an unsettling feeling in the pit of my stomach. Possibly lower, too. It was creepy-gross on Al the Walrus, but creepy-hot on Stefan. Yeah, fine, call me shallow. "For one of our kind, I fear it is rather like a strong drug."

"I thought the nectar of chemically induced emotions was poisonous," Cody observed in his most laconic voice.

Stefan raised one eyebrow. Of course he was one of those guys who made it look effortless. "You have a good memory, Officer. But there is nothing artificial about Miss Johanssen's emotions." His pupils did that wane-and-wax thing again. "Indeed, I suspect they are a singularly pure nectar. And having tasted it, Al is ravening."

"Ravening?" I echoed.

He inclined his head. "Like an addict craving a fix, only more dangerous. It is a condition to which the undisciplined among us are vulnerable. Usually it is triggered by exposure to extreme emotion, and causes the afflicted to seek to provoke further extremity in . . . unfortunate ways."

"Like murder?" Cody asked bluntly.

"No." Stefan turned his ice-blue gaze on him. "There is no sustenance to be gained from the dead. Only the living."

My skin felt cold and prickly.

He looked back at me. "But that is not the case here. Your ordinary emotions are provocation enough. At any rate, do not be concerned. I will attend to the matter."

"Mind if I ask how?" I said.

Apparently, he did. "You have my word. I will attend to it."

Cody shook his head. "Not good enough. I want details."

For the first time since I'd met him, Stefan Ludovic looked irritated. There's a whole hierarchal thing that goes on in parts of the eldritch community, and he didn't like being challenged. "This isn't a matter that concerns mundane—"

Lurine interrupted him. "Oh, now, a little detail or two couldn't hurt, could it?" She took a compact out of her purse and checked her lipstick in the mirror. "Daisy's practically my goddaughter." She gave him a winsome smile. "I'd take it as a personal favor, Mr. Ludovic."

It was a face-saving measure, and it worked. "Oh, indeed?" He eased. "I didn't catch your name, Miss . . . ?"

"Hollister," she said. "Lurine Hollister."

"Is that the name you were born with?" Stefan asked. Not a fan of B-grade horror movies or tabloid gossip, it seemed.

"Is yours?" she countered.

He laughed. "Actually, yes. Very well. I'll have Al picked up this afternoon and confined under guard until the ravening passes. He's only had a couple of brief tastes. It shouldn't take more than ten days. You'll want to avoid accidental contact with him afterward," he added to me. "It could retrigger him."

Oh, great. "Not a problem."

"Does that satisfy you?" Stefan asked Lurine.

She closed her compact with a snap. "Thank you, yes."

He looked at me. "You said a *few* issues."

"Yeah." I glanced at Detective Wilkes and Cody in case either of them wanted to take the lead, but the detective was clearly overwhelmed, and Cody gave me a go-ahead nod. "Okay, here's the deal. We've got a dead boy who was in this bar looking for Ray D two weeks before he died, and we've got eyewitnesses who saw two ghouls, one male and one female, dump the boy's body in the river. Like it or not, your people are involved in this, Mr. Ludovic." I held up my left hand, flashing Hel's rune at him. "Last night I was summoned to Little Niflheim. To put it mildly, Hel is *very* concerned."

"I see." His pupils contracted again, giving him a blind, inward-looking appearance. "I will look deeper into the matter. But I assure you, no one you spoke to the other day lied." His nostrils flared, and his pupils expanded. "I would have known."

Lurine idly jiggled one stilettoed heel. "What about the bartender?"

"Jerry? It's possible," Stefan admitted after a pause, a frown creasing his pale brow. "He's a blank."

I felt ignorant. "What's a blank?"

"He has no sense of empathy." Stefan was silent a moment. "Condemn us as you will; call us *ghouls*." He spoke the word as though it left a bad taste in his mouth, and I remembered Hel calling it an unkind name. Briefly, I wondered what they called themselves, and wished I'd thought to ask her. "We are what we are, victims of our own passions. But we could not exist without being attuned to the emotions of others. This gift is not without its uses." His unnerving gaze settled on me. "One such as you, a skilled and compassionate *ghoul* could assist. One could allow you to safely experience the emotions you fear, Daisy Johanssen."

A shiver ran down my spine. Sheesh, was it that obvious? I cleared my throat. "Yeah, um, this isn't about me. Back to the blanks?"

He shrugged. "Because they lack empathy, we cannot attune to them. So yes, in theory it is possible for Jerry to lie in my presence."

"He's a sociopath." Detective Wilkes had found his voice. "That's what you're saying, isn't it?"

Again with the arched eyebrow. "Is that the correct terminology? Yes, I suppose so."

"Can we subpoena the bartender and bring him in to testify under oath?" Cody asked Wilkes. "Maybe hook him up to the polygraph?"

The detective shook his head. "Based on this? Hell, no. I read the file. He's already given you a statement. You want me to go to a judge and claim he's an uncooperative witness because some, some . . . ghoul . . . says he has no sense of empathy?" He shook his head again. "No. No, I don't think so."

Stefan Ludovic laid his hands flat on the desk. "Speak, Hel's liaison. My services are at your disposal. What will you?"

"Umm . . ." I glanced at Cody.

"The victim was found with a matchbook from the Wheelhouse in his pocket, and there was a phone number written on it," Cody said. "Unfortunately, it was illegible. But someone here gave it to him. We want to know who and we want to know why." His voice dropped an octave, a hint of a growl in it, a reminder that he was a predator, too. "And we want to find Ray D and question him. Badly. Very badly. You claim to be in charge here. Is that too much to ask?"

They had a brief staring contest and it was the ghoul who looked away, although I had the feeling it was more about maintaining self-control than any sense of intimidation. "I assure you, every effort will be made."

For now, it would have to do.

Remembering Hel's warning, I wondered what would happen if he failed.

Eighteen

Knowing what I did now, I couldn't help but check out Jerry the bartender as we left the Wheelhouse.

Bracing his hands on the bar, he fixed me with a long, flat stare. "You gonna blow up my kegs again, blondie? Or do you like what you see?"

In fact, I most definitely didn't like it, because what I saw was *La Araña*, the spider from my mom's reading. An intricate tattooed web covered Jerry's right shoulder and upper arm, the spider squatting amidst it.

Oh, crap.

"Yeah, um . . ." I made myself smile. "Sorry about that."

He shrugged. "Whatever."

I opted to keep quiet about this discovery for the time being. I wasn't sure how much stock Cody put in Mom's reading, and I was definitely sure Detective Wilkes wouldn't approve.

It was a relief to escape from the dark confines of the Wheelhouse to the bright sun outdoors in the parking lot. The driver of the Town Car emerged to hover patiently beside it. Ignoring him for the moment,

Lurine put her sunglasses back on. "Are you done playing with ghouls for the day, cupcake?"

"For now, yeah. Thanks." I paused. "Practically your goddaughter, huh?"

"Well." A mischievous smile curved her lips. "Why not? It worked, didn't it?" Her smile vanished, and she lowered her sunglasses to give me a serious look. "He's an old one, that Stefan, and dangerous, and you're like catnip to these things, Daisy. I wanted to make sure he knows I consider you under my protection. Now he does."

"Do you know him from . . . before?" I asked.

Lurine shook her head. "No. I'd remember. And believe me, so would he. He was just baiting me."

"Ah . . ." Detective Wilkes glanced at his notes. "You said he was old. How old are we talking?"

"Aren't you cute?" Lurine patted him on the cheek, not deigning to answer. "Baby girl, you *call* me next time, okay?"

"Okay, okay!"

She settled her sunglasses in place. "I know you can take care of yourself under normal circumstances, but it's just that you don't have any defenses against this kind of thing."

My hand went instinctively to my straw satchel, feeling the shape of *dauda-dagr* nestled inside it. "That's not entirely true."

Lurine's face paled beneath her sunglasses, and she drew in a sharp breath, her voice taking on that bronze-edged tone it had when she summoned the naiads, making the sunlight seem to shiver over the hot pavement of the parking lot. "Daisy Johanssen, tell me you're *not* thinking of invoking your birthright!"

"No!" I protested. "God, no! Of course not."

She let out a sigh of relief. "Don't scare me like that, cupcake." Behind the dark lenses, her gaze shifted to Cody, softening. "Of course you're not defenseless," she said. "With a big, strong, handsome police officer at your side. My apologies, Officer Fairfax. It was rude of me to imply otherwise."

He blushed. "Please call me Cody."

"Cody." Lurine smiled at him. "I like the sound of it." She pointed at me. "Call me."

"I will!"

She glided back into the Town Car, and the driver closed the door after her. Cody and Detective Wilkes stared after it as it pulled away.

"All right." The detective gave himself a shake. "I think . . . I think I need to rethink this case and how we're going to handle it." He stared at his nice leather-bound notebook. "I'm at a bit of a loss here. I'm not sure how to even report on this. Mind if we go back to the station and conference?"

"Not at all," Cody said.

Lifting his head, Detective Wilkes gazed at the highway in the direction the Town Car had gone. "That really was Lurine Hollister, wasn't it? I'd heard the rumor that she lived in the area, but . . ." He glanced at me. "What the hell *is* she? For that matter, what are *you*? And what did she mean about invoking your birthright?"

"Nothing germane to the case," I said firmly. And yes, I was a bit pleased with myself for remembering the word *germane* and using it correctly in context. My old teacher Mr. Leary would have been proud. "Shall we go?"

Back at the station, we sent out for sandwiches and conferenced, the chief sitting in on our discussion. Away from Lurine oozing preternatural, predatory charisma all over the place, and the glittering eyes of ghouls, Detective Wilkes regained a measure of confidence.

"You weren't kidding about this one, Dave," he said to the chief. "It's a tricky son of a bitch."

Chief Bryant nodded. "Told you."

Detective Wilkes spread one hand over the open pages of his notebook. "Here's what I'm thinking. For now . . ." He raised one finger for emphasis. "For *now*, I'd like to leave this eldritch angle under wraps and let your people handle the fieldwork on it."

"Sounds good." The chief bit into a ham sandwich on marbled rye.

"Any ordinary *human* leads, my team will run down," the detective continued. "We'll run a background check on that bartender. . . . What was his name?" Lifting his hand, he squinted at his notes. "Jerry Dunham. And there's the name the vic's younger brother gave us, too. Matthew Mollenkamp, the Triton alum from Van Buren College. That whole secret-society-within-a-society, Masters-of-the-Universe business. I don't see any follow-up here. You looked into it yet?"

Cody shook his head. "No time."

"Make time."

The chief chewed and swallowed a bite of ham sandwich, taking a swig of water and clearing his throat. "Speaking of time, how much time are we talking about, Tim?"

"Not a lot." Detective Wilkes gave him a bleak look. "Four, five days. A week at best. I can't keep it under wraps forever."

"Gonna get ugly if it blows up."

"I know." The detective sounded sympathetic. "At some point, we're going to have to bring those boys back in for questioning."

Chief Bryant grimaced. "When?"

"Give it another day or two. Let's see what more we can dig up." Detective Wilkes took another peek at his notes. "No leads at all on the whereabouts of this Ray D? Not even a last name to go on?"

"It's hard enough tracking down a human member of the Outcasts," Cody said. "Or any biker. Most of them go by nicknames or aliases. It's ten times harder when it's a ghoul. The majority of them are at least a hundred years old. Any official ID they had is ancient history. And you know what motorcycle clubs are like."

The detective nodded. "There's a pretty fierce code of loyalty at work. Was this Ray D involved in the meth lab we busted back in April?"

"Yeah, but no one would finger him." Cody turned his hands

palms-up. "Never been able to bag a ghoul. Humans won't flip on them."

"Maybe they would if they didn't know what they were doing." For the first time in hours, the shrewd light was back in the detective's eyes. He tapped his notebook. "Let me make some inquiries down at county, see what I can shake loose."

"The ME released the vic's body today," the chief observed. "Funeral's scheduled for tomorrow afternoon. Thought it might be good politics for me to attend it. Be interesting to see who else is there."

"You think Ray D might show?" Detective Wilkes asked.

Chief Bryant shrugged. "It's the kind of thing a ghoul would do, especially if he's the perp." His heavy gaze slid over to me. "Daisy, I thought you might come with me. See if there's anything hinky. Any eldritch presence."

"It's not likely," I said. "Not outside Hel's sphere of influence. The funeral's in Appeldoorn, right?"

"South side," he said. "Along Big Pine Bay. Cuypers and Sons. It's on the outermost limits, but it's in range."

I sighed. "I'll go. But I didn't, um, exactly make a good impression on the family." I picked up the copy of the *Appeldoorn Guardian* still sitting on the table. "And we're not exactly their favorite people."

"That makes it more important than ever to keep up appearances," the chief said. "Pay our respects."

"And intrude on their grief," I said morosely.

He wasn't cutting me any slack on this one. "No one ever said this job was easy."

"Right." Tim Wilkes closed his notebook and stood. "All right, I've got enough to get started on here. I'll be in touch. Meanwhile, keep me in the loop."

"Will do," Chief Bryant promised.

Once the detective had gone, Cody rose, too. "Chief, if it's all right with you, I've got a couple more possible leads to run down.

Known associates of Ray D that I didn't get to yesterday. Probably no point, but . . ." He shrugged. "No stone left unturned, right? Daisy, I think it's best if you lie low until we get word from Ludovic that Al's off the streets. Stay here, maybe catch up on some filing."

"Wait." The chief raised one meaty hand. "Back up a minute. Al?"

At his insistence, we filled him in on the attack of Al the ravening ghoul and its aftermath. I left out the part where Cody got a little furry and toothy in the process, and Cody tactfully avoided mentioning Lurine's presence. It warmed my heart a little to see him honoring the unspoken eldritch code, which in turn made me think of Jen with a guilty pang. I checked my phone surreptitiously.

Nope, no messages.

Chief Bryant agreed with Cody that I should lie low. "No point in taking unnecessary risks," he said pragmatically, lumbering to his feet and heading for the conference room door. "And Patty could use a hand in the front office. With everything going on, she's backed up."

I sighed again.

Daisy Johanssen, part-time file clerk. Last week I wouldn't have minded a bit. Now it felt like a bit of a letdown.

Cody grinned at me, his gold-flecked topaz eyes crinkling at the corners. "It's for your own good, Pixy Stix. Don't worry; it's only temporary."

"Hang on." I caught him before he left, remembering Jerry the bartender's tattoo. "There's something I wanted to tell you."

He listened, looking skeptical. "It doesn't prove anything, Daise."

"It fits the reading," I said. "So did the bottle. That's the one solid piece of evidence we have that the kids were lying."

It was Cody's turn to sigh. "Yeah, it does. But we can't bring him in for questioning on the basis of your mom's reading a deck of *lotería* cards any more than we can a ghoul's say-so. Understand?"

"I guess."

"Have you looked into other possible interpretations?" he asked.

"I meant to," I admitted. "No time."

"I know." Cody lowered his voice. "As long as we're being honest, you didn't mean me, did you? In the parking lot?" he added when I looked at him with confusion. "When you said you weren't entirely without defenses?"

"No."

"Didn't think so." From his mild tone, he took no offense. "What, then?"

Opening my satchel, I showed him the gleaming, rune-etched length of *dauda-dagr*, its keen edges already fraying the satin lining. "Hel gave me a weapon last night," I said. "Its name means 'death day.' It can kill the undead. She thought I should have it."

Cody sucked in his breath, phosphorescent green flashing behind his eyes. "Because you'll need it?"

I shrugged. "Maybe."

He stared at it. "Daisy, do you have the first idea how to handle an edged weapon?"

My tail twitched with indignation. "I have a general idea. After all, it's pointy, right?"

He exhaled hard. "Okay. Later this evening, we're going to have a little lesson." His tone turned firm. "No arguments, all right?"

"All right," I agreed.

Nineteen

I spent the afternoon catching up on a backlog of filing, skimming the reports for any telltale signs of eldritch involvement. As far as I could tell, all was quiet on that front. The community was lying low.

A little after three o'clock, there was a commotion on the block outside the station, a flurry of excited shrieks and gasps.

"What the hell's going on out there?" the chief called from his office.

Patty and I exchanged a glance. "I'll go take a look," I volunteered, jumping at the chance to take a break from filing.

The source of the commotion turned out to be none other than the head ghoul himself. Stefan and two other members of the Outcasts had parked their motorcycles halfway down the block, and were approaching the station on foot.

That was why the tourists were shrieking. I couldn't blame them. There was no mistaking the trio for human. It was a bona fide eldritch sighting. In broad daylight, the underlying ghoul pallor was more pronounced, and an otherworldly aura that even an untrained mundane could recognize surrounded them.

Especially Stefan. And I realized, watching him walk down the sidewalk like a victorious warrior returning from battle, that I didn't respond differently to him just because he was gorgeous.

He was *different*. Lurine had said he was old. Maybe it was age that had slowly altered him, turning the dull and creepy carbon of a ghoul like Al the Walrus into something hard-edged and glittering, like a scary diamond.

Okay, a bit of a mixed metaphor, but you get the idea.

At any rate, the tourists continued to point and exclaim and take photos. Courtesy of the misapprehensions of popular culture, I heard the word *vampire* thrown around with delight. Vampires in daylight? Trust me, it does not happen.

Ignoring the tourists, Stefan halted in front of the station to greet me, inclining his head. "Miss Johanssen."

I couldn't help but notice that his chest rose and fell as he took a slow, patient breath. Unlike vampires, for example, Stefan lived and breathed. For a being whose entire existence was predicated on some kind of complicated spiritual loophole, he seemed very physically present. Very much there, very much alive. There was actual blood beating in his veins. And I could not help but be very, very aware of it. So aware it made my skin tingle.

I tried not to think of the Seven Deadlies, especially lust. Which was hard to do, what with the tingling and all.

"Um . . . hi. You can call me Daisy," I said. "Is everything okay?"

"Yes, of course." He nodded toward the station's front door. "I have come to report. May we go inside?"

"You came in person?" I asked.

Stefan raised his brows. "You are Hel's liaison. Proper protocol requires more than a phone call."

The crowd was beginning to get bigger, so I ushered Stefan and his . . . his lieutenants, I guess, into the precinct. At the front desk, Patty stared, openmouthed. The chief poked his head out of his office, but he withdrew with a shrug when I waved him off.

I closed the front door. "So what's up?"

"I wish to notify you that Al has been secured and is under guard," Stefan said in a formal tone. "When the ravening has passed, you will be informed. As I said, it is best you avoid contact with him."

"As *I* said, not a problem."

One corner of his mouth lifted, a dimple forming in the crease. *Oh, crap.* "These are my lieutenants." He indicated the two ghouls with him. Got the terminology right—yay for me. "Rafe and Johnny. If ever you do encounter a problem and I am unavailable, they can be trusted."

"Hi," I said to them.

They nodded in reply. Rafe looked like he might be part Native American, with black hair, a pale coppery hue to his skin, and dark eyes that should have partially hidden the wax-and-wane ghoul effect, but somehow didn't. Johnny had long, sandy-blond hair caught back in a ponytail and an expression that might have been congenial if it weren't for the dilated pupils glittering in his eyes.

Avid, but in control. Still, it made my skin stop tingling, giving way to the creepy-crawlies.

"I spoke to Jerry." Stefan withdrew a folded piece of paper from a pocket inside his leather vest. "After some questioning, he admitted to having given the boys Ray D's phone number."

My pulse quickened. "Did he say why?"

All three ghouls' pupils dilated further. *Uh-oh.* Best not to get too excited around these guys. Stefan's contracted pretty quickly. "He claimed the boys were looking to score."

The word *score* sounded oddly anachronistic coming from him. "Meth?"

His jaw hardened. "Yes. He claimed he merely gave them the number to get rid of them, knowing that I disapproved of such matters being discussed on the premises and that Ray D hadn't been seen for months."

"Did you believe him?" I asked.

"No. But I cannot disprove it." The words were clipped; I think the admission cost him. "Not without resorting to means outside the law, which I am loath to do under the current level of scrutiny. And as a human, he is under the jurisdiction of your mundane authorities, not mine."

"Ray D's one of yours," I observed.

"Theoretically, yes." Stefan inclined his head in acknowledgment. "And I will continue to search for him. But I cannot even confirm that he remains in Pemkowet." He handed me the folded paper. "The telephone number Jerry provided me goes unanswered. Assuming it is valid, I trust your people can trace it."

Not my area of expertise, but I certainly hoped so. Unfolding the paper, I saw a phone number written in a precise, blocky hand with the sort of penmanship you just didn't see in this century. Beneath it, the bartender Jerry Dunham's name and home address were written in the same hand.

I glanced up inquiringly.

"I dismissed him from his position," Stefan said in answer to my unspoken question. A look of distaste flitted across his face. "But I thought you might wish to know where to find him."

"Thanks."

His expression eased, and he smiled. "You're welcome . . . Daisy." His smile widened a little. *Gah!* Ghouls weren't supposed to have dimples. "If I learn anything further, I will contact you."

"Thanks," I said again. "I appreciate it."

"Have you given thought to my offer?" he asked me.

"Your offer?" Belatedly, I remembered Stefan telling me at the Wheelhouse that I could benefit from the assistance of a skilled and compassionate ghoul, that I could experience my emotions safely. It was appallingly tempting. A hot flush ran over me. "Jesus!" I lowered my voice. "Do you know what I *am*?"

Stefan's face was grave. "Yes. At first I was not sure. But I made inquiries. Your story is known."

I waved one impatient hand at the ceiling, at the invisible presence of the Inviolate Wall far, far above it. "Then you know what's at stake?"

He arched that eyebrow. "You are what you are, Daisy. In and of itself, passion is no sin. It is deeds that matter in the end."

"What deed did you commit?" I asked him. "For heaven and hell alike to reject you?"

He was silent.

Behind him, his lieutenants shifted from foot to foot, glancing uneasily at each other with waxing-and-waning eyes.

I winced. "Sorry. We don't know each other well enough to ask that, do we?"

"No." Stefan Ludovic accorded me a courtly little bow. "But it was I who overstepped the bounds of propriety first. It's just . . ." His nostrils flared and his pupils dilated, then shrank to highly controlled pinpoints. "Forgive me?"

I nodded.

He bowed again. "My thanks."

With that, the trio of ghouls took their leave, lieutenants Rafe and Johnny falling in behind their commander. I waited, listening for the inevitable shrieks of the tourists followed by the coughing roar of three Harley-Davidson motorcycles being kicked to life, throttles open, chugging out of town.

"Damn!" Behind the front desk, Patty Rogan fanned herself. "What have you gotten yourself into, Daisy Jo?"

"Trouble," I said briefly. "Okay if I clock out for the day, Patty? I've got some research to do."

She made a face. "Go ahead."

I called Detective Wilkes and left a voice-mail message for him with Ray D's purported phone number.

I studied the autopsy report, and confirmed that the tox screen of Thad Vanderhei's blood didn't turn up anything but alcohol. No methamphetamines, no drugs of any kind.

Okay, so maybe they didn't score. Or maybe if Jerry the bartender was lying, he was lying about the meth, too. The Tritons had a reputation as a hard-partying fraternity, but crystal meth wasn't exactly a common collegiate drug, especially at a conservative place like Van Buren College.

But if they weren't looking for Ray D to score drugs, what the hell *were* they looking for?

I had a feeling Detective Wilkes was right: We needed to look into this Masters of the Universe angle. I also had enough sense to know better than to tackle it on my own, which is why I decided to look into spider mythology instead. Maybe Jerry's tattoo symbolized a connection.

For that, I had two choices. I could take my chances at the library with the Sphinx. Depending on her mood, she would either direct me toward the appropriate research materials or pose me an indecipherable riddle. Or I could ask Mr. Leary. Depending on his level of sobriety, he would either treat me to a long series of rambling anecdotes or give me a succinct answer in a lot less time than it would take to do the research. All things considered, I decided on the latter option.

Mr. Leary lived in a charming little cottage in East Pemkowet, and in case you're wondering, yes, Pemkowet and East Pemkowet are technically two separate towns. Because Pemkowet proper is divided by the river, their boundaries overlap in a crazy-quilt fashion. Every other decade, someone proposes combining them into one entity, and every time it happens, one side or the other votes it down.

Anyway.

The shade garden in Mr. Leary's front yard was looking good, which was a hopeful sign. I made my way up the walk past the arching fronds of ferns so tall they looked almost prehistoric, and immense broad-leaved hosta plants in every hue of green imaginable, some of them sending up narrow shoots of pale blue flowers.

"Daisy Johanssen!" Mr. Leary greeted me with delight when I

rang the doorbell. He had a drink in hand, but he was steady on his feet and he sounded lucid. "How is my favorite little eschatological time bomb?"

For the record, no, I don't know exactly what that means. It happens a lot with Mr. Leary. But I always appreciated the fact that he never, ever talked down to his students. A lot of teachers did, especially if you happened to have a single mom who waited tables and took in sewing for a living or an abusive handyman dad. Not Mr. Leary. Jen and I had always liked that about him. We might not have been his best students, but we studied hard for his classes. I was proud of those B-pluses.

"I'm good, thanks," I said.

"No," he corrected me. "You're doing well, thank you very much."

I hid a smile. "I'm doing well, thank you very much. And you?"

"I'm doing splendidly, thank you kindly." Mr. Leary hoisted his drink in response. He was tall and lean, in his late sixties, with a long, mobile face and a leonine head of white hair, kind of like a more benign-looking Donald Sutherland. "Come to pick my brain, have you?"

I nodded. "Do you mind?"

"Not at all." Stepping back, he gestured. "Come in, come in. Can I offer you a gin rickey?"

"No, thanks."

"Ah." Mr. Leary gave me a broad conspiratorial wink. "Of course, you're on the job." He shook his glass, half-melted ice cubes tinkling. "I hope you don't mind if I refresh my own. Can I offer you something else? Club soda?"

"I'm fine," I said. "But please go ahead."

Watching Mr. Leary make a drink was like how I imagine watching a Japanese tea ceremony must be, every movement precise and ritualized. He emptied his glass, washed it under the tap, and dried it with a tea towel, then folded the tea towel just so and placed it on the counter. Three ice cubes were plucked from an ice bucket with a pair of silver tongs and placed one by one in the glass. Half a lime was squeezed with a fancy little juicer and poured atop the ice, followed by an exactly measured one and a half ounces of gin, topped with club soda until it fizzed to the rim.

I waited patiently, knowing there was no rushing him. Actually, it looked pretty damn refreshing.

"Ahh!" He sighed in bliss at the first sip. "There's no finer libation on a hot summer day. Are you sure I can't tempt you?"

"I'm sure."

In the living room, he took a seat on the overstuffed sofa, the arms and back covered with old-fashioned antimacassars. I sat opposite him on a matching chair. "Is this about the Vanderhei boy?" he asked me.

"You know I can't comment on that," I said.

Mr. Leary's wide mouth curved in a saturnine smile. "It's always worth a try. Curiosity may have killed the cat, but satisfaction brought him back. What can I do for you, Daisy?"

"I'm looking for a spider."

"A spider." He didn't ask me to elaborate; he didn't have to. I'd come to him with this kind of puzzle before. He simply set his glass neatly down on a coaster, tilted his head back, and closed his eyes in thought.

Despite being a regular full-blooded human, Mr. Leary knew more about mythology, religion, and folklore than pretty much anyone in the eldritch community except the Sphinx, and he was a lot more loquacious. And yes, that's another one of his vocabulary words. According to the folk wisdom of Mrs. Browne, madmen, poets, and drunkards all have half a foot in the eldritch world. I figured Mr. Leary qualified on at least one count, and I had a suspicion he might write poetry, too.

Beads of condensation formed on the glass containing his gin rickey, trickling slowly down. "There's Arachne, of course," Mr.

Leary said without opening his eyes. "I should hope one of my students would have thought of *her*."

"I did," I said. "It's not her. It might be something more literal."

He steepled his fingers. "There's *Argiope aurantia*, also known as the writing spider, rather fetching specimens with bright yellow and black markings. I had one in my garden a few years ago. I named her Agatha."

"Not Charlotte?" I couldn't help but ask.

Mr. Leary cracked one eye open at me. "The full name of the eponymous heroine of *Charlotte's Web* was Charlotte A. Cavatica, a reference to *Araneus cavaticus*, also known as the barn spider."

"Oh."

He closed both eyes again. "*Argiope aurantia*'s web has a distinctive jagged vertical lattice pattern in the center, and legend has it that the writing spider weaves the name of a member of its human household into the lattice as a warning of said member's impending demise."

I shook my head. "Not that literal, I don't think."

"Fascinating how many local superstitions revolve around our own mortality, isn't it?" he observed. "I'm thinking of writing a book."

This time I kept silent, hoping to keep him from pursuing that particular tangent.

"Very well." Mr. Leary sighed. "West African folklore gives us tales of the trickster Anansi, tales which spread throughout the Caribbean in various permutations. I believe the Lakota people have a similar deity whose name escapes me at the moment, while the Navajo creation myth features Spider Grandmother. In Islamic lore, there is a tale of a spider that spun a web across the mouth of a cave to protect the prophet Muhammad. Additionally, I suspect there may be some farther-Eastern spider lore with which I fear I'm unfamiliar. I'd have to consult my library." His eyes snapped open. "Is any of this of assistance?"

"I suppose we could be talking about a trickster," I said. "Can you think of any likely reason for one to be in Pemkowet?"

"No." Picking up his gin rickey, he took a long sip, eyeing me. "But then, there are a good many unlikely creatures in Pemkowet."

"True."

Mr. Leary took another drink, easing one of the ice cubes into his mouth, crunching it with relish, and swallowing. "And yet, since you ask, I must confess that I do think it quite unlikely." He set his glass back down on the coaster with the careful, controlled motions of a practiced drinker. "By and large, it appears that lesser deities retain a measure of cultural affiliation. That being the case, I cannot see why an African or a Lakota trickster god would venture into the domain of a Norse goddess."

"Yeah, I know," I agreed. "Pemkowet's a bit on the homogenous side."

"Alas, our lack of diversity is one of the few shortcomings of our fair community, at least in terms of ordinary mortal culture and ethnicity." He regarded me with an owlish look, or the way I imagine an owl might look if it were wise and slightly drunk. "And although you most pointedly did *not* ask, I will say that I am wholly unaware of any connection between mythological spider lore and drowned young men. If I were you, I'd be looking for a naiad." His voice deepened, taking on an oratorical resonance. "Think ye of Hylas, the noble companion of bold Heracles—charming Hylas, whose hair hung down in curls!"

I smiled. "Thank you, I will. I appreciate it."

Mr. Leary saw me to the door. "You're welcome to visit anytime. In the meanwhile, may you continue to be well, Daisy." He hoisted his glass to me. "Indeed, given your particular ontological dilemma, may you continue to be *good*."

That one, I think I got. Stretching on tiptoes, I kissed his cheek. "I'll do my best."

Twenty

Outside Mr. Leary's cottage, I checked my phone. No messages, and it was only a bit after four thirty in the afternoon.

Okay, so spider deities were a probable no-go. Mom had said her reading was likely to be pretty literal.

Mr. Leary's writing spider might be a little *too* literal, but we had a literal bottle, and a definitely involved bartender with a literal spider depicted on his literal shoulder. We had missing but implicated ghouls, and according to the cards, we were still looking for a pair of crossed arrows and the elusive mermaid *La Sirena*, an alluring woman in distress.

Right now, none of it added up.

And speaking of ghouls . . .

I was in serious need of some girl talk. I really, really wanted to talk to Jen. If I could get her to accept my apology, at least it would be a start. I thumbed my keypad, composed a message, then changed my mind and deleted it.

Instead, I called her mother. "Oh, hey! Hi, Mrs. Cassopolis. It's Daisy." I cradled the phone under my ear. "Is Jen still at work? Can you tell me where she's working today? I need to talk to her, and she's not picking up."

Bless her heart, she did.

I drove over to the summer home on the lakeshore where Jen was working alone, banging on the door until she answered. Her expression was sullen. "I don't want to talk to you right now, Daise."

"Hear me out?" I pleaded.

She hesitated, then tossed a rag at me. "I'm running behind. The family's due back any minute. Help and I'll listen."

"Deal."

I followed Jen upstairs to the master bathroom. Without speaking, we fell into a familiar rhythm. I set about polishing the chrome fixtures while she tackled the sunken Jacuzzi bathtub. It felt like being back in high school, when I'd helped her out plenty of times, except in high school, we would have been looking through the client's cupboards in search of sex toys, giggling uncontrollably if we happened to find any.

"Look," I said to her reflected back in the mirror. "I'm sorry. I was wrong, and you were right. I shouldn't have intervened. And I wasn't exactly a neutral third party."

"Not *exactly*?" She shot me a look over her shoulder, brushing a wisp of glossy black hair out of her eyes. "You were all over him in the patrol car."

"I wasn't *all over* him! I just . . ." Realizing I wasn't helping my case, I bit my tongue. "I'm sorry. It's just that I've had a crush on him for ages. I should have told you."

"Yeah, you should have." Jen pointed with one rubber-gloved hand. "Mind scrubbing the toilet?"

I exchanged my rag and polish for a brush and a bottle of toilet-bowl cleaner. "I'm sorry," I said for a third time. "Truly. I don't know how else to apologize for it. Help me out here?"

Jen detached the showerhead and sprayed down the tub. "Why didn't you ever tell me?" she asked over the sound of the water.

"About Cody?"

"Duh."

I scrubbed diligently at the faint rust-colored ring in the toilet bowl. "I don't know. I guess . . . it just felt safer not to."

Jen shut off the water, then turned around and sat on the edge of the tub. "See, that's what hurts, Daise. Since we've been friends, when have I ever not had your back? Since when can you not trust me?"

I flinched away from the genuine pain in her brown eyes. "It's not you—"

"—it's me?" she finished bitterly. "Yeah, where have I heard that before?"

I sighed. "It's not what you think." Closing the toilet-seat lid, I perched on it. "Cody's a werewolf."

She stared at me, lips parted. "You're telling me Cody Fairfax is a fucking *werewolf*?"

"Yes," I said. "I'm violating the entire eldritch code of honor to tell you that Cody Fairfax is a fucking werewolf. That's why he dropped out of basketball when his hormones went into overdrive. That's why he cut classes at least once a month. That's why the chief never schedules him for duty during a full moon. And that's why he never dates anyone for more than a month or two, which is why I didn't want you to go out with him, because I knew you'd only get hurt."

"It still wasn't your call to make," Jen said automatically.

"I know."

She peeled off her rubber gloves. "Why's he such a closet case?"

I shook my head. "I don't know. It's complicated. His whole clan—"

"His whole *clan*?"

"Yeah," I said. "The whole Fairfax clan. I think they're pretty secretive by nature, but they've got reasons for it."

"It does explain a lot about them," Jen said in a thoughtful tone.

"I know, right?" I stuck the toilet brush back into its container.

"Look, that's why I didn't want to talk about Cody. I didn't trust myself not to tell you, and it wasn't my secret to tell."

"You didn't trust me to keep it?"

I spread my hands. "I'm trusting you now, aren't I?"

She made a face. "*Now*, yeah."

"I know, I know," I said. "And for the thousandth time, I'm *sorry*. I've got a lot going on, okay? I didn't expect all this to come up. I didn't expect the Vanderhei kid to drown. I didn't expect to be working so closely with Cody." My tail lashed with pent-up agitation, and I felt pressure rising in the air around me. "And that whole 'it's not you; it's me' thing? It's true. He meant it. Turns out werewolves only mate with their own kind, so if it's any consolation, I'm no more eligible than you are. And there's this guy I just met, this other guy, Stefan—actually, he's a ghoul, but before you—"

"Daise," Jen interrupted me. "You're babbling." She glanced uneasily about her. "Calm down before you burst a pipe."

Taking a deep breath, I envisioned myself pouring out a glass filled with my roiling emotions. "Okay, okay. So this ghoul, Stefan—"

Downstairs, the front door opened. "Yoo-hoo!" a bright, cheery woman's voice called, accompanied by the sounds of a family returning from a day at the beach. "Hello! Are we just about finished here?"

"On my way out, Mrs. Kleinholtz!" Jen called back downstairs to her. "Sorry—just running a little late!"

I helped Jen scramble to pack her cleaning supplies into a plastic carryall, then followed her downstairs, where the highly manicured and impeccably tanned Mrs. Kleinholtz blinked in perplexity at my choice of attire—I was still wearing the linen sheath dress I'd put on this morning—but insisted on tipping me alongside Jen nonetheless, pressing a ten-dollar bill into my hand.

Outside, Jen cocked her head at me, her expression soft and open for the first time since we'd fought. "Look, I've got to go home and shower. Do you want to meet at the Shoals in an hour and get a drink? Talk?"

I did. I *so* did.

But *dauda-dagr* was fraying a hole in my straw satchel, and I had promised Cody he could give me a lesson in handling edged and pointy weapons this evening. More important, I needed to tell him what Stefan had discovered, and what I'd learned—or hadn't learned—from Mr. Leary.

"I can't," I said reluctantly. "I wish I could, but I can't."

Jen sighed. "Oh, for fuck's sake!"

At that moment, my phone rang. Glancing at it, I saw it was Cody. "I'm sorry. I have to take it."

I thought Jen might bail on me, but she waited while I confirmed with Cody that I'd meet him at his place in half an hour.

"Okay," I said after I ended the call. "I really, really am sorry. I should have put our friendship before the eldritch code, and I didn't. But as much as I'd like to, I can't put it before this investigation. There's a lot at stake. And if we don't get to the bottom of it fast, it's going to get ugly."

"I know." Her face was somber. "Everyone's talking about it. Are you in trouble, Daise?"

"Honestly?" I asked. "Yeah, I think maybe so. But I'm not sure what kind."

"Anything I can do?" Jen asked steadily.

"Yeah." I smiled at her. "You can accept my apology. That way at least I won't be checking my phone every ten minutes."

"Okay, okay!" She blew out her breath, setting wisps of hair dancing around her face. "Look, I'm not quite ready to hug it out yet, but if you want to talk later, call me. I have to admit, I'm curious. I mean, seriously? A *ghoul*?"

Gah! I really wished I had more time. "I'll call you," I said. "Thanks, Jen."

"You're welcome." She got into her car, an old Chrysler LeBaron convertible with God knew how many miles on it. "Daise?"

"Yeah?"

"Be careful," she said in a serious voice, turning over the ignition. "Okay?"

"I will."

Jen's hand hovered over the gearshift. "And listen, I won't say anything to anyone about Cody. But if you really like him, I think you should go for it. All these rules and codes . . ." She shrugged. "They're kind of stupid, and they get in the way. Sometimes you've just got to follow your heart, you know?"

"Maybe," I said ruefully. "This isn't the time for it. Like I said, there's a lot going on. But so far, there's no evidence he feels the same way."

She put the LeBaron in gear. "Well, think about it."

Twenty-one

I drove home and changed into jeans and a scoop-necked T-shirt, then drove out to Cody's place.

Collectively, the Fairfax clan owned a big tract of property out in the countryside that bordered the county game preserve. Exactly how they divvied it up, I wasn't sure, but Cody had his own place with a couple acres of woodland within shouting distance of his brother Caleb's place. His mother and father's house was a little way down the road, and beyond that, I thought there were an aunt and uncle, as well as a few cousins and their families.

"Hey, there, Pixy Stix!" Cody greeted me from the front porch as I pulled into his driveway. "C'mon up."

Oh, crap.

He looked different in his own element, more at ease in his skin. He wore faded old blue jeans that fit him in all the right ways and an equally faded plaid flannel shirt, washed until it was paper-thin and soft, worn open over a white wifebeater tank top with Timberland boots on his feet.

In other words, a poster boy for a woodsy "Men of Pemkowet" calendar.

"Beer?" he asked as I approached the porch, dangling the neck of a bottle from one hand.

"Yeah, thanks." I accepted it with gratitude, trying to ignore the way his damp, freshly washed bronze hair curled around his ears. I tipped the bottle and took a long drink, slaking a thirst that had plagued me since I'd visited Mr. Leary. "Any luck this afternoon?"

"No. You?"

"Yep." I handed him the folded paper Stefan Ludovic had given me. "Jerry the bartender confessed to giving the kids Ray D's number. No answer at the number, but that's it. And that's the bartender's home address."

Cody scanned it, his topaz eyes intent. "Did he say why?"

I nodded. "Drugs. He claims he was just looking to pass the buck and get rid of them."

He looked up at me. "You believe it?"

"No." I shook my head. "Neither does Stefan. That's why he fired Jerry and gave us his address. He thought we might want to have a talk with him."

"Oh, Stefan, is it?" Cody's voice was light, but there was an edge to it.

I took another swig of beer, eyeing him. "Uh-huh. We're on a first-name basis now. He came to report in person. Caused a bit of a commotion downtown."

He ignored my comment. "What about Al?"

"Al's in custody."

Cody exhaled. "Good. I'm glad to hear it." He tapped the paper. "Did you give this number to Detective Wilkes to trace?"

"I left him a message," I said. "And I also paid a visit to Mr. Leary to run down any possible mythological spider leads. There's nothing that fits the bill. He told me to consider Hylas and look for naiads. That we've already done. So I think we're looking at Jerry Dunham and his spider tattoo, Cody."

He frowned at the paper. "But for what?"

"I don't know," I admitted. "I double-checked the autopsy results and confirmed toxicology was negative for drugs."

"Could have been a deal gone south," he mused.

"Could have been," I agreed.

"Oh, fuck it." Cody refolded the piece of paper and shoved it into the back pocket of his jeans. He grinned at me, baring his teeth. They were very white and very strong, and maybe a little more pointed than usual. The slanting sunlight of early evening caught his eyes, making them blaze to amber, gold-flecked life with a hint of green behind them. "I'm tired of this case. I'm tired of *talking*. Let's have some fun for a change, Daisy Jo. Did you bring the dagger?"

"Uh-huh." I patted my fraying satchel.

Cody beckoned. "Let's take a look at it in my workshop."

I followed him through his house, which was exactly what I would have predicted: small, rustic, tidy, wood flooring, and lots of plaid fabric. His workshop was in an outbuilding behind it.

As long as I was predicting, I would have guessed Cody dabbled in carpentry. I would have been wrong. "You work with leather?"

"My family collects a lot of hides," he said dryly.

I picked up a half-finished bag from the workbench. "You make *purses*?"

He scowled and took it from me, setting it aside. "It's a messenger bag, and yes. I sell them online, okay? Now, let's see that dagger."

Easing *dauda-dagr* from my satchel, I laid it on the workbench. The runes running the length of it seemed to flicker in the sunlight, while the keen edges were faintly blue. The leather-wrapped hilt was shiny with wear, but the rest of it looked like it might have been forged yesterday.

"God, it's gorgeous," Cody murmured. "What does it say?"

"I don't know for sure," I said. "I assume it spells out its name, but I haven't learned to read runes yet."

"Death day, right?" he asked. I nodded. "It's a perfectly balanced blade by the look of it." He glanced at me. "Can I touch it?"

I shrugged. "Your guess is as good as mine."

Reaching out with one reverent hand, Cody closed it around the hilt, and let go quickly. "Jesus! It's *freezing*!"

"It is?" I hefted it experimentally. "It's cold, but I wouldn't call it freezing."

He shook out his hand, then showed it to me. There was a reddened imprint of *dauda-dagr*'s hilt on his palm and fingers. "At a guess, I'd say it's not meant for anyone but you to wield."

I winced. "Good to know. Sorry!"

"Not your fault." Cody studied the dagger. "It didn't come with a sheath?"

"Nope."

"Let's see if we can't improvise something." He spread a piece of muslin on the worktable. "I'll make you something more permanent later."

At his instruction, I laid *dauda-dagr* on the muslin and traced a pattern. It actually wasn't that dissimilar from helping my mom with her seamstress work. Once we had a workable pattern, Cody transferred it to a piece of soft deerskin and set about cutting and stitching with practiced expertise.

"This won't last long," he said, poking one big-ass curved needle through the leather. "The hide's too soft. But it will do for now, and I'll use the pattern to make something better with a heavyweight hide."

I watched his strong, capable hands at work. "Are you going to make me a belt to go with it?"

"Sure, if you like." Cody grinned at me. "I could even make you a bag with a built-in sheath for everyday wear."

"Really?"

"I do custom work on commission." He handed me the deerskin sheath. "See how that fits."

I slid *dauda-dagr* into it. "Perfect."

"Excellent." He beckoned again. "Now let's go out back and play."

In the grassy clearing between the house and the woods, Cody proceeded to instruct me in the finer points of knife fighting, of which there were surprisingly few.

"First and foremost, if you think you're going to need to use it, draw it before you *know* you do," he said. "Because if you get attacked, you won't have time to draw it."

"Did they teach you that at the police academy?" I asked him.

"No." He adjusted my stance. "Knife-hand foot forward, rear foot at a forty-five-degree angle. Left hand up to shield your chest. With your right hand, hold the dagger like you'd hold a hammer."

I obeyed. "Where, then?"

"When Caleb and I were kids, there was a guy in the neighborhood who was an ex-marine." Cody circled me in a predatory manner, setting my tail to twitching in an involuntary reflex. "We used to bug him to teach us stuff."

I peered over my shoulder at him. "I would have thought you and your brother had your own . . . defenses."

"Not as kids," Cody said. "That came later." Coming around in front of me, he showed his teeth in another cheerful grin. "The second-most-important thing? Get them before they get you."

If he hadn't warned me, I wouldn't have known it was coming, but he did, which was why when Cody charged me, I was able to turn to one side, hook his leg, and execute a perfect takedown, following him to the grassy ground and placing the sheathed edge of *dauda-dagr* against his throat.

"Duly noted," I said sweetly. "So what's the third-most-important thing?"

Cody's taut, hard-muscled chest heaved beneath mine as he drew an indignant breath, which I must admit felt pretty good. His face conveyed a mixture of dismay and amusement. "You said you didn't know anything about fighting!"

"No," I corrected him. "I said I didn't know the first thing about handling edged weapons, which is true." I withdrew the sheathed dagger and sat upright, straddling Cody's lean hips. And yes, that felt pretty damn good, too. I smiled at him. "When *I* was a kid, I was a star pupil in Mr. Rodriguez's Li'l Dragonz tae kwon do class four years in a row. Mom thought it would be a good way for me to get out my aggression."

Cody laughed. It was a good laugh, full-throated and deep, his topaz eyes sparkling. "Was it?"

Reluctantly, I climbed off him. "Yeah, actually. It was."

"Okay, my bad." He bounded to his feet and shook himself all over. "Shall we try it again?"

We did.

It was fun, it was sexy, and it was educational. By the time we finished, I was a lot more comfortable handling *dauda-dagr*. I was also tired enough to collapse on the ground. I hadn't exactly kept up with my Li'l Dragonz training in the past decade or so.

"You're not half-bad, Daisy." Lying on his back, Cody folded his arms behind his head. "How did you become Hel's liaison, anyway?"

"She asked me," I said simply.

"Really?"

I nodded. "Really. I'd already started helping out the chief with a few cases. It came to her attention, and she summoned me. She gave me the choice. I took it." Surreptitiously, I scratched my rune-marked left palm. "I said yes."

Cody turned his head toward me. "Why?"

The sun was hovering low above the tree line, gilding the bronze stubble on his cheeks and throat. His gold-flecked eyes, so close to mine, were wide and questioning. The clean fragrance of pine hung in the air.

"Because I wanted to believe there's some purpose to my existence," I said softly. "Because I want to side with order and good. You know?"

He nodded. "I know."

It was a moment.

And maybe it could have been more, except it was the exact moment that Cody's brother Caleb arrived with his family in tow.

"I forgot to tell you," Cody said in an apologetic tone. "I thought it might be nice. Take a little downtime with family, grill a few steaks. You don't mind, do you?"

On the one hand, I did; on the other hand, if my initially reluctant partner in crime fighting wanted to introduce me to his family, I wasn't going to object. Rising and retrieving my satchel, I stowed *dauda-dagr* away. "No, of course not."

Caleb Fairfax was several years older than Cody and a bit broader, with thick rusty auburn hair, and, as I remembered, he was indeed rocking the muttonchops. On him, they looked good. Or okay, anyway. If Cody was laconic, his brother was downright taciturn. Not in an off-putting way, just in the manner of a man inclined by nature to silence.

His wife, Jeanne, was slight and delicate, with straight, sleek light brown hair that framed her face in an old-fashioned look. The faint tingle of otherness in her aura identified her as eldritch, but if I hadn't known, I'd never have pegged her for a werewolf. Dryad, maybe, but definitely not a wolf.

"It is a pleasure to meet you, Daisy," she said in a grave little voice with a trace of an accent when we were introduced.

"You, too," I said, shaking her hand. "You're not originally from Pemkowet, are you?"

"No." She flushed slightly, glancing at Cody, and then away. "Montréal."

"Oh."

"We met at a gathering of the clans," Caleb said quietly.

Just like Cody had met the only woman he'd dated in earnest, Caroline Lambert, shot by a hunter. I felt . . . awkward.

"It's okay," Cody said. "Hey!" He tousled the hair of a pair of boys who looked to be about five and six. "Meet my favorite nephews. This is Stephen and this big guy's Elliot. Boys, this is my friend Daisy."

Both boys stared at me with an intense focus that was unnerving in such little ones, their nostrils flaring and twitching in unison.

"Hi, guys," I said to them.

Elliot, the older of the two, tugged at his mom's sleeve. When Jeanne leaned down, he whispered in her ear. "That is not a question we ask in polite company, *mon chou*," she said in her Québécois accent.

At an educated guess, I figured he'd asked her what I was. "It's all right. I don't mind."

Jeanne gave me an apologetic look. "Forgive me, but your particular nature . . . I am not sure I'm ready to discuss it with them yet."

Oh, great. A Canadian werewolf on the down-low was playing the morality card with me. My temper stirred.

She placed a slender hand on my arm. "I mean no offense. You understand that explaining such matters to children is complicated?"

I shrugged. "My mom never had a problem with it. But then, she wasn't ashamed of me."

Phosphorescent green flashed behind Jeanne's mild hazel eyes. Yep, now I could see the wolf.

"Okay, no one said anything about shame," Cody interjected. "C'mon; let's go up to the deck. Let the boys play while we fire up the grill." He gave me a warning look. "Sound good to you, Daisy?"

"Yeah." Tip the mental glass, pour away the irritation. "Sounds great."

Elliot tugged at his mom's sleeve again and whispered another question in her ear. This time, Jeanne's expression eased. "Yes, of course. It's perfectly safe." She made a shooing gesture. "Go, go play."

The adults retired to the deck, where Cody fetched a round of beers before firing up the grill. I sat with his brother and sister-in-law, who watched indulgently as their young sons played in the glade.

I understood why Elliot had asked whether it was *safe*. The boys didn't play like human children, not exactly. They chased each other, tussling and scuffling and rolling on the grass, accompanied by yips and yelps and playful growls.

"They're cute kids," I said to Jeanne. "Very . . . energetic."

"Yes." She smiled ruefully. "They're too young to shift, of course. In some ways, it will be easier when they are older. When they are able to give true voice to the wildness inside them. But of course, that brings its own dangers." She glanced in the direction of the grill. "The clan is lucky to have Cody in a position to protect us."

"No doubt." I racked my brains for a topic of discussion. "So, how do you like living in Pemkowet? It must seem awfully small after Montreal."

"I like it," Jeanne said. "I find it peaceful here. I like the seclusion."

Beside her, Caleb nodded. "City's too big. Too busy." He shuddered. "Too many eyes watching."

Oh-kay.

"Are the boys in school yet?" I asked.

"Oh, no!" Jeanne gave me a startled look, green glimmering behind her eyes. "No, I do not think that is advisable. We will homeschool them."

"Pemkowet's school system isn't so bad," I said. "Look at Caleb and Cody. They turned out okay."

"Boys'll be safer at home," Caleb said briefly.

Okay, point taken; that was the end of that discussion. Even though it was none of my business, I was just trying to make polite conversation. I tried and failed to suppress a returning surge of irritation. "Did Cody tell you we ran into an old girlfriend of yours, Caleb?" I asked. "Rosalind says hi."

"Rosalind?" He looked blank.

"Rosalind Meeks," Cody supplied. He was in the process of placing six obscenely large T-bone steaks on the grill. "I think you dated her toward the end of your senior year. She's tending bar at Bazooka Joe's."

"Oh." Caleb shrugged. He and his wife held an unspoken exchange that consisted of a faint glance of inquiry on her part and a slight, dismissive headshake on his.

I sighed inwardly.

No matter what Jen said, the rules and codes of the eldritch community were rigid and ingrained, and it was evident that the Fairfax clan was a closed society, even to other members of the community.

A little later, we dined on the ridiculously oversize steaks, cooked rare and bloody, the Fairfaxes holding them with both hands to gnaw on them. Steaks, and nothing but steaks.

"Would it have killed you to serve a little potato salad?" I asked Cody. "Or maybe a green vegetable?"

He grinned. "Sorry. I wasn't thinking."

I felt guilty. "It's okay. I'm being an ungracious guest."

"I don't usually have guests," he admitted. "I guess the lack of practice makes me a thoughtless host."

It made me feel better. "So we're even?"

Cody nodded. "Definitely."

His brother and sister-in-law glanced back and forth between us, silent and watchful. Disapproval might be too strong a word, but I got a distinct feeling of discomfort and uneasiness from them. Whether it was because I was a hell-spawn or merely an outsider, I couldn't say, but I have to admit it was a relief when they said their good-byes as the sun was sinking low, taking their rambunctious wolf-cub boys with them.

I helped Cody carry the dishes, which basically consisted of six plates swimming in bloodred juice, into the kitchen. "Can I help you wash up?"

He shook his head. "No need. Go home; get some sleep. After yesterday and today, you must be tired."

Actually, I was. It was hard to believe it was only last night that Hel had summoned me. "Okay." I hesitated. "Thanks, Cody. This was really nice."

His mouth quirked. "No, it wasn't."

"It was a nice *idea*."

"Look." Cody laid his hands on my shoulders. "Don't take it personally, Daisy. My family is very . . . insular."

I raised my eyebrows. "You don't say?"

"I'm glad you came." He let go of me. "This investigation's been tough on all of us. I know I had reservations at the outset, but I wanted you to know that I'm glad we're working together."

It wasn't exactly what I wanted, but I'd take it. "Me, too."

Cody showed me to the door. "Tim Wilkes has called another conference for tomorrow morning. See you there?"

I made myself smile. "Bright and early."

I drove home to my empty apartment. My neighbors across the hall were engaging in another bout of noisy lovemaking. Mogwai was nowhere to be found. On the plus side, at least I didn't have to worry about any ravening ghouls lurking around the Dumpster or in my stairway. I had to say, Stefan had come through on that score.

I thought about Stefan and his oh-so-tempting offer.

Cody, too.

And I thought about calling Jen to talk about both of them, or my mom, just to hear her voice, but I *was* tired.

Instead, I poured myself a couple inches of scotch and put on some music. Sometimes you have to go old-school and let a genuine queen of the blues give voice to your melancholy. I put on a scratchy old recording of Bessie Smith singing "Salt Water Blues," her world-weary voice accompanied by the spare, droning wail of a muted trumpet, and opened my case file to study Thad Vanderhei's photo.

Thad's bland, ordinary face gazed back at me. His hair still bore the impression of a ubiquitous baseball cap. Tomorrow I would attend his funeral. And I still didn't have the first idea why he was dead.

"That doggone salty water," I mused, echoing Bessie. "Why salt water? What the *hell* were you up to?"

Not drugs.

Something else.

But I didn't know what.

Twenty-two

When I reported to the station in the morning, there were protestors outside it. Not many, only three or four, but it gave me shivers to see the signs and hear their chants.

"No more lies, no more evasion!" the protestors called in unison, marching in a circle and hoisting homemade placards. "No more sanctuary for Satanism!"

I slipped past them.

The mood in the station was grim. In the conference room, the chief slammed both hands down on the table. "Tell me we know something," he said. "Tell me we're making progress."

Detective Wilkes cleared his throat. "Let me give you a rundown. Thad Vanderhei, Mike Huizenga, and Kyle Middleton are clean, no priors, no red flags. Ditto for Matthew Mollenkamp, the Triton House alum the brother cited. We've got no references on the Masters of the Universe. As far as anyone knows, it's nothing but an old cartoon. We also ran the number Miss Johanssen gave us for Ray D, but it's a dead end. Prepaid disposable cell phone, no longer in service."

"Sounds like it's time to bring the vic's friends back in for another chat," Chief Bryant observed. "We've got enough leverage to make them sweat."

"It's not going to be easy." The detective looked disgruntled. "The Middleton boy's parents picked him up and took him home to Indiana. The Huizenga boy's been sent off on a church retreat." He slid a piece of paper from a file. "And the Vanderheis have lawyered up on behalf of both of them. They've already given sworn statements. Looks like anything further's going to take a subpoena. And given the fact that our key eyewitnesses are, um, undines, that could be a problem."

"What the hell is wrong with these people?" the chief said in frustration.

"I don't think they *want* to know the truth," I said quietly. "Parental instincts are telling them they're not going to like it. And I have a feeling they're right."

Chief Bryant heaved a sigh. "Despite the collegiate culture of prolonged adolescence, in the eyes of the law, those so-called boys are grown men. One way or another, they will be held accountable. What else have you got, Tim?"

The detective ran a finger over his tidy mustache. "A possible lead on another known associate of the elusive Ray D. According to one Bruce 'Red' Henderson, a member of the Outcasts currently enjoying a stay in the county correctional facility, Ray D had recently acquired an unusual lady friend, a fellow ghoul by the name of Mary Sudbury. Where you find one, you'll find the other. Red was quite adamant on that score."

"Ring any bells?" I asked Cody.

"No," he said. "My contacts weren't as forthcoming. But it's definitely worth checking out. Your undines did say there was a man and a woman in that boat. What about the bartender? Jerry Dunham?"

"Now, there's an interesting character." Tim Wilkes laid a file on the table. "A bit of a drifter, it seems, and he's fairly new in town. A handful of priors, six months served on an assault charge four years ago in Seattle. Here's the interesting part: Until it closed, he was a carny with Dr. Midnight's Traveling Sideshow."

Cody frowned. "Now, that *does* ring a bell."

"They applied for a permit to hold a performance here a couple of years ago," the chief said. "The town council turned them down. It wasn't exactly, ah, family-friendly entertainment."

I was intrigued.

Detective Wilkes nodded. "It was billed as an old-fashioned sideshow with live freaks and geeks. They traveled on a national circuit, but they were based in Seattle. Late last fall, the Seattle authorities shut them down on charges of abusing and exploiting the performers."

"Whereupon this Dunham decided to move to Pemkowet and begin consorting with ghouls?" Chief Bryant said sourly. "It doesn't add up."

"Seattle has an underworld," I said. "Where else did Dr. Midnight's Traveling Sideshow perform?"

Wilkes checked his notes. "Larger venues, mostly. Chicago, New York, Denver . . . a few oddities, too. Fresno, Leavenworth. Nothing as small as Pemkowet."

Cody and I exchanged a glance. "They're all sites in the U.S. with functioning underworlds," he said.

My skin prickled. "So there's an eldritch connection. I bet there was something in that sideshow that wasn't human. Oh, hell! I'm sure there was. It's right there in the name."

Everyone looked blank.

"Dr. Midnight's Traveling Sideshow?" I said impatiently. "It's a reference to *The Last Unicorn.*"

"Let me guess," Cody said. "A movie?"

I successfully fought the urge to glare at him. "As a matter of fact, yes, but it was a book first. My mom read it to me when I was a kid. The Midnight Carnival was a traveling sideshow full of illusion, but it had one true thing in it."

"What was it?" he asked.

"A harpy," I said.

He raised his brows. "Now we're looking for a harpy?"

"No. I don't know. We're looking for *something*." Glancing around the conference room, I could see I was losing the crowd. "I'm just speculating, okay?"

The chief propped his chin on one meaty fist. "All right. Where are we on the aquarium angle, Tim?"

"Still tracking down leads," the detective said. "We've got a possibility or two, but we're waiting on the ichthyologist's report on the scales found under the Vanderhei boy's fingernails. That will help us narrow it down."

"Okay." Chief Bryant dislodged his fist from beneath his chin and looked at his watch. "Let's run with what we have. Cody, Daisy, I want you to shake down this Dunham character, see what comes loose. Just be back in time for the funeral."

Cody nodded. "Both of us?"

"No, just Daisy." The chief leaned back in his chair. "Cody, Bart's out with the flu, and I'm going to need you back on patrol tonight. But see if you can't chase down a lead on Mary Sudbury. Have the two of you looked into this Masters of the Universe business yet?"

"No," Cody admitted. "Sorry, Chief. We still haven't had time."

Chief Bryant leaned forward, his chair creaking beneath the shift in bulk. "Let's make it a priority. Might be something more substantial if we need to subpoena the witnesses for further questioning. In fact . . ." His deceptively sleepy gaze slewed my way. "Daisy, maybe it's best we don't go to the funeral together. Let's keep your options open."

"So you don't want me to go?" I asked hopefully.

He dashed my hopes. "Oh, I want you to go. Just not with me. If we need to go nosing around Triton House later, it might come in handy to have a pretty girl who can pass for a college student."

"The family's already seen me," I reminded him. "Huizenga and Middleton, too."

"Since the vic's friends are under wraps, I'm assuming they won't attend. The Vanderhei family will have bigger things on their minds. That leaves plenty of others who couldn't ID you, including this Matthew Mollenkamp. It's worth a shot." He levered himself to his feet. "Cuypers and Sons, two o'clock. Don't be late."

I sighed. "I won't."

Dismissed from the conference, Cody and I exited past the protestors and drove to the address for Jerry Dunham that Stefan had provided us.

It was a run-down little rental property a few miles north of town. Not only was Jerry Dunham in residence, he was in the driveway doing something mechanical to one of the most beautiful motorcycles I'd ever seen. It was a vibrant, glossy red, the color deep and saturated, with a teardrop-shaped gas tank, sweeping oversize fenders, and a black leather seat with rivets around it. I actually felt a pang of regret when Jerry scowled at the sight of us and dragged a cover over it.

"Jerry Dunham." Cody peered past him into the garage, where the covered forms of two more bikes lurked, along with a third that was uncovered, a gleaming black number. "Mind if we ask you a few questions?"

Jerry picked up a remote and closed the garage door. "Yeah, Ossifer. I do."

"Got a reason to?" Cody asked.

"No." He wiped his hands with a greasy rag. "Don't need one."

"Stefan Ludovic said you gave the Vanderhei boy Ray D's phone number."

"So?"

"When I showed you the boy's photo, you said you hadn't seen him," Cody said mildly. "Why'd you lie?"

Jerry shrugged and tossed the rag onto the driveway. "I must've forgot. All them college boys look alike."

"You get a lot of college boys in the Wheelhouse?"

"Some."

Wow, this was a scintillating exchange. Since it didn't seem to be going anywhere, I decided to try blindsiding Jerry. "Hey, I'm curious. What was the star attraction in Dr. Midnight's Traveling Sideshow?"

There was the slightest of pauses before he turned his flat, dead gaze on me. "A headless chicken." Somehow, the casual lack of menace in his tone made it all the more menacing. He made a slicing motion across his throat. "Little fucker got the ax, but it was still alive. Used to run around and flap its wings, trying to peck at shit without a head. We fed it through its gullet with an eyedropper. You should've seen it, blondie. You'd have loved it."

Okay, ew!

"So the circus closed down and you lost your chicken," Cody said. "What made you decide to move to Pemkowet?"

The bartender gave him a smile that didn't reach his eyes. "Let's say I had a taste for some wholesome small-town living."

"Including acting as a go-between for a known meth dealer?" Cody pressed him.

Jerry shrugged again. "Some boys were looking for a man; I gave them a man's phone number. None of my business what they did with it." His face tightened. "Got 'em off the premises, didn't it? So they wouldn't offend Mister High Lord Muckety-Muck's delicate sensitivities. A lot of thanks I got for it."

"See, here's the thing, Jerry." Cody rested his hands on his utility belt, his tone taking on a harder edge. "I'm pretty sure you're lying. And I'm pretty sure those boys weren't looking for drugs."

"See, here's the thing, Ossifer." Jerry mimicked his pose, hooking his thumbs in the belt loops of his jeans. "I'm pretty sure I don't give a flying fuck."

I glanced at the windows of his rented house, slatted blinds drawn. "Have you got any houseguests, Jerry?"

"Nope."

I cocked my head. "How about an aquarium? Do you keep fish?"

Another infinitesimal beat passed before Jerry unhooked one hand and scratched his opposite shoulder, the spiderweb shoulder. "No. Why would I? What the fuck would I want with *fish*?"

"I don't know," I said. "What did you want with a headless chicken?"

He gave me his flat stare. "It was a job. That stupid fucking headless chicken made money for us."

"What happened to it?" I asked.

Jerry smiled, and this time it was genuine. Creepy, but genuine. "It died. Everything does, blondie. Eventually."

Ew and double ew. My skin crawled.

"About Ray D—" Cody began.

"I don't know nothing more about Ray D, Ossifer." Jerry Dunham dusted his grease-stained hands together. "Look, I did my part. I gave Lord Muckety-Muck the only number I had, the same number I gave those boys. If it's no good . . ." He spread his hands. "Not my problem."

"So you knew—"

"Bye-bye, Ossifer." Jerry waved to us, turning for the front door. "Unless you have a warrant, I think we're done here."

In the patrol car, Cody let out a growl of pent-up frustration, his hands gripping the wheel tightly. "He's lying, Daisy. And he's involved in this somehow. I feel it in my gut. Did you see those bikes?"

"Yeah," I said. "That red one was beautiful. But I'm not sure where you're going with this."

"Unless I'm very much mistaken, that *red one* is a 1940s-era Indian Chief," he said grimly. "I went through a bike-worshiping phase when I was in high school. And I don't know if you caught a glimpse of the black one, but I'm pretty sure it's a Vincent Black Shadow. No telling what he had under the other two covers."

"Still not following," I admitted.

Cody shot me a glance. "Those are some very, very expensive and highly collectible bikes. No way he came by those on a bartender's or a carny's wages."

"You think he stole them?"

"It's possible." Cody's fingers drummed on the steering wheel. "It's certainly a popular activity among outlaw motorcycle clubs. But the odds of his finding a Vincent Black Shadow out on the street . . ." He shook his head. "There were only seventeen hundred of them made, every one assembled by hand."

"So he's a collector," I said slowly. "That's his passion. That's the one thing he cares about."

"Right." Cody nodded. "We can check out the registration. Assuming it's legit, where the hell did he get the money?"

"Which brings us back to drugs," I said. "Except neither of us thinks it was drugs the boys were after."

"Lot of coincidences going on here," Cody said. "Jerry Dunham and Lord Stefan Muckety-Muck turn up in town right around the same time Ray D disappears? I don't like it. Not a big believer in coincidence."

"There's no love lost between those two," I said. "Did you see Dunham's face when he talked about Stefan? It's the only time he showed emotion." I shuddered. "Except for the part about the headless chicken dying."

Cody looked skeptical. "He was just trying to get under your skin. You didn't believe that bit about the chicken, did you?"

"Yeah," I said. "Actually, I did. Not that it was the star attraction, no. That, I'd like to know."

"Why?"

I shrugged. "Call it a hunch. I'm interested in knowing what Dr. Midnight's one true thing was."

Cody drove across the bridge that divided Pemkowet and East Pemkowet. The river was sparkling in the sunlight, its surface ruffled with little waves. Sailboats scudded along before the breeze. Darting Jet Skis dodged the more graceful vessels, throwing up rooster tails of water behind them. Seagulls wheeled and squalled overhead. The massive form of the SS *Osikiyas*, once a passenger steamship that plied the Great Lakes, now a tourist attraction, maritime museum, and a venue for private functions, sat in its permanent berth, its keel resting on the riverbed, presiding benevolently over them all.

It was a very pretty picture, but today, it felt fragile. Vulnerable. I couldn't shake the memory of the protestors. Only three or four, but if we didn't solve this case, their numbers would grow.

"We need a break, Daisy," Cody said in a low, quiet voice. "Before this blows up even worse."

"I know."

Twenty-three

Thanks to Jerry Dunham's lack of cooperation, I had some time to kill before attending Thad Vanderhei's funeral.

After changing into a black linen pencil skirt with a cream-colored sleeveless top and a little black cardigan, I paid a visit to the Sisters of Selene occult shop to check in with the Fabulous Casimir, finding him unwontedly subdued.

No turban, no wig, no bling—not even false eyelashes. It was more than a little unnerving.

"Hey, Miss Daisy," he greeted me, attempting to summon his usual flair and falling short of the mark. He just sounded tired. "Tell me something good, girl."

I shook my head. "Sorry. You?"

The Fabulous Casimir shrugged. "I've got a whole lot of nothing, darlin'. At this point, I'm just glad I don't have protestors on my doorstep."

"Cas, have you ever heard of Dr. Midnight's Traveling Sideshow?" I asked him.

He pursed his lips. "Maybe."

I perused his shelves idly, reaching high to pick up a shrunken, tallowy claw that was labeled as a genuine Hand of Glory. Turning it this way and that, I examined it. "What was their one true thing?"

"Girl, don't go touching that nasty thing!" Casimir swooped down to take it away from me, stretching to put it on an even higher shelf. "You of all people ought to know better than to go messing with the black arts. It is *not* safe for you."

"Dr. Midnight?" I pressed him.

"I don't know," he admitted. "All I ever heard was rumors."

"Rumors of what?"

Casimir shrugged again. "Rumors that they had a genuine attraction. Like you said, something real." He rubbed his forefinger and thumb together. "Something worth the mundanes paying to see. But that circus never came to town, and what it may have been, I cannot say. That's all I know, Miss Daisy. I swear. You know I'd tell you otherwise."

"How about the Masters of the Universe?" I asked.

The Fabulous Casimir looked blank. "The *He-Man* cartoon? Oh, please. Only that Prince Adam was obviously a total closet case in every sense of the word." He gave a discreet cough. "Not that I'm old enough to remember it, of course."

I smiled. "No, of course not. Thanks, Cas. If you do hear anything about either, let me know, okay?"

"I'll ask around." He shook a finger at me as I left. "No matter how bleak it looks, you stay away from temptation, Daisy Johanssen! I mean it."

"I will," I called over my shoulder, bells tinkling as I exited the shop. "I promise."

Temptation.

What the hell did that mean, exactly? There were always the Seven Deadlies, which I struggled with on a daily basis, always trying to control my temper. But behind them lurked the greater presence of my birthright.

I could invoke my father, Belphegor.

I could claim my birthright.

My tail twitched at the mere thought of it, swishing back and forth beneath my linen pencil skirt. Until this case came along, I'd never really chafed at the lack of material powers that came with my half-breed status. Oh, sure, I'd entertained a few revenge fantasies in my teen years—what adolescent hell-spawn wouldn't?—but I always knew it would be wrong. And I always had my mom there to guide me. But what if I could claim my demonic birthright and put my powers to work in the service of *good*?

It was a heady thought, and I was pretty damn sure it was a dangerous one, too. I wished Casimir hadn't put it in my mind. As much as I loved Pemkowet, it wasn't worth risking a breach in the Inviolate Wall to save the town's reputation.

So I pushed the thought aside, got into my car, and drove to Cuypers and Sons to attend Thad Vanderhei's memorial service.

The funeral home on the southern edge of Appeldoorn was a gracious old family-owned establishment. I'd cut it closer than I intended, and the chapel was already quite full. I recognized the Vanderhei family in the front pew, and Chief Bryant's bulky, uniformed figure a few rows behind them, as well as a thickset couple who might have been the Huizenga boy's parents. It was hard to tell from behind. Otherwise, there was no one I recognized, except . . .

I narrowed my eyes at a tall man alone sitting in the rearmost pew. He was good-looking with high, rugged cheekbones, longish black hair caught back in some kind of silver clasp.

He looked familiar, and yet not. He wore an impeccably tailored black suit, a black shirt, and a black satin tie, and, oddly, a pendant on a silver chain over it, some kind of smoky quartz crystal. He was sitting quietly, calm and collected, his eyes half-closed.

And . . . there was a glamour over him.

With an effort, I made myself see through it. His skin took on an otherworldly pallor and his features came into sharper focus.

I slid into the pew beside Stefan Ludovic. "What the hell are you doing here?" I asked under my breath.

Stefan's eyelids remained lowered. "Much the same thing you're doing, I imagine," he murmured. "Do you mind being quiet? It's difficult to concentrate this close to the fringe."

"You're *tasting* them?" I whispered in horror. "What happened to not feeding on the unwilling?"

At that, his ice-blue eyes opened. "I am siphoning off a measure of raw grief," he said with soft precision. "It is an ancient compact, and a service for which a wise and experienced funeral director knows to be grateful. In this instance, I am also sifting through it for unexpected strains of guilt or denial."

I regarded him. "Since when can a ghoul spin a glamour?"

"Since never." Stefan touched the pendant that hung from his neck. "The charm is in the stone. It was a gift from a dear friend long ago. Now, if you wish me to share my findings with you, I suggest you heed my words and keep silent."

Since the service was beginning, I heeded.

It was long and painful. No matter what Thad Vanderhei may have done, he was a young man cut down in the prime of his youth, and those who had known and loved him were grieving deeply. I sat and listened while his family and members of the community offered tributes, painting a portrait of a daring, adventurous, high-spirited boy who had lived life a little too recklessly and paid the ultimate price for it.

As I listened, I scanned the crowd for any twinge or tingle of eldritch presence, but the only two beings present who weren't fully human were me and the ghoul beside me, who sat motionless with half-closed eyes and sifted through the mourners' grief, breathing slowly and deeply, his lips slightly parted.

When it was over, the family exited the chapel for the reception room, the crowd following slowly, the chief among them.

As the last mourner passed us, Stefan opened his eyes. "Do you wish to pay your respects to the family?"

"I'm not sure that's a good idea." Beyond the door came the sound of raised voices. Curiosity and prudence warred in me, curiosity scoring a swift victory. "Hang on; let's just see what's going on."

Stefan followed me past the threshold of the reception room, where we found an ugly confrontation between Chief Bryant and Jim Vanderhei in progress, the latter stabbing at the chief's broad chest with one indignant finger.

"You've got a hell of a lot of nerve showing up here!" the victim's father was saying, his patrician face flushed with fury.

The chief raised his hands. "Mr. Vanderhei, I assure you, I'm here out of the utmost respect to convey—"

"To convey what? More lies and evasion?"

"Our investigation—"

"I don't give a damn about your investigation!" Spittle flew from Jim Vanderhei's mouth. "Your town *killed my son*!"

There were a disturbing number of *amen*s and righteous murmurs of agreement.

A surge of anger rose in me, fierce and irrational, with no regard for the grief that fueled the ugliness. I fought to suppress it, but my nerves were strung too tight. Even the effort made my fury slip further out of my grasp, spiraling out of control. My hair lifted with static electricity, and the scent of ozone crept into the room as the air pressure tightened. I could see the chief glance around uneasily. A framed portrait of Thad Vanderhei rattled on its easel, and a montage of photos tacked to a display panel began fluttering around the edges.

Sue Vanderhei let out a piercing wail.

Oh, crap!

If I was outed as a hell-spawn with anger-management issues at Thad Vanderhei's funeral, Pemkowet's reputation might never recover from it. For sure it would be the end of Chief Bryant's career.

"Daisy." Stefan laid one hand on my shoulder, turning me toward him. His pupils dilated like dark moons. "I can help if you will allow me. Do you permit it?"

"Yes!" I gave him a frantic nod. "Hurry!"

It was nothing like it had been with Al. Stefan took another slow, deep breath, and I felt my violent emotions spill out of me, to be swallowed in the boundless depths of his ancient yearning, a transaction tempered with discipline honed by centuries of practice. It was incredibly intimate without being in the least invasive. I consented and he accepted, and yet, it went both ways, too. The pressure surrounding me eased softly, gently, the tightly wound coil of anger unspooling into the cool, still place that was Stefan Ludovic.

It felt . . . good.

I can't explain it. It was like my anger was a raging fever, and Stefan's essence was a cold, deep well that quenched it. Or maybe a nuclear reactor, and . . . whatever cools down nuclear reactors. I could sense an echo of his pleasure, of the sustenance he took from the exchange, vibrating between us. I had the feeling that if it went on long enough, I could get lost in the reflected sensations, like staring into one of those infinity mirrors. At the same time, I felt safe. Protected, at peace.

His pupils shrank to pinpoints, and he gave the faintest of shudders. I think it was good for him, too. "Better?"

I nodded again. "Much. Thank you."

Stefan's hand tightened on my shoulder. "I think it would be for the best if we left. Do you agree?"

The portrait on its easel was quiet, the photo montage still once more. But people were beginning to talk in hushed tones about witchcraft, supernatural doings, and Thad Vanderhei's restless ghost.

"Definitely."

Twenty-four

Outside Cuypers and Sons funeral home, Stefan offered to buy me a cup of coffee.

"You're serious?" I asked him. *"Coffee?"*

"Is that not the convention of the day?" He raised his eyebrows. "We should talk, Hel's liaison."

I ran my hands over my face. Now that the moment had passed, I felt acutely aware of the unique intimacy Stefan and I had just shared. "Okay. Yeah, sure. Meet me down at Callahan's Café."

Approximately twenty minutes later, he did, roaring into town on his Harley-Davidson.

At this hour of the afternoon, Callahan's was quiet. Stefan slid into the farthest corner booth opposite me.

Even with the glamour lending him human semblance, dimming his aura and his ridiculous good looks, he was eye-catching. Tina, the waitress on duty, hastened to bring him a brimming mug of coffee.

Stefan sipped it. "Dear God. This is dreadful."

"I know." I poured creamer into mine. "But the refills are free. Did you learn anything today?"

"No." He took another tentative sip. "No, I'm afraid not. Did you?"

"No." I wrapped both hands around my mug, determined to keep this on a professional level. "Not there. But we spoke to Jerry Dunham. He wasn't very cooperative, but he's got a whole lot of fancy motorcycles he shouldn't be able to afford. And it looks like the two of you turned up in Pemkowet around the same time, which is also the same time Ray D disappeared. Quite a coincidence, don't you think?"

Stefan blew on the surface of his coffee. "You don't trust me?"

"I don't *know* you," I said. "I don't know anything about you."

"Untrue," he said. "You trusted me today. Did I give you cause to regret it, Daisy?"

I shrugged. "Desperate times, desperate measures."

His ice-blue eyes gazed at me with disconcerting directness. "Very well, Hel's liaison. What do you desire to know?"

"Ever been to Seattle?" I asked him.

He shook his head. "I haven't had the pleasure."

"So you'd never met Jerry before?"

"No. He was already employed at the Wheelhouse when I arrived." He lifted one shoulder in a half shrug. "I had no previous cause to dismiss him."

"Did you have anything to do with Ray D's disappearance?" I asked.

"No." Stefan's tone took on an edge of asperity. "In fact, I'm quite perishingly weary of being questioned about someone I've never met."

"Your territory, your responsibility," I reminded him. "How about Mary Sudbury?"

He blinked. "Who?"

I stirred my coffee. "Remember the undines said there were two ghouls in the boat that dumped the body? One male and one female? Apparently, she's Ray D's lady love. Something none of your fellows have seen fit to divulge thus far."

Something subtle altered in his expression. "He's in love with another ghoul?"

"So it seems," I said. "Does it matter?"

"It changes things." Following my lead, Stefan stirred creamer into his coffee, frowning. "Two *ghouls*, as you call us, two of our kind cannot sustain each other. For both to attempt to feed on each other, it creates . . ." He gestured absently with his plastic stir stick. "I believe the term your modern science accords it is a closed feedback loop. Call it emotional cannibalism if you like. Ultimately, it is an unsustainable system."

Okay, now we were getting somewhere. "So what's the fix?" I asked him. "An outside source, right?"

"Yes."

"Like killing a mortal boy?"

Stefan shook his head. "I told you before, Daisy. There is no sustenance to be gained from the dead. A pair of ghouls in love would require a sustainable source of emotion."

"Like what? Some kind of hostage?"

"Possibly," he admitted. "Have there been reports of missing persons in recent months?"

"No." I blew out my breath. "Okay, how about Dr. Midnight's Traveling Sideshow. Ever heard of it?"

His face was blank and innocent. "No."

"You're sure?"

"Yes."

I studied him. "Okay, here's an easy one for you. I get the impression *ghoul* isn't exactly a polite term. So what should I call you?"

It startled a faint smile from him. "Over the ages, there have been many names for our kind. *Ghoul* is among the less flattering, but it is the term that has endured. In truth, there are far too many of those among us deserving of the name. You may as well continue to use it."

"What do *you* call yourself?" I pressed him.

Avoiding my gaze, Stefan pondered the depths of his coffee mug.

His black hair was no longer bound in a clasp, and it swung forward to obscure his features with a perfection an anime illustrator would have envied. "Outcast," he murmured. "I number myself among the Outcast."

I was pretty sure he wasn't talking about the biker gang. There were a lot of emotions behind the words, all of them intense, all of them held fast with steely discipline in that cool, still place inside him. I knew because I'd caught a glimpse of it, and my emotions were still resonating like a tuning fork. Which, frankly, unnerved me a little. I fought the urge to stroke a lock of hair back from his temple and focused on the issues at hand. "Stefan, who are you and where did you come from? Why are you here? I don't mean to overstep my boundaries, but I'm trying to figure out what the hell brought you to Pemkowet."

Stefan's head came up, but there was a guarded look in his eyes. Yep, definitely overstepped my boundaries. "My story is a long one," he said at length. "And I do not intend to tell you the whole of it yet. *My* trust must be earned, too, Daisy. For now, let it suffice to say that most recently, I lived a comfortable existence in a town in Poland."

"There's a functioning underworld in Poland?" I asked, trying to steer the conversation back to safer ground.

It worked. He gave me a look of mild reproof. "Is that any stranger than Michigan? Yes. In Wieliczka, Poland. Many of the major elder deities fled Europe during times of upheaval, but there are lesser ones who remained. Peklenc is one such."

"Never heard of him."

He smiled wryly. "As I said, he is a lesser deity, forgotten even by many Slavic folk."

I propped my chin on one hand. "So why did you leave?"

"To put it simply, I was bored," Stefan said simply. "I sought a greater challenge. I sought meaning."

"In *Pemkowet*?" I was skeptical.

"Your country is young and brash, unsophisticated. Nowhere more so than in its rural areas." He shrugged. "Such ghouls as are made here are born of extreme faith rooted in considerable ignorance. Believing themselves betrayed by their faith, they embrace the role of the Outcast to the fullest extent, leading lives of lawlessness and pointless mayhem. The motorcycle club's name is no coincidence. It may be that I can help change this and teach them that there are better ways to live. Perhaps I may even find a purpose to my existence in it. That is the challenge I embraced."

"Yeah, but why Pemkowet?" I asked. "I mean . . . seriously?"

Stefan smiled again, this time with dimples. "I thought it best to start small. Does that answer your question?"

It did if I believed him. I found it a bit hard to believe that he was the ghoul—or Outcast—equivalent of a crusading do-gooder.

On the other hand, he was taking steps to crack down on the ghoulish drug trade, so that was something. And he did appear to be doing his best to assist us. And there was that whole moment-of-emotional-intimacy thing.

On the *other* other hand, the entire reason the chief had wanted me at Thad Vanderhei's funeral was to spy out any eldritch presence there. As he'd said, attending a funeral was the sort of thing a ghoul would do, especially if he was the perp. And surprise, surprise, who did I find in attendance? I had only Stefan's word to explain his presence there, not to mention his assertion that he'd learned nothing. And for all I knew that sense of intimacy I'd experienced was just another predator's weapon, like a vampire's hypnosis.

"You speak pretty flawless English for a Polish ghoul," I said. "And you ride a mean Harley."

He looked amused. "There are motorcycles in Poland, Daisy, and I spent time paying my dues among the Outcasts' club before I earned my colors. And over the course of centuries, it is not uncommon to master many tongues." One eyebrow arched. "As, no doubt, your protective friend Miss Hollister could attest."

Out of the blue, that gave me an idea. "That glamour-casting pendant of yours. How does it work?"

Stefan looked surprised. "You must hold the image you wish to project in your mind to invoke it." He touched the crystal lightly. "It cannot fully conceal the truth, merely blur it. I cannot change my likeness entirely, but it allows me to pass as mortal beneath mundane scrutiny at need. Why?"

I eyed the smoky quartz. "Would it work outside of Hel's domain?"

"For a time," he said. "No longer than a day or so. Then its magic would begin to fade, as with anything. As below, so above. May I ask again, why?"

"I'd like to borrow it," I said.

Stefan's face turned unreadable. "You ask more than you know. I told you it was a gift from a dear friend. It is not the sort of thing to be loaned on a whim."

"I'm not asking on a whim." Okay, that was kind of a lie, but I thought it was a pretty good whim. "If you want me to trust you, trust me."

He hesitated, then nodded at my straw satchel on the booth beside me. "Then give me a token of your trust in trade. Tell me what item hidden in your bag sends a shiver of ice the length of my spine."

I hesitated, too, but Hel hadn't said anything about keeping it a secret. "A dagger."

"What manner of dagger?"

I looked squarely at Stefan. "One capable of killing the undead."

Even beneath the glamour, he paled. "I see. That explains why I sense its presence." He inclined his head. "Hel places considerable trust in her young liaison."

"Desperate times," I said for the second time. "Desperate measures. Do we have a deal?"

"We do."

Twenty-five

First of all, I called to check in with the chief. I reported on what I had and hadn't learned today, and then I told him I planned to do a little undercover sleuthing at Triton House that evening.

There was a long silence on the other end of the phone. "I didn't mean for you to fly solo on this, Daisy."

"I won't be."

"I can't spare Fairfax," he said. "We're too shorthanded and the town's restless. I can't take him off patrol tonight."

"I didn't mean Cody. It's, um, a member of the community." I cradled the phone against my ear, peeling the lid off a bowl of ramen. "Look, you said to make the Masters of the Universe a priority. And like you said, I can pass for a college student."

"Not without backup," he said.

I flashed on the image of Lurine in the river, her splendid coils thrashing the water as she summoned the naiads in a bronze-edged voice. "Oh, I'll have backup, sir. Trust me? I saw what happened at the funeral. We need to move on this."

Chief Bryant grunted and ended the call.

I took it as a yes.

While my ramen noodles cooked in the microwave, I called Lurine. "So, how bored are you?"

"On a scale of one to ten?" she asked. "Oh, maybe a seven. What's up, cupcake?"

I fished out my bowl of noodles and stirred them, then stuck them back in the microwave. "Want to help me play Nancy Drew at a frat house? I need backup, and I could really use the skills of a good actress."

"Love to," Lurine said promptly and regretfully. "But, honey—"

"I know," I said to her. "Outside of certain werewolves on the down-low, college students are probably your biggest audience." Picking up the chain of Stefan's pendant, I let it dangle from my hand as I regarded it, the cloudy facets glistening dully. "What if I could guarantee you wouldn't be recognized?"

There was a brief pause. "I'm listening."

I told her my plan.

"Okay, cupcake. It sounds like fun." Her voice was filled with light, playful menace. "Shall I send the car for you?"

I smiled. "Lurine, we can't take a car and driver. I'll drive. I'll pick you up in half an hour, okay?"

She sighed. "I hate Method acting."

Half an hour later, I pulled up to Lurine's gated drive. I'd exchanged my pumps for strappy sandals, my linen skirt for a denim mini, and shed my demure little cardigan. After announcing myself, I was buzzed through the gates.

As usual, Lurine looked fabulous. She had poured herself into a clingy black spandex dress that hit her at midthigh. When I arrived, she was checking her flawless makeup in an immense lighted mirror at her vanity table.

"Hey, baby girl," she greeted me. "Let's see this magic necklace."

I handed her Stefan's pendant. "He said you have to hold the image you want to project in your mind to invoke it."

Lurine glanced in the mirror and pursed her lips. "This *is* the image I want to project."

"I just need you to dial it down a few notches," I said. "Just for tonight."

"I know, I know." She examined the smoky quartz. "Interesting. I don't recognize the signature."

"It has a signature?"

"All magic has a signature. Okay, let's give this a try." Lurine lowered the chain around her neck, the pendant nestling in her cleavage.

The shift was subtle and instantaneous. As Stefan had indicated, it didn't change her likeness entirely, but Lurine looked . . . different. She looked like she could have been her own younger sister: not quite as gorgeous, not quite as glamorous. A little less intimidating, a little more approachable.

She made a face in the mirror. "Well, it works."

I smiled. "You look perfect."

"Come on." She grabbed her clutch purse. "Let's go meet some frat boys."

I drove north toward Appeldoorn. There was a brief frisson as we passed out of range of Hel's domain: a sense of loss, like a little of the brightness had gone out of the world. I stole a quick glance at Lurine to confirm that the pendant's charm was still working. It seemed to be holding just fine.

Lurine sniffed disdainfully and wriggled in the passenger seat. "Ah, back into the mundane world."

"It can't bother you that much," I said. "You spent years in it."

She shrugged. "I'm an immortal monster, cupcake. It would take more than a few years for me to run the risk of fading away without an underworld beneath me."

"You're not a monster," I said automatically.

"Actually, I am," she said in a pragmatic tone. "As surely as you're a demon's daughter. That's one of the reasons I'm so fond of your mother, Daisy. When I saw how determined she was to love her hot-tempered little hell-spawn . . ." Affection filled her voice. "Gods, you were a handful!"

"So I've heard."

"An adorable handful, if it helps." Lurine reached over to tousle my hair with the careless lack of respect for personal boundaries that was part of her charm. "Even in the middle of a temper tantrum, you were a cute little brat. But I'm serious, Daisy. Your mother reminded me that there are people in the world with enough heart and courage to love even a monster." She gave a lock of my hair a sharp tweak, her voice sounding a different note. "For that alone, I'd do anything in my power for either of you."

Batting her hand away, I stole another glance at her to see whether she was kidding me. She wasn't. "You *are* serious."

She smiled at my incredulous expression. "What can I say, baby girl? I'm proud of you. I know what you're trying to do. You're doing your best, and it isn't easy." She waved one hand in the general direction of Appeldoorn. "And the rest of the world isn't going to make it any easier."

I thought about the headlines, the protestors, the righteous *amens* at the funeral. "That's for sure."

It was around seven o'clock when we parked on the campus of Van Buren College, the warm summer air promising another long, balmy evening gliding ever so slowly into the soft lavender twilight. Actually, it was a lot like the night Thad Vanderhei had died. Right around this time, I'd been headed down to the gazebo to meet Jen and listen to Los Gatos del Sol, fighting an unexpected surge of jealousy at seeing Cody Fairfax flirt with my best friend, warning an irascible milkweed fairy against stealing a changeling child.

God, that seemed like a long time ago.

But counting backward in my mind, I realized it was less than a week ago. It felt like so much had happened, so much had changed.

And if we didn't catch a break soon, there would be a lot more change coming, none of it good.

On the sidewalk, Lurine waited patiently for me. "Ready?"

I nodded. "I'm ready."

She winked at me. "Showtime, cupcake."

Triton House wasn't actually located on the Van Raalte campus, which was charming and stately on a modest scale, with lots of red brick buildings designed to emulate the town's old Dutch architecture. The fraternity house, a gift of some wealthy fraternal alumnus, was a few blocks away, all the better to avoid being under the aegis of the college's public safety department. But since it was part of my cover story that I was considering transferring to Van Buren, I thought it best to park on campus and walk the few blocks.

The house itself sat on a tree-lined street. It was a big, rambling place that had probably once housed multiple generations of a family, now identified by the stylized Triton symbol proudly displayed beneath the eaves. There were a few guys on the front porch drinking beer from plastic cups, and through the screen door, I could see a handful more inside. The mood seemed pretty somber, which, under the circumstances, was to be expected.

"Sorry, ladies," one of the beer drinkers said as Lurine and I approached the porch. "Private party tonight."

"No offense," another added, sounding genuinely regretful. "We're holding a wake."

I shaded my eyes with one hand. "For Thad Vanderhei?"

The second beer drinker leaned over the porch railing. "You knew Thad?"

"Yeah." For all the effort I put into avoiding lying, doing it came surprisingly easily. "We were in youth group together before my family moved. Thad and I stayed in touch. I'm here visiting because I was thinking of transferring. We were supposed to meet up." I smiled sadly. "He said he really wanted to introduce me to you guys."

"Shit, I'm sorry." Looking stricken, he beckoned. "Come on up. I'm Dale."

I hesitated.

"We don't want to intrude," Lurine said apologetically. "And I'm sorry; I didn't know Thad." She laid one hand on my shoulder. "I'm just here to chaperone."

"No, no!" Dale insisted. "Come on; you've absolutely got to have a drink with us."

Within a minute's time, we were on the porch, plastic cups of tepid beer pressed into our hands.

I introduced myself as Lisa Trask and Lurine as my older sister, Sara. The Tritons asked a few cursory questions about my acquaintance with Thad, but they had other things on their minds.

"You know this is some seriously fucked-up shit you've walked into, right?" Dale asked me.

I shook my head. "I only found out yesterday. I called his home number when Thad wasn't answering my texts."

He stared into the distance. "Shit."

I took a sip of beer. "I just can't believe it."

"No shit." His mood darkened visibly. "Everything about this is pretty fucking hard to believe."

For a fleeting moment, I wished I'd asked Stefan to come with me instead of Lurine. It would have been useful to have someone who could read emotions. But then, I still wasn't sure I could trust him, or how well his gift would function outside of Hel's domain, without the presence of an underworld to sustain it. As the eldritch saying goes, as below, so above.

"I thought it was an accident," Lurine said in a voice so soft and tentative, I couldn't believe it was coming out of her mouth.

Dale glanced at her. "You don't think there's one hell of a cover-up going on down there?"

She gave him an apologetic look. "I'm sorry; I don't know anything about it."

That opened the floodgates. The three Tritons on the porch gave vent to a confused mishmash of conspiracy theories about Thad's death, fueled by grief, anger, and beer, compounded by reports of

Thad's restless ghost protesting the chief's presence at his memorial service.

Lurine and I listened wide-eyed, prompting them until I was reasonably sure none of these three knew anything.

I wanted to ask about Matthew Mollenkamp and the Masters of the Universe, but I didn't want to press my luck without an opening, and there were more Tritons inside the house.

"Mind if I use your restroom?" I asked when there was a brief lull in the outpouring of grief and fury.

"I could use a potty break, too," Lurine added.

"No, yeah, of course not." Dale put one hand on the small of my back. "Come on; I'll show you where it is."

Inside, he introduced us to the six or seven Tritons lounging on battered furniture and milling in and out of the kitchen.

Bingo.

I recognized Matthew Mollenkamp as one of the funeral attendees, and I'm pretty certain I would have ID'ed him even without the introduction. For one thing, he was older, in his mid-twenties and likely an alumnus, but mostly it was about the way the others deferred to him and the air of entitlement he exuded, even slouching in an armchair with a beer in one hand. Also, he was the only guy in the house with the balls to check out Lurine blatantly.

"Sisters, huh?" He gave us a weary half smirk. "Come back and talk to me, Trask sisters. I could use some consoling on this bleak motherfucking day."

"Amen, brother," one of the Tritons on an adjacent couch muttered.

Lurine and I ducked into the bathroom, which was . . . *gah*. Pretty much what you'd expect from a frat-house bathroom. I wondered what it was like during the regular school year at full occupancy. Using a square of toilet paper, I flushed the toilet gingerly, then waited a decent interval while Lurine peered at her face in the mirror, wrinkling her nose with displeasure.

"He's the one, right?" she asked me. "Mollenkamp?"

"Uh-huh." I flushed the toilet again.

"Okay, baby girl." She applied a fresh coat of lipstick. "Let's go see what he has to say."

At the outset, not much. Despite his request, Matthew Mollenkamp was content to slouch in his armchair, drinking steadily while the other Tritons shared fond memories of Thad, most of which involved booze-fueled exploits.

Outside, the sunlight began to fade, dusk rising.

"Enough beer," Matthew said abruptly, and the room fell silent. "Let's have a real toast. Denny, get the scotch."

A Triton in a backward-facing baseball cap hurried into the kitchen, returning with three bottles of Macallan and a stack of paper cups. Yeah, I know. Sacrilege.

After a ceremonious round of shots were poured and distributed, Matthew Mollenkamp rose to his feet. Everyone followed suit, including Lurine and me.

"To Thad," he said.

"To Thad," we chorused.

Everyone drank. With a couple of beers already in me, I would have faked it if I could, but Matthew was watching. He was a good-looking guy, tall and rangy, but there was a guarded look behind his hazel eyes that made me uncomfortable.

"Again," he said.

Twice more, Denny the Triton circulated to refill our paper cups with twelve-year-old single-malt scotch with which we toasted Thad Vanderhei before Matthew Mollenkamp sank back into his armchair.

"Jesus," he murmured. "Jesus fucking Christ."

I blinked, wishing I weren't starting to get more than a little drunk. Maybe I wasn't cut out for undercover work.

"Poor boy." Lurine perched on the overstuffed arm of Matthew's chair, stroking his hair with idle fingers. "I know it's awful."

He glanced up at her. "You don't know shit."

She gave him a faint smile. "Try me. I might surprise you."

His mouth curled, but it wasn't a smile. "Anyone ever tell you that you look like Lurine Hollister? Only not as hot."

"Oh, is that that pickup-artist thing where you pretend to compliment a girl, then insult her to undermine her confidence?" Leaning down, Lurine kissed his cheek. "Honey, it's okay. You don't have to pretend tonight. I know you're in a bad way." She plucked the paper cup from his hand. "But if you're going to keep drinking, let's get you a proper glass so you can drink like a big boy."

Matthew tilted his head back, narrowing his eyes. "So you think you can handle me, huh?"

She regarded him. "Yeah, I do."

One of the other Tritons, a doughy, thickset guy sitting on the couch beside me, laughed. "You don't know who you're messing with." He hoisted his cup. "All hail Lord Matt, the original Master of the Universe."

Someone said, "Hear, hear," and drank; someone else attempted to hush them. Most of them looked uncertain.

"That's what Thad said," I offered. "The last time he texted me. He said he was gonna be a Master of the Universe. I just thought it was, you know, a figure of speech. Is that, like, a thing with you guys?"

There was a little silence, broken by the doughy Triton next to me bursting into low, racking sobs.

Unsure what else to do, I rubbed his broad back.

"Jesus!" Matthew Mollenkamp pressed the heels of his hands against his closed eyelids. "Ron, Ronny, man, get it together. Get ahold of yourself. I know, okay, I know. But at least Thad went out trying; he went out a *man*."

"It's just—"

"I *know*." He lowered his hands, glaring. "I need a drink. I need a motherfucking drink."

Lurine slithered upright and beckoned to me. "Come on, baby sister. Let's go find some glasses."

I followed her into the kitchen, leaning on the counter to stabilize the spinning room while she ransacked the cupboards. "Ummm . . . I'm not so sure this is a good idea anymore."

Examining dingy glasses, she glanced at me. "You're a little drunk, huh?"

I peered at her. "You're not?"

"Sweetheart, do you have *any* idea what my actual body weight is?" Lurine asked, buffing a glass with a semiclean towel.

"No," I admitted. "Not a clue."

She laughed. "To be perfectly honest, neither do I." Lurine lowered the towel, her gaze serious. "This was your idea. If you want to leave, we'll leave, Daise. It's okay; I can drive. But if you want to stay . . ." She shrugged. "These boys are almost drunk enough to reach the confessional stage. You might not have another chance like this."

"True."

Lurine yanked a bag of pretzels out of the cupboard and poured some in a bowl. "Here. Eat."

I shoved a handful in my mouth. "Thanks," I said around a mouthful of dry pretzel crumbs. "You're the best ex-babysitter, sort-of godmother, and pretend sister ever. Seriously. I really, really appreciate your doing this."

"Oh, gods." She sighed. "And *you're* at the maudlin-drunk stage."

"Nuh-uh!" I shook my head. "I'm serious!"

"Okay, cupcake." Lurine patted my head. "Maybe it's best if you let me do most of the talking for now."

When we returned to the living room with clean glasses and a bowl of pretzels, the ranks had thinned. I was sorry to see that the doughy Triton who'd burst into tears was gone. If anyone was going to crack tonight, he'd seemed like the best bet. But Lurine zeroed in unerringly on Matthew, solicitously pouring a glass of scotch for him and resuming her perch on the arm of his chair.

His glassy-eyed gaze skated slowly up and down her spandex-wrapped figure. He might be playing it cool, but he wasn't immune to her charms. Even dialed down a few notches, Lurine was still Lurine.

"How come you're being so nice to me?" he murmured. "It's not like I've done anything to deserve it."

"You're hurting." She wound her fingers gently through his hair. "People lash out when they're hurt."

He exhaled a long sigh, closing his eyes.

"Plus, I've never met a Master of the Universe before." Lurine's tone was light and soothing, somehow maternal and seductive at the same time. "I thought that meant guys in the finance industry pulling down seven-figure salaries. Is that you?"

His eyes opened. Beneath the sheen of drunkenness, there was a cynical light in them. "Is that what you're looking for?"

"It wouldn't hurt." She bent over and placed a lingering kiss on his lips. "But I'm guessing your answer is no."

"I do all right."

"I'm sure you do."

"Masters of the motherfucking Universe." Matthew leaned his head back against the chair as though it were too heavy to hold upright, his eyes half-slitted. "The true sons of Triton. You know who Triton was, Trask sisters?"

"Some Greek god, right?" Lurine, who was in all likelihood related to the deity in question, hazarded a guileless guess.

"Like in that movie?" I added. *Clash of the Tritons?*"

He laughed soundlessly. "Old Triton blowing his wreathed horn, right? Blowing his horn over the waves, summoning all the sea nymphs, every one of them bowing down before him, every one of them hoping to be chosen, every one of them hoping to get fucked by a motherfucking god. That's what it's all about. *That's* what it means to be a Master of the Universe."

Lurine and I exchanged a glance.

"Is that how Thad died?" I asked softly. "Trying to become a Master of the Universe like you?"

"Yeah." Matthew's eyelids flickered, sinking closed, then opening again. "I mean, I don't know. Hell, I wasn't there. But I think so." He hoisted his glass, scotch slopping over the rim. "He died trying, anyway."

I felt sick.

Twenty-six

Half an hour later, Lurine and I made our exit from Triton House. We didn't get anything more out of Matthew Mollenkamp or the other Tritons. Having divulged that much, they retreated from the subject and settled for drinking themselves further into oblivion. But as far as I was concerned, it was a good start.

I concentrated on putting one foot in front of the other, steadied by Lurine's hand beneath my left elbow. "You think he was telling the truth?"

"No." She steered me over an uneven patch of pavement. "But I think he was telling the truth wrapped in a lie."

"Oops." Despite Lurine's guidance, I tripped over a jagged crack. "Yeah, me, too." I peered into the darkness. "Hey, is that my car?"

"It is." Lurine held out her hand. "Keys, please."

Rummaging in my straw satchel, I found my car keys beneath *dauda-dagr*'s deer-hide-wrapped length and handed them to her. "Thanks."

"Your mom would kill me if I let you drive in this condition." Lurine slid behind the wheel. Glancing in the rearview mirror, she eased Stefan's pendant over her head. The subtle glamour faded, restoring her features to their usual unsubtle beauty. "Ah, that's better." She handed me the pendant. "Put that somewhere safe for the head ghoul in town. Been seeing a lot of him, have you?"

I tucked the pendant in an inner pocket of my satchel. "Not a *lot*."

"Hmm." Lurine turned the key in the ignition and began easing the Honda out of the parking lot.

"What does 'hmm' mean?"

"Just be careful with him, Daisy." She gave me a serious look. "I told you, you're like catnip to these things. He may be older and have more control, but that just makes him more dangerous."

"Like you?" I asked as she turned onto the street. It was probably a boundary-crossing question, but what the hell. Drunk as I was, I had an excuse.

Lurine didn't answer right away. The passing streetlights illuminated her face intermittently, and she looked different in their glow. Not older, exactly; for as long as I'd known her, Lurine had looked about twenty-seven or -eight, and assuming I remained resigned to accepting my own mortality, it wouldn't be all that many years before I'd be able to pass for her older sister, which was sort of an unpleasant thought.

Anyway, it was a sense like age, as though I could see the shadows of antiquity stretching behind her.

"In some ways, yes," she said eventually. "We do what is necessary to ensure our survival. In others, no. I am no danger to *you*. That does not mean I'm not dangerous to mankind." She turned her gaze on me. "Do you really want to know more?"

The streetlights caught a hypnotic glitter in her pupils: not the avid hunger of a ghoul, but the steady predator's gaze of a snake fixing its prey.

"Umm . . ." I swallowed. "I'm going to go with no."

She turned her attention back to the road. "Daisy, you're Hel's liaison, and I will tell you anything you truly wish to know. But in the eldritch community, it's not wise to ask questions if you don't want to know the answers."

"Gotcha." The thought occurred to me that if Lurine had shed her borrowed glamour and turned that basilisk stare on Matthew Mollenkamp, he would have peed in his pants, begged for his mommy, and told us the whole unvarnished truth instead of bragging about being a true son of Triton. Of course, that probably would have resulted in half the town of Appeldoorn camping outside the infamous Lurine Hollister's estate with pitchforks, which was the point of the glamour in the first place. "So what do you think about Lord Matt's Masters of the Universe story?"

Lurine pursed her lips. "It all comes down to sex, doesn't it? That's the one thing that boy wasn't lying about."

"Uh-huh." I attempted to nod sagely, and found my head was still a bit wobbly on my neck. "But with who? Or *what*?"

"Nothing human." She pulled adeptly onto the highway. "But there's no way it was one of the local water elementals." She shook her head. "They wouldn't dare lie to me. And there's no way those boys could catch or lure one."

"No." I rubbed my temples, feeling the lurking onset of the hangover that awaited me. "But you're right. That's what they were looking for in Pemkowet. Not drugs. It all comes down to sex."

Lurine crossed the invisible threshold that marked the return to Hel's domain, and both of us relaxed a bit, feeling brightness restored to the world even in the dark of night. "It so often does, cupcake."

The cards from my mom's reading danced behind my eyes as I tried to put the pieces together. *La Calavera*, the victim's grinning skull. Had it been just earlier today that I'd attended Thad Vanderhei's funeral? Yes, it had. *La Botella . . . Urgh*. My stomach turned sour at the thought of it.

La Araña, the spider in its web sprawling over Jerry Dunham's shoulder, his flat, dead gaze meeting mine as he spoke of headless chickens, and that had been this morning, too . . .

Las Jaras, the arrows.

I didn't have a fix on that one at all.

After that . . .

Lulled by the soft, steady sound of the Honda's engine, I drifted into sleep, waking only when Lurine pulled into the driveway of her gated estate and put the car in park, shutting off the engine.

Lurine eyed me. "Under the circumstances, I think we'll put you up for the night in one of the guest rooms, okay?"

I yawned, too tired to protest. "Okay."

Ten minutes after we pulled into the drive, I was nestled in the depths of a bed with a feather-cushion mattress, ironed sheets with a ridiculously high thread count drawn up to my chin. Everything smelled fresh and clean and faintly of lavender. I wriggled with contentment and snuggled deeper into the mattress, my tail twitching in gentle approval. It made a nice swishing sound against the sheets.

Lurine deposited a glass of water on the bedside table. "There are toiletries in the guest bath. Got everything you need?"

"Uh-huh."

"Good." Stooping, she kissed my forehead, sort of like she used to do when babysitting me, only not quite. "I'll be out for a while."

With an effort, I propped myself up on my elbows. "Where?"

"Down to the beach." A dreamy look crossed her face. "Night's the only time I can swim freely."

"Oh." Now, that would be a sight to see: Lurine in all the splendor of her true form, diving and cavorting through the white-crested wavelets of Lake Michigan on a midsummer night, the iridescent scales of her muscular coils glinting in the moonlight, their joyous rainbow hues muted to a complex monochrome palette. I was a little sorry to miss it and a little relieved, too. "Have fun."

She smiled. "I will."

I slept.

It seemed as though no more than a few minutes had passed before my phone chimed an incessant alert, but when I squinted my way awake, there was a faint, gray daylight behind my eyelids.

I fumbled for my phone. " 'Lo?"

"Daise?"

It was Jen, and she sounded scared. I dragged myself upright against no fewer than five very soft down pillows. "Yeah, I'm here. What's up? Is it your sister?"

"No, it's Brandon."

"Your brother?" I was still half-asleep.

"Mom and Dad had a fight. He took off in the middle of the night. I only just realized it."

"Hang on." I downed at a single gulp half the glass of water Lurine had left for me. "Okay, so Brandon's missing. Did you report it?"

"Of course I did!" Now Jen sounded impatient. "Officer Mallick said boys will be boys. He told me to call back if Brandon wasn't home by lunchtime."

I pressed the cool glass of water to my temples. "Do you know where he went?"

Although I couldn't see it, I knew that on the other end of the phone, Jen gave a helpless shrug. "Where does he always go?"

I knew the answer to that question.

In times of trouble, of which there were many in the Cassopolis household, Jen's brother, Brandon, fled into the woods and marshes behind their house, where he could hunker down and hide. It was exactly the kind of stupid, dangerous place that appealed to an eleven-year-old kid, but he'd never stayed away for long.

Overnight was a record. Overnight meant he ran a serious risk of encountering something very unpleasant.

"Okay, okay! Don't panic." I scrambled out of bed. "I'm going to call Cody."

"He's not on duty," Jen said. "I asked."

I squirmed into my denim skirt. "I'm going to call him anyway. We need a tracker."

There was a little silence. "Do you think he'll do it?"

"I don't know." I switched the phone to my other ear so I could squeeze my right arm into my sleeveless top, then switched back to do the other, yanking it over my head. "But I'm sure as hell going to ask. I'll call you back."

Cody picked up on the second ring, sounding surprisingly alert for a guy who'd worked patrol on the night shift.

I explained the situation to him. "I thought maybe you could shift and track him for us. See . . ." I winced. "Jen knows."

There was a silence, and it wasn't little. If it weren't for the slow, steady sound of his breathing, I would have thought he hung up.

"I'm sorry!" I said. "It's just . . . Oh, crap, I'll explain later. But she won't tell anyone. And the thing is, it's dangerous out there. If Brandon hasn't come home yet, it probably means he's in trouble."

"What kind of trouble?" Cody asked curtly.

"The green, slimy, and pointy-toothed kind," I said. "There's a mucklebones in the marsh."

"A *what*?"

"A Jenny Greenteeth. Only Jen didn't like sharing a name with it, so we called it Meg Mucklebones, which, yes, is from a movie. . . . *Gah!* It's a marsh hag, Cody. They drown and eat children. Are you coming or not?"

"I'll be there." He hung up.

I was leaving a note in the kitchen when Lurine drifted out wearing a sheer, lacy nightgown and robe straight out of a Victoria's Secret fantasy, only probably ten times as expensive. "What's up, cupcake?" she asked in a sleepy, sultry voice. Honestly, I don't think she was even trying for sultry; it was just her default mode. "I heard you talking to someone."

"Sorry," I said. "I didn't mean to wake you. Hel's liaison is on call. Got a possible eldritch emergency."

Her gaze cleared and sharpened. "Do you need help?"

I shook my head. "Cody's on his way to meet me."

"Oh, good." Yawning, Lurine stretched languorously. "Then I'm going back to bed." She smiled at me. "I had a *goood* swim last night."

Okay, that time she was trying. I suppressed a faint shiver. "All right, I'll talk to you later. Thanks again."

"Anytime."

Twenty-seven

The sun was only just clearing the horizon when I left Lurine's place, the sky a pale eggshell-blue. It was a still, quiet morning. Below the bluff, Lake Michigan was calm and glassy, its waters unusually translucent.

It would have been lovely if I weren't hungover, my head throbbing and my stomach roiling. Undercover work was definitely not my strong suit.

The Cassopolises' house was on the outskirts of East Pemkowet, verging on a tract of undeveloped wetlands. Given Mr. Cassopolis's temper, I had to admit I was glad to see Cody's pickup truck already in the driveway. A patrol car would have been even more reassuring, but he was off duty.

Inside the house, it was uncomfortably obvious that it was a scene of domestic violence. Jen's father was glowering, barely managing to keep his temper under wraps in the presence of a police officer. Her mother sported a bruised lump on the side of her jaw.

She wouldn't press charges, though. She never did. She'd probably already told Cody she fell and hit her chin on the table.

Jen met my gaze ruefully, confirming my suspicion. "Thanks for coming, Daise."

"Of course." I gave her a quick hug, whispering in her ear, "Do you have something of Brandon's? Cody's going to need it to track his scent."

She nodded. "I'll be right back."

While Jen left to fetch an item of her brother's, Cody turned to me. His expression was studiedly neutral, and I couldn't tell how angry he was. "Got something for you, partner." He handed me a sturdy, finely worked belt with a metal-trimmed scabbard hanging from it. "Try that on for size."

"What in the world?" Mrs. Cassopolis said faintly. Her husband silenced her with a glance.

Feeling more than a little silly, I buckled the belt over my denim miniskirt. Although the leather was stiff, the belt fit well and sat perfectly on my hips.

"It will soften with wear," Cody said briefly. "And I'll give you some oil for it. Try the dagger."

Dauda-dagr caught the early-morning light as I eased it out of the makeshift deerskin scabbard, its etched runes flaring. It slid into the new scabbard as if . . . well, as if it were made for it.

Both the Cassopolises stared.

And suddenly I didn't feel silly anymore. I was Hel's liaison. The Norse goddess of the underworld had marked a rune onto my left palm with the hand of life, and she had given me *dauda-dagr* with the hand of death, a badge of status visible for all to see, eldritch and mundane alike, a symbol of her trust. I had the right to bear it openly, maybe even a duty. I found myself standing a little straighter, a little taller.

At that moment, Jen returned to eye me with disbelief. "Jesus! Way to accessorize, Daise."

Okay, maybe it didn't exactly go with a miniskirt. "It's a magic dagger," I informed her. "And it has a name."

"Okay." She processed that without blinking. "Shall we go?"

Cody gave a brusque nod. "Time's wasting. Show me which way you think your brother went."

The Cassopolises' backyard was small and overgrown, boasting a rusty swing set that I was pretty sure had been there when they bought the place decades ago. Beyond it, a faint trail led into the woody underbrush.

It wasn't a nice wood, not like the old forest in the game preserve near the Fairfax compound. It was a scrubby, dank wood. We picked our way along the trail until we'd gone far enough that the house behind us was hidden from view, and Cody called for a halt.

"Here?" I asked.

He shrugged, removing his off-duty shoulder holster and stripping off his T-shirt. "It's as good a place as any."

If I'd thought about it, which I would have if I weren't so ungodly hungover, I would have realized that asking Cody to shift meant asking Cody to get naked first. And I probably would have imagined a scenario in which he asked Jen and me to turn our backs or look away for modesty's sake.

I would have been wrong.

Cody took off his clothes with an utter lack of self-consciousness that gave me a brief flash of insight into werewolves' relationship with their own physicality. And yes, he looked very good naked, all lean, hard muscle and sinew, not hairy except for that treasure trail leading down from his belly toward even more tempting parts, which I commended myself for not checking out.

Folding his briefs, he placed them carefully atop a stack of clothing on a fallen tree trunk. "You've got something for the scent?" he asked Jen.

She nodded, wide-eyed, fishing a boy's worn and misshapen sweat sock out of her pocket. "Here."

Iridescent green flashed behind Cody's eyes. "Hold on to it for me."

Jen nodded again, wordless.

Cody shifted.

It wasn't like in the movies, with bones straining, flesh melting, and sinews cracking. I thought it would be, having caught a glimpse of Cody's self-control faltering when Al attacked me. But this was a deliberate and controlled transition, swift and flawless. One form flowed into another.

One second, naked man. There was the quickest image of him dropping to all fours, his skin pale in the dappled morning light.

The next second, wolf. And I do mean *wolf*.

Long and rangy in the limb, lean-sided, with tawny-gray fur, a long muzzle full of teeth, and prick-pointed ears. There was nothing human looking out of those amber eyes, but there was intelligence, keen and alert and waiting.

"Show him the sock," I whispered to Jen.

"*You* show him the sock!" she whispered back, shoving it at me.

Reluctantly, I took it from her and held it out toward wolf-Cody, letting it dangle from my hand. "Find Brandon?"

The wolf sniffed the sock, crescent-shaped nostrils working, then turned tail and sniffed the ground. It set off down the trail at a steady trot that didn't look particularly fast, but was. In seconds, it was out of sight.

Clearly, I hadn't really thought this through.

Jen and I followed at a run, at least until we ran out of trail. Luckily, the wolf had paused to let us catch up to it before it darted into the underbrush. From then on, it got pretty pathetic. We crashed through branches and blundered under them, tripped over vines, squeezed past brambly, thorny bushes. The sun was climbing higher and it promised to be a hot day. I could almost smell the beer and scotch sweating out of my pores, which made me feel even more nauseated.

"God, I really need to join a gym or something," Jen muttered between gasps. "Do you see him?"

"No." Straining my eyes, I caught a flicker of tawny movement ahead. "Yeah. Up there."

"It thins out ahead," she said. "But it gets grosser."

"I remember." When Jen and I had been younger and stupider, we'd explored back here, too. That was how we knew about Meg Muckle-bones, although we'd been careful to keep our distance. "Jen, you really need to think about moving out and getting your own place."

"I know, I know! It's just—"

"You worry about your mom and Brandon," I finished for her. "I know."

She sighed. "Sucks to be me, huh?"

Reaching back, I found her hand and gave it a squeeze. "Yeah, it does."

After that, we saved our breath for the effort of clambering through the scrub. Once it thinned out, it did indeed get grosser, the damp ground turning to gray muck filled with decaying foliage. It reeked of rotting vegetation and threatened to pull my cute little strappy sandals right off my feet. Thank God at least they were flats. Dead or dying trees rose out of the muck, and clouds of mosquitoes hovered whining over puddles of stagnant water.

"Hang on." I halted, panting, and took the opportunity to bend over and tug the heel straps of my sandals in place. "Lost him again."

"You're not exactly dressed for this, are you?" Jen commented, pushing her dark hair back.

"Didn't exactly plan on it." Straightening, I scanned the bleak landscape for a glimpse of the wolf.

"Oh, my God!" She gave me a smack on the shoulder. "Daisy Johanssen, is this a walk-of-shame morning? Is this about that *ghoul* you mentioned?"

I shook my head, which wasn't a particularly good idea, as it set off a wave of dizziness. "I wish." Oh, I did, did I? *Huh.* That had certainly come out of my mouth without any conscious thought on my part. "No, I spent the night at Lurine's."

"Well, how very fabulous of you." There was a slight note of envy in Jen's voice. "Was there champagne and caviar?"

"No," I said. "Beer and pretzels. Hold on; be quiet a moment. I think I hear something."

She fell silent.

Both of us strained our ears until we heard it in the distance: a sound like the screech of tree limbs rubbing together. If you'd never heard it before, you might think that was all it was. But it was a still morning, not a breath of a breeze stirring over the marshy wood. And Jen and I *had* heard it before.

We exchanged a glance.

"Oh, crap," I said.

Jen swallowed. "It's her."

We set out at a run across the gray muck, splashing and slipping and floundering. I lost one sandal and then the other, abandoned both of them, and hoped there weren't any nasty, splintery bits of wood underfoot.

On the verge of a scummy pond covered with bright green algae and choked with weeds, I caught sight of the wolf hunkered down beneath a deadfall and skidded to a halt, my bare feet plowing through the mud, Jen stumbling into me from behind. The wolf-Cody glanced up at me, that inhuman intelligence in its eyes.

Beyond it . . .

Meg Mucklebones was even bigger than I remembered, towering above the pond, green, slimy skin stretched over a frame that looked like it had been built of twisted roots. Long, veiny arms reached impotently for her prey, her voice creaking and screeching. A mere foot beyond her grasp, eleven-year-old Brandon Cassopolis clung like a terrified spider monkey to the trunk of a dead pine tree jutting out of the pond, arms and legs wrapped around it, his eyes squeezed tightly closed.

"How did he—" I saw a second barren pine trunk angled across the pond, caught in the branches of Brandon's perch. "Oh, crap."

Jen shuddered. "Daise?"

A policeman with a gun would have been helpful right about now.

A wolf, not so much. I was pretty sure wolves could swim if they had to, and pretty sure they weren't at their fighting best when they did. But without the wolf, we wouldn't have found Brandon.

I really, really hadn't thought this through.

I glanced down at wolf-Cody. "If you can understand me, now would be a good time to go back for your gun."

Apparently he could, since he shot out from beneath the deadfall and headed back across the muck at a rapid pace.

In the center of the pond, the marsh hag abandoned her futile effort to reach Brandon and wrapped both massive, long-fingered claws around the trunk of the upright pine tree. Brittle wood screeched and splintered alarmingly as she tugged on it, sounding a lot like the marsh hag herself.

"Daise!" Jen's voice was high and tight with panic.

"Okay. Okay!" I reached for *dauda-dagr*'s hilt and drew it. It felt cold against my palm, but in a good way. The dagger cleared the scabbard with a faint singing sound. "Hey! Hey, Meg! Or Jenny, or whatever your name is! Over here!"

She turned, dripping and oozing, looming up into the morning sky. Her sunken gaze found me.

I held up my left hand, showing her Hel's rune. "You're out of line, bitch! Let the boy go."

It took a moment to identify the rhythmic creaking sound as laughter. The marsh hag bent toward me, baring a mouthful of hideously pointed teeth and a disturbingly withered tongue. "I am within my rights!" she rasped at me. "The boy ventured into my territory knowingly! It has happened many times. Many times! Again and again, he has trespassed. This time, I have caught him." She gestured at Brandon with one slimy, taloned claw. "That makes him my rightful prey, Hel's liaison." Her voice dropped to a low, slithering, contemptuous tone. "Do you dispute it?"

It made me angry.

Seriously angry.

And this time I didn't try to contain it. I didn't even think about the Seven Deadlies. I let it rise, the air pressure tightening around me, pressing on my eardrums, my hair lifting with static electricity. Nearby trees made whining, cracking sounds, residual sap heating and bursting the bark. "You're damn right I do," I said grimly. I didn't know if she was telling the truth or not, and I didn't care. "Pemkowet can't afford this. Not now."

She screeched.

It was an earsplitting, soul-shaking sound, and I still didn't care because I was *pissed off.* I was sick and tired of being lied to by sociopathic bartenders and megalomaniac frat boys, sick and tired of being torn between friendship and the eldritch code, sick and tired of the eternal balancing act that was my life.

"You want a piece of this?" I beckoned with *dauda-dagr.* "Come and get it."

Meg Mucklebones lunged at me.

Jen screamed.

But I was already in motion, scrambling up the angled length of the fallen pine tree, the bark rough and scaly beneath my bare feet.

And the world . . . changed.

I don't know how to explain it. It was like a glamour falling or a scrim descending on a stage. Looking through it, I could see that I was perched precariously on a slanted log, an expanse of scummy pond water beneath me, *dauda-dagr* in my hand, and Meg Mucklebones turning back toward me.

But looking *at* it, I saw myself treading a narrow bridge over a lake of fire, a fiery whip trailing from my hand, black, bat-veined wings extended for balance.

In the one vision, I looked more than a little ridiculous and painfully vulnerable.

In the second, I looked powerful. Dangerous. Deadly, even.

My right palm felt either blazing hot or icy cold. To be honest, I couldn't tell which it was. I flexed my fingers impotently, trying to determine whether I held the hilt of Hel's dagger or the butt of hell-fire's whip. From somewhere or nowhere, laughter arose: not the marsh hag's, but a slow, rolling bell toll of dark mirth that resonated deep in my chest.

An image of my father's face flashed behind my eyes. Belphegor, lesser demon and occasional incubus.

I had an unhealthy suspicion that I shouldn't have unleashed my temper to *quite* this extent.

Belphegor wasn't here, not really. Not in physical form, anyway. But my rage had weakened the Inviolate Wall and called out to my father across the ether, and it felt like it was real. Black eyes, as black as the pits of hell, bored into mine.

Daughter.

"I'm busy!"

His head dipped forward, inclining the curved, pointed horns that sprang from his temples in my direction. Although I'd never admit it aloud, they were actually sort of cute in a totally demonic way.

All that you behold, you could become. You have but to ask.

My shoulder blades twitched involuntarily, mourning their lack of wings. Yeah, wings would be nice. Even bat wings. So would a fiery whip.

I sighed.

With a truly prodigious effort, I wrestled my temper under control. I did the visualization thing, wrapping my anger into a tight package of butcher's paper, tying it with twine, and throwing it into the algae-covered pond, where it bubbled and sank beneath the depths.

Belphegor's presence faded, and the real world came crashing back to the sound of a gunshot.

On the shore, barefoot in jeans and a T-shirt, Cody took careful aim at Meg Mucklebones and fired again, sending a second bullet through her chest. It sent her staggering and opened a hole in her torso like a knot in a moss-covered tree trunk.

"Stupid wolf!" the marsh hag screeched at him. Dripping slime sealed the wound closed with a distinctly unpleasant sucking sound. "You should know better! You cannot kill me that way!"

He fired again. "Oh, yeah? I can try."

She reeled under the impact, flailing and sending up gouts of foul-smelling stagnant pond water.

"Brandon!" I called, taking advantage of the distraction. "Come down!"

He pried his eyes open. "I *can't*."

I held my left hand out to him. "Yeah, you can."

After a long, agonizing moment of hesitation, he climbed down and took my hand, his fingers folding into mine, his brown eyes wide and terrified. "I'm scared."

"Yeah," I said softly. "I know. But it's okay. It's going to be okay."

I wished it were true. I wished there weren't things in Brandon's life so scary that he fled to a marsh hag's lair for sanctuary.

As we began inching down the trunk, Meg Mucklebones made one last desperate lunge, reaching for us with her huge, dripping hands. And I didn't hesitate. Shielding Brandon with my body, I did what Cody had taught me and struck without thinking. Wielding *dauda-dagr* in a sweeping blow, I slashed it across her slimy green fingers and watched Meg shrink back to cradle her seeping hand against her chest, wisps of frosty mist rising from the wounds. Unlike bullets, apparently *dauda-dagr* was capable of inflicting actual damage.

"You hurt me." Her voice was small with disbelief. "You *hurt* me!"

"Sorry," I said in an unapologetic tone. "Here's the deal, Meg, or Jenny, or whatever your name is. I don't care what the rules were back in the olden days on the old sod." I pointed *dauda-dagr* at her. "This is Hel's domain. And there will be *no* drowning and eating of children. Ever. Understand?"

The marsh hag sank low into the pond until only her head protruded, weedy hair floating atop the bright green algae. Her sunken eyes glowed a reptilian yellow in their woody sockets, and she licked her lips with her withered tongue. "Can I still frighten them?"

"Yeah," I said. "You can still frighten them. So do we have a deal? Do I have your word?"

Meg Mucklebones sank even lower into the murky water, submerging the bottom half of her face. "Yes." The word rose in a dank, sullen bubble, bursting on the surface with a whiff of vegetal putrescence—another vocabulary word Mr. Leary would be proud of me for remembering. A series of equally smelly, equally sullen bubbles followed. Her eyes held a resentful glow. "You have my word."

I smiled. "Excellent."

Twenty-eight

Within seconds, I had Brandon down from the trunk, both of us standing on what passed for solid ground in the wetlands.

Jen gave her brother a fierce hug, alternating between exclaiming over him in relief and scolding him. He endured both with an eleven-year-old's guilty embarrassment, squirming in her embrace.

Cody and I exchanged a glance.

"Nice work," he said to me.

"Thanks." I was filthy, spattered with muck and slime from head to toe, but I actually felt pretty good. Nothing like a surge of pure adrenaline to chase away a hangover, I guess. "You, too."

He holstered his gun and pulled a clean bandanna from his back pocket. "Might want to clean off your magic dagger, Pixy Stix."

I wiped *dauda-dagr*'s gleaming blade clean of sticky green ichor before sheathing it. "Thanks. Love the belt, by the way."

Cody's mouth twitched. "It suits you."

I peered down at it. "Really?"

"Uh-huh." Shoving his hands into the front pockets of his jeans, he rocked back on his bare heels. "Is it just me, or did something weird happen out there? Weirder than usual, I mean?"

I winced. "You saw it?"

"I saw *something*."

"Yeah, I know what he means. I didn't exactly see it, but I heard it. Halfway up the tree trunk, you yelled, 'I'm busy,'" Jen supplied helpfully. "What was that all about?"

I sighed. "Dad."

Both of them stared at me, with Brandon dividing his attention between the three of us, his gaze darting back and forth. In the pond, Meg Mucklebones continued to lurk, mostly submerged, her eyes glowing across the scummy water.

"Temptation scenario?" Jen asked in a low voice.

See, there are reasons to stay good friends with the people who know you best in the world.

"Yep."

Her luminous brown gaze was steady. "But you passed?"

I nodded. "I passed."

Jen gave me an approving punch in the arm. "Good job, Daisy-cakes. Hey, Brandon!" She nudged her brother. "This is Officer Fairfax. He helped us find you even though he's off duty, so say thank you to him, okay?"

"Thank you," Brandon said in a contrite tone. "I'm sorry."

There was no indication that he'd noticed anything unusual about the particulars of Cody's involvement in his rescue. We were lucky he'd had his eyes closed through most of the altercation. I hadn't thought that part through either.

Cody gave him a brusque nod. "Just don't do it again, okay?"

"I won't."

Together, we trooped, sloshed, and slogged our way back across the marsh and through the damp woods to the Cassopolis house-hold. My sandals were a total loss, having vanished into the mire.

Cody was able to retrieve his neatly arranged Timberlands and socks, tugging them onto his muddy feet.

"You want to tell me about this temptation scenario?" he asked me. I shook my head. "Maybe later."

Mr. and Mrs. Cassopolis were grateful and relieved to have their son restored to them, although I could see the threat of paternal anger looming.

Cody could, too. He fixed Mr. Cassopolis with a steely stare. "I hope you're not thinking of punishing the boy." He laid a protective hand on Brandon's thin shoulder. "He's had a pretty bad scare."

"Of course." Mr. Cassopolis reined in his temper, affecting a smooth charm. He was good-looking for an older guy, with the shiny black hair and rich olive-hued skin tone Jen and her older sister, Bethany the blood-slut, had both inherited. "I'm just sorry he caused such trouble."

"It's no trouble," Cody said briefly. "It's my job." He handed one of his departmental business cards to Mrs. Cassopolis. "If you ever need anything, call me," he said to her. "Day or night."

With a furtive glance at her husband, she tucked it into her apron pocket.

"Just to be on the safe side, you might want to tack some cold iron over your doors," I added. "An old horseshoe or whatever you have handy. I don't think Meg's going to be a problem anymore, but . . ." I shrugged. "You piss off one fairy, others might take issue. They can be pesty."

Jen followed Cody and me into the driveway. "Thank you," she said to him. "Thank you *so* much. I know—"

"Thank Daisy." His voice was still curt.

"Oh, yeah, of course!" She sounded surprised. "It's just—"

Cody glanced at his watch, then at me. "Look, I've got to go. Daisy, anything to report?"

"Actually, I do. You?"

He nodded. "Yeah. Go home; wash up. I'll do the same and meet you at the station in half an hour."

"Okay."

"Hey!" Jen's voice rose as Cody turned to go. "I don't know how you were raised, but when someone thanks you, you say, 'You're welcome,' Officer Fairfax. And, um . . ." Now her voice dropped until it was barely audible. "I'm not going to say anything, okay? Daisy's not stupid; she knows she can trust me." An unexpected flush touched her cheekbones. "And just so you know, you make a beautiful wolf."

Cody looked startled. "You're right. I'm sorry. You're welcome. And, um . . . thank you."

We watched him get into his pickup truck and drive away.

I glanced at Jen. "A beautiful wolf, huh?"

She folded her arms across her chest, looking slightly defensive. "I just wanted him to know I was okay with it. That I wasn't freaked-out. You okay with that?"

I smiled wryly. "I don't know. Are you ready to hug it out yet?"

Jen's expression softened. "Duh. Daise, you were *awesome*. You totally kicked ass today. And I so totally owe you. If we hadn't gotten there in time . . ." She shuddered. "I don't want to think about it. Let's just say you rock, girlfriend."

"Deal."

We hugged.

"You've really got to go?" Jen asked. "No chance of staying for a cup of coffee?"

"No. I wish."

She blew out her breath, wisps of hair rising from her brow. "Okay, but when this is over, we *seriously* need to talk."

I nodded. "You have no idea."

Besmeared with muck and mire, I drove home and parked the Honda on a side street, padding barefoot to my apartment, *dauda-dagr* hanging in its scabbard from my new belt, tourists staring as I cut across the park. Mogwai emerged from beneath a rhododendron bush to greet me with a plaintive howl.

"You think you're hungry?" I said, scooping him up ignominiously beneath one arm. "I don't even remember my last meal."

Dangling, Mogwai wailed.

Upstairs, I plunked him down and filled his bowl with kibble. I removed my belt and set it carefully aside, then stripped off my filthy clothing and climbed into the shower, letting hot water pelt me.

Clean and restored, I checked the time and realized I was due at the station in ten minutes. Scavenging in my refrigerator, I found a lone hard-boiled egg. I couldn't remember how long it had been there, but it smelled okay when I peeled it, so I doused it with salt and pepper and ate it standing over the sink. When this was all over, I really needed to do some major grocery shopping.

Believe it or not, I actually do know how to cook. Mom taught herself from books she got out of the library, and she let me help from the time I was old enough to control my temper in the kitchen. But for now, a hard-boiled egg would have to do.

On the whole, I felt okay.

Yeah, I was tempted by my father's scenario. Yeah, I liked the image he had shown me. But I didn't need bat wings and a fiery whip. I was Hel's liaison, dammit. That was enough. And she trusted me. That meant a lot.

I put on jeans and a scoop-necked T-shirt, buckling Cody's belt through the loops, *dauda-dagr* hanging from my left hip, its leather-wrapped hilt at the ready, waiting for my hand. It felt good. It felt right.

I looked at myself in the full-length mirror in my bedroom. Damned if I didn't look kind of badass. A magic dagger definitely went better with jeans than a miniskirt. And I'd used it. I'd actually wielded *dauda-dagr*. Okay, it wasn't exactly in a major ending-the-life-of-the-undead way, for which I was grateful, but I'd done it. I'd drawn blood, or ichor, or whatever sticky green sap ran in

Meg Mucklebones's veins. I'd backed down a marsh hag and saved a kid.

"Yay, you," I said to my reflection in the mirror.

My feeling of well-being lasted for as long as it took me to walk the few blocks to the station. There were half a dozen protestors outside the doors today, marching with their placards. Tourists were giving them a wide berth. This was definitely some bad publicity for Pemkowet.

Inside, the news got worse.

Detective Wilkes had come to inform us that the county sheriff's office had issued an ultimatum. Come Monday, Sheriff Barnard was going to announce that his office was taking over the investigation in its entirety, and would no longer be collaborating with the local Pemkowet police department.

"So he's throwing me to the wolves," the chief said, his face impassive. "I'm sorry to hear it."

"I'm sorry to tell you." Tim Wilkes sounded sincere. "He's under a hell of a lot of pressure."

"Exactly how does he plan on getting the eldritch community to cooperate?" I asked indignantly. "They won't talk to just anyone. They'll just make themselves scarce."

Wilkes glanced at me. "He's not planning on following up on that angle. He's trying to shift the focus back to the human element. He thinks it's the best thing for Pemkowet and everyone involved." He shrugged. "The autopsy results prove the Vanderhei boy's friends were lying. We'll charge them as accessories if we have to."

"Ross Barnard can shift the focus all he likes, but it's not going to change the truth," Chief Bryant said. "Is he calling for my resignation?"

The detective hesitated. "Not yet."

I looked around in vain for a calendar, and counted days on my fingers instead. "But today's . . . Friday, right?"

Cody stirred. "Right. So we're not finished yet. We have three days before the case gets yanked."

"Correct." Tim Wilkes nodded. "And until then, I'm still autho-rized to share my findings."

The chief leaned forward, an alert glint kindling behind his de-ceptively sleepy gaze. "Which are?"

Wilkes slid a piece of paper across the conference table. "Ichthy-ologist's report on the scales found under the vic's fingernails. Says he's never seen anything like it. Says the closest living relative would be the coelacanth. You know what that is?"

"Yeah," Cody said. "I watch the Discovery Channel. It's a prehis-toric fish, right?"

"Right."

I shivered.

The chief drummed his fingers on the tabletop. "We're not talking about a hobbyist's aquarium here, are we?"

Lost in reverie, I didn't hear the reply. My thoughts chased one another. I examined all the pieces of the puzzle.

Jerry Dunham, the dead-eyed former carny from Seattle, his con-nection to Dr. Midnight's Traveling Sideshow, and his collection of expensive vintage motorcycles. Matthew Mollenkamp, Van Buren slacker alumnus extraordinaire and self-proclaimed Master of the Universe and true son of Triton. A pair of ghouls in love, locked in an unsustainable loop of closed feedback, requiring a hostage to sur-vive. A dead boy, a callow young man drowned in salt water, with a bellyful of booze, scratches on his back, and impossible fish scales lodged under his nails.

My own words, echoing Lurine in the car. *But you're right. It all comes down to sex.*

It so often does, cupcake.

One by one, the pieces of the puzzle fell into place like cards. Mom had told me it was likely the reading was unusually literal. I should have seen it before. According to rumor, Dr. Midnight's cir-cus had one true thing—one true thing that fulfilled the require-ments of Triton House.

La Sirena, upside down. An alluring woman in distress, that was my mom's interpretation. But the card didn't just depict an ordinary woman. It depicted a woman with a scaled fishtail bobbing in the saltwater sea.

In other words, it depicted a freaking mermaid. It had been right in front of me the whole time.

I inhaled sharply. "It's a mermaid. We're looking for a mermaid."

All three men stared at me.

"It *fits*," I said impatiently. "It fits with what Lurine and I learned at Triton House last night. That whole Masters of the Universe thing, it's about having sex with an immortal, preferably of the aquatic variety. That's how you get to become a Master of the Universe and a true son of Triton. Mollenkamp admitted as much. He tried to play it off like Thad drowned trying to seduce a naiad, but he was lying."

"Miss Johanssen . . ." Detective Wilkes seemed at a loss for words.

I threw up my hands. "Is it any more unlikely than a coelacanth?"

"No," he admitted. "But I'm telling you, we've been looking into this, and there's no one in the area with an aquarium that size. It's not something you can hide easily. They require maintenance and upkeep."

Cody leaned back in his chair and ran a hand over his chin, rasping against his stubble. "What if Jerry Dunham brought it with him from Seattle?"

I eyed him. "You think?"

He shrugged. "He had to hire some sort of moving truck or trailer to transport those bikes. Why not an aquarium? If that's what he was in charge of in the circus, he might be doing the maintenance himself." He gave Wilkes an inquiring look. "Think we can get a search warrant for his house, Detective?"

"Based on this? No."

"Based on suspicion of trafficking in stolen motorcycles and parts," Cody said. "Hell, I saw the evidence with my own eyes. It's in the report."

The detective stood. "I'll see what I can do. But as far as we can tell, Dunham holds legal title to those bikes. If I were you, I'd go with reasonable suspicion and worry about the paperwork later." He glanced around at all of us. "Good luck to you. You'll need it."

With that, he made his exit.

Chief Bryant sighed. "A mermaid, eh?"

"It's a guess," I murmured. "But I think it's a pretty good one, sir. And if it's true . . ." I swallowed. "I'm guessing she's in a pretty bad way. And that's not a priority the county sheriff's office is interested in pursuing."

He met my gaze. "No, it's not. But *I* am."

"So do we bring this Mollenkamp in for questioning, or do we cut to the chase and go back to Dunham's?" Cody asked me, his upper lip curling to reveal a hint of gleaming white incisor.

I shook my head, successfully fighting the urge to say, *Down, boy!* "No, I mean, yeah, of course, let's check it out, but if she exists, I don't think she's there, Cody. I could be wrong, but I don't think Jerry Dunham gives a shit about anything but collecting his fancy motorcycles. I don't think he ever has. He doesn't care. He's not interested in suffering except as a means to an end."

"So who is?" the chief asked me. "Who *cares*, Daisy?"

It wasn't a rhetorical question.

I took a deep breath. "About suffering? Ghouls, sir." I glanced sidelong at Cody. "See, I think we're still looking for Ray D. Stefan said two ghouls in love would create a closed feedback loop. They'd need a hostage to sustain them, and if you ask me, Jerry Dunham doesn't seem like the type to let a couple of love-struck ghouls crash on his living room floor. I think we should question Matthew Mollenkamp."

Both of us looked at Chief Bryant.

He pursed his lips in thought. "Did you come up with any leads on Ray D's lady love?" he asked Cody.

Cody nodded. "Yeah, I did. It seems Mary Sudbury's got a sister who lives in town. I thought we could talk to her."

The chief folded his meaty hands. "Check out the sister and Dunham's place. Assuming this hostage exists, let's make her a priority, since no one else will. Gather as much information as you can. If we can find her on our own without stirring the pot further, so much the better; if not, bring in Mollenkamp for questioning. If he's in collusion with Dunham, maybe he can give us an address. But the good citizens of Appeldoorn are already up in arms, and I'd like to avoid adding fuel to their fire." He grimaced. "I took quite a shellacking at the Vanderhei boy's funeral. It wasn't pleasant."

I touched *dauda-dagr*'s hilt. "Let's go."

"Hold on." Chief Bryant forestalled me. "Daisy, I had a call from Amanda Brooks. She wants to meet with you."

Oh, crap. Amanda Brooks was the head of the Pemkowet Visitors Bureau, intense, high-strung, and, to make matters worse, she'd hired her daughter Stacey, who happened to be one of my high school nemeses, as her assistant. The incident in the girls' locker room with the bursting hot-water pipes that got me suspended? That was all Stacey Brooks.

I made a face. "Me? Why me?"

Leaning back in his chair, the chief shifted his folded hands over his belly. "She's got some ideas she wants to discuss with Hel's liaison. I promised you'd be in touch today. Understood?"

I sighed. "Yes, sir."

Twenty-nine

There was yet another commotion taking place outside the police station, leading me to wish, not for the first time since the Vanderhei kid had drowned, that it wasn't centrally located on downtown Pemkowet's main street.

Stefan Ludovic.

He was leaning against the seat of his Harley, booted ankles crossed. A pair of dark wraparound sunglasses bisected the unnatural pallor of his face. It should have looked cheesy in a Eurotrash kind of way, but it didn't.

He looked . . . hot.

A dozen tourists snapping eager photos agreed with me. Half a dozen wary protestors weren't so sure, and neither was Cody.

"What's *he* doing here?" he complained.

I fumbled in the inner pockets of my purse for Stefan's smoky quartz pendant. "Oh, I kind of borrowed something of his yesterday. He probably wants it back. He said it was special to him."

"You *what*?"

Cars squealed to a halt to let Stefan amble across the street with loose-limbed grace. He inclined his head to me. "Daisy."

I was hoping my emotions wouldn't start jangling in his presence. No such luck. I cleared my throat, handing him the pendant. "Stefan."

It dangled from his fist. "Did it suit your needs?"

I nodded. "Yeah, it did. Thanks. I really appreciate it. Um . . . did you think I would forget to give it back?"

"No." He stashed the pendant in the pocket of his leather vest, then removed his sunglasses, revealing dilated pupils in those ice-blue eyes. "I felt a great outpouring of anger from you this morning. It concerned me."

"It most certainly didn't concern you," Cody muttered.

I ignored him. Yep, definitely still jangling. "You . . . felt that?"

The protestors had abandoned their marching and chanting, and stood milling around us, craning to hear.

"Now that you've willingly allowed me to taste you, I'm attuned to you, Daisy," Stefan said calmly. "Of course I felt it."

"You *what*?" Cody repeated. "You let him *taste* you?"

I felt my face get hot. "It was an emergency, okay? And you might have mentioned that little side effect before you let me say yes," I added to Stefan.

He didn't exactly smile, but a dimple came and went alongside the corner of his mouth. "I might have. As you observed, it was something of an emergency. But you are well, I trust? Nothing is amiss?"

"I'm fine." I glanced around at the gawking protestors and tourists. I sure as hell wasn't going to mention Meg Mucklebones in the middle of this crowd. "Thanks for checking on me, but we've really got to go."

"We should share information again, Hel's liaison," Stefan said. "Where are you bound? I'll follow you."

My temper stirred. "Look—"

Cody tapped my shoulder. "Actually, Daisy, this gives me an idea. Go ahead and follow us," he said to Stefan. "I've got a request for you."

"Of course, Officer." Stefan's face took on a neutral expression. "I'm pleased to assist if I can."

As he turned to go, one of the protestors found an unexpected surge of courage and stepped forward to confront him. She held up a pendant of her own, a shiny gold cross, thrusting it toward Stefan's face.

"No sanctuary for Satanism!" Her voice shook a bit, and the cross trembled in her hand, but she stood her ground. "Begone, fiend!"

Several tourists on the outskirts said, "Ooh!" And I swear to God, a pair of teenage girls were dipping into bags of caramel corn and shoving it into their mouths like they were watching a movie.

More protestors joined the bold one, closing ranks with her. "Go back to whatever hell you came from!" one shouted. "Leave the mortal world to God's children!"

Once again, the chant arose.

"No sanctuary for Satanism! No sanctuary for Satanism!"

Stefan went very still.

It was the same deep, cool well of stillness I'd felt when I let my anger pour into him at Thad's funeral, but this time it radiated outward, encompassing the protestors and the gawking tourists.

The chant faltered.

I had a feeling I had a lot to learn about ghouls. At least, centuries-old ghouls with ironclad control.

Stefan's pupils waxed until they were glittering black moons surrounded by a thin rim of pale blue, then shrank to pinpoints. He fixed the young woman who'd first confronted him with that icy, blind-looking gaze. "You are very much mistaken as to my nature, madam. Once upon a time, my faith rivaled your own. But there are tales of heaven and hell that your priests will not tell you, and mine is such a one."

She gaped at him.

With one pale finger, he pushed aside the gold cross she still held outthrust in his direction. "May I pass?" he inquired. "Or would you prefer that I drain away a measure of this unhealthy terror and spite of the unknown that bedevils you?" His nostrils flared as he inhaled deeply and flicked his lower lip with the tip of his tongue. "It would be a pleasure to provide such a service."

The young woman made an "Eeep!" sound and stepped aside rapidly, the other protestors tripping over one another in their haste to follow.

"Thank you." Stefan put on his wraparound sunglasses. A handful of tourists reached for their cameras and phones.

"East Pemkowet!" Cody called after him. "We'll meet you on the other side of the bridge."

The Harley roared to life in answer.

Once he was behind the wheel of the patrol car, Cody permitted himself a brief, satisfied grin. "You know, for that I could almost bring myself to like the guy."

"Me, too."

He glanced at me. "Seems like you like him well enough already, Pixy Stix. You let him *taste* you?"

I slouched in the shotgun seat. "It was at the funeral yesterday. I was about to lose it. So what's this idea of yours?"

Cody took a left at downtown Pemkowet's only stoplight, which, by the way, is in operation only during tourist season. There's actually a ceremony involved. "I'm thinking maybe Lord Muckety-Muck can send someone to check out Dunham's house without spooking him. At least he's got an in."

I straightened. "Not bad. You trust him?"

"No," he said. "But I've been thinking. You're right: I don't think he's working with Dunham. From what I've seen looking for Ray D, there's still a power struggle going on under the surface in ghoul-world, and for better or worse, Ludovic's thrown his lot in with our side in this investigation. It's worth a try. We can always follow up on our own."

"Okay." I stole a look at him. "So, um . . . on a scale of one to ten, how mad at me are you?"

"For outing me?" Cody asked. I nodded silently. He turned onto the narrow highway. "Pretty much a ten when you called me this morning," he said. "After seeing the way things stand in the Cassopolis household . . ." He shrugged. "Maybe a three. You were right. I'm sorry. I didn't realize how bad things were there. And I didn't realize friendship was so important to you."

"Jen was right, too," I said softly. "You do make a beautiful wolf."

He shot me another glance. "Thanks. You ready to talk about this temptation scenario yet?"

I shook my head. "There's not enough time."

"Okay."

On the far side of the bridge, Stefan's Harley was idling in the parking lot of the little roadside market that sold fresh local produce and flowers. He pulled out and fell in behind us as we crossed the river, following us to a cottage in East Pemkowet only a couple blocks away from Mr. Leary's place.

We held a quick conference on the sidewalk in front of the cottage. I still wasn't sure how much *I* trusted Stefan, but we were running out of options. He readily agreed to send one of his lieutenants to Jerry Dunham's house in search of possible hostages.

"I will send Johnny on the pretext of delivering Dunham's back wages," he said. "If there is anyone being held captive on the premises, he should be able to sense it at close range."

I had an uncomfortable thought. "It won't send him ravening, will it?"

Stefan raised his brows. "The possibility exists. It would depend upon the degree of suffering to which he was exposed. But if it does, you will have your answer, will you not?"

"I guess." I hadn't mentioned the suspected nature of the hostage. "What happens to the hostage if it does?"

"Nothing worse than has already occurred," he said. "Either the captors would share their bounty or there would be a struggle for dominance among those involved, with the winner continuing to feed upon the hostage's suffering. But I think it is unlikely. Like many of the unfeeling, the blank Jerry Dunham has a well-developed sense of self-preservation. I do not think he would keep a victim hostage under his roof."

"What happens to the loser if there's a fight?" Cody inquired.

Stefan glanced at him. "The loser would seek . . . another source, until he or she was contained and the ravening allowed to pass."

"Does it always?" I asked. "Pass, I mean."

He hesitated. "No. Not if the exposure was prolonged and sustained. It would take many months of solitary confinement, but it is possible for one of our kind to starve. To succumb to madness, to devour our own essence until nothing remains and the corporeal body vanishes. It is one of the only ways in which our existence can truly be ended."

Huh.

"Your way is kinder." Stefan nodded at *dauda-dagr* hanging from my left hip in its sheath. "Swifter." A faint, wistful look crossed his face, so briefly I might have imagined it. "And perhaps it may grant us a second chance at heaven or hell rather than the eternal void of nonexistence."

Well, okay, then. I cleared my throat. "It's not *my* way, by the way. I haven't killed anyone."

"And yet the dagger is blooded since last we met, is it not?" Stefan asked in a courteous tone. "Or do my senses betray me?"

"Um . . . no."

"Decision time," Cody interjected impatiently. "Do we take the risk or not?"

"As I said, I believe the risk to be small," Stefan repeated. "But the choice is yours. I do have one request in exchange for the favor. I wish to accompany you on the interview of Mary Sudbury's sister."

Cody gave me a suspicious look.

"I didn't tell him!" I protested. "How did you know?"

Stefan pointed to the mailbox with the street address and then held up a cell phone. "I looked up the address. The resident is listed as one Emma Sudbury."

"Oh." I felt sheepish. Somehow, a centuries-old ghoul using modern technology seemed like cheating. "How did you know it was her sister?"

He smiled. "Statistically, it was likelihood. But it was a guess, which you have now twice confirmed."

Oh, great. Good job, Daisy.

"Oh, for God's sake!" Cody sounded disgusted. "Fine. Let's do it. Call your henchman and send him to check out Dunham's place. Let's go see if Emma Sudbury has any idea where her sister can be found. You can serve as our human lie detector, Ludovic."

He inclined his head. "Of course."

I hadn't had time to form any expectations of what the female ghoul Mary Sudbury's sister might be like, but if I had, I'm pretty sure they would have been wildly off base. We traipsed up the front path of the cottage through a neglected, dying garden. Thick brocade drapes curtained the windows. I saw them twitch at our approach, the narrowest of peepholes drawing closed.

Cody rang the doorbell.

For a long time, there was no answer. At last, the door opened a few inches to reveal a chain-bolt lock and a slice of an elderly woman's face, haggard and fearful, one red-rimmed eye showing. "Yes?" she asked in a quavering voice. "What is it?"

"Emma Sudbury?" Cody asked politely.

"Yes?"

He showed her his badge. "I'm Officer Fairfax. These are my associates, Miss Johanssen and Mr. Ludovic. May we come in?"

The chain-bolt lock remained in place. "Why?"

Cody kept his tone gentle. "We just have a few questions for you, ma'am. It's about your sister, Mary."

The rheumy eye blinked, watering. "Oh, dear God! What has she done now?"

Good question, I thought.

"We're not sure," Cody said. "But—"

"Emma." Stefan's voice dropped an octave. It was beyond gentle: low, deep, and soothing. Once again, I could feel that calm, cool stillness radiating from him. "It's all right. It's been hard, I know. So very, very difficult. And I can tell that you have tried, my dear. You've tried so very hard. But it's all right. You don't have to carry the burden alone. We're here to help."

It shouldn't have worked, of course. Now, Cody, okay. That I could see. Handsome Officer Down-low looked reassuring in his dark blue policeman's uniform. There shouldn't have been anything remotely reassuring about a tall, ice-eyed ghoul with a vaguely European accent clad in motorcycle boots and a black leather vest with outlaw-biker-gang colors turning up on an old lady's doorstep and telling her everything was all right.

But it did work.

Emma Sudbury's chin quivered. She closed the door long enough to disengage the chain, and opened it to admit us.

At close range, she looked even worse. Her skin was sallow, her thinning white hair lank and yellowish, plastered to her skull. She closed the door, her gnarled fingers trembling as she knitted them together. "Have you found her? Have you found Mary? Oh, God! What has she done?"

My heart ached for her, and I had an itchy feeling along my shoulder blades. If I'd had wings I would have wrapped them around her. "That's just it, ma'am," I said softly. "We're looking for Mary. What can you tell us?"

Her voice shrank to a whisper. "She's gone."

"Can you tell us—" Cody began.

Stefan held up one hand, unexpected compassion in his ice-blue eyes. "It's all right. It's your story, too, Emma. Will you tell us? Will you let us help you?"

She did.

And yeah, it was a pretty terrible story.

Mary Sudbury, younger of two obedient daughters raised in a

Pentecostal household in southern Indiana, had wed young in the 1950s in an environment wherein women were encouraged to submit to and obey their husbands, even if they were harsh and abusive, as Mary's husband proved to be. Still, she did her duty. She left her family and moved with her husband to a suburb of Chicago, bore him a son, and did her best to raise the infant until the day her mind snapped and she heard the voice of God telling her what to do to save herself and her infant child.

"She drowned him in the bathtub," Emma whispered. "Drowned the babe and cut her own wrists. But she came *back*."

"She was a true believer," Stefan murmured. "And neither heaven nor hell would have her."

She nodded. "She came *back*."

He touched her liver-spotted hand. "I know."

"*Why*? And *how*?"

"I don't know." He shook his head. "No one does."

I got angry. And yes, it was predictable, and yes, it's my go-to emotion, my own particular default mode. But if I was right, someone or something was suffering for Mary Sudbury's sins. If you ask me, heaven and hell have a lot to answer for. "Do you know where she is now?"

Emma Sudbury gave me a stricken look. "Gone. I tried. All these years, I've tried to provide for her. God knows, I've suffered."

"But she met someone, didn't she?" Cody prompted her. "Someone like her?"

She nodded again. "She said it was love. True love, even though it was forbidden to the likes of them."

I glanced at Stefan. "Forbidden?"

He shrugged. "Ill-advised, for reasons you and I have discussed. No doubt that is why Ray confided only in a mortal companion. Had I known, I would certainly have done my best to end it."

"What can you tell us about him?" Cody asked. "Name? Description? Where did they meet?"

"She said his name was Raymond." Emma shook her head. "But I'm afraid there's not much I can tell you. Mary was . . . secretive. Most of the time, she was docile. But every year, around the anniversary of . . . of her son's death, it got bad. I couldn't control her. I'd find her . . . I'd find her in places where you'd find children. Playgrounds, schools. Staring at them with that . . . that *hunger*." She shuddered. "And I was always afraid . . . She didn't, did she? It's not a missing child you're looking for, is it?"

"No, ma'am," Cody said. "It's nothing like that. We're actually looking for this Raymond. We think your sister may be with him."

A measure of tension went out of her body. "Oh, I'm sure of it. She said he would provide for her, for both of them. She said she knew what a burden she'd been to me, and that it wouldn't go on any longer." She smiled with sorrow, gazing into the distance. "It's true; it got harder and harder as I grew old and Mary remained unchanged. I worried terribly about what would happen when I was gone. And yet, now that it's Mary who's gone, I fear and worry nonetheless, and there is no one to take the fear away."

"You took a heavy burden on yourself," Stefan said to her. "One no one was meant to bear alone."

"She was my sister," Emma Sudbury said simply. "And there was no one else. It wasn't her fault she was broken."

"No," he agreed. "It wasn't."

Cody cleared his throat. "Any information you have might be helpful to us, ma'am. Any detail, no matter how small. Do you have any idea where Mary is now?"

"No." Tears glistened in her eyes. "Mary cut off all contact with me. She said it was for the best." Her tears gathered, spilling over the reddened lower lids. "That she was finally able to set me free."

"And when was that?"

She looked at him, seemingly unaware that she was weeping. "April, I believe."

"And there's been no contact since? Letters? Phone calls? Has anyone reported seeing her?"

"No." A tear etched its way into a wrinkle. Finally registering her tears, Emma pulled a tissue from her sleeve and dabbed at her cheek. "We kept to ourselves, Officer. No one in Pemkowet knew Mary's story. We wanted to keep it that way."

"I understand," Cody said, circling back to an earlier question. "About this Raymond—do you know where she met him?"

"Oh!" She dabbed at her other cheek. "Yes, I'm sorry. She met him at Our Lady of the Lake."

"The Catholic church?" Cody couldn't keep a note of surprise from his voice.

"They have a youth ministry," Emma Sudbury said, as though it explained everything. "There were children there. And it was the anniversary."

"What the hell would Ray D be doing at a Catholic church?" I wondered aloud. It didn't exactly seem like the haunt of choice for a meth-dealing ghoul.

"Our relationship with faith is a complicated one, Daisy," Stefan said quietly. "Raymond would not be the first of his kind to seek to reconcile it. And I have spoken with Father Domenico. He strikes me as an enlightened fellow who is sympathetic to the unique needs of his parish. Indeed, given your particular circumstances, I'm surprised you have not sought him out."

Again, huh.

"My mom was raised Lutheran," I said. "I think she was afraid the Catholics might try to exorcise me or something."

"Some might," he admitted. "Not all."

"Is there anything else you can remember, ma'am?" Cody asked Emma. "Anything at all Mary might have said?"

She shook her head, then reconsidered. "She said Raymond meant to keep her like a queen."

"But not where?"

"No." She regarded the damp tissue wadded in her hand. "No, Mary didn't want me to know. She *is* in trouble, isn't she? Something bad has happened."

"It's possible," Cody said gently. "But we don't know the extent of your sister's involvement."

Emma Sudbury took a deep breath, releasing it in a long, shuddering sigh. Her gaze shifted to Stefan, and her voice took on a note of bitterness. "You're like her, aren't you? Why aren't *you* broken?"

Stefan met her gaze without flinching, his pupils fixed and unwavering. "We remain what we were, my lady. I fear your sister was broken before her death. My circumstances differed. I was not."

"But you died?" she asked him. "Died, and came *back*?"

He inclined his head to her. "I am Outcast, yes."

There was a terrible hunger in her lined face: an addict's hunger. "I miss her, you know. Oh, God, I miss her! It's not fair. It's not fair that I should have become dependent on her to ease my misery, is it?"

"No."

Emma knotted her hands together, shredding the tissue, a look of desperate cunning creeping into her eyes. "You could help me, couldn't you?"

Stefan hesitated. "In the greater scheme of things, I would be doing you no favor, my lady."

She made a cracked sound that was half laugh, half sob. "Do I look like someone with the luxury of thinking about the greater scheme of things in the years to come, Mr. Ludovic? Please. You would do me a kindness."

He nodded. "So be it."

Cody and I exchanged a quick, uncertain glance as Stefan rose and stooped on one knee to cradle Emma Sudbury's head in his hands. His lips parted and his pupils waxed alarmingly as he drank in her fear and worry.

Her expression eased, her face softening. In a totally creepy way, it was sort of like she was receiving a benediction.

Stefan closed his eyes, hiding his own reaction. And yes, I was grateful for that. After a long moment, he released her and took a step backward, his hands loose and open at his sides. He opened his eyes, his pupils steady, dilated, and glistening. "You should embrace your freedom, my lady. Lay down your long burden. You belong to the world of the living. Return to it."

"After so long?" Emma Sudbury murmured. "I'm not sure I know how."

"You will find a way," Stefan assured her. "I promise you."

She gazed trustingly at him. "And Mary?"

His ice-blue eyes were grave. "There, I make no promises."

Thirty

I t's fair to say that at least two of us breathed a sigh of relief on the sidewalk outside Emma Sudbury's cottage, free of its dark, frowsty confines and the weight of fifty-some years' worth of accumulated suffering, misery, and guilt.

Cody shuddered and shook himself all over like a dog, his service pistol, flashlight, portable radio, and various other items on his officer's utility belt rattling in their respective holsters. "Damn!" he said fervently. "It's just so . . . awful."

Stefan's expression was indecipherable. "Yes."

I might not be able to read his face, but there was something new in his voice. "You're worried, aren't you?"

He glanced at me. "I had not realized Mary Sudbury's case would prove so . . . extreme. For an infanticide to be Outcast is rare."

"Yeah, about that," Cody said. "I'm a little hazy on how this whole business works. Mary Sudbury killed her child and committed suicide. So why does hell give her a pass? Not guilty by reason of insanity?"

"In a sense." Stefan's voice was somber. "Over the years, I have spoken to priests and philosophers alike. And I spoke the truth when

I said no one fully understands the how and why of our existence. Not even we ourselves. This I will tell you: Due to Mary's madness, she committed a mortal sin as an act of profound faith. Heaven does not admit unrepentant sinners, and hell does not welcome true believers. Like all of the Outcast, Mary fell between the cracks."

I cleared my throat. "Hel . . . I mean Hel the goddess . . . said that gh—" Damn, I felt guilty saying it now. "That the Outcast were mortal beings slain at height of great passion. I have to admit, I don't get how this fits."

Stefan's gaze rested on me. "Despair is a passion unto itself, Daisy," he said softly. "Do not doubt it."

"Okay," I said. "So what does it all mean?"

His phone rang, chiming with a baroque phrase of classical music I couldn't even begin to identify. Reaching into the front pocket of his jeans, Stefan gave me an apologetic look. "Excuse me."

Cody and I exchanged glances again, both of us still thinking about the haunted figure of Emma Sudbury.

"My mom's got a friend who volunteers at the senior center," I offered. "Sandra Sweddon. Mom's doing the dresses for her daughter Terri's wedding. I could ask her to ask Sandra to look into contacting Emma Sudbury. They've got an outreach program for seniors living alone. Whatever happens, I have a feeling poor Emma's going to need it once this is over."

"Good idea." Cody raised his eyebrows. "Terri Sweddon's getting married? I hadn't heard."

"Yes, you did," I reminded him. "You were right there when Mom told me."

"I must not have been paying attention," he admitted. "Who's she marrying?"

"Cory Dalton."

"Really?"

"I think so." I counted on my fingers. "Curtis, Cameron . . . Cory's the youngest Dalton boy, right? He was a year behind you."

He nodded. "And Terri was a year ahead of you? She has a sister who's younger, too. What's her name?"

"Sherri?" I hazarded. "Yeah, I think that's right. Terri and Sherri. She was a couple years behind me."

Having concluded his discreet conversation, Stefan Ludovic, who was already several centuries old when Cody and I were attending Pemkowet High with the Dalton boys and Sweddon girls, strode back down the sidewalk, his bootheels ringing against the cement. "That was Johnny," he announced. "He says that the place that Jerry Dunham was renting appears to have been abandoned."

Oh, crap.

"What about the bikes?" Cody demanded. "He wouldn't leave without them."

Stefan shook his head. "Gone. All gone."

"He checked the garage?"

"Yes, of course." Stefan tilted his head, narrowing his ice-blue eyes. "He is an Outcast. The garage was the first thing he checked."

It took me a few seconds to realize he meant biker-gang Outcast, not heaven-and-hell Outcast. The overlap was a little confusing.

"Shit." Cody hit his palm with his fist. "We spooked him."

"Yep."

"It is as I said," Stefan said in a matter-of-fact manner. "The unfeeling have strong senses of self-preservation. If Jerry Dunham was involved with some nefarious scheme, I do not doubt he had an exit plan in place."

"Oh, I'm pretty sure it was nefarious, all right." Within the confines of my jeans, my tail lashed with righteous outrage. I stilled it with a conscious effort, curling it between my thighs. And in case you were wondering, yes, it does feel kind of good there. I try not to think about it at inappropriate intervals. "So what now?" I asked Cody. "Do we try to bring in Matthew Mollenkamp for questioning or interview the priest?"

"*I* pick up Mollenkamp." He pointed at me. "*You* call Amanda Brooks at the PVB—remember?"

Double crap! I'd managed to forget that particular assignment. "Don't you think the chief would think this was more important?" I asked hopefully.

"No." Cody squashed my hopes without a trace of remorse. "I don't. And I think it would be better to spring you on Mollenkamp after we've had a chance to question him for a bit. I don't imagine he'll be a particularly cooperative witness, since he's not going to be eager to implicate himself in this. Let the element of surprise work for us."

"Okay, fine." With a sigh, I fished my phone out of my purse.

Despite my fondest wishes, Amanda Brooks took my call immediately and asked in a brisk, no-nonsense tone if I could meet with her in her office in half an hour, and despite my deepest reluctance, I agreed.

And in the midst of our brief discussion, Stefan Ludovic took the opportunity to make his exit.

"Damn." Ending the call, I gazed after the vanishing taillight of his Harley. "Where's he going?"

Cody shrugged. "Places to go, people to feed on. Does it matter?"

"It might." I gave him a sharp look. "I would have liked to know more about why Mary Sudbury has him worried."

"I have a feeling the word *ravening* plays into it." Cody allowed himself another brief shudder, shaking off the last remaining dregs of Emma Sudbury's misery. "Come on, Pixy Stix. I'll give you a ride to your car. I want to swing by Jerry Dunham's and confirm it for myself before I head up to Appeldoorn."

Approximately half an hour later, I pulled into the little parking lot of the Pemkowet Visitors Bureau.

It was a quaint, shingle-sided building situated on riverfront property along the main entrance to the downtown. Inside, the decor was modern and streamlined, everything designed to suggest a tasteful degree of wealth and sophistication unusual for your average small Midwestern town. Glossy magazine-size visitors' guides were spread across the low table in the reception area, featuring a darling blond toddler in a sun hat engrossed in building a sandcastle, the sparkling waters of Lake Michigan beckoning in the background.

On the downside, my old high school tormentor Stacey Brooks was seated at the sleek front desk, speaking ostentatiously into a wireless headset perched atop her cascading ash-brown curls, a little blue light blinking on the earpiece. She glanced at me with a look of disdain, raising one finger in a dismissive wait-a-minute gesture.

On the plus side, there was a visitor seated in the reception area, and he was cute. Short dreads, high, roundish cheekbones, cocoa-dark skin, maybe a year or two older than me. Definitely not a local or I would have known him. He nodded at *dauda-dagr* with a cheerful grin and greeted me in a Jamaican accent. "Nice cutlass, sistah."

My hand fell to the hilt. "Thanks."

"You have much call to use it, do you?" He sounded amused, and I felt self-conscious. Funny how a cute guy checking out your magic dagger can have that effect.

"I hope not."

"Oh?" He tilted his head back, appraising me, his grin giving way to a curious look. I felt the slightest tingle of *otherness*, so slight it was barely there. He was human, all right—there was no glamour to see through—but there was definitely the faintest hint of the eldritch, like shadow cast from afar, the way it did with certain people.

Behind the front desk, Stacey Brooks cleared her throat. Apparently she'd concluded her important call. "Hel-*lo*? Daisy, my mother's ready for you. She's very busy, you know."

I leveled a stare at her. "Look, I didn't ask for this meeting."

Stacey sniffed through her pert, perfect nose. "Do you actually think *she* did?" she asked in a snide tone. "Chief Bryant passed her on to you when she called him. That man is *so* going to lose his job. You're lucky there are people like my mother who truly care about this town."

I bit my tongue. "I'm sure—"

She tapped her headset, her voice turning chipper. "Pemkowet Visitors Bureau! How can we brighten *your* day?"

Oh, gah.

Amanda Brooks emerged from her office. She was one of those whippet-thin older women with clavicle bones that looked sharp enough to cut glass. Actually, she reminded me a bit of Thad Vanderhei's mother, only instead of brittle fragility, she radiated a tightly wound intensity. Her hair was the same ash-brown hue as her daughter's, augmented with blond highlights, but like Sue Vanderhei's it was drawn back in a bun so tight it had to tug on her scalp. Maybe it served as a temporary face-lift. She regarded me through a pair of chunky, retro-chic, expensive-looking glasses, looking me up and down. "Daisy Johanssen?"

You would think that since her daughter was responsible for getting me suspended from school, she might remember me, right? I mean, there were forty-seven people in my graduating class, and the other forty-six were fully human. But I made myself answer politely. "How can I help you, Ms. Brooks?"

Her expression suggested she doubted I could. "Come into my office, won't you?" She turned toward the cute guy. "I'll be with you in a short while, Mr. Palmer. Thank you for your patience."

He shrugged, tapping a fist to his chest and giving her a charming smile. "No haste, mother. All respect."

Amanda Brooks flushed slightly before ushering me into her office and closing the door behind us. She took a seat behind her desk.

I took a seat opposite her, facing the river. If it were my office, I'd have arranged it to have the river view myself, but I suppose it was all the better to impress visitors. Amanda Brooks was clearly willing to sacrifice on behalf of her job.

She leaned forward, bracing her forearms on the desk. "Let me cut to the chase, Daisy. We're in the midst of a publicity crisis here."

"I know."

She gave me a tight, grim smile. "I'm not sure you do. We've had cancellations. Bookings are down. Business owners are panicking. There's a growing perception that Pemkowet isn't a safe destination for paranormal tourism."

"That's because it's *not*," I said. "It never has been."

"With a little more cooperation, it could be." With laserlike focus, Amanda Brooks studied me through the lenses of her chic glasses. "According to Chief Bryant, *you're* the designated liaison to the eldritch community, and unlikely as it seems, it appears that it's you I need to talk to."

For that, I could have throttled the chief. "He may have overstated the case," I said. "I'm Hel's liaison. It doesn't mean I represent the entire eldritch community."

Her gaze was unblinking. "But you represent Hel's authority?" she asked. I nodded. "Do you have credentials? A license?"

"No." My tail twitched. "Not one you can see, anyway. But I have a dagger no one else can wield. Hel gave it to me herself with her left hand, the hand of death." I drew *dauda-dagr* and reversed the blade, proffering the hilt. "Would you care to try it?"

Dauda-dagr's blade shone in the sunlight angling off the river, silvery runes shimmering, its edges glinting blue. It felt pleasantly cold against my palm. Little wisps of frosty mist rose from it, hovering in the bright air.

Amanda Brooks shivered and shrank back, gooseflesh rising on her bare arms. "No." Picking up a gilded letter opener, she poked at *dauda-dagr* like she was poking at a snake with a stick. "Put it away, please."

I sheathed it.

"Here's what I'm thinking," she said without preamble, recovering effortlessly. "The young man in the lobby, Mr. Palmer, has filed a request for a license to operate a tour bus in Pemkowet. A paranormal tour. And I think it's a good idea. I think if we could guarantee sightings, *benign* sightings, it would do the town a world of good. It would help us weather this storm." Her intense gaze fixed on me. "Do you agree?"

I sighed. "It's not that easy."

"It could be. Think of the possibilities, Daisy!" She leaned forward again. "Look at the success of Mrs. Browne's Olde World Bakery. What if we offered a package deal with baking classes with Mrs. Browne herself?"

I shook my head. "That would never happen."

"Why ever not?"

"Because she's a *brownie*!" I said. "Brownies only offer their services at will, never on demand, and never when people are watching. Never. You can't ask them for favors. It's dangerous to even acknowledge them with thanks. You can't ask them for anything. She'd vanish if you did."

"Okay. Okay." Amanda Brooks settled back in her chair, crossing her legs. "So help me out here. Let's brainstorm. What *will* work?"

I thought over the possibilities. Closeted werewolves were out, obviously. Unless we were talking about moonlight tours, vampires were out. Lurine was too recognizable to take that kind of risk; there was no way I'd ask her. "There's a new head ghoul in town," I said. "He seems interested in improving their image; he might be willing to have his people work with us. Oh, and there's Gus the ogre. I bet he'd do it if my mom asked him."

She shuddered. "Oh, for the love of God! Were you even listening? We need *benign* sightings, Daisy. We need nymphs splashing in the river, playing catch with bubbles; wood nymphs flitting through the forest. We need pixies sitting on toadstools. We need pretty, sparkly fairies. We need—"

"Unicorns and rainbows?" I suggested.

Amanda Brooks raised her brows at me. "Don't be glib. I don't expect you to control the weather. But a unicorn would be nice, yes. Do we have any?"

"No," I said. "Not that I'm aware of. And a lot of those pretty, sparkly fairies have sharp teeth and bad tempers. I don't think you understand what you're asking. The eldritch community *isn't* benign. They're not here to serve as tourist attractions. They're here because Pemkowet has a functioning underworld, which allows them to exist in the mortal world without the risk of fading."

She tapped her letter opener on the desk. "Don't you think it's in their best interest to keep it that way?"

"Of course."

Setting down her letter opener, she reached for a copy of the latest *Appeldoorn Guardian* and pushed it across the desk at me. "Look at the poll results."

Reluctantly, I took a look. It seemed that fifty-three percent of respondents thought that it was time to explore the possibility of cutting down Yggdrasil II, razing Pemkowet's underworld, and banishing the unholy eldritch influence from Michigan for good. My mouth felt dry. "It's just a poll. It doesn't mean they can *act* on it."

"No." Amanda Brooks adjusted her stylish glasses. "But it means we're losing the battle of perception. We need to push back against it. Anything you could do to help would be . . . helpful."

I nodded. "I understand. I can't guarantee results, but I'll see what I can do."

"Good." She rose. "I'm glad we're on the same page." Opening her office door, she called out to the cute guy. "Mr. Palmer? May we have a word?"

He sauntered into the office, hands in his pockets, and gave her another charming smile and a disarming shrug. "Any word you like, mother."

"Ah . . . yes." Again, she flushed. "Sinclair Palmer, Daisy Johanssen. Mr. Palmer, Ms. Johanssen has agreed to work with the eldritch community in an effort to . . . enhance . . . the tours you propose."

Sinclair Palmer regarded me. "Is that so, sistah?"

"Yep."

His lips twitched in an effort to suppress a smile. He had nice lips, full and juicy. "I an' I look forward to it."

"So do I and I," I said in reply. "But I'm kind of busy right now. And I can't make any promises."

"Understood." He tapped his chest with his fist. "Respect, eh? What will be will be. Jah bless."

"Um . . . right."

"Good, very good." The matter apparently concluded, Amanda Brooks hastened to usher us out of her office. "I'm glad we were able to come to consensus. Look, I've got a dozen fires to put out. I'll leave it to the two of you to coordinate. Mr. Palmer, I promise I'll see your license is granted. Go ahead and plan accordingly. The sooner you're in operation, the better. Daisy . . ." She sighed. "Do whatever you can. Think pretty. Think sparkly. If they have to smile with their mouths closed, that's fine. Just—"

"Unicorns and rainbows," I said softly. "I get it."

A fleeting look of gratitude crossed her face. "Good luck. Oh, and Daisy?"

I turned back. "Yeah?"

"I thought you might have a word with the powers that be out at the House of Shadows," she said. "Ask them to lie low for a while. Make sure there are no vampires prowling the streets at last call."

I sighed. "Really? Are you serious? You want me to dictate terms to Twilight Manor?"

"Really." Amanda Brooks's expression hardened. "You took on this role. While I recognize my limitations, I'm not entirely ignorant of what goes on in Pemkowet. I realize most vampires are looking for a long-term blood-bond relationship. But there are always paranormal tourists looking for a short-term thrill. And sometimes they find it. That doesn't necessarily work out well for them, does it?"

"No," I admitted.

She nodded at me. "So let's take that off the table for now. Unless you think Hel would disapprove?"

"No," I said honestly. "I don't."

Thirty-one

Finding Stacey Brooks immersed in another phone call, I took the opportunity to make a hasty exit from the PVB office with Sinclair Palmer close behind me. Stacey's gaze followed us jealously. Deprived of the chance to get in one last verbal dig, she lifted her right hand, hooked her fingers, and flashed a devil-horns sign at me.

Apparently in certain circles, that one never got old. I really, really didn't miss high school.

Outside in the parking lot, I blew out my breath. "Sorry—that was a little messy. Welcome to Pemkowet."

Sinclair shrugged. "Eh, it's not so bad. Just a little cuss-cuss."

I eyed him. "Are you really Jamaican?"

He returned my gaze evenly. "Why you think I'm not, sistah?"

"I don't know," I said. "I have to admit, pretty much everything I know about Jamaica comes from watching *Cool Runnings*, and I'm guessing a Disney movie about Olympic bobsledders isn't the most accurate reference material." I nodded at his hair. "But something about your commitment to dreadlocks strikes me as a recent development."

Sinclair laughed. "I tell you true, you do the same?"

"Sure, I guess." I figured he'd find out sooner or later. I'd prefer later, but I was curious about him.

"Yes and no." He dropped the accent. "I was born in Jamaica, but I grew up in Kalamazoo with my dad. He immigrated when I was three. My mom still lives in Kingston." He tugged on one of his dreads. "And yeah, these are only a few months old. My turn?"

I nodded, braced for the inevitable question, but it wasn't exactly what I expected.

"I see auras." Sinclair's gaze roved around me. "But I've never seen one like yours. What is it?"

"Is that a pickup line?"

He grinned. "Do you want it to be? No, I'm serious. Most people just have a little shimmer flickering around their edges. You've got a five-alarm fire, and I do mean a fire." He gestured in the air, tracing invisible lines. "The flames are shot through with these twisty veins of gold. Definitely nothing I've seen before. And definitely not entirely human."

"Is that where you got the idea of doing a paranormal tour?" I asked. "Because you can see auras?"

"Sort of." Sinclair shrugged. "I've always been able to see things other people couldn't, and I've always been drawn to Pemkowet. When I came across a sweet deal for an old tour bus on craigslist, it all came together. Are you avoiding the question?"

In fact, I was. "Hell-spawn," I said reluctantly. "Daughter of Belphegor, minor demon and occasional incubus."

"Really?" He looked surprised. "Well, that explains the flames."

At least he wasn't freaked. "So why the Jamaican act? Or sort-of act?"

"You jestin', sistah?" He rolled his eyes. "People eat that shit up, especially white people." He pointed at the PVB building. "You think that Mrs. Brooks would be fluttering and blushing over plain old Sinclair Palmer from Kalamazoo?"

"Probably not," I agreed.

"Everyone loves a magical Negro," Sinclair said in a cynical tone. "Until they meet one in real life."

I blinked. "Excuse me?"

"You've never heard the term?" he asked. I shook my head. "It's a black character who uses his unique wisdom or special gift to help the white hero achieve his goal. Pretty common in popular culture. *The Green Mile, The Legend of Bagger Vance, Driving Miss Daisy—*"

"Ooh, ooh! Scatman Crothers in *The Shining*?"

"Yeah, exactly."

Cute, and a movie buff, too. We stood in the parking lot smiling awkwardly at each other. The thought occurred to me that it might be nice to take an interest in someone entirely human and almost normal for a change.

I wondered if the tail would freak him out.

"Hey, can I buy you lunch, Daisy?" Sinclair asked. "I'd love to talk about my ideas for the tour and get your input. And I'd love to hear more about your . . . um, unusual heritage." He nodded at *dauda-dagr*. "Not to mention the story behind that mighty cutlass, sistah."

At that inopportune moment, my phone rang. I glanced at it. "I've got to take this; sorry."

It was Patty Rogan calling from the station. "Cody's bringing in a witness," she said. "The chief wants you here in twenty. Okay?"

"I'll be there." I ended the call. "Sorry," I said with genuine regret. "I'd love to; I really would. But I'm sort of on duty and we're in crisis mode. Rain check?"

"Sure." Sinclair frowned. "Who do you work for, exactly? I'm sorry; I'm a little confused."

"I'm Hel's liaison." I patted *dauda-dagr*'s hilt. "That's Hel the Norse goddess of the dead," I clarified, seeing a look of alarm begin to dawn on his face. "Not the infernal realm, okay? But in terms of drawing a paycheck, I actually work for the Pemkowet Police Department."

His expression turned to bemusement. "As what?"

"Mostly a part-time file clerk," I said. "But lately a full-time investigator. Let me see what I can do, and I'll call you."

"Okay."

After we exchanged numbers we parted ways, me in my Honda and Sinclair Palmer on a bicycle, pedaling industriously. Nice legs, too.

Gah! Everything was moving too fast, and there was too much to be done. I wished I could slow down time for a few days, or at least take a day for myself. I could use some quality mother-daughter time. I desperately yearned for an intensive session of good old-fashioned girl talk with Jen. I needed to sort through my feelings about Cody. I actually liked the working partnership and mutual respect that we were developing. Did I still want it to be more, or was it just my long-standing crush at work?

I'd let Stefan *taste* me, for crying out loud, and now he was attuned to me, and I didn't know how I felt about it. Okay, on a primal girlie level, there was something flattering about having him turn up like some magical fairy-tale protector, but I hadn't known that was what I was signing up for. Had he tricked me? Had I agreed to it on a subconscious level?

I didn't know.

Now I'd met a mostly normal human guy with whom I felt a few sparks, and I didn't know what to do about that, either. I couldn't even remember the last time I'd gone on a date, and I was getting way ahead of myself just thinking about it. I didn't even know whether he was single, let alone interested.

I drove around town, looking for a parking space. "Focus, Daisy," I murmured to myself. "It's not about you."

It helped.

If I was right, if Mom's reading held true, there was an eldritch creature being held hostage out there somewhere, not so very far away. *La Sirena.* And I had a good idea that she was suffering pretty badly.

My shoulder blades prickled at the thought, and I felt a surge of anger that left me light-headed, although as I finally found an empty spot and maneuvered the Honda into place, it occurred to me that the latter might have something to do with the fact that I was running on adrenaline and fumes. After a dinner of beer and pretzels, I needed more than one not-so-fresh hard-boiled egg to keep me going.

Luckily, there was a hot-dog stand on the way to the station. I grabbed a chili-cheese dog and ate it on the go, dodging tourists on the sidewalk. Say what you will, but as far as I'm concerned, while fake cheese sauce may be seven kinds of disgusting, it's also one of the ultimate hangover foods.

By the time I reached the station and squeezed past the protestors, I felt calmer and more grounded. Yep, I definitely needed food.

If this were a movie, I'd have a chance to watch Cody and the chief interview Mollenkamp in the interrogation room through a one-way mirror before staging a timely intervention, but the Pemkowet Police Department doesn't have a one-way mirror, or even an interrogation room.

"They're in the conference room," Patty Rogan greeted me. "Chief says he'll send Cody for you when he's ready."

"Thanks, Patty."

She dabbed significantly at the corner of her mouth and gave a discreet nod in the direction of the restroom. "You might want to freshen up first."

Oh, great. The bathroom mirror revealed a veritable clown smile of chili grease and cheese sauce plastered over my lips. Thank God I'd had a chance to shower earlier, and was no longer sweating out stale beer and twelve-year-old single-malt. I washed my hands and face and rinsed my mouth in the rust-stained porcelain sink.

When I emerged, Cody was waiting for me, his expression somber. "Hey, Daise. This guy's got some major attitude."

"Yeah, I know." I wiped my still-damp palms on my jeans. "He's not cooperating?"

He shook his head. "He's denying everything. You and I are trading places. The chief figures it's time to spring you on him. Ready?"

I touched *dauda-dagr*'s hilt again. The coolness it radiated was reassuring. "Yeah, I'm ready."

Inside the conference room, Matthew Mollenkamp was slouched in a chair. Although he looked a little worse for the wear after a hard night of drinking, everything about his body language exuded the same sense of privilege and entitlement. Still, he stiffened perceptibly when I entered the room.

"Hail, true son of Triton," I said to him. "Nice to see you again."

His eyelids flickered.

Chief Bryant smiled a slow, sleepy smile. "Well, now, son. I'd like to introduce you to our special associate, Miss Daisy Johanssen. In fact, I believe you may already be acquainted. Are you still inclined to claim you've never heard of the Masters of the Universe?"

Mollenkamp gave a short, choked laugh. Stalling for time, he ran his hands over his face and through his hair. "I take it you're not a potential transfer student, are you?"

I took a seat. "Nope."

His hazel gaze fixed me. "Where's the other Trask sister? The *hot* one?"

It was meant to hurt, and to be honest, it did. But that was exactly what he intended. I had a feeling he liked his women off-kilter and insecure. I decided to give it right back to him. "Do you know who *you* remind me of?" I asked him. "Matthew McConaughey."

He smirked at me. "Yeah, I get that sometimes. The name helps."

"Did you ever see *Dazed and Confused*?" I asked. "No? It's been a while, but I watched it with my mom years ago. McConaughey plays a guy who still hangs out with high-school students even though it's sort of pathetic at his age. Glory days and all that, I guess, you know?" I shrugged. "You remind me of him. Only he pulls it off better. But then, it's a movie. Real life is different. Don't expect a happy ending here. Thad Vanderhei found that out the hard way, didn't he?"

Mollenkamp glanced at the chief, his smirk fading.

The chief ignored him, examining his fingernails and maintaining a heavy, impassive silence.

I think it was at that moment that Matthew Mollenkamp knew he was in trouble. With the weight of silence pressing on him, his gaze flitted around the room, coming back to me. "Okay." He raised his hands in mock surrender, his tone striving for bitter levity. "Okay, you got me. Busted. I made up some bullshit and a few of the alumni brothers played along. You didn't actually *believe* it, did you?"

"Yeah," I said. "I did."

"It wasn't true," he said in frustration. "It's not my fault if Thad Vanderhei believed me! It was an accident!"

I shook my head. "Not the kind his buddies claim it was."

Mollenkamp sank deeper into his chair. "So why don't you talk to them? I wasn't there. I don't know what happened."

"You sent them there."

He shrugged. "I made up some bullshit story about a secret society within the brotherhood. What the hell? It sounded good at the time. They got punked, okay? No one was supposed to die, and believe me, I feel like shit about it. If I could take it back, I would. I'd give anything to take it back, okay? But it was just another kind of hazing. *I* didn't dare Thad to swim the river. For Christ's sake, I don't even know why—" His voice cut off.

I glanced at the chief. He nodded at me, giving me permission to continue. "You don't even know what Thad and the others were doing at the river, do you?" I asked softly. "Because that's not where you sent them. That's not where you expected them to be."

Mollenkamp looked away. "I wasn't there," he muttered. "Why the fuck are you talking to me? Talk to Kyle and Mike."

"Oh, we are." The chief shifted his bulk, making his chair creak ominously. He was good at that. "But you could be charged as an accessory, son."

"To *what*?" His voice rose. "Thad's death was an *accident*!"

"Maybe," the chief allowed. "But like Miss Johanssen observed, it wasn't the kind of accident it seemed. Not the kind those boys claimed it was. Wherever Thad Vanderhei drowned, it sure as hell wasn't the Kalamazoo River. And covering up the cause of death, even an accidental death, is a crime."

In the aftermath of Thad's death, there hadn't been any opportunity for Kyle Middleton and Mike Huizenga to confer with their Triton brothers face-to-face, but they could have exchanged calls or texts or e-mails. I didn't know whether they had, or if so, how much they'd revealed about what had transpired. Until that moment, I hadn't been sure whether Matthew Mollenkamp knew exactly how Thad had drowned.

Now I knew he hadn't. I saw the realization dawn over his features, a sickening awareness he couldn't hide. "Thad didn't drown in the river?"

Chief Bryant gave me an imperceptible shake of his head.

I kept silent.

"Oh, God." Mollenkamp swallowed, turning pale and sweating visibly. "Oh, fuck! I think I'm gonna be sick."

Wordlessly, I passed him the wastebasket. I was kind of hoping the whole about-to-puke thing would turn out to be an idle threat, but it wasn't. My stomach lurched in sympathy as he gagged and retched, bringing up a thin stream of clear liquid and bile.

The chief cleared his throat. "Daisy, would you be so kind as to fetch Mr. Mollenkamp some paper towels?" I rose. "And maybe something cold to drink?" he called after me.

I grabbed a couple of paper towels in the bathroom and rummaged in the departmental fridge for a can of 7UP.

"Are you getting anywhere?" Cody asked me impatiently. "Is Mollenkamp showing any signs of cracking?"

"Yep."

He sighed. "God, I wish we had a one-way mirror!"

In the conference room, I passed Matthew Mollenkamp the paper towels and the can of soda. He wiped his mouth, then rolled the cold 7UP can over his temples before cracking it open and drinking thirstily.

"Feel better?" Chief Bryant asked solicitously.

"Yeah." Mollenkamp set down the can. "Thanks."

"Ready to tell us what you know, son?" the chief inquired.

Now that he was refreshed and restored, his expression turned defensive. "About what? Thad's death? I keep telling you, I wasn't there!"

The chief gave me a slight nod.

I leaned forward in my seat. "So tell me, Matt. How do you feel about rape charges?"

He blanched. "You can't—"

"Why?" I asked steadily. "Because she wasn't human? Because she was a mythological creature without a birth certificate? Because she has no legal rights? But that doesn't mean she doesn't exist, does it? How did it feel? How did it make *you* feel? Like a god? King of the world? Like a true son of Triton, a Master of the Universe?"

"Don't—"

Righteous anger stirred in me. "Don't what? Tell the truth? Tell me, Matt: How *did* it make you feel? We're not talking about a naiad. We're talking about a mermaid, aren't we? Don't lie to me; I know she's out there. Thad drowned in *salt water*, Matt." As my wrath rose, the air pressure in the conference room intensified, smelling of ozone. Seven Deadlies be damned; I could *use* this. Stefan had once told me that in and of itself, passion was no sin. It was deeds that mattered, and this was a deed worth doing. I felt the pressure building against my eardrums and the insistent pulse of my blood beating against them. Chief Bryant grimaced and Matthew Mollenkamp winced, drawing his shoulders in tight, his hands gripping his opposite elbows. I stared at him, keeping my anger intent, focused, and under control. "Go on—tell me! I'm curious. Did you know she was unwilling? A captive? Did she struggle? Did that make it good for you? Did that make it *better* for you?"

"*No!*" he shouted. "Jesus, what's *wrong* with you?"

Trusting my own instincts this time, I didn't answer, letting my anger drain away. The chief remained silent.

That day, I learned that it's never pretty to watch someone break down entirely. Matthew Mollenkamp began to shiver, breathing fast and shallow, sweat dampening his hair. He picked up the soda can, but his hand was shaking so badly he had to set it back down. He closed his eyes and began murmuring under his breath, rocking back and forth in his chair.

It took me a moment to recognize the words to the Lord's Prayer.

The chief let him finish. "All right, son," he said in a gentle voice. "How did you get drawn into this mess?"

Mollenkamp's lips moved soundlessly. He paused, then tried again, the words emerging in a faint whisper. "There was a website."

Chief Bryant shot me an inquiring look, and I shook my head. I had no idea what he was talking about. "What website?"

"Jesus!" Mollenkamp pressed the heels of his hands against his eyes, then took a deep breath. "Oh, God!" He lowered his hands. "Okay. Okay. It's called Schtupernatural-dot-com."

"Are you serious?" The words escaped before I could censor them. "Is it what it sounds like?"

He looked at me, his mouth clenching in a rictus. "Yeah. It's a forum where anyone can post about sexual encounters with . . . things that aren't human. Photos, too. And, um, want ads, I guess you'd call them."

My tail lashed in a violent reaction. "That's sick!"

"I guess." He shrugged wearily. "What do you want? It's human nature to wonder about it."

The chief pushed a notepad across the table toward me. "So what happened?"

I fished a pen from my purse and jotted down *Schtupernatural* *.com* with a note to confirm the spelling.

Avoiding our eyes, Matthew Mollenkamp stared at the ceiling. "We used to check it out, try to guess which shots were real and which were Photoshopped. It was kind of a running joke. One day, a couple of months ago, there was a post about a Schtupernatural opportunity in Pemkowet."

Bit by bit, as the chief questioned him, the details unfolded.

The gist of it was that for three thousand dollars, the bartender at the Wheelhouse with the spiderweb tattoo would provide the buyer with a phone number and a money-back-guaranteed opportunity to fuck a real live mermaid.

La Sirena, the mermaid. It really had been right in front of me all along.

"You spent three thousand dollars on a phone number?" I murmured.

Mollenkamp lowered his gaze to give me a sickly look. "Yeah. Me and Ron. You met him last night. Three grand apiece."

"Was it worth it?" I asked.

He swallowed hard and shook his head. "No. No. It was . . . horrible. But we got what we paid for."

"And you told Thad Vanderhei and the others it *was* worth it," I said quietly. "Didn't you?"

He nodded. "What else was I supposed to do?"

I couldn't even begin to reply.

"Walk us through the sequence of events," Chief Bryant suggested. "Step by step, starting with the phone call."

Although I had high hopes, unfortunately Matthew Mollenkamp's candor was circumscribed by the reality of his limited information. He'd made the call and spoken to a man who called back after confirming that Matt and Ron had made the required payment to the bartender. A midnight rendezvous in the parking lot of the East Pemkowet public beach was arranged. The Wheelhouse matchbook with the phone number served as proof of their identity and their admission ticket to the main attraction. From the parking lot, Matt and Ron were blindfolded, ushered into a truck, and driven to an unknown destination.

There, their business was concluded. And the less said about *that*, the better.

The two things Mollenkamp was able to confirm were Ray D's identity and the fact that there was also a female ghoul present at the scene, presumably Mary Sudbury. Now that he was being honest, it was obvious that the ghouls had shaken him deeply.

"The sick thing is, we needed them there," he said, licking lips gone dry. "To take away the . . . horror. I couldn't have gone through with it otherwise."

"Poor baby," I said without sympathy. "Your precious horror was just a fucking appetizer. It's *her* suffering that's keeping them fed."

Mollenkamp looked away.

The chief scratched one ear, tugged on a thick lobe. "So you told your fraternity brothers you had a fine old time becoming Masters of the Universe, and they decided to follow in your footsteps?"

Closing his eyes, he shook his head. "Only a few, only the ones who claimed they had access to that kind of money. But when Thad called the number, it was out of service." He was silent a moment. "He accused me of bullshitting him, of making the whole thing up. I should have let him think it."

"But you didn't," I said.

"No." Mollenkamp opened his eyes. "I told him to go down to that fucking ghoul bar and ask for Ray D himself."

"Did he?" the chief prompted him.

"Yeah." He licked his lips again. "Him and Mike. That bartender, the guy with the spider tattoo, he told them to shut the fuck up, that that wasn't how it worked. That he'd give them Ray D's number, his new number, for the cash. I didn't think. . . . I don't know." His voice cracked a little. "Is that what got him in trouble? Is that why they killed him? For asking about that ghoul?"

"Is that what you think happened?" Chief Bryant asked. "You think they killed him on purpose? That it wasn't an accident?"

"I don't *know*!" Matthew Mollenkamp took a deep, shaking breath. "I don't; I really don't. I swear to God, I don't know anything about what happened that night. For Christ's sake, I thought Thad drowned in the river! I thought maybe . . . I thought maybe it was an accident that happened afterward, or maybe . . . maybe he just couldn't live with it."

"So Thad and Mike paid the bartender for the new number?" I asked him. "And they set up a meeting with Ray D?"

"Yeah." He turned his gaze back to me, eyes dull. "They did. Three grand apiece for the two of them and Kyle. It took them a couple of weeks to work up the nerve to make the call."

"Bet you gave them a hard time about that," I murmured.

Matt didn't answer.

I was pretty sure it was true. And I was pretty sure it wouldn't be easy to live with, either.

It damn well shouldn't be.

Thirty-two

After having exhausted Matthew Mollenkamp's store of information, we cut him loose. He declined the offer of a ride home, preferring to call a friend.

In the conference room, Cody slid into a seat beside me. "So what do we know?"

"Well, he confirmed a lot of what we suspected," I said. "Two ghouls, one Ray D and one unnamed female matching the description of Mary Sudbury. And they were working with Jerry Dunham." I glanced at the chief. "Do you think there's any chance Thad was killed for asking about Ray D?"

"No." Chief Bryant's rebuttal was immediate and certain. "It doesn't add up. No reason to let the others live if it were. I'm sure we're looking at an accidental death and a cover-up. And I'm afraid Daisy was right."

"They've got a mermaid?" Cody asked in a tense tone.

"Yeah." I felt sick all over again, a leaden weight in my belly. I shouldn't have eaten that hot dog. "They've got a mermaid. That's how you become a Master of the Universe and a true son of Triton."

Green flared behind his eyes, and his voice dropped to a fierce growl. "*Where?*"

"Take it easy, Cody," the chief said to him. "Keep a cool head. Don't let it get personal."

He struggled to contain himself. "With all due respect, sir, I'm not sure that's possible. I'm not sure you can understand."

I wondered whether Chief Bryant knew Cody had lost a girl he might have loved, a girl whose killer would never be brought to justice because she was a wolf when he shot her.

"We're not out of the woods yet, son." By the compassion in the chief's voice, maybe he did. "We don't have a *where*. The boys were blindfolded and driven to the destination. Daisy?"

I consulted my notes. "Mollenkamp said it was maybe a ten-, fifteen-minute drive from the parking lot of the East Pemkowet beach. The vehicle made a lot of turns, so they could have been driving in circles. He remembers hearing the wind rustling in the trees when they got out of the truck, so we're looking for a wooded area."

"That doesn't exactly narrow it down," Cody muttered. "What about the site?"

"Ground floor of a residence," I said. "He said it looked like a high-end rec room, the kind you'd design if money was no object. Pool table, built-in bar, home theater . . . and an industrial-size fish tank that wasn't part of the original design."

Cody looked as sick as I felt. "Jesus!"

"I'm thinking they must be squatting somewhere," Chief Bryant said. "My best guess would be a house for sale that's been off the market since the spring. Or maybe an unoccupied summer home."

"Any way to get a list of those?" Cody asked.

The chief shrugged. "Start calling local Realtors. As far as summer homes go, other than the local grapevine, not much way to tell as long as they're paying their property taxes. Maybe try the township clerk, see if anyone's delinquent. That could be an indicator."

"Okay. Okay." Cody ran a hand over his bronze-stubbled chin. "What about the Vanderhei kid's friends? At this point, we've got more than enough evidence to subpoena them."

"We do." The chief nodded. "But time's not on our side. I'll put a call in to Sheriff Barnard and let him know exactly what we're dealing with here." His expression was somber. "I don't think any of the families involved will be interested in seeing this play out in the public eye once they know what their sons have been up to."

Cody shuddered. "No, I wouldn't think so. How the hell did this even *happen*? How did a bunch of frat boys from Van Buren end up here?"

"According to Matthew Mollenkamp, there was a website," I said. He gave me a blank look. "A website?"

"Uh-huh." I went to fetch the department's laptop, opened a browser, and typed in *Schtupernatural.com*.

Yep, there was a website.

All three of us stared at it in fascinated revulsion. The banner at the top featured a graphic with someone's idea of a fairy, a pretty, sparkly fairy with gossamer wings that Amanda Brooks would approve of, kneeling in ecstasy as a faceless mundane man hammered her from behind, her head thrown back, her silvery lips rounding in orgasmic pleasure. The protruding green nipples and cobweb hair were a nice touch.

The site was cross-indexed by species and locale. I clicked through a handful of links. Some of the posts were obviously fake, like the entire vampire forum. I'm sorry, but vampires simply don't show up in photographs.

Others looked . . . real.

"That's not right." Cody pointed a shaking finger at a photo of a werewolf in midshift braced between the spread thighs of a mortal woman, a ridge of sprouting hair running down his spine, his snarling, distorted face pressed against her shoulder, all wrinkled muzzle and pointy teeth. "It's not!"

"It's all right, son," the chief murmured. "Daisy, I think we've seen enough."

I found the want ads. "I just want to check something." I did a quick search for Pemkowet and came up empty. "Okay, the site's been scrubbed. Dunham must have deleted his posts."

"As Lord Stefan Muckety-Muck observed, the unfeeling have a strong sense of self-preservation." Cody's tone was bitter.

"Yeah." I closed the laptop. "Someone tech-savvy could probably retrieve them if it came to it. So what now, Chief? How do you want us to proceed?"

He leaned back in his chair, his deceptively sleepy eyes half-lidded. "At this point? As far as I'm concerned, we have two priorities." He lifted one finger. "The first is finding the remaining victim in this tragedy. If she's out there, we need to find her. Fast. Before they decide she's too big a liability and get rid of her. Cody?"

Cody nodded. "I'm on it, sir."

"The second is keeping a lid on the tension in town." His gaze shifted to me. "How did your meeting with Amanda Brooks go?"

Unable to help myself, I made a face. "She wants me to keep vampires off the streets and put pretty, sparkly fairies on them. Preferably at prearranged times suitable for paranormal tourism."

The implacable weight of his gaze pressed on me. "I'd say that's a damn fine idea if it's doable. Is it?"

I sighed. "I'm on it, sir."

Although it felt like it ought to be nearly time for bed, in fact it was barely past two o'clock in the afternoon yet. Checking my phone as I exited the station, I found a voice mail from Mom, sounding a bit worried. Feeling guilty at having neglected her, I called her on my way to the Fabulous Casimir's shop.

"Hey, Daisy, baby!" Her voice brightened. "Everything okay?"

"Yeah. Just busy. I've been working long hours."

"I know." She sounded sympathetic. "Lurine told me. She said you stayed at her place last night, and left at the crack of dawn."

I yawned. "Don't remind me."

"But you're all right?"

"Yeah." I smiled fondly at the concern in her voice. "Remember Meg Mucklebones? From behind the Cassopolises' place? She almost got Jen's little brother, Brandon, this morning."

She drew a sharp breath. "Oh, Daisy!"

"It's okay." Tucking the phone under my chin, I touched *daudadagr*'s hilt. "Honest, I swear. I got her to back down." I wanted to tell her about my father and the whole temptation scenario, bat wings and fiery whip and all, but with tourists already eyeing the girl with the phone pressed to her ear and the rather large dagger on her hip, I figured it had better wait. "Look, I can't talk long. I just wanted you to know I was fine. And your reading's been really, really helpful."

"Oh?"

I nodded. "Yeah. Pieces are falling into place. Everything but the arrows. *Las Jaras*, right? Any thoughts?"

"No," she said apologetically. "I wish I did. Has everything else been as literal as the bottle?"

I thought about *La Sirena*. "Very much so."

"Keep it in mind," she suggested.

"Thanks. I will." I'd arrived at Casimir's shop. "Okay, I've got to go. Love you!"

"Love you, too, Daisy, baby!" Mom blew a kiss into the phone. "Be careful. Be safe, honey!"

"I will," I promised before ending the call.

Bells chimed as I opened the door to the Sisters of Selene. The Fabulous Casimir, leaning on one elbow behind the counter, glanced up as I entered. Today he was sporting powder-white makeup, a geisha-style wig, and an ornate kimono.

I found the sight heartening.

"Hey, there, Miss Daisy," he greeted me. "I've been asking around in certain circles, and I have a piece of news for you." He shook his finger at me. "I didn't know whether or not I should call the station with this. And you didn't give me your personal phone number."

"I didn't?"

"No."

Well, that was an incredibly stupid oversight. *Way to go, Daisy.* I winced. "Oh, crap. I'm sorry. What do you have for me?"

Casimir fished a file from under the counter, passing it to me. "I got this from a coven in Seattle and printed it out for you. Dr. Midnight's Traveling Sideshow's one true thing."

I flipped through the file.

The images were grainy and low-resolution, scans of screen captures. But all of them showed the same thing: a mermaid in a tank, her face contorted with an expression that was meant to convey pleasure, but was more likely distress. And on every image, there was a different phone number to call.

Casimir watched me beneath his artificial lashes. "They were pimping her, Daisy. Is that what's happening here?"

"Yeah," I said softly. "We think so. How did this happen, Cas?"

He shook his bewigged head. "All anyone knows is that she vanished after Dr. Midnight's carnival was shut down in Seattle. What do *you* know?"

I stared at the images. "I think someone stole her. One of the carnies." I glanced up at him. "Thanks—this helps. And I promise we're doing everything we can to find her. But that's not why I'm here."

The Fabulous Casimir arched his painted eyebrows. "Oh?"

"I need cowslip dew," I informed him.

He looked dubious. "It's expensive. And it doesn't work as well as it does if you harvest it yourself."

"I know." I fully planned on invoicing the PVB for the cost. "But I need it in a hurry. Do cowslips even grow around here?"

"No, but primroses work. Didn't you ever try it when you were little?"

I sighed. "Yeah, and I'll gather the acorn caps myself, but I don't have time to harvest that much dew. How much is it, anyway?"

Casimir withdrew a little key on a long chain from beneath the folds of his kimono and emerged from behind the counter to unlock an apothecary case with glass doors. He plucked a stoppered flagon filled with clear liquid from an upper shelf. "It's three hundred dollars an ounce, Daisy," he said with sympathy. "And I can only get it in three-ounce containers."

Gah! "Can you sell me a third of a bottle?"

"No can do, sweetheart," he said. "Once the seal's broken, the magic starts to evaporate."

"Okay." Nine hundred bucks for a bottle of dew. I took out my credit card, calculating how much I had left on my limit. I really, really hoped the PVB didn't quibble at the cost. Also that they paid their invoices promptly, or I was going to have a hell of a time making my rent next month. "There's no invocation, is there? I never used one as a kid, but it didn't always work, either."

"No, but to do it properly, you need a spotless, round white tablecloth, preferably Irish linen." The Fabulous Casimir nodded at the door with a sour look. "Try across the street. I used to stock them, but they undercut my prices."

An Irish linen tablecloth from the Elegant Table set me back another eighty bucks. I was beginning to realize I'd gotten off cheap summoning naiads. Apparently fairies were a lot pricier when you went the commercial route. No wonder the naiads took offense.

After depositing my purchases and the file on Dr. Midnight's star attraction in my apartment, I ducked into the park, where there were a couple of spectacular old oak trees. I hunted around beneath their shade, scrabbling my fingers through the thin grass that grew there, rooting in the hard-packed dirt. In mid-July, it was harder than you might think to find acorn caps.

"Whatcha doin'?" a small voice asked me.

I looked up to see a chubby boy some six or seven years old, wearing a striped shirt, khaki shorts, and kid-size Crocs on his feet, watching me gravely. "Looking for acorn caps."

"Why?"

"Because I want to have a tea party for some fairies." I sat back on my heels. "Where are your parents?"

He pointed toward a pair of exhausted-looking women seated on a park bench surrounded by shopping bags. "That's Mom and Aunt Nancy. They've been shopping all day long. Can I come to your tea party?"

"No," I said. "I don't think that's a good idea. Fairies are very shy."

"Oh." With perfect unselfconsciousness, he rooted around in one nostril with his finger, and okay, ew, but I kind of liked the kid's aplomb. He pulled out his finger and inspected the tip. "Can I help you look?"

The nearby rhododendron bushes rustled, and Mogwai deigned to make an appearance, winding around the boy's Croc-strapped ankles and purring.

Boogers notwithstanding, I felt an inexplicable surge of tenderness. "Sure, why not? What's your name?"

He beamed at me. "Jake."

"Hi, Jake." I smiled back at him. "I'm Daisy."

It turned out to be a smart move. When it came to finding acorn caps, Jake was like one of those truffle-hunting pigs in France. With his help, I soon had a good twenty-some nubby, hollow caps.

With the pockets of my jeans filled, I walked him over to the park bench. His mother looked up wearily. "I'm sorry. Was he bothering you?"

"No," I said. "Not at all."

She did a double take as *dauda-dagr* registered, nudging Aunt Nancy with one elbow. Both of them gaped at me.

I ignored them. "Thanks, Jake. You were a big help."

He nodded, his eyes wide and earnest, his bangs flopping over his forehead. "Will you say hello to the fairies for me?"

"Absolutely," I promised him.

Thirty-three

I had everything I needed, and I had an idea.

No, two ideas.

First I called Jen. I got her voice mail. "Hey, girl!" I said. "Looks like I'm on a mission for the PVB, and I've got to pay a visit to Twilight Manor tonight. If you want to ride shotgun, let me know."

She might or she might not. I wasn't sure. We'd gone out there a few times over the years to check on her sister, Bethany, and try in vain to convince her to leave. But let's face it: It's a scary and deeply creepy place. After this morning's adventure, Jen would either be more inclined than usual to give Bethany a piece of her mind for abandoning her family, or more inclined than usual to let her waste away out there. Either way, I couldn't really blame her.

Next, I called Sinclair Palmer. "Hi," I said when he answered. "It's Daisy Johanssen. We met earlier today?"

He laughed. "You think that's something I'm likely to forget, sistah?"

I smiled. "Look, the chief of police wants me to get on this PR business. I'm going to try doing a little outreach with some pretty, sparkly fairies for you. Want to come?"

There was a brief silence on the other end. "Are you kidding? I'd give my left hand for the chance."

"Not worth it." I shook my head. "Trust me. Where are you? I'll pick you up."

He gave me the address of a rental house out in the countryside just north of town. Ten minutes later, I pulled into the driveway and parked next to an old double-decker tour bus. It was bright yellow, red, and green, with PEMKOWET SUPERNATURAL TOURS painted on either side.

"Wow," I said as Sinclair emerged from the house. "You must have been pretty confident."

He shrugged. "I took a chance. My father works at a custom auto shop." He patted the bus. "The paint job was a birthday present."

"Nice. Are you and your dad close?"

"Yeah, I guess so." There was a faint note of reservation in his tone. He laughed self-consciously. "And I guess I have to say I hope you aren't, eh?"

"Oh, believe me, I'm not. But my mom's great. What happened with my father wasn't her fault." I glanced at my watch. "We should get going. Ready?"

"Ready." In the Honda, Sinclair pulled out a folded map of Pemkowet produced by the PVB. "I've mapped out a route that covers a lot of historical highlights." He traced it with one finger. "That ancient librarian's been a big help with the research. You know the one I mean? Looks like she's a hundred and fifty years old? I think she actually remembers a lot of this stuff."

"The Sphinx?"

He looked startled. "Is *that* what she is?"

"That's what I've always heard." I was curious. "What does her aura look like?"

Sinclair frowned. "It's very . . . muted. I assumed it was because she's so old. Sometimes that happens when people are near the end of their lives. But maybe it's because she's powerful enough to suppress it."

"Is that how it works?" I asked.

"I don't know," he admitted. "I'm learning as I go. If I'd stayed with my mother—" He fell silent.

Ohh-kay. I had a feeling it wasn't a time to pry. "Don't worry," I assured him. "I'm making it up as I go along, too. I can't guarantee this summoning will work, and even if it does, it could backfire. Asking fairies to conform to anything that resembles order is a lot like herding cats."

He tapped the map on his thigh. At the risk of repeating myself, I have to say it was exactly the right kind of muscular. Must be all the bicycling. "Was it incredibly stupid of me to bring a *map* to show them?"

"Honestly?" I said. "I have absolutely no idea."

The destination I'd chosen was an overgrown meadow behind a site just off the highway where a small motel had once stood. It had been condemned and torn down ages ago, and no one had developed the property since. The nature preserve might have seemed like a better bet, but at this time of day, there was a good chance of running into tourists, and I needed privacy.

We hiked past a stand of pine trees and into the center of the meadow, which was filled with indigenous plants and wildflowers— Queen Anne's lace, chicory, butterfly weed, hawkweed, joe-pye weed . . . come to think of it, a lot of perfectly lovely flowers with rather unfortunate names. We even passed one of Mr. Leary's writing spiders, almost as big as the palm of my hand, with vivid yellow and black markings, sitting in the center of its web. Sure enough, a zigzagging ladder bisected the spiral orb of its web. I checked discreetly to make sure nothing was written there.

With Sinclair's help, I trampled down a circle and spread the white linen tablecloth on the ground. Emptying my pockets of acorn caps, I placed them around the rim of the cloth, making sure they were spaced evenly and nestled securely in place.

Sinclair watched with a bemused look as I pulled the stopper on the flagon, breaking the seal, and began carefully filling each acorn cap to the brim. "What is that?"

"Nine hundred dollars' worth of cowslip dew," I said, concentrating on not spilling it. "So let's hope this works." When I was finished, I still had half a bottle of dew left. Not sure what to do with it, I left it open and placed it in the center of the tablecloth.

"Okay," he said. "What happens now?"

I sat cross-legged in front of one of the acorn-cap place settings, and pointed at the setting opposite me. "We wait."

Still looking bemused, Sinclair took a seat on the other side of the tablecloth.

Although it was late afternoon by now, in mid-July the sun was still high. It beat down on us. I could hear birdsong and the faint drone of cars on the highway. Even through my jeans, the meadow grass was prickly. Minutes passed, feeling like hours. Hell, maybe it was hours. I fought the urge to shift and scratch. My pent-up tail wriggled in futile protest.

Maybe this was a stupid idea—

No, wait.

"*There,*" Sinclair breathed, his brown eyes widening. "Behind you!"

I swallowed. "Behind *you.*"

His gaze shifted. "And there—"

"And over there," I added.

Okay, I'd dealt with fairies before, but never so many at the same time. And I'll admit it was surprisingly intimidating. Emerging from the meadow and shedding their glamours, a dozen or more descended on the feast I'd laid out for them. Tilted catlike eyes glittered feverishly. Long, attenuated fingers with too many joints snatched up the acorn caps, tossing back the contents into mouths lined with unnervingly keen little teeth. Translucent wings fluttered, making the air around them sparkle. Golden sunlight fell on green skin, lavender skin, pale blue skin. And yes, they were very, very pretty—but scary, too.

Sinclair Palmer gazed around him in wonder, and then yelped. "Ow!" he said in protest. "Hey! You pulled my hair!"

"Ooh, look," one of the lavender-skinned fairies said to another, stroking Sinclair's short woolly dreads. "It's already in elf-locks."

"Ooh!"

I cleared my throat and raised my rune-marked left hand. "Hello? Hel's liaison. Can we talk?"

The fairy nearest me sported greenish skin, an aureole of lacy white hair, and deep-purple eyes. She eyed *dauda-dagr*'s hilt and hissed, baring her pointed teeth. "It's cold and it *hurts*, half-breed!"

"Too bad," I said ruthlessly. "We need your help."

Her narrow nostrils flared. "Take thy weapon away!"

I shook my head. "Not a chance."

"Daisy?" Sinclair's voice was faint and uncertain. "Um . . . help?"

Be careful what you wish for, right? Fairies swarmed him, laughing and shrieking and buzzing like a flock of locusts, crawling over him, stroking his hair and skin, tugging fondly at his dreadlocks. One with a fiery shock of red-orange hair the color of hawkweed helpfully refilled an acorn cap with dew and shoved it between his lips, forcing him to drink, spluttering.

I drew *dauda-dagr*. "Enough!"

There was a pause. I experienced a fleeting moment of satisfaction.

"Uh-oh," murmured a fairy with pale purple hair piled atop her head in clumps, looking for all the world like a stalk of joe-pye weed. "Uh-oh!"

All of them gazed in the same direction.

I did, too.

Oh, crap. It wasn't my drawing *dauda-dagr* that had given the fairies pause after all. It was something a lot more imposing. I hadn't reckoned on eldritch royalty, but apparently that was what I'd gotten. He stood motionless on the far outskirts of the meadow beneath the dappled camouflage of trees.

Time slowed down.

"Daisy?"

I climbed to my feet, beckoning for Sinclair to follow suit. All the fairies kept silent as the Oak King approached, not so much as a single wing fluttering.

I'd heard rumors of the Oak King's existence, but I didn't know anyone who claimed to have seen him—and believe me, you'd remember. His skin was acorn-brown, his hair the color of oak leaves in autumn, antlers rising from the thick, springing curls over his temples. A long cloak hung from his shoulders. One minute it appeared to be deerskin; the next, it looked to be woven of leaves and moss. He moved soundlessly across the meadow, and it seemed almost as though the meadow shrank at the same time, the trees pressing in closer around us. When he reached us, or we reached him, leaf shadows still stippled his tall figure.

I went to one knee without thinking, according him the same respect I would to Hel herself. Sinclair did the same without being prompted.

"Hel's liaison, I believe." The Oak King's voice was deep and resonant, but there was a hushed quality to it, too, like the stillness at noon in the depths of a forest. "What is it you come seeking?"

I rose, sheathing *dauda-dagr.* "Aid, Your Majesty." As I stood in front of him, the specifics of the request sounded too ridiculous to put into words. "I don't know if you're aware—"

"A boy has died, yes." He inclined his antlered head. "You seek justice for him." He gestured at the fairies, quiet and clustered together, looking for all the world like misbehaving children sobering in their father's presence. "But you will find none here. My people are innocent in this matter."

I cleared my throat. "Um, yeah. I know. Actually, we're here to ask for their help with public relations."

"Oh?" There was a world of patience in his deep brown eyes. It gave me courage to voice the absurd.

"Tourists come to Pemkowet looking for wonder," I said. "And your people are among the most wondrous. We're asking that some of them reveal themselves. At, um, regularly scheduled times and places. This is Sinclair Palmer," I said, indicating him. "He's proposing a . . . a tour bus route."

Sinclair got to his feet and offered a stiff bow. "I have a map," he added faintly.

The Oak King stood motionless for a long time. At last he lifted his gaze to the sky, then glanced around the meadow, settling it on the clustered fairies. They huddled closer together, wings vibrating ever so slightly. "There is too little wonder left in the world," the Oak King said in a thoughtful tone. "It should be cherished and protected. I realize that this requires the cooperation of mortals, who are so often quick to destroy what they fear. These smallest of people are not always mindful of this."

My tail twitched hopefully. "Does that mean you'll help?"

He looked at Sinclair. "Let me see this . . . map."

Sinclair pulled it from his pocket, unfolded it, and held it out in one trembling hand. "I've, um, marked the spots I thought might be suitable, Your Majesty. And, uh, tours would leave every hour on the hour between ten a.m. and four p.m."

The Oak King took the map from him, and I swear to God, it turned into a parchment scroll in his hand. He studied it.

I held my breath.

"Yes," he said at length. "In these times, I find this to be a reasonable request." He returned the scroll to Sinclair, whereupon it promptly turned back into a map. "I will see to it. It will be done."

I let out my breath.

"Thank you!" Sinclair's voice was joyous. "Thank you, thank you!"

The Oak King held up one hand. "I make no promise in perpetuity. It stands for as long as I deem it reasonable." His gaze shifted to me, deep and grave. "Are you near unto finding justice, Hel's liaison?"

I nodded. "Very close, Your Majesty."

His gaze fell on *dauda-dagr*. "You bear a dire weapon, one that chills even my immortal soul. Hel places great faith in you."

"I'm trying to be worthy of it," I said humbly.

"That is well." Unexpectedly, the Oak King reached out and laid one brown, sinewy hand on my brow. I felt a rush of warmth, rich and golden, filled with all the green, growing scents of summer. "As below, so above." He withdrew his hand, turning it palm upward. A silver whistle in the shape of an acorn lay nestled within it. "Accordingly, I give you my own token. You have but to blow it to beseech an audience."

I took it gingerly.

He smiled. "Well done, Hel's liaison."

"Thank you, Your Majesty. And, um . . . it's Daisy," I said. "Sorry, I forgot to introduce myself. Daisy Johanssen."

The Oak King's smile deepened. "Yes, I know. Well done, Daisy Johanssen."

"Thank—"

He was gone.

It happened . . . *Oh, gah!* I don't even know how to describe how it happened, other than fast. Between the space of one breath and the next, the Oak King was gone and the meadow got bigger again. Sinclair Palmer and I stood staring at each other beside a white table-cloth scattered with acorn caps and a huddle of fairies.

A soft breeze blew over the meadow, bending the grasses and wildflowers.

The fairies stirred.

One of them, the Queen Anne's lace fairy with the white hair and purple eyes, snatched the half-empty flagon of cowslip dew from the center of the tablecloth. "Thou hast what thou came for," she spat at me in disdain, clutching the flagon to her narrow chest. "I claim the spoils of thine endeavor!"

"Go right ahead." I pocketed the silver acorn whistle the Oak

King had given me, and began folding the tablecloth. "Oh, and by the way? A little boy named Jake says hello. He helped me put this feast together, so if you ever meet him, be nice."

She hissed at me, baring eel-sharp teeth.

I eyed her. "Also? If you make an appearance, be sure to smile with your mouth closed."

Thirty-four

Sinclair and I didn't speak much as I drove him home, both of us pretty well awed by what we'd just witnessed.

"That was extraordinary, wasn't it?" he asked when I dropped him off. He still sounded dazed. "Tell me that was extraordinary, because if it wasn't, I'm really bugging out here, and I don't bug out easily."

I nodded. "Yeah. That was extraordinary. I don't know anyone who's seen the Oak King. What did his aura look like? Was it muted, too?"

Sinclair shook his head. "No. No, it was . . . huge. Like the sun rising behind a mountain." He gazed into the distance. "Or maybe setting," he added softly. "Like maybe it rose a long time ago."

I thought I knew what he meant. "Let's hope it doesn't set anytime soon."

"Agreed." Returning from the distance, he gave me a fist bump and a grin. "Respect, sistah! I and I owe you one."

I fist-bumped him back. "I and I'll keep it in mind."

It wasn't quite five o'clock by the time I returned to my apartment. I checked my phone and found a text from Jen saying she wanted to come with me tonight, and would swing by around ten p.m. I sent her a text to confirm, then called the station in case there was some news no one had thought to pass on to me.

There wasn't, so I decided to do the sensible thing and take a nap. It had already been an incredibly long day, one in a series of very long days.

I drew the curtains and put Patsy Cline on the stereo. Not traditional blues, I know, but close enough. Something about the effortlessness of her vocals and the soulful ache beneath them works for me. I drifted to sleep to the sound of Patsy singing about walking after midnight and searching, always searching, and had a long, confused dream in which I was walking endlessly down moonlit country roads, beneath the rustling shadow of oak trees, searching for something or someone I never found.

When I woke, it was close to sunset. The awe of my encounter with the Oak King lingered, but I felt melancholy, too. I flipped through the printouts Casimir had given me, studying the mermaid's distorted face.

Patsy Cline may have been looking for her true love, but *I* was looking for a captive mermaid. And if we didn't find her in time, I had a bad feeling about her chances for survival. For all we knew, it was already too late.

With a reluctant sigh, I set the file aside. Maybe Cody had found a lead or two today, and we could run them down tomorrow. Right now, there was nothing I could do for her, and the chief had been very clear that he wanted me working on the PVB's requests.

I managed to wash my face and slurp down another container of microwaved ramen noodles before I heard the familiar sound of Jen's old LeBaron convertible pulling into the alley and dashed downstairs to join her. "You okay with driving?"

She shrugged. "Might as well. It beats trying to find a parking space."

"Okay."

In some ways it felt like old times, taking the LeBaron out to the House of Shadows on a balmy summer night. Even though I'd done it before, I still had a knot of anxiety in the pit of my belly. Vampires will do that to you. The first time had been the hardest, with fear of the unknown making my entire body fizz with nervous energy. But this time was different, too. It was my second time making the trip as Hel's liaison, but this time I had *dauda-dagr* on my hip, a weapon capable of killing the immortal undead, a weapon that chilled even the Oak King's soul. Not to mention the Oak King's token in my pocket.

"So why's the PVB sending you out to Twilight Manor?" Jen asked, pulling onto the highway.

"Damage control," I said. "I'm supposed to tell Lady Eris to make sure her bloodsuckers stay off the streets for a while."

She shot me a startled look. "Really?" I nodded. "Damn, Amanda Brooks has bigger balls than I realized."

I laughed. "No kidding."

"Did you see the delightful Stacey?" she asked.

I flashed a devil-horns sign at her. "Yep."

"Oh, for God's sake." Jen made a face. "She didn't! Grow up already."

"Oh, yes, she did," I said. "But I met a new guy there, too. We're working together a bit on this PR thing. He's kind of cute, and actually a normal human being." Well, except for seeing auras, and whatever secret he accidentally alluded to regarding his mother.

"So what happened to the hot ghoul?"

"Nothing," I said. "Except, um, I let him taste me, and now he's sort of tuned in to me. And I'm kind of weirded out about it."

"You *bonded* with him?" Jen's voice rose in alarm. "Jesus, Daise! You of all people ought to know better!"

"I didn't do it on purpose! It was an emergency. And it's not like a vampire blood-bond," I assured her. At least, I didn't *think* it was. "There's no binding obligation or anything. It's just . . . Okay, like this morning, when I blew up at Meg Mucklebones, Stefan sensed it. And he came to check and make sure I was all right. End of story."

Jen yawned. "Sorry. Wow, was that really just this morning?"

"Yeah," I said. "Long day for you, too?"

"Yeah." Lifting one hand from the wheel, she knuckled her eyes. "On top of getting up at the crack of dawn this morning and dealing with Brandon's near-death experience at the hands of Meg freaking Mucklebones, we've got owners coming into town for two different properties this weekend. Both of them needed a full top-to-bottom scouring."

"Bummer—" I smacked my forehead. "Oh, crap! *Crap!* I'm an idiot."

She glanced at me. "Huh?"

"Your dad works as a caretaker, right?" Jesus, even allowing for lack of sleep and a hangover, I really was an idiot for not having thought of it right away. "So if there are summer homes sitting empty for months on end, he'd be the guy to ask about it?"

"Sure." Jen looked confused. "I mean, he subcontracts some of the long-term stuff that doesn't require a lot of hands-on maintenance, but yeah. Anyway, he should have records somewhere. Why?"

I shook my head, fishing in my purse for my phone. "Can't tell you. Sorry, no offense. It has to do with the case." I dialed Cody, got his voice mail, and left him a terse message about interviewing Mr. Cassopolis.

Jen stole another glance at me as she turned off the highway. "Girlfriend, I have the feeling you've got *way* too much on your plate."

I leaned back against the headrest. "You can say that again."

All jokes about Twilight Manor aside, the House of Shadows really *was* a mansion. It was built near the Lake Michigan coastline by a wealthy inventor in the 1920s as a summer getaway capable of housing his entire extended family, and sold off after his death and the decline of the family's fortune in the 1940s.

Drawn by the irresistible magnet of a functioning underworld and the promise of a lack of the scrutiny that the close confines of urban living entailed, a brood of vampires moved into the estate. The actual purchase was made by their mistress, the wealthy and beautiful Lady Eris, surname unknown, original birth name probably something far more prosaic, like Rhoda or Michelle.

It was fully dark outside when Jen pulled into the long driveway, but all the many lights in the windows of the House of Shadows were ablaze, the sounds of music and laughter emanating from the mansion.

There were a handful of cars in the drive. We parked beside an impressive water feature, a circular pond with fountains jetting, koi fish idling beneath the dimpled surface, their scales glinting gold and crimson and ivory in the illuminated green water.

Jen shuddered in the warm air.

"You okay?" I asked her softly.

"Yeah." She got out of the LeBaron, her expression grim. "Let's do this. I want to give Bethany a piece of my mind."

I touched *dauda-dagr*'s hilt. "Okay."

I rapped vigorously on the door knocker, and despite everything, I found myself catching my breath when a vampire opened the door in answer.

He was just so . . . undead.

You don't realize how much you take for granted the fact that people, including the vast majority of eldritch beings, have pulses until you encounter someone who doesn't, someone who doesn't even breathe unless it's to speak. And suddenly I was sixteen again, filled with more bravado than courage, brimming with fear, righteous anger, mortal loneliness, and the simple human desire to impress a potential friend. I hated when that happened.

Steeling myself, I raised the rune-marked palm of my left hand. "Hi," I said. "Daisy Johanssen. Remember me?"

The vampire inclined his head. "I do."

"May we enter?" I asked. "My friend Jennifer would like a word with her sister, Bethany. And I need to speak to Lady Eris."

The vampire hesitated. He was a tall guy with longish blond hair, strong, aristocratic features, and that bloodless, milk-white pallor to his skin. His gaze dropped to the dagger on my hip. "You are not welcome bearing that weapon," he said in a stiff tone. "Remove it, and you may enter."

Oh, good. I felt badass again. "Hel gave this to me with her own hand," I said. "The left hand, the hand of death? It stays." I raised my eyebrows at him. "Or if you like, we'll wait outside. You can send them out to us. We can talk on the terrace."

Like many eldritch, vampires are big into the whole hierarchical thing, maybe bigger than most. He curled his upper lip at the implied insult, revealing the tips of his fangs. "The mortal girl may wait for her sister if she wishes. But Lady Eris does not come to you, halfling. *You* go to *her.*"

"First of all, halflings are hobbits," I informed him. I'd had enough of that particular erroneous slur from the naiads. "I'm a half-*breed*, thank you very much. Second . . ." I slid a couple inches of *dauda-dagr*'s shiny blade clear of the sheath. "I gave you two options. Pick one."

He actually took a step backward. "Wait here."

"Um, I'd be fine with talking to Bethany out on the terrace," Jen volunteered. The vampire closed the door in our faces. She shot me an apologetic look. "Sorry. Didn't mean to undermine you."

"It's okay," I said. "I don't blame you."

Several minutes later the blond vampire returned with Bethany in tow—or, more accurately, draped over his arm. I winced at the sight. She was a pretty girl. She and Jen looked a lot alike, actually, only Bethany was far too thin, brown eyes overbright in sunken hollows, her skin ashen. A set of fresh puncture wounds on her throat looked black in the light spilling from the open door.

"Hey, sister buzz-kill," she said languorously to Jen. "What crawled up your ass and died?"

"I don't know," Jen retorted. "What died and crawled up *your* ass?"

There were times I regretted being an only child. This wasn't one of them.

The vampire peeled Bethany off his arm and gave her a little shove. "Go speak with your sister."

She pouted at him. "Do I have to?"

"Yes," he said ruthlessly. "Our mistress has acceded to the request. Do you wish to disobey her?"

Her eyes widened and she shook her head like a scolded child. "No, no! I'll go. I'll talk to her."

Jen and I exchanged a glance.

"Lady Eris will receive you, *half-breed*," the vampire said disdainfully to me. "Sheath your blade and follow me."

Oops. I shoved *dauda-dagr* all the way back into its sheath and followed him into the House of Shadows.

One thing about vampires: They definitely know how to throw a soirée. As far as I could tell, life at the House of Shadows was an ongoing party—only the party favors were human. I tried not to look too closely at what was going on in dimly lit corners as the blond vampire led me up a majestic staircase to the ballroom upstairs.

In its own macabre way, it was an elegant scene. Vampires are a picky bunch. Oh, they'll feed on pretty much anyone in a pinch, but they're very choosy about who they change. As a result, they tend to be quite attractive, aside from the whole creepy undead vibe they give off. They move with a preternatural grace that hints at their predator's speed and strength. They dress well, too, although they tend to favor clothing that looks like it comes from a different century.

Predictable, yes—and yet effective.

Lady Eris was ensconced on a thronelike chair with a high back of padded red velvet at the far end of the ballroom, clad in a black lace gown with a plunging décolletage that showed off her motion-less cleavage. I'd met her briefly the first time we'd come here, just long enough for her to confirm that I was indeed a member of the eldritch community before dismissing me as not worth her while.

I had a feeling this time it would be different.

Her gaze pinned me as the throng of partygoers parted at my approach, shying instinctively away from *dauda-dagr*'s presence. Lady Eris's delicate jawline tightened and her long white fingers drummed on the arms of her chair, but she showed no other signs of discomfort. She looked younger than I remembered, but then again, I wasn't a teenager anymore.

"Welcome." Her voice was neutral. "Pansy, isn't it?"

"Daisy."

"Daisy." Unexpectedly, her voice shifted out of neutral into drive, which, for a vampire, means full-on hypnotic seduction mode. *Uh-oh.* The weight of her gaze intensified. Lady Eris curved her red lips in a smile, careful not to show teeth. "Come." She indicated an ottoman before her. "Take a seat."

"Thanks, but I'd rather—"

"Sit," she crooned.

Oh, great. My vulnerable mortal half betrayed me. I found myself sitting on the ottoman without any conscious recollection of having done so, gazing up at Pemkowet's vampire mistress. Lady Eris was straight out of central casting, with wide-set eyes almost as black as my own, raven tresses caught back in a chignon, and bone-white skin so luminous it almost seemed lit from within.

Those white, white fingers stroked my cheek, cold and undead, and yet . . . *gah.* My tail twitched with involuntary pleasure. Okay, so maybe it wasn't just the mortal half. Goddamn eldritch Kinsey scale. "Such warm skin," she mused. "You run hot, little half-breed. It makes for a delightful contrast, don't you think?"

A shiver that wasn't entirely distaste ran over me. "I don't know," I managed to say. "But it sure as hell freaked out my pediatricians."

Her crimson fingernails raked over my skin. "Do you really wish to offer me further offense?" she inquired.

My mind had gone temporarily blank. "Um . . . no?"

"You wished to speak to me." One finger pressed lightly against my temple. My obedient head bent sideways, baring my neck. "So, speak." Leaning down, Lady Eris inhaled deeply and deliberately. "Or not," she whispered in my ear, her fangs grazing my earlobe. "I suspect that your blood must taste deliciously of brimstone and ichor, my dear."

Such a cliché, right? What I wanted to say was that someone had been watching a few too many episodes of *True Blood*. And yet . . . *gah!* I couldn't even begin to make myself formulate words. The blankness in my mind spread to make way for wonderfully depraved thoughts. I'd never really gotten how someone like Bethany could so readily enter into a blood-bond with a vampire, but I'd never been the target of an attempted seduction before. The shadows pressed in on me, a dark voice whispering how *good* it would feel when those fangs pierced my skin and sank deep into my flesh, those ice-cold lips pressed against my throat to drink—better than sex, better than anything, an intimacy and ecstasy beyond anything I could imagine. My blood throbbed in my veins, begging for release.

A rill of unholy laughter ran around the ballroom, amused and contemptuous.

It pissed me off.

I sat with my head craned at an awkward angle. "Okay, all appearances to the contrary, I do *not* consent to this," I muttered.

"You're sure?" Lady Eris sounded dubious.

"Very." With a considerable effort of will, I shifted my left hand to *dauda-dagr*'s hilt, wrapping my fingers around it. It emanated a different kind of cold, clean and bracing. "You've made your point," I said under my breath. "I'll go along with the public humiliation if you accept my apology."

Backing off a few inches, she stared at me without blinking. "And if I don't?"

My neck was starting to ache. I nudged an inch of *dauda-dagr* free. "I'll make it perfectly clear I'm not in your thrall, and you'll lose face."

For a moment, I wasn't sure if Lady Eris would go for it. She sat without blinking or breathing, motionless and . . . just really, really freaking undead. I began to wonder what would happen if she refused. The idea of fighting my way out of the House of Shadows against an entire vampire brood wasn't very appealing.

Then she drew a breath and released me. "Very well, Hel's liaison. I accept your apology."

A murmur of disappointment echoed through the ballroom.

I sat upright, exhaling with relief. "Thank you."

Lady Eris arched one perfectly shaped eyebrow. "Consider it a much-needed lesson in diplomacy."

Okay, what is it with the undead and the eyebrow thing? "Duly noted."

She made a magnanimous gesture. "What brings you to come seeking audience at the House of Shadows?"

I fought the urge to tilt my neck from side to side and work out the kinks. "A request, my lady. A reasonable one, I believe. I don't know if you're aware—"

"Yes, of course." Lady Eris interrupted me impatiently. "A boy has died. I assure you, it's nothing to do with *us*."

It crossed my mind that Pemkowet's vampire mistress could use a much-needed lesson in courtesy from the Oak King. Wisely, I kept my mouth shut on that thought. "I know," I said instead. "I'm just here to ask that you keep your people off the streets until this blows over. That's all."

She studied me. "On whose behalf do you ask this?"

With the memory of Stacey Brooks flashing me the devil-horns sign fresh in my memory, echoing a hundred times I'd endured similar taunts in high school, it was oh, so tempting to pin this on the PVB. But the fact was, no matter how much I disliked Stacey, her mother was right. Amanda Brooks was good at her job. This was a simple, smart precaution to take.

And if I didn't own it, *I* stood to lose face, which could come back to haunt me in future dealings with the House of Shadows.

"I stand before you as Hel's liaison to request this small favor," I said steadily. "Do you assent?"

Another long moment passed.

The music that had been playing in the background had stopped. A multitude of candles flickered soundlessly, casting moving shadows against the walls, reflected in the tall arched and paned windows with their blackout curtains drawn for the night. The ballroom was filled with the unnatural silence of the pale, pulseless, and breathless undead, broken only by the sound of their mortal playthings breathing, and the occasional soft, unnerving giggle.

Lady Eris inclined her head. The part in her black hair was ruler-straight and perfectly white. "Let it be heard and known!" she said, raising her head and lifting her voice. "Until such a time as I decree otherwise, there shall be *no* hunting on the streets of Pemkowet. Is this understood, my people?"

A dozen vampires grumbled without breath, but they bowed to their mistress, acceding to her wishes.

"Well, Hel's liaison?" she asked me, her expression unreadable. "Does that suffice?"

I nodded. "Thank you, my lady. It does."

Thirty-five

Outside, I gulped down air.

All in all, I hadn't done a bad job. Okay, apparently I was more vulnerable to vampiric seduction than I'd realized, but I'd managed to hold my own. And I'd gotten what I came for, which was the most important thing.

On the far side of the parking terrace, Jen and Bethany were still immersed in conversation, perched on the fountain's ledge. I drifted near them and hovered, unsure whether or not to approach.

"It's just *so bad* at home, Beth!" Jen said, her voice breaking. "Dad—"

"So *leave!*"

"I can't!"

Bethany huddled into herself, crossing her forearms and hugging her elbows. "Yeah, you can! *I* did."

"For what?" Jen gestured futilely at the manor. "This?"

Her sister glared at her. "It's better than—"

"Than what?" Jen touched the puncture wounds on her sister's throat. "This? It's just another addiction. Just like Dad and his drinking."

"You don't understand!"

"The hell I don't!"

"You *don't*."

I cleared my throat. Both of them fell silent and looked up at me. "You're both right," I said to them. "Jen, I think we underestimated the allure." I rubbed the side of my neck where my pulse still beat hard, my skin yearning to be pierced. "A lot. But, Bethany, I think Jen's right. It *is* an addiction. And I bet it's one that can be beaten."

She gave me a stony look. "How many addictions grant you eternal life, devil girl? Geoffrey's promised to change me."

"Your goddamn bloodsucking boyfriend's been promising to change you for eight years!" Jen said grimly. "Wake up and smell the plasma, Beth!"

"He's waiting for me to reach my prime!" she retorted.

I gazed at her emaciated figure with sorrow. "Honey, the way you're going, you've already passed it. He's not going to change you; he's going to trade you in for a younger, healthier model."

That kindled a spark of alarm in her hollow eyes. "He wouldn't do that. He loves me!"

"Yeah, and I love a good bottle of scotch, too," I said. "But when it's empty, I throw the bottle away."

She looked confused. "You don't recycle?"

Jen rolled her eyes.

I sighed. "Yes, I recycle! It's a metaphor, okay? Listen . . . you know how they say absence makes the heart grow fonder? Why not put it to the test?" I patted the LeBaron's folded top. "Come home for a few days. Rest up, get some beauty sleep, eat your mom's good home cooking." I'd never actually eaten Mrs. Cassopolis's cooking, but I assumed it was good. Her husband probably wouldn't stand for anything less. "Give Geoffrey a chance to realize what he's missing."

Bethany eyed me suspiciously. "If you're right, he'll just choose someone else for the blood-bond."

I shook my head. "Not right now, he won't. Lady Eris just issued a no-hunting decree. Believe me, there'll never be a better time."

Her gaze shifted back and forth between Jen and me. "Is this a trick?"

"No trick," I promised.

"Cross our hearts and hope to die," Jen said wryly. "Bethany, *please*? Just for a few days?"

A deeply buried longing surfaced behind her eyes. "I'll . . . Okay, maybe I'll ask Geoffrey about it."

"No asking," I said. "You've got to tell him. Make him think you're strong enough to walk away if he doesn't keep his promise."

"But I'm not," she said in a small voice.

"It's okay, Beth," Jen said, her tone gentle. "He doesn't have to know that. You just have to make him believe it."

She hesitated. "You *swear* this isn't a trick? You won't, like, try to deprogram me or send me to rehab? You'll let me go anytime I want?"

"Yes!" both of us said in unison. I was pretty sure both of us were lying through our teeth. I knew I fully intended to research breaking a blood-bond at the first opportunity, and I wouldn't put it past Jen to lock her sister in the basement. But we'd deal with that when the time came.

"Okay." Bethany came to a decision. "But only for a few days. And I have to tell Geoffrey. I can't just *leave*."

Great, back into Twilight Manor. "I'll go with you." I didn't trust her not to change her mind.

"So will I," Jen said with determination.

The blond vampire looked irritated to see all three of us back on the doorstep, and all the more irritated when Bethany announced her intention in a tremulous voice, but he went to fetch her boyfriend into the foyer.

Geoffrey Chancellor had the whole Edwardian-rake look going: fancy suit, waistcoat with a chain and watch fob, immaculate ascot, and slicked-back hair. He was very good-looking in a totally supercilious way. I'd met him before and I didn't care for him. From what I could tell, the feeling was mutual.

When Bethany told him she planned on visiting home, he scowled at her. "It is foolish and unnecessary. Everything you need is here."

"It's just for a few days," she pleaded.

"It is contrary to my wishes." From the way he said it, I was pretty sure that if we weren't there to witness it, he would have forbidden her outright.

Bethany wilted anyway. "All right. It was just a thought."

Geoffrey smiled with satisfaction. "Good—"

"No," I interrupted him, laying my hand on *dauda-dagr*'s hilt. "*Not* all right. She expressed a clear desire to leave."

He looked down his nose at me. "She changed her mind."

"I changed my mind," she agreed weakly.

"*You* changed her mind," I said to him, ignoring Bethany. "Do you want me to inform Hel that the House of Shadows is now detaining mortals against their will?"

Geoffrey fixed his gaze on me, and I felt the tug of vampiric hypnosis coming into play. He wasn't as powerful as the mistress of the house, but it still made the blood sing in my veins, and I was glad I already had my hand on the reassuring chill of *dauda-dagr*'s hilt. "After Lady Eris's display with you upstairs, I confess, I'm not terribly impressed with your authority, Hel's liaison." He curled his lip, baring his fangs in a manner that was both a threat and a promise. "You heard her. She changed her mind. Now either go away, or stay and play."

Oh, crap. That was what I got for being diplomatic: a supercilious pretty-boy vampire calling my bluff.

Jen gave me an uncertain look. "Daise?"

"I'm thinking." If I drew *dauda-dagr* and backed him down, Bethany might change her mind. Or she might not, in which case everyone lost face. *Damn!* This was way too complicated.

While I was still in the throes of indecision, there was a knock at the front door—not just any knock, but a slow, ponderous knock heavy enough to make the old windowpanes tremble in their lead molding.

Looking annoyed and vaguely alarmed, the blond vampire opened the door.

Mikill the frost giant stood on the doorstep, his icicle-laden beard dripping, wisps of frost rising from his bluish skin. Ducking his head, he entered the House of Shadows without waiting for an invitation, his slush-colored gaze seeking mine.

"Daisy Johanssen," he said in his booming voice. "I am bidden to summon you to an audience with Hel."

I suppressed a grin, silently blessing him for his excellent timing. "Of course, Mikill. Just as soon as we've finished our business here."

Looming over mortals and vampires alike, Mikill swung his massive head around to take in the scene. His hair and beard continued to drip onto the marble floor of the foyer, a puddle forming beneath him. "What is at issue?"

"No issue," I assured him. "Geoffrey here was just saying good-bye to his blood-bonded girlfriend for a few days." I smiled sweetly at him. "Isn't that right?"

He gave me a poisonous glare, but he wasn't stupid enough to challenge my authority in the presence of an actual inhabitant of Little Niflheim, especially not one who stood eight feet tall. "Be good," he said to Bethany, trailing one finger down her throat. "And come back soon. I'll miss you, poppet."

"I hope you do." She sniffed. "I hope you miss me a *lot*. Maybe it will make you remember your promise."

Mikill's gaze returned to me. "Is your business now concluded, Daisy Johanssen?"

"Yep."

He inclined his head. "That is well."

I thought so, too.

Back outside in the warm summer night, I said good-bye to Jen. Bethany sat in the passenger seat of the LeBaron, staring straight ahead, while Mikill waited patiently beside his dune buggy and dripped onto the driveway.

"Are you going to be okay?" Jen asked me.

"I'll be fine. Mikill will drive me home." I made a shooing gesture at her. "Go on; get Bethany out of here before she changes her mind again."

Jen wasn't entirely satisfied. "What did Geoffrey the prat mean about Lady Eris's display with you?"

"Nothing," I said. "She tried to put the bloodsucker whammy on me. I let them think it worked."

She looked suspiciously at me. "Did it?"

"No!"

Jen grabbed my chin and lifted it to inspect my throat.

I batted her hand away. "Okay, it worked a little! But I was able to break it. Now get out of here, will you?"

"All right, all right. Call me."

"I will."

I waited until the LeBaron's taillights turned out of the driveway before getting in Mikill's dune buggy. The frost giant solicitously handed me a fur coat.

"Thanks." I squirmed into it, pushing back the overly long sleeves. "Where's Garm's doggy treat?"

"It is at your feet, Daisy Johanssen."

Oh, so that was what I was stepping on. I reached down and fished up a crusty loaf of bread, hoping the hellhound wouldn't mind that it was slightly flattened. "Good timing," I said as Mikill put the buggy in gear. "How did you know where to find me?"

"I am able to sense *dauda-dagr*'s presence. The timing was incidental."

I rubbed the side of my neck again. "Well, it was good anyway."

"That is well."

A frost giant of few words, Mikill drove without speaking to the Pemkowet Dune Rides, breaking his silence only to utter his customary warning to hold fast as we departed from the graded trails to jounce over the untamed dunes, Garm's full-throated howl arising in the darkness before us.

At least this time I was ready for him. "Here, boy!" I shouted as the slavering figure came into view, yellow eyes aflame. Winding up like a pitcher, I threw the bread loaf as far as I could, watching the hellhound bound after it. "Go get it!"

And then we were spiraling down the massive trunk of Yggdrasil II, past the rushing wall of heartwood, past the Norns doing their Nornish thing, drawing water from the well and tending to the roots of the giant pine. I gave them a wishful glance as we passed, wondering whether they would speak to me this time, maybe utter a little sooth.

"No," Mikill said in answer to my unvoiced question. "They have no counsel for you yet, Daisy Johanssen."

"Will they ever?" I asked him.

He turned his patient, slush-colored gaze on me. "Perhaps. Perhaps not. I do not know."

I sighed.

I know, I know. But I couldn't help it.

This time, there were *duegars* lining the streets of Little Niflheim, dwarves with forms as hard and knotty as tree roots. They gazed at the dune buggy with expressions that contained equal parts hope and despair.

"Mikill?" My voice sounded faint. "Why are they staring at us? They never stared at us before."

The frost giant pulled up before the abandoned sawmill. "It is the first time you have come carrying Hel's gift of death upon your hip, Daisy Johanssen," he said somberly. "In the coming battle, you will serve as Niflheim's champion."

Now my voice rose with alarm. "Coming battle? What coming battle?"

Mikill ushered me into the sawmill. "Whatever battle is coming."

Gah! If I could have reached his neck, I would have throttled him.

As my eyes adjusted to the dim light of the bioluminescent lichen on the walls, the sight of Hel on her throne banished whatever petty mortal exasperation I was feeling. "Welcome, my young liaison." Her voice echoed in the rafters, where a handful of roosting blue jays squawked and ruffled their feathers. "I would hear what news you bear. My harbingers tell me that matters are coming to a head."

I went to one knee, bowing my head. "Harbingers, my lady?"

Hel raised her fair and shapely right hand, the hand of life, indicating the roosting jays. "My eyes and ears in the mortal world."

"Blue jays?" I felt foolish saying it aloud.

The right side of Hel's mouth curved in a gentle smile. On the left side of her face, her blackened lips remained set in a grim line. "They are kin to ravens, the favored harbingers of my kinsman Odin."

"Oh."

Hel waited.

Okay, so apparently I was supposed to make a report. I collected my thoughts, wiping my damp palms surreptitiously on the fur coat. "You're right, my lady. Matters are coming to a head. It appears that a mortal man, with the assistance of a pair of ghouls, has been holding a mermaid captive and selling access to her."

"Access?" Her voice dropped to a note so deep it made the old timbers shudder in protest.

I nodded. "We believe the Vanderhei boy drowned in an . . . an act of sexual congress with the unwilling victim."

Hel's left eye, her ember eye, blazed a furious crimson in the black, withered ruin of the left side of her face. "Have you found the offenders?"

"Not yet, my lady," I said. "I believe we're close. We're hoping to find them in time to save the captive."

"That is well." Her ember eye closed briefly so that she might gaze at me with her compassionate one, but then it winked open again, red and baleful. "Are you prepared to dispense justice in my name, Daisy Johanssen?"

I swallowed. "Justice?"

"The offenders cannot be permitted to endure." Her voice was implacable. "The mortal man I cede to mortal authorities. But the ghouls who violated my order must be dispatched."

"Oh," I said again. *Dauda-dagr* tingled on my hip. "By me?"

Both sides of Hel's face were stern. "By you or the newcomer who lays claim to authority over their kind."

"Stefan?"

Hel tilted her head slightly. In the rafters, blue jays squawked and muttered. "Stefan Ludovic, yes. Unless he is complicit in this?"

"No." Funny how quickly that denial came out of my mouth. I amended my words honestly. "Forgive me, my lady. I cannot be entirely sure. But I believe him to be innocent in the matter."

Hel regarded me with both eyes, the compassionate and the baleful alike, and I had the feeling she could see straight through my vulnerable mortal flesh to the dense and conflicted knot of pride, anger, desire, fear, confusion, and a thousand other tangled emotions that lay within my restless hell-spawn's soul, always fighting for ascendance.

I half hoped that she would say something painful and insightful to sever the knot. I half feared that she would dismiss me from her service as unworthy. Or maybe it was the other way around.

Instead, she made her voice gentle. "It is well that you possess hope, Daisy Johanssen. Do not lose it."

"I'll try not to, my lady."

Gentleness fled, and Hel's ember eye blazed, eclipsing the compassionate one. "It need not be done by your hand, but it must be done. Bear a message from me to this Stefan Ludovic. If he fails to administer my justice to his kind, he *will* be banished from my domain. Is that understood?"

I nodded. "It is."

"And if he fails?" Hel asked me.

My left hand dropped to *dauda-dagr*'s leather-wrapped hilt, my fingers closing around it for comfort. Death day. Its bracing coolness seeped into my palm.

Could I kill?

It wasn't a threshold I'd ever imagined myself crossing. But I thought about what I had seen on Schtupernatural.com, about the printouts Casimir had given me, the mermaid's distorted face above an anonymous phone number. About the anguished hunger in Emma Sudbury's eyes, the entire span of her mortal life sacrificed in service to her sister's needs. About Twilight Manor, and Bethany's emaciated frame and hollow-eyed gaze.

Yeah, maybe I could.

"If he fails, it falls to me," I said steadily. "And I will *not* fail you, my lady."

Hel inclined her head. "You may go."

Thirty-six

The frost giant Mikill was wrong about one thing. As we approached the sacred well at the base of Yggdrasil II, one of the Norns set down her bucket and beckoned to us. I glanced at Mikill, who lifted his massive shoulders in a shrug and braked the buggy.

It was the oldest of the Norns, the one who looked like a kindly old grandmother except for the fact that her fingernails were long, silver talons and, now that I got a closer look, the fact that her eyes were as colorless as mist.

"Yes, my lady?" I said politely.

"Listen well, young Daisy." Her voice sounded like it came from far away, like some whole other dimension. Maybe seeing the past, present, and future simultaneously will do that to a person. "When the time comes, think on the words the vampire spoke to you today and find a key hidden within them."

Okay, not what I expected. "Umm . . . any chance you could be more specific?" I asked her. "At least point me in the direction of the right vampire?"

The Norn gave me a vague smile. "The answer lies within you."
With that, she picked up her bucket and resumed her duties.

Huh.

Mikill revved the engine and cautioned me to keep my limbs inside the vehicle as we raced back up Yggdrasil II's hollow interior.

"You said the Norns wouldn't have any counsel for me yet!" I shouted above the sound of the engine as we emerged.

"So I said upon your arrival," Mikill replied. "Perhaps you are not entirely the same person upon your departure, Daisy Johanssen."

Between coming and going, I'd pledged to kill if necessary, something so grave it made worrying about the Seven Deadlies seem trivial. I let that thought sit in silence for the rest of the drive home.

Mikill delivered me to the alley at some late o'thirty of the night, only just too early for Mrs. Browne to have fired up her ovens. I thanked him for the ride, and the dune buggy sputtered away in a fine mist of frozen pellets, the frost giant's beard wagging in the wind of its passage.

I climbed the stairs to my apartment, my steps leaden. Despite having taken a nap, I was tired beyond tired. It wasn't just that this was the longest day of my life and I'd begun it sleep-deprived and hungover. From Meg Mucklebones onward, the day's seemingly endless series of encounters had taken a serious toll on me.

Mogwai was nowhere to be found, and the apartment felt empty. I filled his bowl, then went straight into the bedroom. I unbuckled my belt and sheathed dagger, laying them carefully on the dresser. I tried to reconstruct every conversation I'd had at the House of Shadows tonight, but I was just too damned tired to concentrate. Instead, I fished the Oak King's token from my pocket. That was certainly the day's highlight. I took a moment to sit on the edge of my bed, gazing at the silver acorn in wonder. I couldn't resist raising it to my lips, letting my breath mist the gleaming metal.

Okay, Daisy. Put down the magic whistle.

I stashed it in the jewelry box atop my dresser, stripped off my clothes, crawled into bed, and fell into a deep, dreamless sleep.

It seemed like only minutes had passed before the unmistakable roar of a Harley chugging into the alley below awakened me, but sunlight was streaming through the gaps in the drapes.

Swearing, I scrambled back into yesterday's clothing, opened the drapes, and flung the window wide. "Stefan?"

The black leather-clad figure on the bike below cut the engine and removed his helmet, revealing a blond ponytail. Not Stefan, but his lieutenant Johnny. "Sorry to wake you, ma'am," he called up in a faint drawl. "Stefan's been trying to reach you, but he's not getting any phone reception out in the boondocks. He found out where Jerry Dunham's gone and holed himself up."

A spike of adrenaline jolted me alert. "He did?"

Johnny the ghoul nodded. "He sent me to fetch you." His expression was grim. "Said to make sure you brung that dagger of yours."

"Are they all with Dunham?" I asked. "Ray D, Mary Sudbury, and . . . the hostage?"

"We think so." He shrugged. "Stefan didn't want to move in on them without talking to you first. Hel's liaison and all. It's a courtesy, I reckon." He didn't sound particularly approving, but he didn't sound particularly disapproving, either. "You coming or not, ma'am? One way or another, this is going down. And I still got to swing by Rafe's place and pick up reinforcements."

I buckled *dauda-dagr* around my waist, settling the belt on my hips. "Give me the location. I'll call it in to the station."

Johnny hesitated, scowling up at me. "This ain't police business."

I pointed at him, banging my fingertip against the screen. Smooth, I know. "Not your call, Johnny. I spoke to Hel last night and she was very clear about leaving Dunham to mortal authorities." I didn't mention that she had a pretty serious message for Stefan, too. That, I'd deliver to him myself. "What's the address?"

With another shrug, he gave it to me.

I called the station and relayed the address to Patty Rogan with orders to pass it on to the chief and Cody, then clattered down the stairs.

Johnny's pupils dilated briefly in his gray-blue eyes, then contracted to pinpoints as he wrestled himself under control. He shoved the helmet back onto his head, buckled it, and handed me a second one before straddling the Harley. "You need to hold on to something, ma'am, best you hold on to the sissy bar," he advised me. "Not me. I don't need no extra temptation. Okay?"

Donning the helmet, I sat gingerly behind him, trying to minimize contact between us. "Not a problem."

"All right, then." Johnny turned the key in the ignition and kicked the bike into life, opening the throttle. I caught a fleeting glimpse of Mogwai crouching beneath the rhododendrons, his fur bristling, before we roared out of the alley.

It had been years since I'd ridden on the back of a motorcycle—since Mom's old boyfriend Trey Summers, who had introduced me to the blues, had been killed. It was a car accident involving a drunk driver that took his life, but he'd had a motorcycle, too. Sometimes, with Mom's permission, he'd take me for rides. I'd forgotten how exhilarating it could be. I leaned back against the upright sissy bar, away from Johnny, reaching behind me to take a tight grip on the bars.

The streets of downtown Pemkowet whizzed past us. We pulled out onto the highway, crossing the bridge.

The river sparkled brightly in the sunlight like a promise.

At East Pemkowet's only stoplight, which unlike its sister stoplight in downtown Pemkowet doesn't have a changing ceremony of its own, Johnny turned his head and shouted something incomprehensible to me, pointing in the direction of the lakeshore. All I caught was a few words about Stefan's second lieutenant, Rafe, and reinforcements, but he'd mentioned it earlier.

I nodded. "Okay!"

We roared toward the lakeshore and along the bluff above Lake Michigan. Today it was windy and there were whitecaps, long, rolling breakers curling toward the shore. It would be a good day for bodysurfing. I felt a burst of nostalgia, yearning for the sun-kissed days of childhood, when Mom would take me to the beach on her day off and I'd spend the entire day building sandcastles and frolicking in the waves, my only concern making sure I kept my tail securely tucked in my bikini bottom. The arching canopies of the grand old trees lining Lakeshore Drive made it seem like we were driving through a green tunnel. Johnny drove with impressive competence, weaving around joggers and dog walkers. We passed Lurine's gated driveway and kept going.

A half mile later, Johnny pulled into a long driveway leading to a McMansion nestled in the woods, parking alongside five or six additional motorcycles.

Call me dense, but that was about the time my tail started twitching with suspicion.

I scrambled off the back of the bike, unbuckled my helmet, and hung it on the sissy bar. "Awfully nice place Rafe has here."

"You think a ghoul can't have nice things?" Johnny asked in a mild tone, taking off his own helmet. "Can't live in a nice house?"

I took a few wary steps backward. "Nooo . . ."

He beckoned. "Come on; it'll just be a moment."

Two things caught my eye. The first was the most beautiful motorcycle I'd ever seen, with a teardrop-shaped tank painted a deep, glossy red. Cody had identified it as a 1940s Indian Chief.

The second was a stone placard hung beside the front door of the McMansion announcing it to be the residence of the Locksley family, complete with a faux-heraldic crest with a Latin motto and pair of crossed arrows on prominent display. Yeah, crossed arrows—the missing piece of the puzzle from my mom's reading. *Las Jaras*, the destination.

Oh, crap.

Johnny's pupils dilated a split second before I bolted, and he was on me before I'd gotten ten steps toward the road, tackling me, his greater weight bringing me down. I hit the driveway hard, banging my chin and seeing stars. He rolled me over effortlessly, straddling my waist and pinning my arms with his knees. I fought a surge of pure panic, channeling it into fury.

"Whatever happened to being Stefan's trusted lieutenant?" I spat at him.

Johnny inhaled deeply and grinned down at me, his pupils wide and black. "What can I say? I'm afraid I had a change of heart. Got an offer I couldn't refuse." He cracked his knuckles and drew back one fist. "Sorry about this, *ma'am*."

His fist crashed down against my temple.

And everything went black.

Thirty-seven

My consciousness filtered back slowly. All I knew at first was that my head ached fiercely, and I felt sick and dizzy. Disoriented, I opened my eyes and tried to make sense of what I was seeing.

Water, murky and greenish. Huh. It didn't feel like I was underwater. I took an experimental breath. Yeah, that worked. Okay, so I definitely wasn't underwater.

A woman's face swam into view inches from mine, gray-green and eerie, dark hair swirling around her head, pale translucent membranes over her eyes.

"Gah!" My body convulsed in a futile attempt to scramble backward, which was when I realized I was lying on my side, my hands tied behind my back, my ankles bound together. With an effort, I levered myself to a sitting position.

"She's awake," a man's voice said with the same relish you might use to announce that dinner was ready.

Focusing, I made out the figure of Al the Walrus, his eyes glittering in the dim light. *Oh, crap* didn't even begin to sum it up.

"Leave her be for now, you greedy bastard," a laconic voice retorted. Jerry Dunham thumped the top of what I now realized was an enormous aquarium tank. "You need to feed, feed on good old Rosie here."

"Ring around the rosie, pocket full of posies!" a woman's voice sang dreamily. The infanticidal ghoul Mary Sudbury stooped before me, pupils enormous in her blue eyes. She'd died young, pretty, and insane. "Can't I have just a taste?" she crooned. "I'm ever so tired of mermaid. Her despair's gone all stale."

"No. Get off her." Dunham gave Mary a ruthless shove.

"Hey, man!" another ghoul protested, tall and whippet-thin. Ray D, I presumed. "You don't treat her like that."

"Or what?" Dunham calmly pulled a pistol from the waistband of his jeans.

Ray D laughed and spread his arms. "Go ahead, shoot."

"Oh, I'm not gonna shoot *you*." Dunham shifted his stance and aimed the gun at my head. My mind went blank with terror. "First I shoot the girl; then I shoot the fish, and you ravening motherfuckers can starve."

Across the room came the sound of a shotgun being pumped. "Do it and I blow your head off, Dunham," Johnny said. "And there's no coming back for *you*. Stick with the plan."

"That's exactly what I'm trying to do, you dumb hillbilly." Jerry Dunham turned to face him with a sociopath's utter lack of fear. "You promised me you could keep your ghouls under control long enough."

Johnny gritted his teeth, his pupils waxing and waning. "And I will. No feeding on the girl," he warned them. "Not until this is over."

"Oh, but she's *so scared*," Mary Sudbury crooned, circling back to stroke my cheek. "Poor little thing." A shadow crossed her face. "I bet your mommy's going to miss you ever so much."

"Get off her, Mary," Dunham said again. "I'm not gonna tell you a third time."

She pouted. "Just a taste?"

"Not until it's over." Johnny gestured with the shotgun. "Ray, pull her off."

"Come on, sweetheart." The tall, thin ghoul took Mary by the shoulders, easing her gently backward. "It won't be long." He grinned at me, baring discolored teeth. "And when it's over, we'll have a feast."

Licking my dry lips, I found my voice. It sounded shaky. "Was that the offer you couldn't refuse?" I asked Johnny.

He shook his head. "You're just the icing on the cake. Dunham, you ready to try again? I can't touch it."

"Yeah, I'll have another go." Jerry Dunham shoved the pistol back into his waistband, flexing his hand. There was a bandanna wrapped around it. "Fuck, that fucking hurt. Luke, you got that welding glove for me?"

A ghoul I didn't recognize tossed it to him. I shrank back at Dunham's approach, finding a wall behind me. In the tank beside me, the mermaid pressed her webbed hands against the glass in a gesture of sympathy.

"Quit your cowering," Dunham said to me with disdain. "I'm not interested in *you*." Reaching down with his gloved hand, he yanked *dauda-dagr* from its sheath. Within seconds, he was grimacing. "Motherfucker, that's cold!"

"Can you hold it long enough to do the job?" Johnny asked him.

"Oh, yeah." Dunham dropped the dagger on the top of the bar and shook out his hand. "I reckon I might lose a few more layers of skin. But for Mister High Lord Muckety-Muck, I'll manage."

I swallowed. "You're after Stefan, aren't you?"

He turned his flat gaze on me. "Give the little girl a cookie."

"Why?" I asked him. "It seems like an awfully big risk to take."

Jerry Dunham peeled off his welding glove and shrugged. "Well, now, Johnny here's looking to stage a coup and take over in Pemkowet. His accomplices want to go back to doing what ghouls do best, and make other people's lives miserable." He nodded at Ray D and Mary Sudbury, the latter wrapped in the former's arms. "Them two lovebirds just want to be left alone, only they need a source, and I reckon you'll do for a while, since poor old Rosie's gettin' tapped out. And as for me . . ." He cocked his head and looked thoughtful. "You know what, blondie? I just really don't like the guy."

"And that's enough?" I whispered.

Dunham flexed his hand again, contemplating it. "Sometimes you just gotta let the world burn."

Let the world burn. . . .

The words echoed in my ears, evoking yesterday's vision: the lake of fire, the bat wings, the fiery whip.

I shivered. "You don't know what you're doing. You don't know what you could unleash."

His mouth curled. "I heard the rumors. You gonna call your daddy, blondie? Risk unleashing hell on earth?" He shook his head. "I don't think so."

"Ladybug, ladybug, fly away home," Mary sang, swaying back and forth in Ray's arms. "Your house is on fire, and your children are all . . . Oh." Her voice fell silent.

A wave of despair washed over me, fresh and tasty, by the way the ghouls responded. Al the Walrus groaned with pleasure. It was a disgusting feeling.

"Simmer down!" Dunham said sharply. "Whatever she's broadcasting, we need it out there loud and clear, long enough for Ludovic to home in on it."

"Could be a while." There was a sheen of sweat on Johnny's face. "It don't exactly work like a GPS, you know."

"We'll wait as long as it takes." Dunham strode across the room and banged on the side of the aquarium. "Come on, old gal! Muster up a bit of anguish." Stooping, he picked up an extension cord with a frayed end. "Shall I give you a little jolt?"

The mermaid's face contorted with fear and she shook her head, hair waving like seaweed.

The ghouls sighed with satisfaction.

Dunham dropped the cord. "That'll do you for now."

Oh, God. I was alone in a house full of ghouls and a captive mermaid, serving as bait for a trap to lure in Stefan. Too late to try to rein in my emotions now; I'd already loosed a bolt of sheer terror he couldn't have missed. I'd sent the police on a wild-goose chase. The Oak King's token was back home in my jewelry box. I'd lost *daudadagr*, an incredibly dangerous and valuable weapon, to a freaking sociopath. Apparently whatever ancient Norse magic had created a dagger only Hel's chosen could wield hadn't taken Kevlar welding gloves into account. I pulled my knees to my chest, bowing my head against them.

There were no good outcomes here.

Daughter . . .

Belphegor's voice whispered faintly in my thoughts, promising power beyond imagining: powers of temptation, seduction, and destruction. The power to wreak vengeance on my enemies, which sounded pretty good right about now.

You have but to ask.

Yeah, and crack open the Inviolate Wall, paving the way for Armageddon. Turning my head, I gazed at the mermaid. She gazed back at me, eyes a lucent green beneath their nictitating membranes. The scales that covered the lower half of her body were large and gray. A row of gills ran along either side of her torso, starting below the armpit. They fanned open and shut feebly in the murky water, revealing vulnerable-looking inner flesh that was an unhealthy pale mauve color.

I didn't know a lot about mermaids—or fish, for that matter—but I thought she looked pretty damn sickly. I wondered how long she'd been held captive in that tank.

"So what happens when this is over?" I asked Dunham. "You pack up the tank and skip town again?"

"Nah." He shook his head. "Not worth it to hire an experienced crew. I found that out the hard way."

"Bringing her from Seattle?"

Dunham didn't bother to answer. "Just not a big enough market in this Podunk town." He thumped the tank again. "And poor old Rosie's on her last . . . fins." He laughed at his own joke. "My fault for letting a couple of dumb ghouls handle things. I should have kept her in the trailer like I planned."

"We did our best!" Ray D protested. "It wasn't our fault that kid panicked and got himself drowned."

"Sweet, sweet panic," Mary murmured in a melancholy tone. "My sweet baby boy panicked when I held him underwater, but I held him ever so tight until he went to sleep like a good boy."

"They all panic," Dunham said briefly, nudging the extension cord with his foot. "That's part of your fun, ain't it? *Your* job was to keep Rosie in line so she *didn't* struggle."

"So it was an accident?" I asked.

He gave me his flat stare. "You want to play twenty questions, blondie? It was a clusterfuck is what it was." He pointed at Ray. "*You* fucked up giving those first Van Buren boys your name. Them others were never supposed to come looking for no Ray D at the bar. Just a phone number."

Mary hummed and then sang to herself, swaying in Ray's arms. "Operator, could you help me place this call. . . ."

"Ray, can you shut her up?" one of the ghouls I didn't recognize said.

Ray glared, tightening his arms around Mary. "Fuck you!"

"Fuck *you*!"

Johnny swung his shotgun around the room, aiming at everyone and no one. "Shut up, y'all," he said genially. "No point in turning on each other now. For the time being, we're in this together. Once Stefan's out of the picture, you want to fight, fight."

Everyone fell silent.

Surreptitiously, I tested the ropes around my wrists and ankles. Yep, pretty tight. But if no one was watching, I thought maybe I could wriggle my arms over my hips and butt and get my hands in front of me.

And do . . . what?

Daughter . . .

"No!" I said aloud. "No!"

"No, what?" Dunham eyed me suspiciously.

I leaned back against the wall. "Nothing."

"Ludovic's taking his own sweet time." Crouching before me, he plucked the pistol out of his waistband, shoving the muzzle under my chin. "You sure you're plenty scared, blondie?" he mused.

Hyperventilating, I nodded.

"Stefan's not stupid, Dunham," Johnny said. "Don't you make the mistake of thinking so. He ain't gonna come storming in here. He's gonna take his time to assess the situation, rally his troops, make good and sure he knows who's loyal before he makes his move. When he does, you be mindful of what I told you."

"No kill shots." Jerry Dunham sounded disgruntled.

Johnny nodded. "You fire off a kill shot, he'll just reincorporate." He snapped his fingers. "Like that. He's old and strong, stronger than any of us here. Shoot to maim and finish him off with the dagger, you hear?"

"I hear."

Thirty-eight

Time crawled.

My head ached; my chin stung. My shoulders and arms were beginning to burn from having my hands tied behind my back. If the Locksley residence had air-conditioning, it was turned off in their absence.

Sweat trickled down my temples.

Daughter...

I hunched my shoulders toward my ears, trying to block out a sound no one else could hear. I thought about what the Norn had told me: The key lay hidden in something a vampire had said to me yesterday, and whatever it was, it lay within me.

For the life of me, I couldn't think what it might be.

In the wide world outside, the sun reached its apex, baking in the sky. I made an effort to breathe low and slow.

"So how did you find this place?" I asked Ray D in a conversational tone. "It's really nice."

He looked pleased to be addressed. "Oh, I do a little handyman work from time to time. A guy I met at the bar hooked me up with this gig."

"Mr. Cassopolis?"

He beamed. "You know him?"

I rotated my aching shoulders. "Yeah, I do."

"My Raymond's a very good handyman," Mary Sudbury said helpfully, reaching up to stroke his jaw. "Very skilled."

Ray bent his head toward her, and they smiled at each other, a pair of blissful ghouls in love. I might have felt sorry for them if the continued existence of their relationship didn't necessitate generating incredible amounts of anguish and misery, which I was apparently next in line to provide.

Somewhere out there, Stefan was zeroing in on my location. Maybe, just maybe, Cody had tracked down a lead from Mr. Cassopolis after realizing the address I'd phoned in was bogus. Unfortunately, both would lead them straight into an ambush.

Okay, so it was past time to start using my wits. I just wished they didn't feel so scrambled. But whatever cards I held, it was time to play them.

"You two seem really happy together," I said to Ray and Mary. "It's too bad Hel's issued a death sentence for you."

They stared at me. Mary's pupils dilated fiercely. "You shouldn't say such things! Liars make the baby Jesus cry! Liars get their mouths washed out with soap, little lady!"

I'd be willing to bet somebody was channeling an evangelical Mommie Dearest. "I'm not lying," I said steadily. "Read my emotions and see. I'm Hel's fucking liaison, and I'm here telling you that Hel has decreed you're both to be dispatched for your sins."

"For what?" Ray seemed genuinely bewildered.

I nodded at the mermaid's tank. "What do you think? For *that*."

"But we needed her!" he protested.

"No." I shook my head. "You *wanted* her. You wanted this—this whole sick Sid and Nancy scenario. And you were willing to overturn Hel's order to have it."

"We didn't do anything!" Mary said indignantly, pointing at Dunham. "He's the one who did everything. We just took care of her."

An incredulous laugh escaped me. "Took *care* of her? Is that really what you're going to call it?"

Mary might just be crazy enough to believe it, but I saw a slow awareness dawn on Ray's face. He was stupid, but he wasn't that stupid. "Them boys didn't really hurt her none," he mumbled. "She's a tough old gal."

I didn't bother to dignify it with a response, glancing at Johnny instead. "Hel's prepared to banish Stefan if he can't administer her justice to his own people. If you take over, these two become your problem."

"Don't listen to her," Dunham advised him.

"Why not?" Johnny cradled his shotgun. "She's telling the truth. I reckon I'll deal with it when the time comes."

"What's *that* s'posed to mean?" Ray asked suspiciously.

"It means I'll deal with it." A note of impatience crept into Johnny's tone. "Don't worry about it, man."

"It means he'll get rid of you when this is over," I informed Ray. "You and Mary. Lock you in solitary confinement for months on end until you starve and devour your own essence. Isn't that how it works? Maybe it won't take as long with both of you trying to feed on each other. Or maybe he'll separate you to make it last longer. Do you plan on separating them?" I asked Johnny.

He strolled over, leaned down, and slapped me across the face, wrenching my head sideways. "All right, now, you shut your mouth, ma'am."

I tasted blood.

Daughter . . .

A spiral of anger rose in me. The pump attached to the mermaid's tank made an alarming sound, hoses bulging. "Or maybe he'll have

Dunham use *dauda-dagr*," I said. "Make it quick and clean. Is that the plan?"

Johnny reversed the shotgun. "Do you want me to use this here stock to smash your pretty little face in?" He was breathing hard, his pupils wavering. "Or do you want me to turn every ghoul in this room loose on you?"

I held my tongue, anger dwindling back to fear. The pump stopped whining and the hoses stopped bulging.

"Ignore her." Jerry Dunham sounded bored. "She's just trying to turn us against each other. Don't fall for it."

"Easy for you to say," I managed to whisper. "You're mortal. You're not subject to Hel's authority."

"She has a point," one of the unknown ghouls muttered.

"It's not too late for you to call this off," I said to Johnny. "You haven't done anything you can't walk away from."

He laughed mirthlessly. "Other than kidnap Hel's liaison? No." He shook his head. "Sorry, ma'am. There's only one way that gets forgiven, and that's to prove you're a miserable failure at the job."

Al the Walrus scratched his head. "Don't that put it back on you once you're in charge, Johnny? Hel's justice and all?"

Johnny gestured impatiently with his shotgun. "I'm telling you, I will deal with it when the time comes!"

"You'd better not try it!" Mary Sudbury called out in an ominous singsong voice, swaying in Ray's arms, her pupils as black as night. "I won't let you hurt my Raymond. Never, never, never." She shook her finger at Johnny. "Naughty little boys get eaten up by the bad monsters."

As the sun inched across the horizon, the ghouls quarreled among themselves, which was a lot more unnerving than it sounds. On the surface it looked like any ordinary argument, but there were power plays I couldn't entirely fathom going on in the hidden depths beneath the words, contests of will going back and forth, all of it fueled by an ever-rising hunger that was barely held in check, on the verge of ravening.

I'm pretty sure Rosie, or whatever the mermaid's real name was, bore the brunt of their emotional ardor. Hour by hour, I could almost *see* her being drained. But I could feel it, too—feel the shifting tides of power, feel the avid hunger that crawled over my skin like the psychic equivalent of drool.

Ew. Just . . . ew.

I leaned my cheek against the warm glass of the aquarium. "I'm sorry," I whispered. "I really, really wanted to rescue you."

The mermaid flattened one webbed hand against the other side of the glass, sympathy in her anguished gaze.

"Daisy and Rosie," Jerry Dunham said in his flat voice. "Ain't that just too precious for words?"

I stared at him with pure hatred.

He chuckled. "You want to do it? Go on, do it. Call your daddy. Let the world burn."

Daughter . . .

I closed my eyes, picturing my mother's face. I clamped down on my emotions, wrapping my will around them like a garrote.

Darkness was beginning to fall when the sound of motorcycles rumbling into the driveway silenced the bickering. Stefan and his posse had arrived. Someone shut off the lights, and the ghouls hunkered down in anticipation of the battle to come. Only Rosie's algae-covered tank glowed, green and murky in the dimness.

One by one, the engines outside cut out.

"It's go time," Johnny murmured, aiming the barrels of his shotgun at the front door. "Let bygones be bygones. Let's do this."

I drew a breath to shout a warning.

The muzzle of Dunham's pistol pressed against my temple. "Scream and I'll shoot you," he said with calm assurance. "You first, and the fish second. Is that the way you want to die, blondie?"

"No," I whispered.

The moment dragged on endlessly. I was acutely aware of the silence, of the breath moving in and out of my lungs, of the circle of Dunham's pistol hard against my temple, of the mermaid undulating helplessly in her tank, her gills fluttering.

The knob of the front door of the Locksley family's summer home rotated an inch . . . and went still.

"What the fuck?" someone said in frustration.

In the woods outside, a wolf howled, one, and then another and another.

Johnny turned slightly. "Shit—"

The front door burst inward with a great, splintering crash of wood and glass, lashed by the impossible force of vast, muscular, rainbow-hued serpentine coils moving at lightning speed.

Oh, crap!

A jolt of pure panic gripped me. "Lurine, *no*! Get out of here!"

And then it was all chaos.

Lurine's coils retracted as fast as they'd struck. Johnny's shotgun boomed several times and Dunham's pistol cracked. Heedless of the gunfire, ghouls poured through the shattered door and leaped through the windows, bursting the screens and smashing the glass panes. I caught sight of Stefan, an actual sword in his hand, his pupils wide and furious in his ice-blue eyes. If he wasn't ravening, he was damn close to it.

Every other ghoul in the place had gone over the edge. They were fighting hand-to-hand and will-to-will, grappling and pounding wildly. Some had weapons; some were using fists. Unable to reload in the mayhem, Johnny was using his shotgun as a cudgel. The Locksleys' rec room was a seething maelstrom of raw emotion and naked hunger, and I could feel myself being sucked into it, my essence swirling into it like water down a drain. It filled me with a terror and helpless fury that served only to fuel the madness.

Except for Jerry Dunham, who was as cool as a proverbial cucumber, waiting for a clear shot.

Stefan was holding the others at bay with his sword, which he wielded with the efficiency of long, long practice, his half-mad gaze sweeping the room, searching for me.

"Stefan, get out!" I shouted at him. "It's you they're after!"

Of course he didn't listen, homing in on the sound of my voice; and worse, I saw Cody was behind him.

"That'll do just fine, blondie." Dunham pistol-whipped me across the cheek, hard enough that I toppled sideways. "Now shut it."

Blood filled my mouth. All I could do was watch, lying on the floor with my hands and feet tied, as Stefan came forward, his sword in both hands, looking like a cross between an assassin and an avenging angel.

Until Dunham lowered his pistol and shot out both his kneecaps with calm precision. "Ray, get the cop!"

Stefan went down, his face twisted with pain. Ray D charged Cody, who braced himself in a shooter's stance. His service revolver fired, and a fine red mist exploded from Ray's chest. He staggered backward and crumpled. Mary let out a shriek, flinging herself toward Cody.

And then time . . . stuttered. I don't know how else to describe it. Time stuttered, and Ray D wasn't dead and shot on the floor anymore. He was on his feet, still charging Cody, wrestling for his gun, aided by Mary.

"Hold him off!" Dunham shouted, putting another bullet in Stefan's sword arm, turning his biceps into a gory mess. "I just need a minute!" He lunged for the bar, dropping his pistol and scrambling for *dauda-dagr* and the welding glove.

My chest heaved in an involuntary sob and I gagged, half choking on my own blood. Hell, I should have stayed at Twilight Manor and let Lady Eris bite me. It would have been better for everyone. I swallowed hard, the taste of blood filling my mouth.

My blood.

I suspect that it must taste deliciously of brimstone and ichor, my dear. . . .

It was more than just a cliché.

Not just brimstone. Ichor, celestial ichor. After all, what was a demon but a fallen angel? That blood ran in my veins, too. The Norn had said the answer lay *within* me. And I was capable of feeling more than fear and anger, capable of feeling so much more.

I met the mermaid's sorrowful gaze behind the glass, inches away from me. I gazed at her with compassion and held tight to that feeling, letting it swell until it filled me. My shoulder blades itched in the place where wings would have been, and my heart seemed to expand within my chest.

Compassion. Tenderness. Love.

Holding fast to all I held dear, from Mom's unrelenting faith in me to Jen's fierce loyalty to Lurine's mantle of protection, I gathered it and let it spill forth. To the timeless sound of heartbroken women singing the blues and sunlight sparkling on the river. To all that engendered wonder, from the mighty scale of Yggdrasil II and Hel's undeserved trust to the Oak King's indescribable majesty. To the ephemeral beauty of naiads and fairies and Garm the hellhound's slavering devotion to his eternal duty. To all that evoked tenderness, from the chief's love of this town to Gus the ogre's crush on my mother to the booger-eating kid who'd helped me gather acorn caps in the park.

Shuddering at the taint of ghoulish hunger devouring my innermost private feelings, I forced myself to offer them up as a sacrifice.

I fed my best and truest self into the maelstrom, and the sounds of fighting faded.

Feeling spent, I levered myself to an upright sitting position. All around the rec room, ghouls had gone still, pupils wide with awe, momentarily sated and blissful.

"What the fuck?" Unaffected by the outpouring of emotion, Jerry Dunham sounded disgruntled. He knelt beside Stefan's bleeding figure, *dauda-dagr* raised in his gloved hand, poised for the killing strike. "Let's finish this!"

Unfortunately for him, there was one other non-ghoul in this fight, and he wasn't affected by what I'd done, either.

"You've got it." Cody leveled his pistol and fired, and Dunham toppled sideways, *dauda-dagr* falling from his hand.

Thirty-nine

The spell broken, the fight resumed at a shambling, incoherent pace. Ray D bolted and ran, dragging Mary behind him by the hand. Outside, there was a hoarse shout cut short and then a higher-pitched scream followed by receding footsteps and the sound of wolves yipping to one another in the woods.

Dunham was a few feet away from me, pressing his left hand to his other shoulder and grimacing, blood seeping between his fingers. *Dauda-dagr* lay beside him where it had fallen, wisps of frost rising from it. With a concerted effort of will, I wriggled my bound arms over my hips, squirming until I was able to pull my legs through.

"Daisy!" Cody was covering the room, unable to pick out a clear target in the fighting. "You okay?"

"Yeah!" With my hands before me, I made an awkward dive for the dagger, the breath going out of my lungs as my belly hit the floor. I spat out a mouthful of blood, inching forward until the fingers of my right hand closed around the leather-wrapped hilt. Its bracing coolness had never felt sweeter.

Cody scanned the room. "Where's Dunham's gun?"

"On the bar." Getting my legs back underneath me, I wedged the hilt between my knees and sawed at the rope around my wrists. *Dauda-dagr*'s blade parted the strands effortlessly. "Stefan?"

Stefan groaned . . . and did the impossible.

Reaching across with his uninjured left arm, he retrieved his sword, grabbing it by the blade and planting the hilt on the floor. Using the sword's leverage, he rolled over, the edges of the blade slicing his palm as he heaved himself to his shattered knees and planted the sword's tip against the center of his chest. His black hair hung around his face, and his breathing sounded labored but steady.

The sound I let out as Stefan lurched forward, using all his strength to impale himself on the blade, was somewhere between a gasp and a shriek. The one I emitted as the sword's tip emerged from between his shoulder blades to tent the back of his leather vest was more of a whimper.

Once again, time . . . stuttered.

It was like watching the flickering images of an old black-and-white film. One instant Stefan knelt impaled; the next, he was on his feet, whole and uninjured, the sword in his right hand. Dead one instant, cast out of heaven and hell and back onto the mortal plane in the next. I'd seen it happen with Ray D, but this?

If I were the fainting type, now would definitely be the time. Instead, I severed the ropes around my ankles.

"Guard the women and keep watch over Dunham," Stefan said to Cody, who nodded, phosphorescent green shimmering behind his eyes. "I will handle the others."

Shrugging off the last of the ropes, I watched him exert his control over the remaining ghouls.

The only one who made a move to resist was Johnny, reaching to reload his shotgun. Stefan was on him in two swift steps, his sword held low, the tip of his blade hovering in the vicinity of Johnny's belly.

What followed basically looked like a good old-fashioned staredown contest, only with a hell of a lot more tension. When Johnny looked away and dropped the shotgun, the tension broke, or at least most of it. By the looks of them and the creeping sensation against my skin, a few of the more undisciplined ghouls like Al were still ravening, but Stefan's control of them held. I guess there were some advantages to this whole hierarchical thing after all.

"It seems after all this time there are things I have yet to learn about judging a man's character," Stefan said in a deadly tone.

Johnny shrugged. "I saw a chance and I took it. You're a warrior. I reckoned you'd understand."

Stefan gestured around the room with his sword. "*This* was not a worthy battle."

"I'd have made it right once I won," Johnny said stubbornly. "I would have!"

"No." Stefan shook his head. "It would already have been too late. Such thinking is why you are, and remain, Outcast."

On the floor, Jerry Dunham gave a short bark of laughter that turned to a coughing fit. "Like you're any better than the rest of them, Lord High and Mighty?" he said in contempt when he regained his voice.

"No." Stefan spared him a single disdainful glance. "But I aspire to it." He turned back to Johnny. "Take your people and go. When the ravening has passed, depart from my territory and never return. Is that understood?"

Johnny gritted his teeth, but he bowed his head. "Yeah."

"Good."

A cold rill ran through *dauda-dagr*'s hilt into the palm of my hand, reminding me of my duties. "Ah, Stefan? It's not that simple. What about the ones who got away? Ray and Mary? Hel's pronounced them under a death sentence."

"The runners?" Cody cocked his head, listening to the sound of yipping drawing nearer. "Unless they're in a mood to get mauled, my kin ought to have them rounded up soon."

"Those are Fairfaxes out there?" I was touched.

He gave me a faint smile. "I invoked clan loyalty. You're sort of my partner, Pixy Stix. I wasn't taking any chances."

Outside the shattered front door, the thick coils of an iridescent tail flicked. Ray D's body sailed through the entrance and landed on the floor, looking slightly . . . squashed. Apparently he hadn't gotten far.

Lurine slithered through after him, bracing her spectacularly naked torso on her hands and arms before drawing herself up to her full height, the rec room suddenly seeming a lot smaller. Her worried gaze sought mine. "Hey, Daisy, girl! You okay, cupcake?"

I nodded. "Yeah, thanks."

She poked Ray's squashed-looking body with the tip of her tail. His sunken chest rose and fell feebly, breath wheezing in his lungs. "I hope you don't mind. I took the liberty of—" Her gaze fell on the mermaid's tank, turning thunderous.

Ghouls scattered as Lurine flowed across the room and wrapped her protective coils around the tank, including me in their circle. She lifted the tank's massive lid as though it weighed nothing, setting it carefully aside.

The mermaid surfaced, her head breaking water, nictitating eyelids opening to fully unveil her lucent green eyes.

Lurine questioned her in one language.

The mermaid shook her head and replied in another, adding, "I listen long time. I speak some English."

"Rosie?" I asked softly, leaning forward.

"Rusalka. It is not a name. It is what I am." With an obvious effort, she lifted one webbed hand toward me. "Thank you."

I clasped her gray-green hand as best I could, tears stinging my eyes. "I'm sorry. I'm so sorry."

The rusalka drew a long, sighing breath. "I know."

If I could have stayed there, I would have. But I was Hel's liaison, and I had a job to do. Reluctantly, I extracted myself from the security of Lurine's coils. "Take care of her?"

Lurine nodded, tightening her coils around the tank. The ominous expression on her face promised a world of agony to anyone who dared entertain the thought of hurting the rusalka again.

Outside, the Fairfax wolves were drawing nearer, herding their quarry relentlessly toward the Locksleys' summer home.

Inside, Ray struggled to draw breath. Unsure how to proceed, I glanced at Stefan. Now that the moment was here, I felt scared and uncertain.

Stefan's stillness encompassed me, cool and soothing. His pupils looked normal, and I could sense the effort it took to maintain his immaculate self-control. "You have a duty, Daisy. Are you capable of carrying it out?"

"I don't know." My voice sounded small. "What happens if I do, Stefan? Do I risk *my* immortal soul?"

He hesitated. "I do not believe so, no. Not for ending the existence of one of the Outcast on the orders of Hel herself. The divine laws that govern the taking of mortal life do not apply in this instance. But I cannot swear it. So I ask again, Hel's liaison: Are you capable of doing your duty?"

I took a shaky breath, gazing around the room. I had accepted this role. I had taken on this responsibility. My hand tightened on *dauda-dagr*'s hilt. "Yes," I said. "If it's what must be done, yes."

Stefan took a knee beside Ray's half-crushed body. "The sentence has been passed, brother," he said gently. "And one way or the other, it must be carried out. You loved, but I fear that you loved unwisely and committed sins in the process. What will you? I give you the choice: starvation and the void of nonbeing, or Hel's dagger and the risk of a second chance at divine judgment?"

Ray D's fingers twitched in my direction. His chest rose, and he whispered something so faint I could barely hear it. "Maybe I can be with her again in hell. . . ."

My hand trembling, I placed the tip of *dauda-dagr* against his breastbone. Stefan reached down to adjust my hand, relocating the tip under Ray's chin. "What I did takes a great deal of physical strength," he said in a quiet voice. "It would be better and quicker to thrust upward into the brainpan."

Closing my eyes, I did it.

And yes, it was awful.

Ray D convulsed, his broken body arching. I felt his death flow into *dauda-dagr*. A final death, a lasting death. The weight of it settled onto my shoulders, into my soul. I had taken a life.

All at once, Ray's body vanished.

It was just . . . gone.

I looked at Stefan. His pupils were wide, and there was hunger and envy and regret in his gaze.

"He has gone to the final death," he said formally, rising to his feet. "But our business is not yet concluded here."

After Cody handcuffed Jerry Dunham's wrists behind his back, we went outside and waited in the driveway. Someone had turned on the outdoor lights, and it wasn't long before Mary Sudbury limped into the circle of illumination. She was barefoot, having lost her shoes or kicked them off to run. Brambles and stray branches had scratched her porcelain skin, tangled her golden hair.

Three wolves sat on their haunches just outside the pool of light, red tongues lolling, eyes reflecting green. Oddly enough, I recognized two of them: Cody's brother Caleb and his wife, Jeanne. Don't ask me how, but I did.

"Thanks, guys," Cody said to them. "We'll take it from here."

The wolves melted into the darkness.

"I'm sorry," Mary said in a little-girl voice, clasping her hands in front of her. "I didn't mean to do anything wrong. Where's Raymond?"

I felt sick.

"Raymond's gone, Mary," Stefan said gently. "And you have a choice to make, a very hard choice."

"I don't understand." Her gaze met his, her pupils fixed and di-

lated. "Raymond promised to take care of me. And I'm *hungry*, ever
so hungry!" She sniffled. "Will you take me home to my sister?"

Stefan shook his head. "I'm afraid that's over. You must choose
your ending, Mary."

"But I don't *want* to!" she said plaintively. "I don't understand! It
isn't fair!"

No, it wasn't. My palm, wrapped around *dauda-dagr*'s hilt, was
slick with sweat. "I can't do this," I whispered. "She's right; it's not
fair. She's ill, for God's sake! She's mentally ill!"

"Life isn't fair, Daisy," Cody murmured.

Mary Sudbury's head snapped up. "Did *you* kill my Raymond?"
she asked me, not waiting for an answer. "Oh, you bad, bad girl! Did
you kill my sweet boy Raymond? I'll eat you up whole, I will!"

I didn't expect her to rush me.

Silly me.

She was a hell of a lot stronger than she looked. Faster, too. The
back of my head hit the pavement with a cracking sound. Mary's
pretty, doll-like face loomed above mine as she inhaled deeply, her
eyes like twin eclipsed moons. "Eat you up whole," she crooned.
"Oh, yes, I will!"

Feeling her hunger crawling over me, I panicked and stabbed her
in the rib cage.

Her pupils shrank. "Ouch!"

"I'm sorry!" I said in anguish. "I don't *want* to do this!"

A strange clarity settled over Mary Sudbury's face, her pupils
dwindling further. It was as though the pain had given her focus. Or
maybe it was something more. Reaching between us, she fingered
the inch of *dauda-dagr*'s blade that wasn't buried in her flesh. "It
burns with cold," she mused. "Yet it purges, too."

I yanked it free, feeling the blade grate against her ribs.

Mary rolled off me, staring into the outdoor lights of the Locksley residence, staring at the night sky, or maybe staring at nothing at
all, not caring that she was injured and bleeding. "I murdered my

son, didn't I? My precious baby boy. I didn't put him to sleep. I drowned him in the bathtub." She turned her head toward me. "I did, didn't I?"

"Yes," I whispered. "You did."

Her hands found mine, wrapped around *dauda-dagr*'s hilt. "Let it burn, so long as it makes an end to it. There has been too much suffering." She guided the tip to a point beneath her breastbone. "Purge me."

"You're sure?" I asked her.

She nodded. "Help us, O God of our salvation," she murmured. "For the glory of Thy name. Deliver us, and purge away our sins, for Thy name's sake." Her hands tightened on mine. "Now!"

I shoved *dauda-dagr* home.

It wasn't as hard as Stefan had led me to believe, not with Mary positioning the blade at the exact right angle, anyway. Up and under the breastbone, not through it. Not as hard as it should have been.

Mary Sudbury sighed, shuddered, died . . . and vanished, her corporeal body taking leave of the mortal plane.

I rolled onto my back and stared up at the night sky, wondering whether Mary had seen the terrible truth of her existence written in the black places between the stars, wondering whether that fleeting moment of sanity would cost her eternal damnation, wondering about the state of my own soul. I had a lot of unanswered questions.

"Daisy?" Cody squatted beside me, feeling at the back of my skull. "You okay? You've got quite a lump."

That and I'd just killed two people. "Yeah, I think so."

He shone his flashlight into my eyes. "Pupils are normal."

For some reason, that made me laugh hysterically. Something to do with having dealt with a dozen or so ravening ghouls, I guess.

"Come on." Cody helped me stand. "Let's get you inside. I've got to call this in."

Leaning on him, I examined *dauda-dagr*. There was blood on it. I wasn't sure whether there would be.

"Here." Stefan handed me a bandanna.

I wiped the blade clean before sheathing it. "I don't understand this," I said to him. "You . . . What *are* you? Are you alive or undead? Are you even *real*?"

Stefan was silent a moment. "These are not questions I can answer," he said at length. "The nature of our existence is a mystery. Is it part of heaven's unfathomable plan or hell's boundless cruelty? Or is it merely a flaw in the divine edifice, a crack through which we have fallen?" He shook his head. "I cannot say. I can only tell you that we think and feel. We possess awareness of self." He laid one hand over his recently impaled heart. "Although I die and am cast back into the world again and again, my heart beats in my chest. Blood courses through my veins. I believe myself to be real."

"Okay." I didn't know what else to say.

"It is a difficult thing you did tonight, Daisy." His voice was gentle. "You did it well. Had you not, they would have continued to prey on the unwilling. Neither of them would ever have found redemption in this world. Perhaps they will find it in the next."

I hoped so.

Forty

Inside, Cody argued for holding Johnny and his rebel ghouls and charging them with kidnapping.

As the kidnappee, I argued against it. "Under Hel's authority, Stefan's within his rights to pass sentence on them. Banishment is a fitting sentence."

"But they broke the *law*, Daisy," he said impatiently. "And you've got rights, too. You've got a birth certificate and legal citizenship."

"I know." My head ached. "But in the eldritch community, Hel's authority supersedes the law. And since her justice has been done, as her liaison I have to decline to press charges against them."

Cody jerked his thumb at Jerry Dunham, who was propped shirtless against a wall, a field dressing over his gunshot wound. "What about him?"

"Him? Oh, yeah," I said grimly. "It's the only thing we *can* legally charge him with."

"Might want to rethink that, blondie." Dunham was pale and shivering with the onset of shock, but as remorseless as ever. "You want this whole clusterfuck coming out in a court trial? Ghouls, werewolves, hell-spawn?"

"No," I said to him as Johnny and his battered troop beat a hasty retreat. "I was thinking you'd plead guilty."

He gave me a rictus of a smile. "Ain't got no incentive."

"I'll give you one." Unless it was to speak to the rusalka in a low murmur, Lurine had been silent during the discussion. Now she uncoiled from around the tank with unnerving speed and loomed over him, her upper body swaying back and forth like an immense cobra's. Her voice had taken on that implacable bronze edge, and I didn't have to see her face to know her eyes were glittering with a deadly basilisk stare. "If you don't, I will hunt you down and find you. And I will crush you, bit by bit, bone by bone." The tip of her tail caressed his cheek with sensuous grace. "You understand a bit about suffering, don't you? I'll make it last for days. Did you know that as long as your heart's still beating and blood's flowing to your brain, you can live for a long, long time?"

"Rather like a headless chicken," I added. "Only with more nerve endings."

For the first time, Jerry Dunham looked well and truly afraid. It was pretty damn gratifying.

Cody shuddered and shook himself. "Jesus!"

"You should get out of here, too," I said to Lurine. "We've got cops and paramedics on the way, and I can't vouch for their discretion."

Lurine glanced at the rusalka, obviously reluctant to abandon her.

"She will be safe until such time as arrangements can be made," Stefan assured her. "I will see to it myself."

A look passed between them, and then Lurine nodded. "My husband was on the board of the Monterey Bay Aquarium. I'll start making calls."

"You're not—" I began in alarm.

"No, cupcake." Her tail circled my waist, giving me an affectionate squeeze. "Of course not. Calls about arranging to transport her safely back to where she came from. Or at least to Puget Sound, which is where she got tangled in a fisherman's net. She's a long way from home."

"Sorry; I don't know what I was thinking."

Lurine squeezed me again. After the fate she'd threatened Dunham with, you wouldn't think that would be entirely comforting, but it was. "It's okay. You've had a rough day, baby girl. I'm just glad you're all right."

For the first time, it occurred to me to wonder how Lurine had gotten in on this, and I asked her.

Releasing me, she nodded at Stefan. "He called me."

"You did?" I asked him.

He inclined his head. "Of course. She declared you under her protection. It was a necessary courtesy."

"Oh."

Lurine shifted, dwindling abruptly from a glorious and terrifying monster to a naked B-movie starlet. "Speaking of courtesies, would you be so kind as to fetch my clothes?" she asked Stefan. "I left them in the Town Car."

I caught Cody staring.

"What?" He shook himself again. "It's just that I've seen all of her movies. Was she really your babysitter?"

"Yeah." I smiled wearily. "Still is, apparently."

"Oh, you're all grown-up now, cupcake." Lurine blew me a kiss. "But do me a favor and call your mom, okay?"

"I will," I promised.

Minutes after Lurine departed the premises, the chief arrived. He stepped through the wreckage of the front door and surveyed the scene without comment for a long, long time before exhaling heavily. "She going to be all right?" He nodded toward the rusalka.

"I hope so, sir," I said. "We've, um, already got someone working on arranging to transport her home."

"Good." His gaze skated over the wreckage again, taking in the shattered glass, Dunham's shivering form propped against the wall,

Stefan, his lieutenant Rafe, and half a dozen other loyal ghouls standing in the shadows by the bar, their eyes gleaming softly in the dimness. Outside, sirens sounded and red lights flashed as the EMS vehicle pulled into the driveway. The chief's gaze shifted to Cody and me. "You two care to fill me in on the details? Wilkes and Sheriff Barnard are on their way."

The paramedics halted in shock at the sight of the rusalka in her tank, although not as much as one might imagine. They were Pemkowet locals, and had seen a few unusual things in their day. Regaining their composure, they worked efficiently to examine Dunham and check his vitals while Cody and I reported to the chief.

It was another matter altogether when Detective Wilkes and the county sheriff arrived. Wilkes turned pale, but at least his recent dealings with the eldritch community had done a little to prepare him. Sheriff Ross Barnard let out an involuntary grunt, as though someone had punched him in the gut, and stood rooted to the spot, staring at the tank. "Holy Mary, mother of God." Since that didn't seem adequate, he repeated it. "Holy Mary, mother of God! Is that thing *real*?"

"I told you that's what we were looking for, Ross," Chief Bryant said.

The sheriff glanced at him. "Yeah, you did. Frankly, I didn't believe you. So that's how the Vanderhei kid drowned? In there? With *that*?"

My tail twitched. "She's not a thing," I muttered. "She's a rusalka."

He looked at me. "A what?"

"A Russian mermaid, sir," Cody offered.

Sheriff Barnard scratched his head. "What in the name of all that's holy is she doing here?"

"Pull up a chair," the chief said. "It's a hell of a story."

While Chief Bryant related it, Cody and I helped the EMTs shift Jerry Dunham onto a gurney, unlocking the handcuffs behind his back and cuffing him to its frame by one wrist before wheeling it out to the vehicle.

"I've got to go with him," Cody said apologetically to me in the driveway. "Are you going to be okay?"

"Yeah," I said. "Thanks."

"Anytime, partner." Cody gave me a hug, resting his chin on the top of my head.

It felt good. Warm, solid, and comforting. I hugged him back, inhaling the scent of pine trees and leather, laundry detergent, a lingering trace of Ralph Lauren's *Polo*, and a faint, underlying musk. I wished he didn't have to leave. Reluctantly, I made myself let go of him. "Hey, we make a pretty good team, don't you think?"

He gave me a crooked smile. "Yeah, we do."

Back in the Locksley residence, Sheriff Barnard looked dumbstruck. Tim Wilkes had recovered his composure enough to begin documenting the scene with a professional-looking camera.

"Are you filing an official report on her?" I asked him.

"I don't know." He shook his head. "I doubt it. But there should be a record anyway, don't you think?"

I placed one hand against the glass of the tank. The rusalka pressed her gray-green hand against mine on the opposite side, webbed fingers splayed. "Yeah. I do."

Wilkes stared at her in horrified fascination. "The thing I don't understand is exactly . . . how it worked?"

"The mechanics of it?" I asked. He nodded. "It's a kind of ventral slit."

He blanched.

In her tank, the rusalka's face was grave with sorrow, her dark, floating hair a nimbus around her head.

"I know," I said. "It makes me sick, too."

"I wish I could talk to her," Wilkes murmured. "Tell her how damn sorry I am on behalf of human men."

I didn't tell him the rusalka had surfaced and spoken to us earlier. She didn't show any inclination of doing so again, and after the abuse she'd suffered, if she didn't want to have dealings with ordinary mortal men, I didn't blame her. Instead, I patted Tim Wilkes on the shoulder. "You're a good guy, Detective."

He gave me a bleak look. "This job doesn't make it easy. Are you ready to give me a statement? We'll need it if we're bringing charges against Dunham." He fingered his mustache. "It's going to be a challenge to figure out how to present the facts."

Wilkes took statements from the ghouls, too, or rather, he took a statement from Stefan, and the others confirmed the details. I had to credit the guy for being thorough. Even if it didn't all go into an official report, I was glad there would be a record of this. Hel's justice had been administered to Ray and Mary, but Jerry freaking Dunham couldn't even be charged for what he'd done to the rusalka. Maybe someday that would change, and if it did, it would be good to have this on record somewhere.

"I think we're done here," Sheriff Barnard said when Wilkes had finished. "I'll prepare a press release declaring that my office's investigation has concluded the Vanderhei boy's death was an accident. When all's said and done, it was." He glanced at the tank and shuddered. "And I'll be in touch about a private conference after I've spoken to all the parties involved."

"Sounds good." The chief shook his hand. "Daisy, you need a ride home?" His voice was kind and concerned. "Or maybe to your mother's house?"

I hesitated. "Can you give me a minute here?"

"I'll be outside in the cruiser," he said.

Once they'd exited through the gaping hole that had once been a front door, I approached the tank. The rusalka rose to the surface again, dank water streaming over her shoulders.

"Hi," I said softly, touching *dauda-dagr*'s hilt in what I hoped was a reassuring gesture. "Would you like me to stay here with you?"

The pale, translucent membranes over her eyes flicked open, and she gazed past me toward the ghouls. "Do you trust them?"

"I trust their leader," I said, realizing as I said it that it was true. "And he's given his word to keep you safe."

The rusalka's gills fluttered weakly. "Him, then. Not the others. I do not want the others here."

"Is that okay with you?" I asked Stefan.

He inclined his head. "Of course. If you wish, Rafe will give you a ride home."

Rafe stepped forward, his dark eyes glittering faintly.

Okay, maybe Stefan's other lieutenant had proved himself to be loyal, and maybe he had the ravening under control, but . . . no. Just no. I wasn't ready to climb onto the back of a ghoul's motorcycle anytime soon.

"Thanks," I said to him. "But I think I'll take the chief up on his offer."

Stefan made a slight gesture with his left hand, still holding the sword in his right. Rafe and the remaining ghouls departed without a word. Outside, a full-throated chorus of motorcycles rumbled to life.

The rusalka sank back into the murky waters.

Stefan came toward me, stopping a few feet away. My chest felt tight. I could see the slit over his heart in his black T-shirt where the sword had pierced it, his skin gleaming pale through the rent. "What you did today took a tremendous effort of will, Daisy Johanssen," he said to me. "And I owe you a great debt."

I looked involuntarily at my hands, still feeling the residual chill of *dauda-dagr*'s hilt, the tremor of death.

"I do not speak of dispatching the Outcast," Stefan said gravely. "I speak of what you did to quell the battle."

"Oh," I said. "That."

He nodded. "You shared a profound glimpse of all that you hold dear. It was a valiant gesture, and I will not forget it." Closing the space between us, he took my hand and placed it on his chest. Beneath the rent in his shirt, I could feel his heart beating. I could sense the deep stillness within him. He gazed at me with his ice-blue eyes, his pupils stable, calm, and perfectly controlled, centuries of patience behind them. "It is as I have said. There are things I could teach you. Methods to ward your formidable emotions, even from the likes of me. We could help each other, you and I."

It felt good, too.

Maybe *too* good. And definitely not comforting. At least what I felt for Cody was familiar territory. What I felt for Stefan scared me.

My tail twitching with suppressed desire, I curled my fingers into the fabric of his torn T-shirt. "There's a part of me that wants that, Stefan," I whispered. "But I'm not ready for it. I saw you *die* tonight."

"I have died many times," he said in a formal tone. "The result is always the same. One day, perhaps it will be different. Perhaps it is you and I together that will make the difference, serving notice to heaven and hell alike that matters have changed."

God, he really was ridiculously good-looking.

I opened my hand, releasing the bunched fabric. "One day, maybe. But not today. Okay?"

Stefan inclined his head. "I can wait."

Forty-one

In the days that followed, things happened.

The press release from the county sheriff's office did a lot to put a damper on unrest in the media. Warned by the sheriff that the details of their son's death would cast Thad in a highly unflattering light, the Vanderheis went silent and ceased to exert their influence. Accordingly, the protesters in downtown Pemkowet vanished.

Everyone breathed easier for it.

Hel summoned me to deliver what felt like unearned praise. When I protested that I'd temporarily lost *dauda-dagr* and nearly botched the entire affair, she merely fixed me with her baleful ember eye and her compassionate eye alike until I got sort of squirmy.

"You upheld my order, Daisy Johanssen," Hel said in her sepulchral voice. "In the end, it is all that matters."

I took the hint and thanked her. Beneath Yggdrasil II's roots, the oldest Norn winked at me on the way out.

Mogwai was less forgiving, treating me with disdain for ignoring his covert bristle-furred warning not to trust Johnny. Privately, I agreed with him.

Sufficiently intimidated by Lurine's threat, Jerry Dunham chose to keep his bones intact and pled guilty to conspiracy to commit kidnapping and assault charges. I breathed a sigh of relief at that, too.

Cody and I delivered the news of Mary's death to Emma Sudbury, who wept tears of mingled grief and release. I talked to Mom's friend Sandra Sweddon about the senior center's community outreach program, and she promised to pay Emma a visit.

Sinclair Palmer's paranormal tour proved a great hit. Under orders from the Oak King, the pretty, sparkly fairies made regularly scheduled appearances, smiling with their mouths closed. Locals got used to waving to Sinclair's brightly painted tour bus while he charmed the tourists with his semi-faux-Jamaican patois.

Lurine utilized her contacts with ruthless efficiency. The day after my kidnapping, a team of marine mammal experts from the Shedd Aquarium in Chicago descended on the Locksley residence, monitoring the pH balance and other chemicals in the water, examining the rusalka to the best of their abilities, once they'd recovered from their initial bout of disbelief and giddy astonishment. In exchange for the unprecedented experience, they had agreed to legally binding terms of secrecy.

I would have thought getting the rusalka back to Puget Sound would be a considerable undertaking, but it's pretty amazing what can be accomplished when money isn't an issue. Lurine footed the bill for the whole thing. A day later, I was there to watch as the Shedd staffers lifted her out of the tank in a stretcher they used for transporting dolphins and transferred her into a specialized water-filled shipping container in the back of the cargo truck that would carry her to O'Hare airport.

"When we had to move our dolphins and belugas during the renovation, we had someone they know and trust ride along with them every step of the way," one of the staffers said to Lurine, looking starstruck and vaguely perplexed by Lurine Hollister's involvement in the entire thing. He was probably dying to tell someone about it. "I don't know how you feel about it, but the, ah, rusalka seems to trust you. . . ."

"Sure." She stepped out of her high-heeled pumps and handed them to him. "Put these somewhere safe, will you? They're Louboutins."

"Okay." Holding her shoes, he stared as Lurine hopped up to perch on the container's ledge, her legs dangling in the water. "Don't you, um, want a wet suit?"

"I'll be fine." She looked amused. "Are you sure you don't want to come along, Daisy? My treat. No sense letting space on a chartered flight go unused."

"Yeah," I said reluctantly. "I'd love to, but I really need to be here for this conference with the families."

"Okay, cupcake." She smiled at me. "Try to stay out of trouble while I'm gone, will you?"

"I'll try." I leaned over the container.

The rusalka surfaced. Already her skin—if that was what you called it—looked healthier, more greenish than gray. Her nictitating eyelids opened, her lucent emerald gaze meeting mine. "Thank you."

I clasped her hand for the last time, feeling the cool, rubbery webbing against my own warm fingers. "Be safe."

The conference took place two days later at the county sheriff's headquarters. Jim and Sue Vanderhei were there, along with Mike Huizenga, Kyle Middleton, and their parents, me, Cody, Chief Bryant, Detective Wilkes, and Sheriff Barnard. I have to admit, it was pretty much the last place on earth I wanted to be. Seattle would have been a lot nicer. The sense of anguished loss and devastating guilt hanging over the room was palpable, so much so that I found myself wishing Stefan were there to siphon off a measure of it, like he'd done at Thad's funeral.

And no, I hadn't seen Stefan or spoken with him since the night it all went down. As he'd said, he could wait.

Silence weighed heavy on the room. Sheriff Barnard and Chief Bryant exchanged a glance. They were cut from the same cloth: big men in positions of power who knew how to use their imposing presence well.

"Anything you boys want to tell us about the night Thad Vander-hei died?" the sheriff asked gently.

Mike Huizenga shook his head violently. Kyle Middleton wrapped his arms around himself and shivered.

"All right, then." Sheriff Barnard nodded at Detective Wilkes, who opened a file and slid a handful of photographs of the rusalka in her tank across the table. "Let *us* tell *you*. Chief Bryant?"

The chief cleared his throat. Leaning forward to prop his elbows on the table and fold his meaty hands over each other, he laid out the whole sordid story from beginning to end, periodically consulting with Cody or me to confirm a detail.

At first, the parents were in utter denial. I couldn't blame them. It really was unthinkable, and all the more so because the young men involved were raised in devout Christian households and taught to re-vile the very existence of the eldritch community. But then, I suppose that made the temptation posed by forbidden fruit all the stronger.

At any rate, it wasn't long before the boys' reactions made it im-possible to deny the truth. Kyle simply shut down, going into a state of glaze-eyed catatonia and refusing to respond to his parents' insis-tent questions. Mike Huizenga broke silently, tears streaming down his broad face, his linebacker's shoulders shaking.

The room got very quiet.

"So it's true," Jim Vanderhei said after a long moment. No one answered him. "Whose idea was it to put Thad in the river?"

Chief Bryant glanced at me. "That's one detail we don't know," I admitted.

"It was that crazy woman's." Mike's voice was thick with tears, but audible. "The lady ghoul. Then the other one, Ray, he said he'd hot-wire a motorboat once the bars closed and no one would ever have to know. So Kyle and I just grabbed a bottle from the bar and started drinking." Turning his head, he wiped his nose on the sleeve of his T-shirt. I rose to fetch a box of tissues and handed it to him. "Thanks."

"And these . . . *ghouls*?" Jim Vanderhei pronounced the word with profound distaste. "They're to be charged with my son's death?"

"No," I said. The chief hadn't gotten to that part in his narrative. "They were both killed in the course of the raid."

Thad's father eyed me with disbelief. "That's awfully convenient. You're protecting them, aren't you?"

"For what they did to the rusalka?" My temper stirred. "No, sir. Never. Not in a thousand years. I assure you, they're dead."

"But I thought that was impossible," Sue Vanderhei said in a faint voice, surprising me. "I thought they were condemned to eternally prey on the sufferings of others."

Everyone looked at me. "Nothing is impossible," I said. "There are weapons that can kill even a ghoul."

"I give you my word, ma'am," Cody added. "I saw it with my own eyes. They're dead and gone, and they're never coming back."

"So what happens now?" Kyle's father demanded. "What happens to *our* boys? Are they being charged?"

"They could be," Sheriff Barnard said bluntly. "Concealment of an accidental death is a punishable offense. But given the fact that they were subject to unnatural influences at the time, I'm not inclined to bring charges against them." He glanced at Jim and Sue Vanderhei. "Unless the victim's parents insist on it."

Jim Vanderhei hesitated.

"No!" his wife said vehemently. "I won't have it, Jim! I won't have Thad's name dragged through the mud." She pointed at Mike and Kyle, her hand trembling. "These boys didn't make Thad climb in that awful tank with that unspeakable *thing*, and they'll have to live with the memory of what happened for the rest of their lives. Don't you think that's punishment enough?"

Reluctantly, he nodded.

"Then I think we're done here," the sheriff said. "Thank you for your time, Mr. and Mrs. Vanderhei; again, I'm sorry for your loss."

Unfortunately, Sue Vanderhei wasn't finished. She stabbed a

manicured finger in the chief's direction. "None of this would have happened if *he* didn't tolerate a demonic element in Pemkowet's midst! Chief Bryant should be dismissed and that unholy underworld razed to the ground!"

"Amen," Mr. and Mrs. Huizenga murmured in unison.

My tail thrashed, and I could feel the air tightening around me, the scent of ozone rising. I fought to keep a lid on my temper.

The chief glanced at me with his sleepy-lidded Robert Mitchum eyes. "Go ahead, Daisy."

"I'm sorry," I said to the parents. "But none of this would have happened if your sons hadn't thought it was a great joke to spend their time browsing Schtupernatural-dot-com, if they hadn't decided that sexually abusing an eldritch being—a sentient, *feeling* being held captive against her will—would make them Masters of the Universe. The ghouls preyed on the rusalka's emotions, yes. But they relied on ordinary human men like your sons to make her suffer."

There was another silence.

It was Kyle Middleton who broke it, emerging from his catatonic state. "We didn't know," he whispered. "We didn't know what we were getting into. The ad didn't say anything about her being held captive. And Matt, Matt Mollenkamp . . . Matt and Ron said . . . Matt and Ron, they said . . ." His voice cracked. "We didn't *know!*"

"I believe you," I said. "But you went through with it anyway when you found out, didn't you?"

"We tried to, yeah." His haunted gaze met mine. "Or at least, we would have. Thad went first."

I couldn't help it; I felt sorry for him. Sue Vanderhei might be high-strung and intolerant, but she was right about one thing.

It was a lot to live with for the rest of their lives.

Forty-two

Bit by bit, things returned to normal in Pemkowet.

I went back to being a part-time file clerk at the police department, albeit one with a magic dagger on her hip and the Oak King's token strung on a chain of dwarf-mined silver around her neck. Cody went back to working patrol on the night shift, and we saw less of each other. I found myself missing him: the real Cody, the Cody I'd come to know, not just the object of my long-standing crush. Even if I'd wanted more, I'd liked having a partner.

I continued to avoid Stefan.

Stefan continued to be patient. I had a feeling his patience could wear down mountains. Whether or not it could wear down me, we'd have to wait and see. It was going to take me a while to forget the sight of him impaling himself on his own sword, and I still wasn't thrilled about the fact that he was attuned to my emotions.

Lurine returned from Seattle with a satisfyingly stirring tale of seeing the rusalka turned loose in Puget Sound, returning to the wild, and heading unerringly toward her home somewhere in the Bering Sea, free and unfettered.

I wished I could have been there to see it.

After spending a week at home, Jen's sister, Bethany, put on a much-needed ten pounds, copped a healthier attitude toward her bloodsucker beau . . . and promptly caved when Geoffrey the insufferable prat begged her to return to the House of Shadows, vowing for the umpteenth time to make good on his promise to change her.

Yeah, I know. You can't win them all. I started looking into ways to break the blood-bond anyway.

Amanda Brooks at the PVB was outraged at the invoice I submitted for cowslip dew and a linen tablecloth. I stood my ground, reminding her that I'd delivered big-time on her request for pretty, sparkly fairies, and that I could certainly tell them to cancel their appearances if she didn't want to reimburse me.

In the end, she relented and paid it, which was good, since it meant I could pay my rent that month.

Mogwai approved and begrudgingly forgave me, so long as it meant his bowl was filled with kibble whenever he deigned to visit.

Terri Sweddon married the youngest Dalton boy in the Episcopal church, looking like a vision in a sleek Vera Wang–inspired satin gown Mom made for her, flanked by bridesmaids in ivory-hued sheath dresses they might actually wear on another occasion. Even the mother of the bride looked surprisingly stylish.

I know, I know, you don't care, but Pemkowet is a small town, okay? And in a small town, these things matter to us.

Plus, my mom rules.

And my father's voice had gone remarkably silent since the showdown at the Locksley residence.

I was good with that, too. Forbidden fruit and all.

A month after Thad's death, I attended Music in the Gazebo for the first time since the night his body had been found there. I was hoping to shake the association, and Jen needed cheering up after Bethany's defection, so I invited a few other people: Mom, Lurine, Cody, and Sinclair Palmer. Everyone but Sinclair came, and to my surprise, Caleb and Jeanne Fairfax and their two boys joined us, too.

"I hope you don't mind that I invited them." Cody lowered his voice. "I think it's good for them to get out of the woods every once in a while."

"I'm glad they came," I said, meaning it. The Fairfax clan might be insular, but they'd come through for us that night at the Locksley place.

We spread our blankets and set up our folding chairs on the grass in front of the gazebo. The band was called Swing Time Revue, one of the last touring holdouts from the big swing music revival that went on ten or fifteen years ago. Despite the August heat, they had the whole look going on: the high-waisted pegged pants, long coats with wide lapels and padded shoulders, natty hats. The lead singer was sweating buckets as he exhorted us to jump, jive, and wail, but the band was good and the music was infectious.

"Think you still remember how to do it, Daisy?" Mom asked me with a mischievous look.

Cody chuckled. "You took swing dancing classes?"

"No." I pointed at my mother. "She did. She made me practice with her. I was, like, ten years old."

"Twelve," she corrected me, then gave a mock sigh. "But I suppose you're far too grown-up for it now, huh?"

Lurine lowered the oversize sunglasses that rendered her semi-incognito and gave me a stern look. "Oh, for God's sake, cupcake, dance with your mother."

I eyed Mom. "Do you want to lead or shall I?"

She smiled. "I will."

So I danced with my mother on the trampled grass, both of us laughing as we held each other's hands and tried in vain to remember how the basic steps went, eventually giving up and just making it up as we went along while the trumpets wailed and the lead singer mopped his sweating brow.

We weren't alone. Adults danced, some badly, some of them rather well. Little kids danced, entranced by the rhythm. Older kids hung around pretending like they didn't wish they dared to shed their inhibitions and join in the fun.

Cody and Jen danced together, the young Fairfax boy-cubs tumbling around their feet in some complicated feral game of their own invention while their parents watched with a mixture of benevolence and concern. At least Cody's nephews weren't yipping and growling aloud this time.

On the band's first break, Sinclair turned up, picking his way through the crowd when I spotted him and waved. After introducing him to everyone, I scooted over on the blanket to make room.

Sinclair plunked himself down next to me. "Am I imagining things, or is that Lurine *Hollister* you just introduced me to?" he whispered.

I sighed. "Yeah."

"Cool." He nodded. "I didn't know."

"Didn't know what?"

"I can't say for sure, but let's just say she's sporting an almighty powerful aura for a B-list actress who starred in some awfully crappy movies, even if she was the best thing about them," Sinclair said with amusement, his shoulder brushing mine. His voice changed, taking on a different shade of emotion. "Your mom's pretty. Got a pretty aura, too. Tranquil. Not what I expected, I guess."

"Exactly what did you expect?" I asked him.

"I'm not sure." He shrugged. "Given what you are, I guess I assumed she'd seem more like someone inclined to traffic with demonic forces. No offense—I know you said it wasn't her fault. She seems really nice, that's all."

"She *is* nice," I said firmly. "She's the best person I know. And the, um, trafficking was an accident."

The band returned to the stage, expending a tremendous amount of energy endeavoring to invoke a zoot-suit riot. The sun sank in the west, gilding the dome of the gazebo. Soft violet twilight hovered, and the white fairy lights lacing the gazebo's latticework twinkled to life. The steam-wheeler replica *Pride of Pemkowet* returned from its sunset excursion to Lake Michigan, its paddle wheel churning the river's murky waters.

"Hey, sistah! I still owe you." Sinclair bumped me, nudging my shoulder with his. "Maybe I could buy you dinner sometime?"

Cody glanced over at us, a hint of phosphorescent green flashing behind his eyes. Jealousy, maybe? Interesting. But it wasn't like I hadn't laid my cards on the table and given him every opportunity. Maybe a little jealousy wouldn't be such a bad thing. And although I didn't know him well, from what I did know, I genuinely liked Sinclair. Maybe that was worth exploring on its own merits.

"You sure about that?" I asked Sinclair. "I mean, given what I am and all?"

He nodded. "I'm sure."

I looked into his clear brown eyes with their steady pupils. "I'd like that," I said honestly. "It would be nice."

"Nice," he echoed. "All right, then. I'll call you."

Nice.

It shouldn't be a laden word, but in a way it was. *Nice* could be a consolation prize, like Cody's hug in the driveway of the Locksley place. *Nice* could be taking the easy way out, like accepting an ordinary date with Sinclair while avoiding Stefan, who offered something that tempted and scared me.

But *nice* didn't necessarily mean making the safe choice, either.

My mother's niceness was clean and pure and good, and she made a hard choice because of it.

Knowing what I was, having conceived me against her will, she chose to have me anyway.

When I was thirteen or fourteen, some kids at school, Stacey Brooks and her friends, started calling me Rosemary's Baby. I'm sure they got it from their parents, since the movie was, like, twenty years old before any of us were born, and that was right around the time a group of parents unsuccessfully petitioned the school board to kick me out on the grounds that I made the other kids uncomfortable.

Anyway.

I wanted to know what it meant, so Mom and I watched *Rosemary's Baby* together. It left me shaken. If you haven't seen it, it's pretty creepy. Especially the ending, where Mia Farrow finally accepts her destiny and begins rocking the cradle that holds her creepy goat-eyed infant hell-spawn.

It made me cry. I didn't want to be that baby, and I think it was the first time I truly understood that I *was* that baby.

It was Mom who argued that the ending was left open, that no one knew what happened next. That maybe the movie's ultimate message was that the strength and purity of a mother's love was enough to redeem even the spawn of Satan, let alone a lesser demon and sometime incubus like Belphegor. And I believed it, because she believed it.

She still does.

So do I.

And yeah, I was willing to give *nice* a try.